ONLY UNTIL I NEED GLASSES:

The extraordinary life and adventures of Jimmy DeAngelo

Written by

James T. Scarnati, Ph.D.

First published by Dog Ear Publishing
4011 Vincennes Rd
Indianapolis, IN 46268
www.dogearpublishing.net

ISBN: 978-1-4575-4477-4

This book is printed on acid-free paper.

This book is a work of fiction. Places, events, and situations in this book are purely fictional and any resemblance to actual persons, living or dead, is coincidental.

Printed in the United States of America

TABLE OF CONTENTS

PREFACE

Memories and events unwritten are memories and events soon forgotten. Everything has a beginning and everything has an end, but committing words to paper preserves the time between the beginning and the end. None of the characters in this fictional story came from rich families, but they are wealthy in other respects. Their richness is found in being surrounded by good families and good friends. The late 1940s, 1950s, and the early 1960s are innocent, happy days. Life is a continuous adventure and I will recount those adventures with you. Based on actual characters, *Only Until I Need Glasses*, is an uplifting story of joy and a celebration of life. The tale portrays young boys in rural Northwestern Pennsylvania. The narrative describes the shaping of fundamental values and adventures with family, friends, and buddies. The boys experience conflicting and confusing emotions as they evolve into adults. Our guide is Jimmy DeAngelo. Follow the naïve, testosterone-induced boys as they make age-appropriate mistakes, discover their sexuality, and learn to cope with life's curve balls. Jimmy uses explicit language at times, so don't be offended when he describes situations and rhetoric from the vantage point of his preteen and teenage years. However, please don't tell his dad, or he will surely get into big trouble.

PROLOGUE

"Thinking it is the same as doing it," warns Sister Scholasticia. What a predicament. As a prepubescent Roman Catholic boy I don't have to do anything significant to sin. I need only imagine something and it is a transgression. I do horse around in church with my buddy Nick and sometimes we can't help but laugh under our breath. Yes, occasionally we don't kneel straight and the nuns promptly prod us, "You boys straighten up," but these are not momentous violations. Perhaps more serious on the "sin scale" is that period in life when I sit in church having dirty thoughts. Church is unbearably boring, and my mind often wanders. I yield to temptation and become a victim of my fantasies. It must be the work of the Devil.

God knows I have lewd and lascivious thoughts, as do all my friends, but good grief, I never want anyone else to know. I am fairly confident God can keep a secret. Nevertheless, there is one dead giveaway to my wayward thinking—yep, I get what my buddies call a "boner." An out-of-control and traitorous appendage betrays the sanctity of my thoughts. There is definitely a relationship between naughty thoughts and my Pinocchio-like creature − neither is under my control. With a firm nudge from his elbow, my buddy Nick interrupts the rapture of impure thoughts racing through my mind. "Hey Jim," he coyly whispers, "looks like you got a growing problem."

I move away and say, "Ah shut up."

"Just trying to help." Nick snickers. "The nuns will have conniptions when they get a load of that pickle in your pants."

I apologetically say, "It's kinda hard to keep it in the jar." I rapidly regain my composure and retort with a sharp whisper, "Mind your own business and worry about your own pickle." Imagine me worrying what Nick, the king of the pocket pull, is thinking.

I concentrate on ridding myself of the self-inflicted menace. Fearfully, prayers are offered for it to go away. I try purging the malevolent images by meditating and praying a rosary. If discovered in such a decadent state, the Pope will excommunicate me. Unquestionably, the degree of my offense is at the Pope's level. He will personally want a written report that one of his flock has meandered down the road of wrongdoing. Rapidly, nervously, purposefully, the fifty-nine slippery black oval beads glide through my fingers. The accompanying prayers are recited with evangelical zeal, but to no avail. Jumpin' Jehoshaphat, what a dilemma.

Everyone in the church will notice. People will whisper, "Heavens to Betsy, how can that young boy go to the altar and receive communion in that state? Didn't his father teach him better?" Oh my gosh, like a thunderbolt a horrifying thought flashes through my mind. What will Mom and Dad say? Dad warns in the sternest of words, "Never bring disgrace to the family name." If Dad knew my predicament he would vehemently, forcefully, explosively add, "Get rid of that thing right now, do you hear me!" Is this God's way of ratting on me and getting me in trouble?

Fortunately, by the time communion is passed out, God and Mother Nature take care of my little matter and keep my little matter little. It goes away as fast as it appears and I have little to do with its demise. This enjoyable but unpredictable pagan event happens more and more frequently during my preteen and early teenage years.

So you see, growing up is difficult enough for any boy, but being Catholic adds an extra dimension that makes it a maddeningly complex, demanding, and highly unmanageable process. I am a helpless victim and feel guilty about it.

Problems, problems, problems. As a youngster I have more than my share. The weight of the world rests on my shoulders. In the 1940s and the 1950s, traveling the road to adulthood poses unique challenges. Nevertheless, the trials, tribulations, and conflicts experienced are common to the psyche of young boys no matter when they are born.

So how does a young preteen kid get himself into such a psychological stammer? What events led to my guilt-laden church experience, and where am I heading? How is it possible for guilt, fear, and ignorance to intermix and put me in a situation to commit egregious sins against family and community? Is there a conspiracy between my mind and body bent on taking me down the road to hell, and if so, how can it be avoided?

Mom and Dad won't be proud if I end up in hell. Such shameful acts never happened to Jesus Christ or any of the Twelve Apostles—they are holier than holy. All the tea in China couldn't make those guys have a dirty thought. I don't think they ever broke wind or else it would be in the Bible.

How rude of me – almost forgot my manners. I am Jimmy DeAngelo. Mom teaches, "There is never an excuse for poor manners, only poor excuses." Oh, one more thing, please don't let Dad know what I did in church. I know he'd kill me if he found out.

I.

THE FOUNDATION YEARS

CHAPTER 1

BURN IN HELL—NOT ME!

Mother ushers in Sunday mornings by repeatedly singing a deliberately loud, off-key chant to my brother Joe and me. "It's a beautiful day in Brockway, Pennsylvania." I look at Joe snoozing in his bed and yell, "Hey, Joe, it's time to rise and shine." Annoyed, Joe opens his groggy eyes and says, "Leave me alone, ya little squirt, or I'll pulverize you." In a warning voice I respond, "I don't know about you, but I'm getting up before Dad comes up to get us out of bed." Joe, under protest, gets out of bed and dresses for church.

It's a serious crime to miss Mass. Let me tell you about this thing called sin. In the Catholic Church there are two kinds of sin. The unimportant sin is a venial sin, and the serious sin is a mortal sin. As a good Christian, I avoid the mortal sins of the world and pay little attention to the venial sins. The mathematics are simple. By adding up the score I discover venial transgressions are not cumulative or summative. At Sunday Mass I discuss this with Nick. "Nick, my calculations tell me that no matter how many venial sins I commit, they don't add up to a single mortal sin. A venial sin here, a venial sin there, so what's the big deal." Nick ponders the question and responds, "Makes sense to me. They ain't a mortal sin, that's for sure."

As kids we are taught that a mortal sin means burning in hell forever. Tell me this is not motivation for avoiding big-time disobedience to God's law. Nevertheless, I have a problem making sense out of this sin stuff. I can't figure out the reasoning behind missing Mass on Sunday being at the same level of wrongdoing as murder and thievery. Like a sudden flash of lightning, God provides insight into my sin dilemma. "Nick, it seems to me there should be some type of sin between a venial sin and a mortal sin—maybe a 'vemortal' sin."

"Sounds like a good idea for sin," Nick agrees, "as long as we don't have to go to hell to find out."

Every Sunday, Mass is a necessity lest the hellfire be waiting to consume me. I know this to be true because hidden behind the door in Mother's bedroom is a picture painted by a medieval Italian artist

depicting people burning in hell's fire. My sister and I accidentally find it while exploring the house. "Megan, look at those people burning in hell. Pretty yucky, isn't it?"

"Yes, now put it away. I don't want to see it no more," says Megan. The ghastly sight scares us and we are grateful that Mom keeps it hidden. As the fire attacks their body, the people raise their arms toward heaven in hope of being saved. The spectacle of those poor souls burning in hell grates on my mind. During the day the horrifying sight is suppressed, but at night the hidden fears are unmasked.

A week after viewing the picture, I abruptly wake in the middle of the night. My pajamas are soaked in sweat. I experience the worst nightmare of my life. Clearly I see the earth opening, and my falling into an endless, tunnel-like, black chasm. I slowly tumble, and the deeper I fall, the hotter it gets. At the end of the tunnel, I glide to a stop. Red and yellow flames, similar to those in the picture, painfully caress me. If the flames aren't enough punishment, a smiling, red-faced, bearded person with white horns greets me. He says in a deep, echoing voice, "Jimmy boy, I want you. You committed a vemortal sin and now you are mine."

"You mean me? But, I'm not supposed to go to hell for a vemortal sin."

"Well, Jimmy boy, surprise, surprise. I hate to tell you, but you guessed wrong. Vemortal sins are a one-way ticket to the underworld."

At that point I start running, but feel his hot, fetid breath close behind—he's really gross. The guy could use Listerine. Gosh, if caught what will become of me? I don't even have a pocketknife. Luckily, I am jarred out of my dream by a passing railroad train. What a horribly frightening nightmare. Now more than ever, I certainly don't want to go to hell.

To underestimate the power of religion in my life is to underestimate the power of the family influence. In my world, religion and family are interdependent and mutually inclusive. The church reinforces everything taught at home. My parents tell me what is wrong, and the church makes me feel guilty about it. There isn't much wiggle room or shades of gray when it comes to right and wrong—it either is or it isn't.

My first recollection of church is as a preschool tyke. During Mass I sit on the hard wooden bench beside my parents. I have no idea of what all the boring religious mumbo-jumbo is about, but I know I have to be there. Mom orders, "Sit still. Do you have pin worms?" I wiggle and squirm all over the seat. Finally, I find a comfortable spot on the padded wooden kneeler and park my butt; nobody objects. On hidden command from the priest, everyone kneels. From my vantage point near the floor, I notice the lady's legs from the bench in front are protruding into my territory. She wears black shoes, but the disturbing thing is that the seams on her nylon stockings are crooked. I know how fussy and upset Mom gets when her seams are crooked, so I decide to help. As the priest begins the most sacred part of the Mass, an involuntary high-pitched scream, "Ahhhhhhhhh," is emitted from the lady. My helpful hands startle her, but at least her seams are straight. Mom isn't one bit happy. Her lips disappear into the familiar stern line across her face. The privilege of sitting on the padded kneeler is quickly revoked and it's back to the hard bench for me. Sometimes being helpful gets a guy in trouble.

At the age of seven, Church doctrines dictate that I know the difference between right and wrong and pay a price for doing wrong. I begin a yearlong process to make my first "confession of sins" and receive absolution for those sins at my first Holy Communion. If you aren't a Catholic and I tell you to eat the body and drink the blood of someone, you will think I am seriously deranged. Yet, in our church this is what we do when we confess our sins and receive communion with Christ.

I lean over and whisper to Nick, "If we are going to raise a little hell in life, we'd better do it before the age of seven. Up to this point sin is a freebee. Well, it's something to consider." With disdain Nick looks and me and says, "Jim, how can you think of crap like that? In my opinion the age limit should be raised to sixteen. Your brother is a sinner and age sixteen would get him off the hook." Nick is correct. Joe sins a lot more than me, and by the time he's sixteen he will be the world's champion.

The day of First Communion the girls wear white dresses and the boys wear black trousers, white shirts, and black ties. White is the outward symbol of purity and freedom from sin. My school buddies, Nick Manceni and Ronnie Faust, think we look good. "Alright, boys, line up for the processional march into the church," the nuns order. We jab and poke at each other as we linger with our hands together in a pious stance. "You boys knock it off," a nun sternly admonishes.

The nuns are proud of their work. In an Italian-American family this is a big day for their son. After receiving my First Communion, I am watchful since the "dumb little kid" excuse is gone. I am now officially responsible for my actions. Sins are easy to commit, so Sunday Mass, confession, and communion are an expectation, and they are essential rituals to keep my soul ready for heaven.

From first grade until twelfth grade, religious education classes are mandatory. It is a nonnegotiable topic with my parents and there are no alternatives. To energetic kids, religious education is sometimes stupid. Nick expresses his feelings in a more down-to-earth manner. He irreverently says, "This is a crock of shit," but nevertheless he attends religious education classes with me. Even in the summer months, attending daily religion class is mandatory. To me summer religious classes are an injustice. There are other important things I could be doing such as lying in bed, conjuring up dirty thoughts.

We nickname the nuns in their black-and-white habits "walking penguins," and they are prominent in our religious instruction. I attend classes and truthfully a steady diet of religion doesn't hurt me. It's like eating vegetables—I don't like them, but I know they're good for me. Sometimes I am embarrassed at the way we treat the good-hearted nuns. We horse around in class and make fun of the well-intentioned, but preposterous things they try to teach us.

For some reason the nuns certainly are partial to me. Must be my charming personality. Sister Mary asks, "James, have you thought of becoming a priest?" Ya must be joking. Thanks, but no thanks. I politely answer, "No I haven't, Sister, but I'll consider it." I would never show disrespect to her inquiry by saying an outright "No." It is beyond me why anyone would want me to become a priest. I never picture myself as a priest. Batman, Superman, Captain Marvel, or Plastic Man, yes, but a priest never. I am a man of the world, not a man of the cloth. Besides, I don't like the priest's black-and-white stiff, high-collared uniforms. If they wore cotton denim overalls, I would consider it. Nick tells me, "You ain't gonna believe it, but my aunt told me the priests starch their underwear. Honest, that's what I heard." That bit of information cinches it—no priesthood for this guy. Nevertheless, the nuns are persistent little angels. I am awarded the statue of Jesus for my endeavors in religious education, and Mom and Dad proudly boast of my pseudo-accomplishment. Sometimes, having charm is a curse. I must say that I do develop a good sense of right and wrong even though many times I choose to exercise my free will and ignore it. Still, the Church deeply embeds the guilt associated with sin in my psyche, and I carry the heavy burden of a conscience, since I sin often and like sinning.

My first memory of a guilty conscience is placing a baseball-size rock on the railroad tracks, believing the dastardly deed will derail a steam locomotive. I plan a premeditated crime, and the prospect of a lifetime in jail is a distinct possibility. A guilty conscience is a terrible burden. That night I worry about my loathsome deed and do not sleep soundly. Honesty is the stuff I tell myself when nobody else is listening. I visualize the newspaper headlines, "JIMMY DeANGELO DERAILS TRAIN," and the story reading, "A nationwide manhunt for Jimmy DeAngelo is being conducted by the FBI." Thank God a train didn't accidentally derail or I would have certainly thought my stone the culprit. Throughout life I practice drawing a line not crossed at any price, because I am given the precious gift of a value system. I say "practice" since I often stray, but eventually I get it right. The good news is that when committing a sinful act, some guys recognize it as a sin—the bad news is some guys can't. The Church, with all its inhibitions and prohibitions, is relevant in building my ethical and moral foundation for life.

Ritual and symbolism are part of all church activities, and the family rituals mirror those practiced in church. At exactly eight forty-five on Sunday morning, I must be washed, dressed, and sitting in the car ready for church. Dad, wearing his suit, mounts his driver's seat and motors to within a half block of the church. He parks on the street in front of Gene Rose's Barber Shop until the people from the earlier eight o'clock mass clear out. During the ensuing twenty minutes between parking in front of the barbershop and claiming his parking spot, I am subjected to the WCED DuBois Sunday rendition of "The Polka Party" on the car radio. As long as festive polka music is playing, I am forced to listen. Frankie Yankovic is "America's Polka King," but I'll never forgive him for the cruel punishment he foisted upon us. Perhaps my pre-church incarceration is a test of faith. Perhaps it somehow prepares me for Mass, because I would rather go anywhere and do anything other than listen to polka music.

"Ahhh, there it is, Edith. Let's hurry and get there before someone else takes my parking spot. Just hang on—here we go," Dad announces as he steps on the accelerator. "Now, Joe, be careful. Don't get us into an accident just to get that spot," Mom pleads. At a precise moment known only to Dad and God, his favorite parking spot beckons him to enter. As fast as I can escape the polka car, I proudly march into the church, knowing this will make my parents and God happy. As I enter my mind resonates with an absurd polka song.

"I don't want her, you can have her, she's too fat for me—yeah,

She's too fat for me—ho—she's too fat for me.

Oh, I don't want her, you can have her, she's too fat for me—

She's too fat—she's too fat—she's too fat for me."

In our parish, school-age children sit together at the nine-fifteen Mass. The boys sit on the right side of the church, overlooked by a statue of Saint Joseph, and the girls sit on the left side of the church, appropriately guarded by a statue of the Virgin Mary. It is impossible to get comfortable since I am constantly standing and kneeling, sitting and kneeling, and kneeling and sitting. There is continuous mechanical motion to a cacophony of words and phrases spoken in Latin. Maybe it is God's way of keeping me in good physical condition. What other purpose could all the movements possibly serve? I can't understand what the priest is saying, but I know it is serious business. After years of hearing the ritual chants, I am able to recite the verbiage word for word. Away from church Nick and I horse around and irreverently recite the holy Latin verses.

Nick says, "*Dominus vobiscum.*"

I chant, "*Et cum spiritu tuo.*"

Nick replies, "*Oremus.*"

And we end the chant by laughing and howling: "*Amen!*"

Neither Joe nor I want to be altar boys, because it requires one more day to do what someone else wants us to do. I am never comfortable when people order me around. It is okay at home, but not outside my home. Surprisingly, Dad doesn't object to our lack of interest. Besides, altar boys wear unmanly robes that look like dresses. I am forever thankful for Dad's disinterest in this aspect of my spiritual growth.

After Children's Mass, the priest keeps the kids for fifteen minutes and asks questions about the catechism or inquires about our spiritual well-being. Occasionally blowing off confession on Saturday means I can't go to communion on Sunday. In the confessional the priest asks prying questions: how many times do you swear, how often do you get angry, and so on. Confession is a pain in the neck, and I feel I should keep a sin scorecard. Wouldn't you know, I don't keep a scorecard, but the priest keeps a mental count of kids not receiving communion. I am still new to the communion business when Father Goodler calls on me and accusingly asks the dreaded question. "James DeAngelo," he bellows and I obediently stand up. The anxiety of everyone in the church staring at me is unbelievable. "James, why didn't you receive communion today?" Yipes, he's calling me James, I must be in trouble. I freeze and grope for an answer. What should I say? Silence erupts as everyone waits for my reply. Joe, crouching beside me, laughs, hunches forward, and whispers, "Tell him you forgot to go to confession." So I lie to the priest and say, "I forgot." Joe lets out a soft, low moan, "Ohhhhhh noooooo," and I instantly know I blew my lines. I quickly realize that "I forgot" is not an acceptable answer. All I had to say was "I forgot to go to confession," and I blundered. I could be home free if I had only inserted four words. The agony of stupidity weighs upon my shoulders. How could anyone with half a brain forget to get up from his seat and walk to the altar to receive communion? Rhetorically, Father Goodler looks to heaven and rolls back his squinting eyes. "Ohhhhhhhh, I think I heard you correctly, am I right? Hhmmmmm, so you forgot to go to communion—that's interesting, hmmmmm?" The priest frowns, furrows his brow, looks me in the eyes, and lets out another "Hmmmmm, you forgot to go to communion," before moving to the next kid. He knows I lied. Imagine lying to a priest—what is to become of me? Busted again, oh my gosh, I'm in second grade and I'm blowing it. Thank God the lie is only a venial transgression. I still have a chance to stay out of hell, but it is going to be hard work.

In the 1950s everything, including looking cross-eyed at someone, is construed as a sin. Eating meat on Friday, girls going to church with their head uncovered, and having a dirty thought are sins, and the ridiculous list goes on forever. The Church has more ways to commit sin per capita than any other religion in the world.

As a preteen there is a disconnect between real life and the message the nuns try to get across. If the message can be manipulated and misinterpreted, I take pleasure in doing it. The nuns tell us to respect ourselves. Good advice, but they take it to extremes. "Never touch yourself," Sister Mary tells us, and that advice makes us preteen boys snicker and joke under our breath. Nick mocks their warning by whispering, "Fiddlesticks, then how are we going to take a leak? I'll have to tie a rope on to my thing." I know Mom wouldn't want my wild-willie peeing on the bathroom walls and I don't like the rope idea. As budding intellectuals we ingeniously manipulate and transform the nuns' message. "Hey Jim, got something to tell you. You better stop playing with yourself or you will go blind and go to hell." Nick snickers. We ceaselessly cajole each other and jokingly take it one step further. "Nick, I know playing with myself will make me go blind, correct? But, how about only until I need glasses?" Needless to say it isn't good to be a kid with glasses. Oh, by the way, I don't wear glasses and I didn't go blind.

In high school I become doubtful, sarcastic, and cynical. Sometimes I have strange and comical thoughts about religion and how it fits into society. "Hey, Nick, what is the name of the new company formed by the merger between the Yale Lock Company, the Mary Tyler Moore Corporation, the Fuller Brush Company, and Grace Industries?" Nick shrugs his shoulders. "Ya dummy, it's Yale Mary Fuller Grace," I playfully say. "Ya get it, Nick, ya get it?" I laughingly echo. The smirk on his face indicates that he gets it, but my brand of religious humor doesn't tickle his funny bone. No bolt of lightning strikes, so the joke must be okay.

I explore the juxtaposition of the good and evil, but I don't stray to the dark side. The term the nuns use to describe poor decision-making is exercising my free will. "Nick, free will means if I make the wrong decision, I am cut loose as far as God is concerned. Maybe that is why the Church invented the Sacrament of Confession; too many people exercising their free will. Think about it, Nick, free will here, free will there, and relatively soon everybody is in hell. So, starting a 'Sinners Anonymous' group makes sense, but it's too lengthy and inefficient," I say.

"Hell is filled with freewill people," Nick says, "but I don't think the Church wants a Sinners Anonymous Club. The Church needs active sinners, not sinners who have repented."

"You're right. The Church needs a quick mechanism to get people back in good grace and off the sin bandwagon; otherwise, hell will be overpopulated and heaven will be a ghost town. Imagine, a heaven without a population of souls."

"It would be a downer if I went to heaven and no one opened the gate," says Nick.

"No danger," I answer. "At the rate you're going, angel wings are not an option." I know as long as I keep my thoughts stored under lock and key in my head I don't risk excommunication—an automatic "burn in hell" event.

All in all the Church is a positive influence, but the challenge of being raised as a Roman Catholic is daunting. I deal with the innate conflict of doing what I like to do versus what is the right thing to do. Sometimes I win and sometimes I lose. Somehow, losing is more fun, but I always feel guilty about it.

CHAPTER 2

I NEVER WORRIED ABOUT GETTING BORN

To understand the present, you must first understand the past. I was born in 1941 and raised in a small rural Northwestern Pennsylvania town called Brockway. In our moderate climate the summers are not too hot and the winters not too cold. We also enjoy the diversity of nature's four seasons. What more could a person want? The town's population consists of 2,400 people with varied European backgrounds, mostly Slavic, Polish, Italian, and Irish. In my town an alcoholic can't remain anonymous for long. The town is located in a peaceful valley a hundred miles northeast of Pittsburgh and ninety miles southeast of Erie. What I'm telling you is that we are in the middle of nowhere. Now, that's not good or bad; it's just a fact.

Various businesses adorn our thriving downtown district: Beadle's Department Store, Moody's Variety Store, the 5 & 10 Cent Store, the City Restaurant, the E & E Restaurant, two drugstores, and a unique store called Donald's Plumbing Shop. Donald's proudly boasts on the marquee over the front door, "Donald's Plumbing—A great place to take a leak." At the far end of town by the Methodist Church, U-turns are permitted so that a driver can easily change direction on Main Street. The meek and mild Toby Creek flows through the heart of town, and every four years announces it is a force to be reckoned with by flooding homes and stores. Two major highways, the North-South PA Route 219 and the East-West PA Route 28, pass through town, and traffic constantly flows through our peaceful village.

I live in a time before antibiotics, when doctors make house calls. It is a time when people visit and civility is valued. There are two principal occupations in our town. Most people work either in the glass factory or in the clay plant. The glass factory produces jars and glass container products, and the clay plant produces clay pipes in diameters ranging from six inches to four feet. Every able person wanting to work finds a job without ever leaving Brockway.

When I come along, World War II is just beginning. I am told that I am a beautiful baby, but woe and behold, Mother wants a girl. People say, "Sons are put on earth to keep mothers busy until they get their daughters." There may be some truth to this because brother Joe tells me that I have curls until sister Megan is born the following year. Megan fulfills Mother's need to curl someone's hair and relieves me of my long, black, curly locks. In my family everything is a group activity, including potty training. Mother sits on the big person's potty and Megan and I sit in front of her on small metal children's potties. We all talk and do our business. When done, Mother bends us over to wipe and off we go to play. I am one of three children, the middle child. Brother Joe is four years older and Megan is one year younger. Books have been written about the plight of the middle child, but I live the experience. As kids Joe and I often wonder how my parents figured out such an awkward age spread, and we guess our sister might have been one of those so-called "Catholic oops."

Being a middle child is a blessing and a curse. Not old enough to make the first mistakes, but second in line to suffer the consequences—therein is the curse. Joe continually pushes the envelope, and I pay for his sins. I'm not the family's baby, so the cute and cuddly routine does little good. Joe has Mom's complete attention during the first four years of his life, and then I become the focus of attention until the birth of my sister a year later. After Megan's birth I am on my own as far as exclusive attention goes. As a middle child I learn to adapt to a myriad of changing situations and find creative avenues to meet my needs. The middle child's blessing is that I have the opportunity to observe Joe's blunders and thus avoid his pitfalls.

At the age of four my most noticeable physical feature is jet-black hair. A forest of thick, wavy, individual hairs join as a team to produce a prideful sea of black. Aunt Betty comments, "Oh, look how cute he is, and my, doesn't he have beautiful hair." The relatives constantly chatter and fuss about my sister's cute dimple. I try poking my pointer finger into my face but can never create a cute dimple. Some things I either have or don't have and a dimple is one of them.

I walk around our two-story house on cold winter days in footy pajamas and draw pictures on the frosted single-pane windows. To me windows are the 1940s equivalent of a blackboard. Sometimes my sister and I slip upstairs and sneak into Mom's closet to play house. We put on her high heel shoes and play until she discovers we are missing; then everything goes back into the closet. A special day of the week is when the cleaner returns Dad's white shirts. Excitedly, eagerly, and impatiently, I wait for Mom to unwrap them. After extracting the starched shirts, the discarded packaging is transformed into my drawing paper. I love drawing large airplanes and, with the magic of a lead pencil, shoot down the enemy's planes. I am a brave air warrior on paper.

Megan's crib is located alongside my parents' bed. Joe and I have double beds in what is called the boys' room. Our three-bedroom frame house is small, but to a four-year-old, it is a labyrinth of forbidden spaces. The big challenge is walking down the steep steps to the kitchen. Sometimes I trip and tumble down the steps. Mother comes to my rescue. In sympathy she says, "Oh, my poor baby, are you hurt? Let me kiss your boo-boo." She kisses my boo-boo and the hurt miraculously disappears. My sister and I solve the stair problem by learning to slide down the steps, bumpity-bump, one step at a time on our behinds. Sliding is more than a fun game; it is safe travel between floors. I don't have many toys, but I am not the worse for it. The best toys are Mother's clothespins and her pots and pans. With a little imagination and creativity, three clothespins put together in the shape of a T become an airplane. Likewise, the pots and pans are either a boat or a castle. I play for hours with these improvised toys and never feel deprived.

I am a thin, wiry, inquisitive, brown-eyed kid with an easygoing temperament. It doesn't take much to please me, but above all I desire approval and recognition from my parents. Joe says I have the "Italian Good Boy" syndrome. Even at an early age, encouraging words from my parents make me feel like a million bucks. Mom makes me a millionaire every day, but Dad is much harder to please. Tough on the outside, but a marshmallow on the inside, he sets the bar very high and I continually struggle to exceed his expectations. Dad seldom shows feelings, but quickly lets me know if he disapproves of something. He is stingy with compliments, but under that crotchety exterior he wants only what is best for me.

My immature world also contains the dark emotions of fear, insecurity, and greed. Occasionally a vile beast inside flips the switch and releases nasty demons. Before I have the ability to comprehend words, right and wrong messages are delivered in a consistent format. Right is rewarded with hugs, kisses, affections, and nonverbal gestures. A simple smile or a nod lets me know I have my parent's approval. The message of wrong is delivered by a scolding, a slight slap on the hand, or for more serious infringements a swat on the bum. Either way I know my parents care.

Mom and Dad place character building at the forefront of childhood development. As a small kid I can always get away with something, but from an early age, guilt and anxiety are imprinted in my gray matter. To my utter despair, sometimes my conscience intervenes before I can commit a wrongful act. Of course my conscience often calls, but I don't always answer. Adding extra weight to my guilt, Aunt Betty preaches, "You can hide what you're doing from your parents, but you can't hide it from God." Now, that's heavy stuff for a kid. I struggle to balance doing right according to the family and the Church against the earthly desire to stray off the path.

I think I am related to the whole town. Walking a block without running into a relative is a novelty. I call it the "overextended" family. In addition, our family has a unique relationship. You see, Uncle Sam is my father's brother and Aunt Betty is my mother's sister. The DeAngelo brothers married the Gamelo sisters—maybe they worked out a special two-for-one deal. These are the people who helped shape my values and my life.

In 1945, toward the end of my fourth year of existence, the church bells ring throughout the town. No longer is white oleo margarine substituted for real butter; no longer will Joe and I help the war effort by collecting the metal we scrounge when separating tinfoil from the paper of empty cigarette packaging; and no longer does the sun not shine on the brightest of days. Horns honk, the fire sirens blare, people are cheering and yelling, "It's over, it's over." I am accustomed to hugging and kissing among the relatives, but the celebration seems ridiculous. Mom takes me aside and with tears in her eyes explains in kid language. "Jimmy boy, World War II in Europe has ended and today is a special day of prayer and thanks. Our prayer has been answered, and just think, you'll get a chance to meet cousins and uncles you've never seen."

"You mean army guys?"

"Yes," Mother says with a smile.

The Draft Board classified Dad as 4-F because as a young boy he lost most of his hearing in his right ear. Being on the good side of Dad means being on his left side, the good ear side. Some months later many relatives and cousins return from the war. I know cousin Jimmy, a tail gunner in a B17, was shot down somewhere over Germany. He has a metal plate in his head, stuttered speech, and can't remember a thing about his military experiences. Aunt Freda's boys, Abe and Johnny, return home unharmed. Abe was in the Navy on a ship in the Atlantic and Johnny served in the Air Force somewhere in North Africa. War stories are not a topic of family conversation, and veterans rarely discuss their experiences at family gatherings.

In general 1945 is a landmark year forever etched in my memory. Uncle Jim asks Joe and me, "Hey boys, I've got a lot of military insignia and patches. Do you want them?"

"You bet we do," Joe replies, and they become our little treasures from the war. The unfortunate soldiers and sailors who didn't return are listed in a glass-enclosed Honor Roll Memorial located near the high school. To me they are unknown names; but when Mom takes me for walks, she often stops and tells me stories about the people she knew.

At five years old the world is confusing. Immaturity easily allows my brain to be hijacked, and rational thinking overrun by emotions. Like most kids I am egocentric. I think the world revolves around me. On one particular occasion my brain shuts down and I turn into an emotional basket case. It is a mystery why Joe is the only person to receive gifts at his birthday party. Avarice and greed take charge of my entire being when Joe receives a Big Ben pocket watch and I don't. It doesn't matter that I can't tell time, and it doesn't matter that it isn't my birthday. I want that beautiful silver pocket watch to be mine, and it isn't. Swelling within me are powerful and uncontrollable feelings. More than anything else in the world, I want that watch. With trembling lips and a whimper, I begin to bawl uncontrollably. Puzzled, Mom asks, "What's wrong, sweetheart?"

I keep crying. Finally I calm down enough to mutter, "I want a pocket watch too."

"Is that what's bothering you, honey?" she says. So devastatingly serious is the situation that Mother senses my agony. She wisely tells Joe, "Joseph, I'm going to give your birthday watch to your brother. I'll get you another watch tomorrow, sweetie. Is that okay?" To his credit Joe stands quietly and relinquishes his prized birthday gift. When I settle down I feel embarrassed about my selfish behavior. Maybe I am a temporarily insane five-year-old. I painfully think how foolish I acted. Being the good Catholic-in-training that I am, I didn't recognize that it isn't a good idea to covet my neighbor's goods even if that neighbor is my brother.

Visiting the relatives is a favorite family pastime. Dad's sister, Freda, is the spitting image of him except for her long hair and her large chest. Both siblings have midnight-black hair, sparkling rust-brown eyes, lobbed ears, a prominent bent Roman nose, and high foreheads. Freda's house is four blocks away and we visit once or twice a week. Mother sometimes allows me to walk to her house, where Aunt Freda kindly reads me stories from a book of fairy tales. The plump, good-natured lady is my godmother, and that bestows upon me a special status.

Under Aunt Freda's towering maple trees, a three-cushioned glider and five wooden Adirondack lounge chairs are circled on the redbrick patio. Aunt Betty and Aunt Mary live next door to Aunt Freda. Visitors at Aunt Freda's house are a magnetic force that attracts people. Within five minutes a whole mess of relatives and friends magically appear. Animated gestures propel hands to fly in all directions as they chat and joke. I theorize that if everyone sits on their hands, the talking will stop. To my aunts and uncles, talking involves lively, whole-body gestures. Shoulder shrugs, head nodding, smiles, frowns, brows furrowing, arm and hand movement, and for added drama, foot stomping are part of the repertoire that makes conversation dynamic and alive. Family conversations require listening and watching to understand what is said. Often the meaning is in *how* something is said and not *what* is said.

Aunt Freda is a good host. Whenever friends gather she disappears and returns with cookies and iced tea. That's the other part I like about visiting.

Energetic and engaging conversations abound. A local tragedy is the talk of the town. My aunts and uncles thoroughly discuss the circumstances of a neighbor lady's demise. I hang around like an unobtrusive fly on a garbage can and listen to the chatter. So what—a kid's supposed to be nosy. I gather that a middle-aged neighbor committed suicide. The gossip leads me to believe the woman made her final decision because she couldn't get rid of an enormous tapeworm lodged in the pit of her stomach. Aunt Betty put her hands on her cheeks and dramatically blurts out, "Oh my God, I heard that when they cut her open they found this tapeworm—it was fifteen feet long—fifteen feet long—imagine that."

Aunt Freda echoes, "Fifteen feet long. It must have been huge."

"Yes," says Aunt Betty, "fifteen feet—imagine that."

Aunt Betty often ends sentences with "imagine that." No one says how to get rid of a tapeworm, but I think I know. It isn't by shouting, shoo-shoo-shoo, go away. After listening to the conversation I envision the huge, flat white creature wiggling around in my intestines and vow no such animal will ever inhabit my tummy. Hearing the speculative chatter scares me into eating meat well done lest a blood-sucking creature invade my body—imagine that. So you see, gab sessions are both interesting and educational.

Our visit is interrupted when the rug salesperson from Punxsutawney stops to peddle his wares. Sam Jamzees is a likeable guy of Middle Eastern origin. Mostly bald with a fringe of hair around his crown, the ruddy, mahogany-skinned salesman talks with a cigar tightly clenched between his teeth. He also talks with exaggerated hand gestures. The hair he lacks on his head is compensated for by the wild growth on his forearms and earlobes. In a begging voice loud enough to be heard by all, he starts his pitch. "Freda, I have a beautiful throw rug you must see to believe."

"Hmmm, no Sam, not today," she replies as she grimaces and thoughtfully scratches behind her ear.

"But, Freda, I only have a few of these and I may not be able to get this quality of rug again. I want you to have this so much that I'll take twenty percent off the price it sells for in a store."

"Nope, I have no use for it." My aunt doesn't bite at his first pitch, but he has a dozen other articles that she must see to believe. He knows that somewhere in the pond of fish, at least one will bite. Often the ladies purchase one or two of the products he carries in the trunk of his car. Sam is no dummy. He uses Aunt Freda as bait to create a buying frenzy among the women. What a clever guy.

Mrs. Dahrugh also appears weekly to peddle linens and tablecloths. We are visiting and watch the show between the seller and the buyer. Mrs. Dahrugh has olive-brown skin, and the deeply etched lines in her face make road maps jealous. How old she is I have no idea, but she hasn't aged well. She drives me crazy because she calls everyone honey. "Honey, I have some beautiful things I want to show you." In the trunk of her black 1947 Ford, she has a vast array of delicate lace and table linens she hopes will interest the ladies. "Here, honey, feel this lace; it's made of the finest linen you'll ever touch. Look at the color and stitching, honey, this is fine workmanship."

"Yes, I know, but are there any flaws or missed stitches?"

"Honey, you'll find no flaws in this material."

"Yeah, it's good quality, but the color doesn't match my furniture." The bartering and bantering go on for fifteen minutes. Sometime the ladies buy and sometimes they don't. It is a battle of wills to see who will prevail.

Traveling salespeople are ubiquitous. Knife sharpeners, window cleaners, and chimney sweeps are among the cast of characters attempting to sell their services, but Mom is a hard nut to crack. Every April the "umbrella repair man" appears on our doorstep. A song from one of Mom's favorite movies puts it into perspective. "April showers bring May flowers" and I know he bet on the showers. The creative capitalists and peddlers who journey through our town seek to satiate the family's unrequited and insatiable desire for material goods.

Doing business in the forties and fifties is a person-to-person transaction. When buying shoes or clothing, we walk up town and the local business people service us. "We are looking for a nice pair of school shoes," says Mom.

"Jimmy, here is a nice shoe that I think you will like. Try it on," says the salesperson.

Mom bends down and places her thumb on the tip of my shoe. She orders, "Now, Jimmy, I want you to wiggle your big toe," and I comply. "Put on the other shoe and walk up and down the aisle." Again, I do as directed. "How do they feel? Do they pinch or hurt your feet?"

"No, Mom, they feel great."

"Okay, we will take them. Remember, they're for school and church, not for running around." Mom opens her black pocketbook and roots through it until she has the exact amount of cash to purchase the shoes.

Grocery stores are small and compact. The owner behind the counter gets the canned goods or products requested and places them in a paper bag, one item at a time, and one customer at a time. The staccato cackling of voices order, "I'll take a loaf of bread, a box of Corn Flakes, Ranger Joe Cereal, a can of Campbell's Baked Beans, six hot dogs," and so on, directed to the clerk. Glistening beads of sweat race down the side of Tommy the grocer's face as he scurries to procure items from the meat case and the floor-to-ceiling shelves behind the counter. On the walls not adorned by shelving, posters and advertisements fill the void. While waiting for Tommy to fill our order, I entertain myself by reading them. One poster in particular, hidden in the back corner of the store, catches my roving eye and piques my interest. I don't think it is meant for the public to see, but I sneak a peek anyway. The instructions covertly posted on the wall near the walk-in meat locker are a mystery. I ask Joe, "What does 'in case of fire grab your meat and beat it' mean?"

Joe laughs and says, "Where did you hear that? Geez, you're stupid. Well, forget about it. I'll tell you in five years."

I can't figure out why a person would want to do that when the most important thing is personal safety and getting out of danger. A strange set of instructions indeed.

Self-service comes along later in the fifties. Unfortunately, Tommy never adapts and his business eventually fails.

My parents converse fluently in either English or Italian, but speak English at home unless they want to keep something secret. My family is bilingual, but I'm only monolingual. They need to speak Italian because both sets of grandparents are from the old country and speak broken English. My grandfathers worked six days a week, from dawn to dusk, in the coal mines, and my grandmothers stayed home to raise the families. Grandpa and Grandma DeAngelo both die before I am born, so I never know them, except for the stories told around the dinner table. The death of Grandpa DeAngelo was caused by a coal mine accident—I heard my aunts say it was a cave-in. Grandma DeAngelo died after she contracted pneumonia.

In all the years I know Grandpa Gamelo, I only see him in buttoned-down, flannel, long-sleeved shirts. The only adornment to his shirt are the gray suspenders holding up his trousers. In summer he wears a wide-brim straw hat as he works in his garden, and in winter he wears a heavy wool cap. He has a head with hair, but I can't tell the color. Working in the coal mines is back-numbing work, but he does what is necessary so that his family can thrive. A no-nonsense, gruff person, Grandpa Gamelo holds to the security of the old country ways. Life is tough and reality requires dealing with its challenges. With all the hurdles and obstacles my immigrant forbearers had to overcome, they passionately love America. Grandfather

Gamelo tells me in broken English, "Jimmy, in America, if you work hard you can be a success." He has hope and with hope anything is possible.

Grandpa Gamelo often uses colorful language, and I never think much of it. One day in his garden he mutters the most powerful and heinous-sounding word ever spoken. I have never heard anything close to sounding as bad as his utterance. He calls something a "bastard," and I instantly know the word is super bad. Boy this is great, I just learned a swear word from Grandpa. It tickles me because even though I have no idea what the word means, it sounds sinister. So why not experiment and use the word with someone. "Hey, Mom, I got a question." Irretrievably I say, "What does bastard mean?"

"What?" she says as her sharp brown eyes get wide like saucers.

"What is a bastard?" I repeat.

Her lips disappear into a tight horizontal crease across the front of her face and she says with explicit resolve, "Don't you ever use that word again—do you understand?" That ends that, but I do get her undivided attention.

Grandpa Gamelo survives and flourishes in this harsh new country. He has his own garden and grows the fruits and vegetables that his family consumes. Italian beans, string beans, carrots, cucumbers, and tomatoes dominate the garden. Along its perimeter fragrant rosebushes with their thorny stems stand guard. How he gets those plants in rows so straight that the military would be jealous is a mystery. The pungent smell of lye soap permeates his basement. The basement is important in family life. It is the living space where dirty hands are washed in the concrete sink and the garden products are preserved.

The Gamelo family consists of Grandma Gamelo, four girls (Jenny, Betty, Helen, and Edith) and two boys (Jim and Pete). I am told that Pete died of a heart condition before the age of twenty-one. Everyone says I look like Pete and I begin to wonder if I, too, will die young. I never worried about getting born, but I sure do worry about dying.

In addition to his garden, Grandpa Gamelo built a three-hole wooden outhouse, and sitting beside it is the pigpen of Dick the pig.

"Joe, I gotta take a leak—how about coming with me?"

"What's wrong with ya, can't you go to the outhouse by yourself?"

"Yeah, but if I fall in it would sure be nice to have someone there to pull me out."

"You're crazy; it ain't gonna happen. I'll go with you, but you owe me."

"Okay, but I don't owe you if you drain your hose too."

"Where on god's good earth do you ever get all your stupid rules?"

I hate using the outhouse. On a hot day the combined smell of Dick the pig and the outhouse is stifling. Dick is a talkative creature, but his personal hygiene leaves much to be desired. Flies are everywhere, competing with humans for entrance to the privy. The outhouse is not equipped with toilet paper—thank God for the Sears and Roebuck catalog. Unless it is an emergency, I hold whatever I have to do until I get home.

Eventually Dick's time to become a meal for the family arrives. Grandpa cuts up the parts and separates them, some for making sausage and some for cooking and eating. To my delight Dick also serves another purpose. Grandpa takes Dick's bladder, blows it up, and gives it to Joe and me as an inflated ball. For the rest of the day, we play with it as if it is the only ball we've ever had.

I am raised as a Roman Catholic, with a rich Italian-American background that emphasizes values and character. As I grow, having character causes many dilemmas. From early on there is never a doubt between right and wrong. The extended family is the center of my life, and they provide the enrichment, the warmth, and the security needed to thrive. Together these variables reinforce one another and create a value system that I strive to live with, even though my youthful behavior is often at conflict with such values.

Neither my grandparents nor my parents are born spitting dollar bills, yet the families prosper in this great land. An unrelenting belief in their ability to overcome the adversities of life is the foundation for success. The lessons that enable them to prosper are part of their culture, and that culture is transferred to their children. They provide a gift that financial wealth can never buy. Money does not equip a person for the future, but strong families build character. They give me a loving environment in which my mind and my spirit grow and flourish. I could not ask for more.

CHAPTER 3

LIFE WITH THE FAMILY: THE EARLY YEARS

Let me tell you about my family. Dad quit school to start working when he finished the eighth grade. Quitting school to work was common in the 1920s and 1930s. It is the duty of each brother to help support the family. Dad, a husky, confident man, is not a person to be toyed with. He visits Sylvio, the local barber, once a week to keep his black hair, thick eyebrows, and sideburns neatly trimmed. He stands five feet, six inches tall, and his dense, compact body exhibits the physique of a weightlifter. The three DeAngelo brothers (Sam, Joe, and John) start their own businesses and work smart and hard to make them successes. From nothing they create something.

Dad jokingly touts the benefits of self-employment. "I only have to work three-fourths of a day. I can choose any eighteen hours I want and go home anytime I want after two o'clock in the morning." The work the brothers find most lucrative is the restaurant and tavern business. In the early 1930s, at the height of the depression, they start their businesses and they are successful. Dad believes in education, and receives a diploma from the Perry School of Business in 1934. He often states, "The little bit of knowledge I learned at school is great, but there's nothing that can replace experience."

Living through the depression imprints on the brothers an *avoiding debt and saving money* mentality. They practice this philosophy with their children. *Earn your way in life* is a prime tenet. Dad never passes up a chance to lecture. He says, "If it comes too easy, it can't be good. Nobody ever gives you something for nothing."

I whisper to Joe, "I think we are in for one of Dad's lectures."

Joe shakes his head. "How did you ever figure that out, genius?"

Dad continues lecturing. "The stupid mouse is the only one that doesn't know the cheese in the mousetrap isn't free. Even a mouse pays a price when getting something for nothing is the motivating force. I hope to God you're smarter than the damn mouse."

"Oh yes, we're smarter than a mouse," I reply.

Joe mutters, "Shut up and let him finish."

"I think you two boys are intelligent. Do you know the difference between being intelligent and being smart?" Dad keeps going. "An intelligent person recognizes it's raining. A smart person knows enough to get out of it."

Joe leans over and whispers, "We just had our character building for the week. So keep your mouth shut so we can get out of here."

"Okay, Joe, I can take a hint."

Living within our means and accepting responsibility for our actions are important. The town's nickel big shots are characterized as people having a rich man's palate and a poor man's fork. With that in mind Dad makes us work hard for everything. He recognizes that when working for something, you appreciate it. Planned adversity and manageable struggle build character.

The entire family is frugal in the expenditure of cash and materials. A good example of the "making do" lifestyle is the tearing down of the old garage and the construction of a new garage. Dad never considers demolishing the structure. No, no, we take it down board by board, beam by beam, and brick by brick. "Joseph and Jimmy, I want you to pound the nails out of the old boards. When you are done, place them on a brick and hammer them straight. Do you boys understand?"

"Yeah, we ain't completely dumb," answers Joe.

Dad gives Joe an irritated look and says, "Well, get busy." Yes, you guessed it; he recycles both the boards and the nails in the construction of the new garage. After chiseling off the mortar, old bricks are recycled into "new" used bricks. The old solid wood garage door is set aside for later use, but within a year it disappears. Joe says, "No way would Dad ever throw out a door. Ya think someone stole it?" Joe and I wonder what became of the door. While replacing the roof over the kitchen of Father's restaurant, the workmen, to their amazement, find part of the old roof consists of an embedded wooden garage door— imagine that. Dad even buys used cars rather than new ones. He can afford a new car, but a used car is a better use of his resources. Thus, whenever the local banker trades in his pristine car, Dad buys it at a greatly reduced price.

Mom is not totally immune to the thrifty bug. For years every dishtowel and glass in our house are from bonus gifts included in the super-size box of Duz. "Duz does everything," says the radio advertisement for the laundry detergent. The restaurant uses many boxes of Duz a month, and we accumulate a collection of prizes. Duz is the adult version of Cracker Jacks—a prize in every box.

Flour bags are also utilized at the restaurant. In the forties, flour is delivered in twenty-five-pound bags made from patterned cotton cloth. To satiate the thrifty bug, the flour bags are washed and transformed into skirts or blouses for the women. At the grocery store S&H Green Stamps are the rage. For every dollar spent, an allotment of Green Stamps is issued. Once home we huddle around the kitchen table to paste Green Stamps in the booklet. Licking the glue stamps is not my favorite job, but as Mom says, "That's why God gave you a tongue." After the books are full, they are ready for redemption. Redemption day is exciting. Each book brings with it a two-dollar credit, which we take in merchandise. Mom says, "Well, kids, what should we buy with our newfound wealth?"

We unanimously shout, "Oreos."

"Okay, then Oreos it is."

Like all kids we skillfully break them in half and lick the white creamy filling before eating the delicious chocolate cookie. If it is worth saving, we save it.

At home Mom is the heart and Dad is the boss. Sometimes they play the "good cop—bad cop" routine featured in the movies. I am smart enough to know that if I want something I first have to get Mom's approval. Mother loves us and treats us as very special persons. When we are coming in from the outside, she cautions, "Don't slam the door or the cake will fall." Making a chocolate cake from scratch is one of her many ways to show love. "As a special treat I'm going to let you lick the mixing bowl," she announces. Her kitchen is a fascinating place filled with intoxicating smells that signal that something great is about to greet me. Every boy's first love is his mother, and I certainly love mine. In contrast, Dad is the tough guy disciplinarian. My parents never argue in front of us. Dad has the final say on all matters. He is the primo-supremo boss. Absolutely no gender or role confusion exists.

Since Dad is always working, I only see him on Sunday and Wednesday afternoon when either Uncle Sam or Uncle John give him a half-day break. On his half day off he works out, lifting weights with two friends, Joe Forester and Bill Carlson—often I go with him. They lug the weights and barbells through the woods to a clearing behind Joe Forester's house. After pumping up Dad purposely forms his arm in the shape of an "L" and flexes his biceps. "Feel this, buddy boy," he says and I dutifully do. "Ya know, son, if you want something you gotta work for it. Remember, you never get something for nothing."

"I think I heard that before," I reply.

His tan, sweaty arm is as hard as a rock, and he is proud of his accomplishment. I wonder if the scrawny muscles on my skinny arms will ever match his. I may as well tell you, they never do. A picture of him proudly lifting a barbell with me perched on his shoulders is taped to the refrigerator. Dad is a man's man and a strong male role model for his children—there are no wimpy males in my family.

In the morning my official duty is to collect the two quarts of milk left on the front porch by the milkman. "Jimmy, go out on the porch and get the milk," orders Mom. "Be careful so you don't break the bottles and cut yourself and oh, don't forget to shake the milk. Remember, your younger cousin John dropped a milk bottle and fell on top of the broken glass, cutting himself severely," Mom reminds me.

"That's an amazing scar across the top of his nose," I respond.

Shaking the milk gets the cream floating on top to mix with the milk and it is my job. We are puzzled when the milkman tells us the company's milk will be homogenized. I don't know what homogenized means until the first delivery. Surprisingly, I no longer have to shake the bottles—the dairy does that for me. Modern science is wonderful, but in an exceptionally short period of time, my shaking job is lost to a new technology. Nevertheless, someone has to bring the milk inside and that is still my job.

Breakfast is a battlefield, with everybody struggling to get a piece of the turf. Once I place the milk in the refrigerator, the competition begins. I call breakfast a competition because Mother gradually toasts and butters a loaf of bread. The bakers only give two crusts with each loaf, a sinister plot for conflict if ever there was one. Surely, the bakery knows that each of us covets those two end slices. As Mother places the golden-brown buttered toast on the table, the sibling with the fastest hands takes what they can and places it on the chair between their legs. Shazam, like Captain Marvel in the comic book, we turn into greedy urchins practicing a caveman's version of sharing. Once everyone stockpiles the toast, the breakfast beverage is prepared. My secret recipe is two spoons of sugar, one-fourth cup of canned milk, one-fourth cup of regular milk, and one-half cup of weak coffee stirred vigorously. One by one, the toast is spread across its entire face with jelly, folded in half so it fits in the cup, and prepared for my taste buds. I quickly dunk it to absorb the creamy brown liquid and then voraciously chew and swallow the soggy delicacy. That's mighty fine eating.

Another official duty is helping Mom with the laundry. There are no clothes dryers in the late 1940s, so everyone hangs clothes to dry on their backyard clothesline. Living seventy-five yards from the railroad tracks is our challenge. Seven days a week, rain, snow, or shine, steam locomotives parade past our house. The marvelous metal machines hiss and chug with a voice friendly to us. Day and night the powerful beasts haul their freight and boastfully announce their presence by means of a window-shaking greeting. I am so accustomed to the syncopated vibrations gently nudging our frame house that it is difficult to sleep without them.

The soothing huffing and puffing is the fire-eating monster's way of breathing. Steam engines produce good and bad smoke. Good smoke is white, and bad smoke is black. The white smoke is the monster belching steam that harmlessly dissipates into the surrounding air. The black smoke is ash and cinders. On laundry days as soon as Mother sees black smoke rolling toward the house, the race begins. The entire family mobilizes. Everyone scurries outside. "The train is coming—quick, everyone outside to take in the laundry," Mom yells. "Joseph, you get the towels. Jimmy and Megan, get the underwear and take them into the house. Hurry, hurry, here comes the sooty black smoke!" Clothespins fly in all directions as we hurry to free the captive clothes from the clothesline. The black cinders roll through the air in an attempt to soil our clean garments. If I don't hustle the smoke overtakes me and deposits painful cinders in my eyes. Soot invades every nook and cranny of our house. Every week a dusting of the black filth from the inside windowsills is a necessity.

Look hard and you discover that even the most bothersome situation has an upside, and sure enough, we discover an upside to living next to the railroad tracks. The hopper cars transporting white silica sand to the glass factory sit several days on the tracks, and the sparkling sand inevitably trickles out from the bottom of the railcars, forming pyramid-shaped piles that beg to be rescued. We have the best sandbox in the neighborhood and at absolutely no cost.

Sundays are set aside to do what Dad wants to do, such as a trip to Bookville. Mom cooking a mouth-watering roast, with potatoes, ushers in the day. In the kitchen I see a green salad with tomatoes and onions, and dressed with oil and vinegar. While sitting around the kitchen table talking with my aunts and uncles, I hear stories about when the brothers first started their business. "Sam," Dad says, "remember when one of the Blackhand came into the restaurant and shot Billy the Bum while he was eating his apple pie?"

"The guy emptied all six shots into him, dropped the gun, and walked out," says Uncle Sam.

"Yes, I remember, folks said it was 'Big Lips' from Pittsburgh that put the hit on him—imagine that," says Aunt Betty.

"You know what they say about those guys?" Uncle Sam queries. Curling his brow he says, "I think it goes something like this:

"If he's your friend, he's your friend.

Cross him and he will knife you.

Run away and he will shoot you.

Get away and he will find you."

"Oh, how terrible those people are," Mom comments.

"Those bums are the scum of the earth," Dad echoes in a forceful voice.

"What a waste of apple pie," I quip. A little humor lightens the mood.

As owner of the business, Dad has to make sure he never sees what he witnesses. Out of fear of reprisal, no one sees anything. Usually, when the family wants to keep something secret, they talk in Italian, but this time they don't, so they must want us to know the story. There is no doubt how Dad feels about gangsters and we all know it.

The only time I see Father hit Joe is when Joe gets too big for his britches. One Sunday he lets his mouth do the thinking for his brain. Joe continually ventures near the edge of the abyss, and I take great pleasure watching him stumble into the chasm without personally experiencing the consequence. He pushes established boundaries as far as possible, and most of the time it is tolerated, but not this time. To Dad, the Mafia is an embarrassment to all honest, hardworking Italian families—there is nothing to be admired about gangsters, Italian or otherwise.

I watch semi-amused as Joe crosses the line. "Hey, Dad, you're Italian, and I'll bet you were part of the Mafia," he blurts out. Instantly, everyone becomes silent as Joe continues. "Aw, come on, Dad, we know you're related to those Mafia guys." Fire rages in Dad's eyes as he rises and slaps Joe across the face. "Don't you ever talk about those goddamn hoodlums in my house. Do the rest of you understand?" he warns as he looks each of us in the eyes. Joe commits a secular offense that has the potential to tarnish the family's good name. On a religious scale I classify his transgression as a vemortal sin. As long as he learns a lesson, Joe's boyhood foolishness is forgiven. Watching him stumble teaches me many of life's lessons. It also teaches me to keep my mouth shut on taboo subjects.

Sunday also brings with it the dreaded Brookville visit. The visits are a family obligation and a family custom. We have a concentration of relatives living in Brookville, eighteen miles away. I like the relatives, but the visits are dreadfully boring. Nonetheless, wherever Father wants to go, the family travels with him. The worst part is that I have to dress up. Mom orders, "All right, kids, get upstairs and get cleaned up. We are going to Brookville to visit the relatives."

I am loath to hear Dad say, "You boys wear your suits." From time to time he makes me wear my blue hand-me-down wool suit. I detest the scratchy garment. No child of my parents will ever be seen by the relatives as scraggily. Upon arrival we are given the usual, but unnecessary precautionary warning: "Now you kids behave yourselves, I don't want any monkey business out of you." There are other unwritten rules that can only be learned by living with the family. I call them the "Brookville Rules."

Rule 1: The first rule is a nonverbal message that Dad telegraphs as if he has extrasensory perception, and we dub it the dreaded "dirty look." Whenever he disapproves of what we are doing, he squints his eyes, stares at us intently, and furrows his brow. We quickly get the nonverbal cease-and-desist message—the dirty look is never misinterpreted. No words need be spoken.

Rule 2: When visiting, we are not allowed to ask for food or drinks. "I don't want you kids to ask for anything to eat" is always included in the pre-lecture instructions during the ride to Brookville. If refreshments are offered and he approves, we eat and drink what is provided. It would be an insult to Father if we give the perception of begging or in need of anything.

Rule 3: As captives, the requirement is to be in the room with the older relatives and sit like ladies and gentlemen, a hard thing to do for antsy kids.

Rule 4: The last unwritten rule is that children must always be respectful and seen, but not heard. We are well indoctrinated in the protocol and the pecking order of polite conversation with adults.

The colorful and animated conversation includes a covert game of one-upmanship between Dad and the relatives. I classify the bragging as "good lies." Listening to the stories and discussions is similar to listening to the family's history. Nevertheless, to me the conversations are of little interest. I have a voracious appetite, and even though undeniably hungry, I know I must live with it, because the Brookville Rules are never violated—that will only embarrass Dad and make the long drive back to Brockway even longer.

In a small town one day melds into another, but Aunt Jenny coming home makes it a special day. Aunt Jenny is a paradigm for the sourpuss of the year award, but Mom likes her sister. "Joseph, Jimmy, and Megan," she announces, "get ready; we are going to the train station to pick up Aunt Jenny. Come on, hurry up or we'll be late for the train." The oldest of Mom's three sisters, Jenny works as a nurse in Pittsburgh. Once a month she takes the train from Pittsburgh to Brockway to visit her family. "Why don't you get a driver's license and drive home?" Joe inquires. "Why get a driver's license when you can't afford a car," she replies. If God designs a model for a nurse, her picture will appear on His poster. Stern, strict, no-nonsense, and attention to detail describe the nursing part of her. Having her as a nurse is comforting, because she is the most competent nurse in Pennsylvania. Over the years she works her way up to head nurse at the Allegheny General Hospital. She is like a drill sergeant. In nursing and war there is no room for nonsense or error. Her downfall is that she can't separate her work life from her real life. Aunt Jenny never marries, but rumors persist that the guy she loved died; no other details are ever revealed. She accepts going through life as a spinster, and the longer she travels the spinster's road, the more she becomes set in her ways.

Chugging, huffing, and puffing the train pulls into the station. With a final hissing sound, the locomotive lurches to a halt. The stationmaster rushes outside and places steps by the passenger cars, and people begin to get off the train. Aunt Jenny soon appears on the platform with her honey-brown tweed suitcase in hand. The excitement is hard to contain. We know that hidden inside the suitcase is a gift for each of us. Cheaply made Japanese wind-up toys are a favorite surprise and we are not disappointed. I play with my toy for hours, but as with all toys it eventually breaks and I dissect it to see what makes it work. Amazingly, many of the metal toys brightly painted on the outside are nothing but discarded soup cans cleverly reworked into toys. Those Japanese lost the war, but they won the cheap toy market. Although strict, and inflexible, Aunt Jenny is thoughtful when it comes to kids. It doesn't take much kindness to leave a lasting impression on a kid. Kindness always overcomes gruffness.

When my brother, sister, and I are exceptionally good, Mother rewards us with a trip to the movies. "Come on, kids," she unexpectedly says. "Get ready because we're going to the movies," and off we go. The best part of the movies is either the cartoons or a Three Stooges introduction to the main feature.

Mother takes us on the night that they play a form of bingo called Lucky. After the introductory clips, Joe Cosvco, the portly owner of the theater, walks on the stage. "Tonight's Lucky grand prize is twenty dollars," he announces. "Lucky may only be called in the event you have all the numbers in a row, a column, or a diagonal line punched on the cards. If everyone is ready I will commence the drawing of numbers." He calls random numbers picked from a jar until someone declares in a loud voice, "Lucky!" The possibility of winning is exciting. Many times we are close to winning and end the game with an awhhhhhh-hhh-geeeeze as someone calls out *Lucky!*

Movie theaters are a place to see what happened in the world two or three weeks ago. Before the introductory clips is the Movie Tone world news, and this is where I get the news of WWII and the battles fought. Mother's favorite movies are romantic comedies and musicals. Sitting through movies such as *The Egg and I, Cheaper by the Dozen* and musicals such as *Singing in the Rain* is a great escape into fantasyland.

The American model for the girl next door, Doris Day is an innocent blonde who catches my fancy. During the movie I whisper, "Joe, isn't she beautiful?"

"Give me two large things you like about her," Joe replies.

"She seems nice and she will make someone a good mom."

Joe snickers and sarcastically says, "Is that what stands out to you? You sure know what to look for in a girl, you dork."

Initially the movies are in black and white, but by the end of the 1940s, almost all are in color. The movie musical productions featuring Gene Kelly or Fred Astaire intrigue me. I never have the desire to take tap dancing lessons even though the opportunity is offered when Megan begins her tap dancing career. The humdrum clickety-clack, heel-toe, heel-toe, heel-toe is repetitively chanted by Megan as she practices dancing on our kitchen's linoleum floor. With Joe playing his accordion and Megan dancing, I can sell tickets for an organ grinder and monkey show. Only "sissy boys" take tap dancing lessons. No sir, neither Superman, Batman, or the Green Lantern tap dance, and I'm not doing sissy things. Imagine Superman tap dancing before he flies off to stop lowlife criminals. The movies of the 1940s and the 1950s are a positive influence. It is easy to identify good and evil, and good always wins. Even the movies have a message that reinforces family values. Not bad, not bad at all.

CHAPTER 4

HEALTHY KIDS OR ELSE

Father preaches, "Keep your bowels open and your mouth shut. You'll not only be a success in life, but you'll also be a lot healthier." Now that's a real win–win state of affairs. My family practices keeping us healthy rather than having us recover from sickness. There is no playing around when it comes to our health.

"Jimmy, you don't look so good today," says Mom.

"I got a little cold, but honest, I'm okay."

"No, Jimmy, you're coming down with something; you can't fool me. I want you to go over to the restaurant and see your father. I'll call him and tell him you're coming. Go now—now get." Displaying symptoms of an impending illness means reporting to Dad. He initiates a homegrown medical procedure if he believes we are coming down with a bug. "You look a little peaked, young man. Are your bowels open? You look constipated," Dad says as he places his hand on my forehead and looks into my eyes. His philosophy is to get the poison, whatever it may be, to pass through my system, and the best way is with a laxative. Constipation is a word never to be uttered in the family lexicon, lest one experiences its dire consequences. He reaches for a bottle and fills a shot glass. "Here, drink this," he orders.

"I really don't want this stuff. I'm not constipated," I spontaneously blurt out. Oh-oh, one word has sealed my fate.

"I don't care. You look constipated, now drink." How does a guy not look constipated? I don't know, but I must have the constipated look. He forces upon my protesting body a shot glass full of dark brown Italian liquor called Fernet Branca. I despise and detest the licorice-tasting stuff, but it does get me loosened up inside—and rather quickly at that. I'll bet Dad's formula for health would have cured the tapeworm lady. The lasting after-effect is that I cannot tolerate the taste or smell of licorice.

In sharp contrast to Dad's "clean them from the inside out" theory of health, Mother is more scientific about her remedies. The terrible retribution for catching a cold or having a hacking cough is the dreaded mustard plaster. The secret formula is one part Vicks and one part Coleman's Mustard compound spread liberally as an opaque yellow paste on my chest before bedtime. Covering the paste with a wool cloth tied around my neck and waist completes the process. Immediately a carpet of fumes from the Vicks engulfs me and works its way into my sinus. The hot, tingly mustard plaster penetrates my skin and scares germs away; that's a medical fact. The next morning after removing it, I check to see if I have any chest left. I do and I do feel better. The crazy thing about my mother's quirky home remedies is that they work for curing everyday illnesses.

In 1946 a serious illness invades our house. The usual home remedies don't work, and my sister contracts pneumonia. The mysterious oxygen tent over her crib and the serious look on my parents' faces frighten me as she fights for each wheezing breath. A constant vigil is kept at her bedside, but there isn't much my parents can do. Pneumonia is a dreaded killer. Like a shadow I listen as the doctor tells us there is some new stuff called penicillin on the market, but the only place it can be found is in Cleveland, Ohio—about 200 miles away. It is the middle of winter and you may as well ask someone to drive to the moon as to drive to Cleveland.

To our rescue comes Uncle John. Uncle John has his pilot's license and a small single-engine airplane at Brockway's tiny makeshift airport. He volunteers to fly to Cleveland and pick up the medicine. His flight is successful, and he returns with the magic fluid. The doctor loads the hypodermic needle and thrusts it into Megan's butt. In two days her condition improves and the oxygen tent is removed. Megan recovers when many others didn't. The doctor tells us, "Had Megan got sick four years ago, I don't think she would have made it." A frightening thought indeed.

Like all kids, I fear polio. Polio is a mysterious disease and nobody knows what causes it. A girl in our neighborhood contracts polio and it strikes panic in me. What I have previously only heard about is now a reality. At the local movie theater, the March of Dimes and Sister Kenny's quest for money to purchase iron lungs are stark reminders of the mysterious ailment. Miraculously, Dr. Salk finds a vaccine for polio, and all the kids line up in the elementary school to receive a shot. "Ouch," I say as the long needle penetrates the skin on my arm. The slight sting of a shot is a welcome tradeoff to banish the terror of the polio beast.

Debilitating fear and chills run up my spine as Mom informs me: "Jimmy, next month I scheduled you for a checkup with the dentist."

"Oh no, not the dentist—can't we skip it this year? Honest, crisscross my heart and hope to die if I tell a lie, my teeth are really healthy."

"Definitely not," she answers. "James, you're going to the dentist—do you understand? Every year you must have your teeth checked. I don't want you to walk around with just your gums showing because you have poor dental hygiene."

I know the argument is over when she calls me James. May as well be submissive—maybe she'll forget. I count the days. Second only to the fear of polio is a visit to the local dentist. Dr. McGinn is the only dentist in Brockway. He is a tall man with a white moustache, menacing high eyebrows arching over chestnut brown eyes, and thick black-rim glasses framing his face. His white tunic and commanding demeanor make him an imposing godlike figure. The Doc doesn't believe in pain relief, so he never administers a local sedative such as Novocain for routine dental work. For weeks prior to my visit, I am distressed and fixate on the thought of sitting in the dental chair as he probes for cavities.

The dreaded day arrives and trepidation grips my body. I concede and accept my destiny. I enter the stark office and wait for my name to be called. "James, step up and sit in the chair," he orders as he adjusts the overhead light. "Open your mouth wide and let me take a look." Without skipping a beat he begins the quest for holes in the enamel. A glint of the light reflects off the point of his stainless steel probe as he purposefully holds it for me to view. "Yeah, huh-huh," followed by a long "ahhhhh" when he hits pay dirt. "Here's one. Do you feel it when I poke it with the probe?" It may be my imagination, but I detect a smile on his face. Finding a cavity makes him euphoric. He's probably thinking, *Oh boy, I found one, goody, goody for me.*

When the pointed metal instrument penetrates a hole in my tooth, my fearful mind goes blank. He reaches for the drill. The arcane and barbaric belt-driven drill slowly, mercilessly pierces the enamel until it excruciatingly, agonizingly, and horrendously touches an exposed nerve. Oh my God, he's drilling into my brain. At a snail's pace he continues drilling deeper and deeper into the cavity. The process engages my senses because I not only feel the intense live pain, but also smell the acrid stench of the tooth as it is drilled away. *Yoweeee!* I mentally scream. In bitter contrast to the sweat flowing from my armpits, the vibration and noise from the drill give my whole body goose bumps. "Relax," he says calmly as my back arches in the chair. Relax, relax, what a joke. God, will this ever end? The Doc deceptively reassures me time and time again, "This won't take long," and "It will be over in a second." I'm sure it is the same subtly contrived lie he tells patients once he gets them into the torture chair. Thanks to Doc McGrin by the age of twelve I have enough metal in my mouth to warrant avoiding strong magnets.

The dentist visit is where I learn the nature of pain. Still, there are other dental issues that need addressed. Straight teeth are not a priority in the forties and the fifties. It isn't uncommon for people to have functionally crooked teeth, and my front teeth are functionally crooked. I'll be a monkey's uncle if know-it-all Aunt Betty doesn't come to my rescue. Aunt Betty should be in *Life* magazine because she has an answer for almost everything. "Look here, Jimmy, put your thumb on the crooked tooth every chance you get and push in on that tooth. You can do it in school. Your great-aunt Lucia did it when she was a little girl, and it straightened her teeth—imagine that," she reassuringly says. At that point she inserts her thumb into her mouth and demonstrates her tooth-straightening technique. No use telling a person when you can show them. "Now you try it."

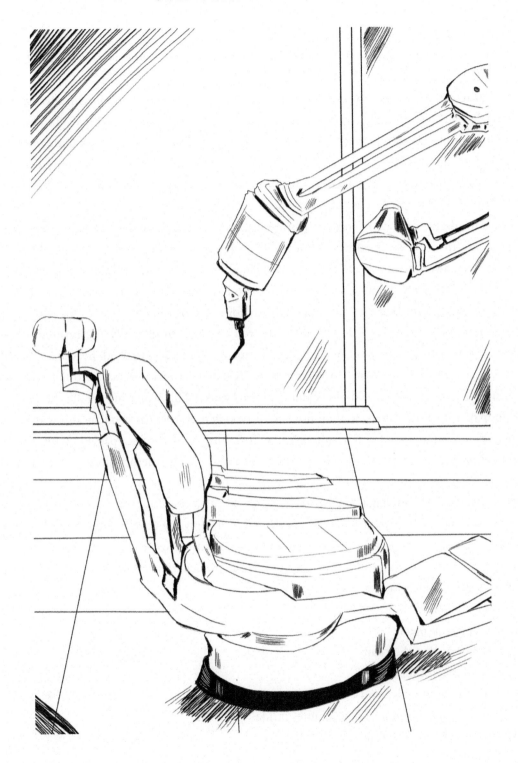

"You mean like this—am I doing it right?" I obediently ask.

"Yes, yes, you got the hang of it. Now do it every chance you get. Just sit in class and keep pushing on those teeth. Do you understand?"

I try her technique for two weeks. There I am at school, sitting at my desk with my thumb in my mouth. Boy, do I feel like a fool. The teacher looks at me and says, "James, are you okay?" I mumble "Huh-huh" with my thumb still in my mouth. The kids start giving me strange looks. I look like I'm sucking my thumb, and worry about what my classmates are thinking. I don't think any of my superheroes suck their thumbs. Then a brilliant idea pops into my mind. Why not invent Captain Thumb Sucker, hero to all boys and girls with crooked teeth? Gee whiz, what a novel idea for a comic book superhero.

Against my digital correction efforts, the stubborn tooth stands its ground. The knowledge that I am doomed to a less-than-perfect alignment of my front choppers is one of nature's flaws that I live with.

I do have an associated problem with overcrowding teeth—too many teeth for too small a mouth. Aunt Betty looks inside my mouth and says, "Yes, you do have crowded teeth; better see a dentist."

My know-it-all Aunt Betty has no home remedy for overcrowding teeth, but Doc McGrin has the answer. Pull four back teeth and that will allow the rest to come in naturally. Fortunately, he does use Novocain for pain management. Four perfectly healthy teeth leave and go to tooth heaven as Doc McGrin anchors his knee on my chest. "Now you relax and this will be over in a minute," he orders as he flashes a tool that looks like one of Dad's old pliers and begins to yank. "This won't hurt at all," he reassures me. Out they pop one at a time, leaving in their place deep, bloody holes. He packs my mouth with gauze until I resemble a puffy chipmunk. After ten minutes he removes the gauze, thrusts a paper cup filled with water at me, and orders me to rinse and spit. "That wasn't so bad, was it," he rhetorically says as he motions me to get out of the chair. At this point I am too old for the Tooth Fairy routine, so there isn't an upside to my yank-'em-and-leave-'em dental experience.

Getting teeth pulled is another one of life's challenges. I apply my introduction to terror to my class-room studies. In school we are doing poetry, and the teacher tells us to write about what we know. Con-stipation is out of the question, so I conjure up the traumatic experience with Dr. McGrin and write a poem titled "Ode to a Dentist."

The dentist is a friend.

He will help you mend.

He told me to sit in the chair.

I said, "You mean over there?"

He said, "Open up wide," and I complied.

Smiling he said, "I'll just be a few minutes inside."

My mind was filled with fear.

But I dared not shed a tear.

After he yanked 'em
I remember Mother said, "Don't forget to thank him."

Pretty nifty poem, isn't it? I believe oral hygiene and straight teeth are important, but fear of the dentist lingers for a lifetime. Doc McGrin is one of those significant life events forever etched in my mind, but thanks to the vigilance of my parents, Joe, Megan, and I grow up fairly healthy.

CHAPTER 5

SUPERSONIC PARTICLE ACCELERATORS AND OTHER GOOD STUFF

At the magic age of eight, Joe and I attend the Saturday afternoon matinee movies. Dad gives me fifteen cents, which in my world is a fortune. What can a person do with fifteen cents? With that type of cash, I go to the movies for five cents, visit Moody's Variety Store afterward and buy a comic book for five cents, and stop by the City Restaurant for a giant ice-cream cone. Cousin Mary Jane works behind the counter at the City Restaurant. "Joseph and Jimmy, what can I get for you," Mary Jane asks.

"I'd like a five-cent chocolate ice-cream cone," I say.

"Coming right up," says Mary Jane as she scans the area for the boss. If the boss isn't nearby, she winks and doesn't charge for the ice cream. With an extra nickel to spend, I am rich.

The movies feature good guys and bad guys. In the forties and fifties, good always triumphs over evil. The dark character of the bad guys is reinforced by the dark color of their clothing. Our favorite movies feature cowboys such as Roy Rogers, Gene Autry, Lash LaRue, The Durango Kid, and Hopalong Cassidy. Each cowboy has a whimsical sidekick, and no, I don't think there is anything odd about two guys traveling together.

The games we play reflect the movies we see. My buddies and I play pretend cowboys and Indians or cops and robbers. Either way we shoot 'em up and banish the bad guys.

I am compelled to keep coming back to Saturday afternoon movies to watch the weekly serial *Rocket Man* or the equally futuristic serial of *Superman*.

"Hey, Nick, Superman is in big trouble. That Kryptonite is mighty bad stuff. Did you see what it did to him?"

"Yep," he replies, "he's gonna bite the bullet this time. Made him wilt like a flower. Gotta admit, this time he's a goner, but we'll find out next week."

Each chapter ends with my hero in jeopardy, and it is critically essential to see if he survives in the following episode. From week to week every kid in town waits in fervent anticipation for the next installment of my heroes overcoming adversity and saving the world from destruction.

Joe introduces me to an experience that I am duty-bound to describe. He takes me to the most frightening and horrifying movie of my life. Nothing in the past or since matches the fear I experienced by viewing *The Thing*. The black-and-white movie delivers a vivid fright to my developing mind. *The Thing* is a cutting-edge horror movie. The monster chasing the good guys at an isolated Alaskan army outpost is a threat to humanity. I visualize The Thing chasing me. "Joe, let's get out of here; this is bad and getting worse. Come on, Joe, let's leave," I beg.

"No," Joe firmly replies. "Piss your pants for all I care. Grow up, mister brilliant, it's only a movie."

"Then give me your coat so I can cover my eyes. Mom will really be mad if you bring me home brain-damaged."

"It's too late for that; you're already an idiot. Here," Joe barks as he hands me his coat, "now will you shut up?" Thank goodness one of the soldiers discovers that The Thing can be fried with electric current. Joe thinks I am silly, but our four-year age difference leaves a huge gap in maturity and how the world is viewed. My suspicion is that he set me up to get a laugh, but he isn't laughing when he has to share his bed with me.

Throughout the movie Joe Cosvco walks up and down the aisles, monitoring our behavior. The worst thing that can possibly happen is to be thrown out of the movies for misbehaving. Getting ejected makes a person a social outcast. If banished, what can a kid possibly do on Saturday afternoon? I deviously learn to fake good behavior. As Mr. Cosvco walks past, I straighten up, fold my hands on my lap, and give the appearance of proper movie-watching decorum. It is the same body language used for faking it in church.

One of the neighborhood kids has a birthday party and Joe and I are invited. I think this will be fun. Little do I know that something starting out as fun will develop into a battle of wills.

I definitely believe mankind's most useful invention is denim overalls. Once washed three times and broken in, the feel of soft cotton on my skin is the greatest. If left to me, overalls would be worn seven days a week. Nevertheless, these decisions are never entirely up to young kids. Mother wants me to dress up to attend the party. That by itself isn't a surprise. I expect to wash my face, comb my hair, and put on clean clothes, but she raises the stakes to an intolerable level. "Jimmy boy, I want you to wear these brand-new knickers I bought for you."

"What? Are you kidding—knickers?" I say defiantly. "Ah Mom, I don't want to wear knickers. How about clean overalls?"

"James, you'll either wear the knickers or you won't go to the party. Your brother is going to wear his."

When she calls me James, I know she is serious and my defiance has crossed the line. I begin to pout and sulk. Knickers—do you hear me?—she wants me to wear *knickers*.

Joe whispers, "Don't be such a dork; wear the damn things so we can get outta here." Those dreaded three-quarter-length corduroy pants fitting over calf-length socks are for kids considered three-dollar bills, and I won't be caught dead in them. Joe must be insane. What is wrong with my parents? Thankfully, Mom chooses not to escalate the situation. She gives me a final ultimatum. "This is your last chance, James. Are you going to wear these new knickers?"

My feelings are so strong that it takes me less than a nanosecond to determinedly answer, "I'm not going to the party." Good gravy, I just told Mom no. Imagine that—I boldly said no—completely out of character for me.

Joe, dressed in knickers, leaves without me. Tearfully I watch him walk up the alley to the party in his goofy knickers and scornfully say, "What a jerk." I won a slight battle, because never again am I asked to get into such an ungodly getup.

Learning to ride a bicycle is another life-altering experience. Dad and Joe hold the bike steady as I climb aboard the two-wheeled beast. After mounting the seat, I place my feet on the pedals. "Okay, now hold on to the handlebars and pedal. Do you understand?" says Dad. I nod my head, yes. "Now, your brother and I are going to give you a little push, and you do what I told you to do, okay?" Together they give me a shove and yell, "Pedal faster, pedal faster, pedal faster!" I do as they instruct and off I go in a straight line. I am as free as the wind. Suddenly I freeze. They forgot to tell me how to steer the bike. In the middle of the large vacant parking lot, a lone telephone pole begs a bike to run into it. I comply. Yes, under extreme duress the innocent pole is hit. Dad yells, "Jimmy, are you okay?"

"Yeah, Dad," I answer. "I was doing rather well until the telephone pole jumped in my path." The good news is that I only get a few scratches. After a few more tries, I get the hang of it and by the end of the day, I am proud of my accomplishment.

The arduous task of maintaining a bike requires constant attention to detail. Checking the tires, adding air, and constantly cleaning my roadster are the obligations of bike ownership. Among my group an ongoing, but meaningless, argument over the best brakes is the topic of discussion. New Departure and Bendix are the leading brakes, and I argue for Bendix because that's what I have. Bicycle tires of the 1940s aren't the best, and a flat tire occurs once a month. Getting up in the morning and attempting to mount my metal steed only to find a flat tire ruins the day. Off comes the wheel, and with two screwdrivers the tire is coaxed from the rim, taking care not to pinch the inner tube. Punctures are easily located by placing soapy water on the inner tube and looking for air bubbles. The real challenge is where to get the twenty-five cents to have the hole patched?

Every kid knows Judd Volpe can repair a flat tire. He is the mechanic at the neighborhood Mobil gas station. If a kid is humble and asks in a respectful manner, Judd interrupts his busy repair schedule to burn a patch on the inner tube. Once repaired, the tire is reassembled and fastened to the bike's frame.

Continuous bicycle improvement is a priority. To give my machine an authentic motorcycle sound, a playing card is taped to the frame and allowed to freely flap between the spokes. Vrooooom is the motorcycle-sound made as the bike accelerates. As I get older, I customize my bike. It is no longer a plain Jane maroon bike, but a beautiful, hand-painted, black with pink accent machine. Pink handle grips with black and pink plastic streamers flowing in the slipstream add a touch of class.

Learning to ride a bike is a liberating experience. Pedal power unshackles me from the limited bounds of foot-powered transportation. My world increasingly expands.

"James," beckons Dad. Oh-oh, this is serious; he's calling me James. I must be in trouble. "James, I want you to take today's deposit to the bank. There's one hundred and ninety-seven dollars in this envelope. I'm putting the deposit slip inside. All you have to do is hand it to Mrs. Mancuso. Wait for her to give you a receipt."

"Okay, I'm on my way." Dad entrusts me with up to two hundred dollars and lets me ride uptown to make the daily bank deposit. With that kind of money, I know the family thinks of me as a man. This simple act nurtures a feeling of importance and reinforces the knowledge of the family's trust in me.

In the summer Joe takes me swimming along with the older boys. There is no public swimming pool, so we hop on our bikes and pedal to our favorite spots. Usually, I am the youngest kid in the neighborhood gang, and the bigger boys generally look after me. The hit movie that summer is *Navy Frogmen* and I pretend to be an underwater demolition expert. To dry off after swimming, I lie in the middle of the hot macadam road. I keep a keen eye out for speeding cars to avoid becoming a splotch on the road. The only time I don't swim is late summer. We call this period the dog days because we believe late summer is polio season. Thank God for Dr. Salk; he gives us extra swimming days.

Sometimes in life you eat the bear, and other times the bear eats you—this time the bear eats me. If possible, Joe and I would swim seven days a week. Swimming is our compulsion. This is where the plot thickens. The situation gets difficult, since Sunday is reserved for the family. Joe is an independent teen, and as his nine-year-old brother, I often follow his example. We are still expected to do the hated Brookville visits, but one Sunday we rebel and take a stand. We challenge the family's authority and place the pursuit of pleasure over family obligations. This is a hill I am willing to die on—and indeed I do die on it.

In incorrigibly wild defiance, we abandon our Sunday duties and go swimming. When we return in the early afternoon, our parents are gone and the house is locked. I am discarded and thrown out of the house. Imagine, nine years old and I'm thrown out of the house. I'm a derelict. I contain my anxiety and ask, "Whadda we gonna do now, Joe?" Cool and calm as ever, Joe responds, "How 'bout we go down to Aunt Betty's house. First let's see if we can get into our house. We're going to need a few things like a toothbrush and underwear." Like thieves in the night we find an unlocked window and break into the house to fetch some clothing. Afterward, we ride our bikes to Uncle Sam and Aunt Betty's house. Joe sheepishly says to Aunt Betty, "Huh, we've been locked out of the house. Can we stay with you?"

"You've been locked out of the house?" she repeats. "Imagine that." She frowns, but does let us sleep over that evening with the codicil that the next day we go home and apologize to our parents. The lesson learned is; before jumping off a cliff, remind yourself that it takes few brains to make the jump, but the fall is going to hurt. So ends my first attempt as a rebellious, independent preteen.

Another lesson learned early is that whenever Joe screws up, I pay the price. Having an older brother creates circumstances hard to overcome. A story I once heard sums up my situation. A mother of an unruly child told the principal, "If my Timmy misbehaves, don't worry. Just slap the child on either side of him and he will straighten up." I forever find myself on one or the other side of Joe. I desperately want a Daisy Red Ryder BB gun like my parents bought for Joe. There is not a boy alive who doesn't. I plead, "Mom, will you buy me a Red Ryder BB gun? I'm the only kid in the neighborhood without one."

"No, you don't need one," Mom tersely answers.

"You heard what your mother said," Dad adds. "Remember what happened to our neighbor's house. Do you want to get into that kind of trouble?" Emphatically he repeats, "You're not getting a BB gun."

The neighbor lady has a hole put through her window by a BB gun. Joe vehemently denies the deed, but as a result, I am not permitted to have a BB gun. It is irrational logic, but it certainly taught Joe a lesson—huh? On every issue where Joe pushes the envelope, I pay the consequences. I finally figure it out. As the first child, Joe is the person my parents practice making their mistakes on, and they are not about to repeat those mistakes with their second child. Rational thinking doesn't make me feel better, but it does explain some of the mystery.

There is one time I shy away from following Joe's example. Uncle Jim, the hair stylist in our family, convinces Joe to get a permanent. I watch intently as he puts curlers in Joe's hair and douses them with something smelling like rotten eggs. "Okay, Joseph, you're finished," says Uncle Jim.

"Can I check out my hair job in the mirror? Wow, it looks different, but I like it," proclaims Joe. Gawking at his fluffy and curly head of hair, I find it hard to keep from laughing—he looks like Harpo Marx, but I'm not dumb enough to tell him that.

"Next? Okay, Jimmy, it's your turn." Uncle Jim beckons me to come forward.

"No way," I emphatically say. I assert my independence from Joe's foolishness and give Uncle Jim an unqualified no. Unlike knickers that are easily discarded, Joe's outrageous curly head will be around for some time. I am not like Joe and won't let myself look like a frizzy Brillo pad.

Music is important to our family—not symphonic music, not contemporary music, but festive Italian or ethnic music. To Dad, the best music comes from the accordion. Father insists that Joe and I take accordion lessons. Joe is four years older and starts taking lessons. This pleases Dad. He loves to hear him play the "Blue Danube Waltz" and "Lady of Spain," but I get sick of hearing Joe practice them over and over. Thanks to his success, a year later I start taking lessons, but I never master the instrument. With the left hand on one side playing the base buttons and the right hand on the keys, the coordination of my scrawny limbs is beyond my capabilities. Even more significant, I don't have a lick of musical talent. Twice a month on Saturday our teacher, Marco, dresses in a black suit and comes to the house to give private lessons. Marco's most significant characteristics are his moustache and the diamond ring he wears on his pinky finger. Except for those details all memories of him are blocked. I frustrate Marco. Why else does his face turn beet red within five minutes of starting a lesson? The family finally recognizes that I don't have the knack to play the instrument when two years are spent on the same sheet of music, "Little Curls," without mastering it. Mother is the first to sense my frustration and counsels, "Son, if you can't play an instrument, don't feel bad. Remember, Jimmy, there have to be good listeners too. Everyone can do something that is important, and so can you."

"That's absolutely true, Mom. Honest, I am trying," I say, even though it isn't entirely true. I always remember Mom's kind words. In the world of instrumental music, I do get good at playing the radio. Finally, after considerable financial investment, Father realizes the folly of fitting a square peg into a round hole and gives up. See? Praying does work.

My celebration is premature. Within a year I am taking piano lessons. I underestimate my parents' perseverance. All I want is to play a tune on the piano, but the teacher has me practicing scales. There is a lack of congruence between what the teacher wants and what I want. Somehow Mother forgot to tell me that I am required to play in a piano recital. Miss Ceretti, my piano teacher, sneaks that in on me. If I can be taught to play a musical instrument, then any person can play. I take the attitude that a guy's gotta do what a guy's gotta do, especially when he's been snookered.

The song I play at the recital is Stephen Foster's "Beautiful Dreamer." The gymnasium is filled with people, and I want to get this dreadful task over as fast as possible. Mother makes sure my hair is combed and that I am dressed properly in a white shirt and a black clip-on bow tie. Dad shines my shoes and I look spiffy. When my turn comes to tickle the ivories, I briskly walk from the back of the gym to the stage and sit at the piano. Quickly, mechanically, without hesitation, I play my song. The audience politely applauds. I smartly bow and in one continuous motion double-time off the stage—my objective to get out of there as soon as possible. Mother is as perceptive as ever. "I thought you were in a bit of a hurry," she comments. "You did run off the stage, didn't you?"

"Mom, when you are a superstar like me, you have to get away from your fans as soon as possible." I have done my duty for the family and within a year beg out of a career as a pianist.

Despite the hardships of paying for Joe's mistakes, there is an upside to having an older brother. He may abuse me, but no one else is allowed to. In elementary school some older boys are bullying a group of us younger fourth-grade kids, and their harassment gets so bad that I ask Joe to intervene. Joe talks to the boys in a language they understand, and they never bother us again. When you don't have the power to intervene, it is good to know someone who does.

Another advantage is inheriting a chain of money-paying jobs as Joe outgrows them and moves on to bigger and better opportunities. For six years I mow the grass for the people living in the neighborhood mansion. Cutting the two acres of grass takes about three hours, and for my effort I receive the lofty sum of $2.00. I am paid by check and keep the canceled checks as a reminder of my first paycheck. The joke among the relatives is that I have the first dollar I ever earned, and they are correct. The touch, feel, and smell of crisp, new one-dollar bills are enjoyable. Donald Duck's uncle, Scrooge McDuck, is my model. There is something about money that I like.

Joe leaves me the legacy, passed on to him from cousin Tom Varni, of scrubbing the floors at the restaurant on Sunday mornings. My custodial duties commence in the eighth grade and continue every weekend until I graduate from college. Joe instructs me, "Jimmy, the job requires more than scrubbing floors. It also requires stoking the coal furnace, taking out the ashes, and filling the coal hopper for the weekend. Your scrub areas are the kitchen floors, the tavern, and the tiled bathrooms, got that? Oh, one more thing: you must also clean the spittoons," Joe says with a smile on his face. In the early 1950s they have these filthy, disgusting, barbaric spitting receptacles. I suit up similar to a spaceperson. Boots and long rubber gloves are worn to escort the spittoons outside for a good scrubbing. The fear of getting splashed and contaminated with the incrusted brownish tobacco crud defies rational reasoning. It is a grimy job, but that's the burden of responsibility. Never will I "put a pinch between my cheek and gum" like they urge on the radio.

In the restaurant business Dad has a standing story. "Do you want to know who the owner of the restaurant is? He's the guy who cleans the bathrooms." To that I add, "And the guy who cleans the spittoons." The moral is that only the owner will do an acceptable job, since he has the most to lose. The good thing is that I get paid for it. The sum of $6.00 a week is good money.

Often my brother and I have fun by ourselves. For instance, when Joe goes to Gene Rose's Barber Shop to get a haircut, I also get a haircut. A haircut costs twenty-five cents, and we want to look good and smell good. To ensure this we have a plan. Joe and I save until we have enough money, two dollars and fifty cents, to purchase a bottle of Mr. Rose's great-smelling emerald green Jeris Hair Dressing.

"Hey, Jimmy, I got the stuff. Let's go in the bathroom and get ready for school. Get in here and close the door before Mom sees us. Here's your ration for today," Joe says as he dispenses four squirts of hair dressing into the palm of my hand. "Rub it into your hair," he instructs. "Good, now rub this Vaseline Hair Tonic into your hair. You're getting the hang of it." To achieve that special manly look, a complex three-step combing ritual is followed.

Step 1: First I run the teeth of my pocket comb through my hair from back to front until it hangs over my eyes in straight lines.

Step 2: This step consists of combing my hair to the right and to the left sides of my head, thus creating a left-sided part.

Step 3: The final step requires special finesse and advanced motor skills. With my right hand I place the comb in the front of my head and quickly move my wrist in a twisting motion up and to the right.

The finishing twist swirls the coarse black hair into an eloquent pompadour. Every morning I follow this routine and liberally apply the special combination of ingredients. Once in place, even a hurricane can't dislodge a single hair—like a Zippo lighter, I am windproof.

Joe and I prefer Vaseline Hair Tonic to Wildroot Cream Oil because Vaseline has a higher shine factor. The scent of the green liquid captured in the Jeris bottle is an outstanding treat for my olfactory nerves. "Guys, what in the world do you have on your hair?" inquires Mom.

"Smells great, doesn't it?" I boastfully say.

"Well, it sure smells, I'll say that for both of you," she replies as she turns and walks away, shaking her head.

On bright, sunny days people squint or risk going blind as the sun bounces off our smelly, but glossy black hair. We are malodorous and proud of it. You can smell us coming long before you ever see us. In my mind I look and smell beautiful, but we probably stink to high heavens.

To finance another of our joint escapades, we pool our money and buy fencing swords advertised in the *Popular Mechanics* magazine. The day our $4.95 package arrives, we hurry home from school and eagerly rip open the box. Feverishly, we remove the packing material and expose our beautiful swords. We are pleased with the fruits of our labor. Joe notices a piece of paper at the bottom of the box. "What's this?" He picks up the paper and reads it: "DANGER, DO NOT REMOVE THE RUBBER PROTECTOR FROM THE TIP OF THE SWORD. WE HOPE YOU ENJOY YOUR SWORDS AND USE THEM SAFELY." Joe gives me an irritated look. "Look at this. A damn piece of paper is giving me a lecture. I'd like to know if there's anyone in this world that doesn't want to give me a damn lecture. Notes like this piss me off. I get enough lectures—I don't need these guys preaching to me."

"Who cares, give me my sword," I plead. "You're acting like some kind of a psycho idiot. It's only a piece of paper—get a life and get over it. Can't you rebel some other time? Flip on your sanity switch and give me my sword." I want my sword and all Joe can do is fixate on the stupid note. He is frozen like a deer in front of headlights.

"They must think we are stupid. What an insult to our relatively mature ability to make levelheaded decisions. I am a swordsman, not a killer."

Nevertheless, our movie hero Zorro doesn't use THE RUBBER PROTECTOR. With gleeful jubilation, we celebrate in unabashed merriment at being the only kids in the neighborhood with fencing swords. With a brown wooden handle, a silver handguard, and a black foil tipped with a rubber protector, these weapons provide hours of pleasure as we transform ourselves into the Three Musketeers, or at least two of them. We defiantly violate the written warning and remove the rubber tip, but blood is never drawn because Mom would surely confiscate our weapons of war.

Moody's Variety Store is a cornucopia of fascinating artifacts that stimulate and energize my mind. Building wooden model airplanes is one of my favorite hobbies. Mr. Moody not only has the best selection of comic books in town, but also the best selection of model airplanes. With single-minded purpose, the wide selection available is passionately examined. Our choice narrows to one airplane, a beautiful mono-wing seaplane. The beauty is purchased and we scurry home to begin the delicate construction process. Carefully we sand the wooden wings, the tail parts, and the pontoon landing gear, before gluing them to the fuselage. With the model fully assembled and silky smooth like a baby's behind, it is ready to paint. We use a paint product called "dope." Joe daringly jokes to Mom, "We have to go uptown to Moody's and buy some dope." God, we boldly push the limits. Even insinuating the purchasing of dope is an imprudently audacious statement. Mom allows us to work at the kitchen table. After painting and putting the decals on our airplane, we ceremoniously suspend it from the bedroom ceiling with clear plastic fish line, giving it the appearance of eternal flight. Hobbies teach me important skills. With a steady hand, colorful paint schemes are created. At a young age I develop a sharp eye for color.

Wherever Joe goes, Mom makes him bring me along. He is responsible for me, but he doesn't mind. When we aren't fighting, we are buddies. "Joseph, keep an eye on your brother," Mom instructs. He responds, "Yeah, I will. Come on, twerp, let's go."

I am more of a go-along than a tagalong kid. Most of the guys in the neighborhood gang are three or four years older, and as I said, they treat me well. All the guys carry black-handled jackknives and so do I. Baseball is a favorite game played with our two-blade pocketknives. Placing the big blade straight out and extending the smaller blade halfway produces the bat. We stick the small blade in the ground so the knife stands by itself. We gather in a semicircle and each kid takes his turn at bat. One finger underneath the black handle provides the power to propel the entire knife spinning through the air. Depending on how the knife lands, the player is awarded anything from a hit to a home run. A knife failing to stick in the ground is an out. Oh, by the way, none of us lose a finger or poke out an eye.

A supersonic particle accelerator is a science fiction name for an intimidating weapon. "Come on, Nick, let's go down to the woods and cut some reeds. They are big enough to be made into bean blowers."

"Yeah, this is the time of year they should be just about right. You got your pocketknife with you?"

"Sure do," I answer. "Wouldn't be caught without it."

Among the hundreds of uses for a knife is cutting hollow-tube bean blowers (better known as supersonic particle accelerators) from reeds that grow in the nearby woods. A supersonic particle accelerator is a science fiction name for an intimidating weapon, and the awesome, nonlethal bean blower propels a projectile accurately to the target at near supersonic speed.

"Nick, there's a patch of elderberry bushes on the other side of the creek. I'll meet you there as soon as I finish cutting this reed. Make sure you get some green ones and some red ones," I instruct. Harvested elderberries in various stages of ripeness are a plentiful supply of ammunition. With my mouth full of elderberries, I propel them rapidly either one at a time or in a staccato *tat, tat, tat*, machine gun spray that insures a hit on the target. "Got ya," I yell after letting loose with a salvo of projectiles.

"No you didn't," Nick protests.

"Oh yeah, then how did you get that red splotch in the middle of your T-shirt?" Let me divulge a secret. Ripe elderberries launched at high velocity leave a bloodred stain upon impact. If a hit is scored I immediately know it.

Supersonic particle accelerators are free to all kids. The requirements for fun are simple: a sense of adventure, a few buddies, and a pocketknife. But do-gooder groups try to form "Ban the Bean Blower" committees, so I wouldn't wait too long to make one.

In the kingdom of kids, rules are important. It is essential that the rule-making process is never disorganized or ambiguous. Meticulously defined screwball rules are observed, lest my juvenile world collapse into utter chaos. "Okay, guys, let's pick up teams," Joe hollers. Getting picked for a team is usually by a coin toss, but in baseball it is a specific ritual performed with a baseball bat. "Who's going to be the captain of the other team?"

"I'll be captain," volunteers one of the older boys.

"Here's the bat," says another guy, as he tosses it to Joe. The bat is tossed to the opposing captain. He catches it with one hand and the selection process begins. Each captain alternatively stacks his hand above the other until the knob of the bat is either completely covered by a hand or can be clutched by one of the captains. If the captain grips and holds the knob with his fingertips, a "throw-off" is in order. "It's a tie—this means a throw-off," Joe announces. "Okay, everybody, get out of the way." A throw-off requires each captain to grip the knob of the bat by his fingertips and throw it as far as possible over his right shoulder. Starting from where the bat lands, it is flipped end over end until reaching the thrower. The largest bat measurement is the furthest distance. The captain throwing the bat farthest gets first pick for his team. "You win," Joe concedes. "That means you get first pick." The origin of this tribal process is unknown. The ritualistic behavior appears strange, but it is effective. Seldom do we argue over first pick.

Too bad cantankerous governments can't problem solve like kids. Imagine the President of the United States and the leader of Russia tossing the baseball bat to settle a dispute. People hold their breath as the radio announcer dramatically counts the bat toss measurements over the airwaves. I think it's a great way to solve conflicts—sure does beat going to war.

Reality is what I perceive and sometimes it doesn't make sense. To the youthful mind the chronology and relationship between time, distance, and space is easily confused.

"Jim, do you know that a Jap Zero crashed in the woods outside of town? He was coming to bomb the glass plant and ran out of gas," Nick informs me.

"No, tell me more. Nick, how many people know about this? Let's keep it a secret; maybe we can capture him and become famous." Somehow incidents taken out of context develop into reality. As the rumor spreads among the gang that a WWII Japanese plane has been shot down near town, we organize search parties. WWII has been over for five years, but we are sure the plane is hidden in the woods. We journey across pastures, through woods, up hills, down hills, constantly moving in our quest to become local heroes. That plane is here and we are going to find it.

Our quest sounds crazy, but the sense of adventure is real. We know the crafty enemy will camouflage and cleverly hide his war machine. This diabolical plot must be unmasked. That's what Captain America would say.

Although our intentions are patriotic, we never find the plane. Maybe it is a good thing that the pilot evades our detection. With only a pocketknife, what would I do if I did find the plane? Perhaps the best defense would be to invite the pilot to a game of pocketknife baseball. The crafty enemy will surely want to do battle, but pocketknife baseball will better test his skills and manhood. We must be out of our skulls to imagine such a preposterous scenario, but there is still an outside chance that the pilot is mucking around in the woods, hiding from us—only time will tell.

CHAPTER 6

FAMILY, FRIENDS, AND FUN

Even though the enemy warplane is not found, it is great to have hills and woods near home. Every summer Joe and I march through cow pastures in our quest to plunder nature's bounty, our secret blackberry patch. When walking through pastures, Joe warns, "Watch out for the cow pies."

"What are cow pies?"

"It's the stuff you're standing in. It's cow shit, ya dummy. Christ, you're stupid."

The numerous cow pies must be avoided because Mom won't be happy if I track nature's droppings glued to the bottom of my high-top clodhoppers throughout her house.

Cows are smart. They strategically camouflage their droppings in high grass. "Joe, when I think about it, what else does a cow have to do all day long except eat and make cow pies? What a great life."

"So you think they spend all day planning where to take a dump so a Sherlock Holmes like you can step in them?" Joe replies, shaking his head from side to side.

At the margin of the forest an old abandoned coal mine guards an area that nurtures the growth of thorny blackberry bushes. We claim the site as our special spot.

Blackberry picking is a tough and lucrative occupation. The thorns are like cat's claws scratching and piercing my skin. It doesn't take long before I wise up and wear a long-sleeve shirt and thick denim trousers. Eventually, I become an efficient blackberry picker and start a business selling them for twenty-five cents a quart. "Hello, my name is Jimmy and I'm selling these fresh-picked blackberries for fifty cents a quart."

"They look old to me. When did you pick them?" says the lady in the doorway.

"Just this morning, lady." She doesn't outright say no, so I know she wants to barter. That's why I always start with the high price of fifty cents. "I'll tell you what I'm gonna do. For you I'll make an exception. You can have them for the bargain price of twenty-five cents a quart."

She pauses, places both hands on her hips, and says, "Okay, but they better be good."

Watching the salespeople haggle under Aunt Freda's trees taught me a lot. Some people gripe if they get a berry that isn't completely ripe, and to aggravate grumpy customers, a few green berries are placed at the bottom of the pail.

As an added bonus the cooks at Dad's restaurant bake fresh pies every day. Now and again the ladies bake me a blackberry pie. The sweet, plump, juicy berries snuggled between the two flaky crusts make a wonderful pie. Every morning the smell of baking pies wafts through the bedroom window, teasing, titillating, and exciting my olfactory nerves. I wake up and instinctively know how to satiate my gastronomical desire. Without hesitation I eat breakfast and before lunch devour a piece of warm pie. Pie is the meal of champions.

Dad's restaurant provides ample time for fun and games. The neighborhood cooks treat me like part of their family. Dad proudly boasts, "In over forty years of business, no customer ever got sick from my food." Often he says to the cooks, "When in doubt, throw it out." Special attention is given not only to the food, but also to my father's personal appearance. Daily he dons a clean, starched white shirt with a black bow tie, shines his shoes, and walks the short distance to work.

Father provides advice for a quick read of people. "You know how to size up a person? Look at their shoes and the wristwatch; they tell a story. Shoes say attention to detail, and if a person cannot take care of personal details, how can they take care of the company's details? A wristwatch tells you the value a person places on time." Although shoes and wristwatches are good indicators for quickly sizing up a person, they sometimes are misleading. Many of the wealthy depression-era customers never display their wealth. The conservative old-timers don't trust banks and keep a great deal of cash on hand in preparation for the next depression.

The best days in the restaurant business are when the produce is delivered. Lettuce is delivered in rectangular 2x2x3-foot wooden crates. The crates consist of three slats on each of the long sides and two solid wood ends. These empty crates become my airplanes. I remove one of the side slats and nail it at the center point on the end of the crate. The slat spins and becomes the propeller. Two slats are nailed at right angles to the sides of the crate to become wings. The remaining slat, placed across the box, is a seat. There, my friends, are hours of fun piloting my airplane. If the airplane crashes, no need to worry since the following week I can build another.

After the morning produce delivery, I look forward to the milkman's visit. His name is Patty Grinnin. As he delivers milk a covey of kids silently gather around his truck. We aren't interested in his regular milk; we are looking for chocolate milk. Chocolate milk is a gift from God. Our folks won't buy it unless there is a special occasion, but Patty, out of the goodness of his heart, gives us each a glass pint bottle to drink. Aunt Betty propagates the myth that chocolate milk isn't healthy for young kids. She preaches, "If you drink too much chocolate milk, you'll get worms."

"You mean I'll get worms like that woman who killed herself? God, I never knew that. I guess I'm pretty stupid," I say tongue-in-cheek. "Imagine, telling us that we can get worms from chocolate milk—how ridiculous. I know those squiggly red creatures live underground and not in chocolate milk."

"Yes, you more than likely will get worms," she says. "You learn something every day, don't you?"

I think the real reason my parents don't buy chocolate milk is that it costs more than white milk.

The milkman is also the iceman. Huge blocks of ice are delivered twice a week, placed in the ice chest, and used as chipped ice for beverages or refrigeration. On hot summer days, Patty chips off some ice and gives it to us to suck on. "Thanks, Patty, this is awesome," I say. Simple things are appreciated.

Monumental events appear unexpectedly. Even though stern, Dad has a sense of humor and we test it. "Megan, I got a great idea. Let's trick Dad tonight and scare him. Wait till you see this." Usually he closes the business after two o'clock in the morning and walks into a dark house. Like clever conspirators Megan and I spend the better part of the evening constructing a life-size dummy. "Here is an old flannel shirt, a pair of bib overalls, and an old hat," I excitedly tell my sister. "We'll buttoned the flannel shirt around the kitchen chair and stuff it with pillows to make it plump like a human chest. On top of the flannel shirt we'll add overalls stuffed with towels. A pair of stuffed gloves attached to the shirt gives our guy hands. A Halloween mask provides the spooky face. Top off the mask with a hat and we have a life-size dummy sitting on a chair." Excitedly we place our fiendish friend around the corner where it can't immediately be seen. The dummy is our version of a Frankenstein monster. Off to bed we scurry, giggling all the way.

In the morning Dad looks at us. He laughingly says, "I came in last night and someone greeted me. Do you kids know anything about this?"

"Not me," my sister and I say in unison. Neither of us is good at telling lies and we bust out laughing.

Dad plays along. "Hmmmm," he says, "that was a frightening sight. It sure did scare me." Pulling one over on him is great.

Not all of our antics are as innocent as scaring Dad. Sometimes Joe and I do taboo things. We dip our curiosity into the pool of forbidden and decadent behavior. A neighborhood kid, Jackie, routinely visits the Mobil gas station to buy cigarettes for his father. He does this daily and there are no questions asked. They take his twenty-five cents and give him a pack of Camels and off to home he goes, except for one day.

"Okay, guys, I got 'em; let's get the hell outta here," Jackie reports to the gang.

"Where we gonna go?" Joe asks.

"Up on the side of the hill near the woods," says Jackie. We agree and hastily make our way to the nearby woods until we are safe from probing eyes. Jackie produces the confiscated smokes. He lights a single cigarette, takes a puff, and passes it to the next guy, who repeats the process. Jackie makes sure we know group-puffing etiquette. "When you take a drag, don't use cow lips," he says. "Make sure you don't get the end wet with your lips—ya understand?"

"Ya mean like this?" I say.

"No, didn't ya hear me? Don't use your cow lips and keep the end dry," Jackie instructs.

Joe looks disapprovingly at me. "Christ's sake, can't you do anything right? Stop being a queer."

Doing something forbidden makes us big shots. We are momentarily exuberant. For that short period of time, we affirm independence from our parents. Dutifully we puff away, thinking we will enjoy dragging on a cigarette. Cigarettes are terrible and there is no joy in choking and coughing. The good news is that we don't burn down the woods. On the "bad-scale" for young kids, smoking is considered a serious offense. The possibility exists that smoking will stunt my growth; at least that's what Aunt Betty tells me.

Every Sunday after Mass I anxiously wait at the front door for the delivery of the thick Sunday newspaper. I am after the Sunday comics. Joe's physical size entitles him to first pick, which means Megan and I get the leftovers. Prince Valiant, Dick Tracy, and the Phantom are my favorite comics. I easily lose myself to my imagination when reading them and know that next week's funnies will be even better. Adding to my explosive world of knowledge is Ripley's Believe It or Not. The things I read in Ripley's comic strip fascinate me.

Al Capp's "Li'l Abner" introduces me to a popular hillbilly comic that includes a teardrop-shaped entity called a "Shmoo." Unwittingly, I find something that can be used to get under my brother's skin. When he starts agitating me, I only have to repeatedly call out, "Joe the Shmoo, Joe the Shmoo, Joe the Shmoo." It drives him crazy. Oh, what a delight. To be really nasty I shout, "Joey the Shmooie, Joey the Shmooie."

"Mom, I'm going to bash that creepy shrimp if he doesn't knock it off."

"James, you stop that right now. You boys be nice to each other," says Mom. I count on her intervention and use my weapon judiciously since he is bigger than I am.

Getting on little sister's nerves is easier. I drive her up the wall with my secret weapon. Whenever she bugs me I take out my pocket comb and run my finger across its teeth. The high-pitched sound of the plastic teeth irritates her in the same manner as someone scratching fingernails across a blackboard. Watching her squirm as I torment her is a joy. "Mom, Mom, he's doing it again."

"I'm not doing anything," I innocently protest.

"Now, Jimmy, stop it," Mom cautions. Megan wises up to my harassing and seeks the protection of Mother whenever the comb is flashed. Imagine, having such power over my brother and sister.

Every neighborhood has a neighborhood pest, and in ours it's Margaret Mary Potter. Dirty yellow hair, thick plastic-rim glasses, and a mouth with protruding buckteeth that give her the appearance of continually sucking on lemons. Being the same age as my sister occasionally makes her an unwelcome guest in our house. Margaret Mary is a bold and obnoxious person with a high-pitched voice that makes dogs howl. She is to be avoided at all cost. Looking out the back door, I see her gray-shingle house less than half a block away. Joe and I have standard procedures if we see her walking down the narrow dirt alley. "Oh

God, here comes Margaret Mary," I alert Joe. Her approach sends us into a frantic frenzy. "Lock the front door. Quick, hide out of sight and wait for her to go away," I say. Her departure usually takes a protracted period of time. She is not easily dissuaded. Her actions are similar to the zombies in *The Night of the Living Dead* as they try to gain entrance into the hero's house. Margaret Mary goes from the front door, to peeking through windows, to knocking on the back door in her quest for entrance. She carefully examines the house for any telltale indication of life within.

One day she catches me off guard and I make the awesome mistake of answering the door. "James, is Megan home?" she asks in her high-pitched, nasal tone.

"No," I curtly reply and slam the door shut. I hate it when she calls me James. Not foiled in her quest, she begins to incessantly ring the doorbell. I again answer and slightly open the door. "I told you she isn't home."

"James, I think you're not telling me the truth," she accuses and sticks her foot in the door so I can't close it. Like Red Skelton in the movie *The Fuller Brush Man,* she gains a foothold to my sacred home and begins her search for my sister. The blatant boldness of this audacious girl amazes me. I am at a loss; what should I do? "Get out, leave now—do you hear me?" I shout in a commanding voice.

"No, I want to talk to Megan and you're not going to stop me," she defiantly responds.

I find myself in a volatile predicament. The situation escalates out of control. Her forced entrance is the camel that breaks the straw's back—I think that's how it goes. This brash invader has pushed me to my wits' end and I tightly grab her arm to escort her from the house. Margaret Mary, not being dumb, initiates a counter-move in the form of passive protest that would make Gandhi proud. Plop, she drops to the kitchen floor. "I'm staying until I talk to Megan, shoo, shoo, get away."

"One way or the other you're leaving," I loudly proclaim.

Her lips curl in a defiant sneer, exposing her gaping teeth. "Leave me alone," she snarls. She momentarily stuns and befuddles me, but she overplays her hand. Fearlessly quivering with fury I confiscate one of her legs, dragging her out of the kitchen. Like a mudslide in slow motion she kicks and screams as I sweep her toward the front door. "Stop that, stop that," she yells. Finally she is positioned near the door, and with one mighty effort I forcefully shove her onto the porch. The Margaret Mary Beast is banished. The sanctity of my home is again temporarily safe from her intrusion. To her credit her foot-inserting effort in the doorway is astonishingly fast and effective. From that time on our house constantly stands in a state of Margaret Mary alert, and the Russians move to number two on our list of deadly threats. Of course Mom always has a way of blunting my dislike of Margaret Mary. "Mom, I hate that Margaret Mary creature," I announce.

"Well, James, the girl you hate the most when you are young is often the girl you end up marrying." There is a sliver of a smile on Mom's face as she taunts me. What a horrible thought—never in a million, billion, zillion years. Fortunately, Margaret Mary's family moves from the neighborhood, and my parting thought as I watch her father escorting the family into his Hudson Hornet is *God bless her new neighbors.*

When I'm not hiking in the woods or picking blackberries, I play marbles or group games. From dusk till early evening, the neighborhood gang plays hide-and-seek. In this game, as on an African safari, a person is either the hunter or the hunted. To start the game straws are drawn and the person with the short straw is the seeker. I wait my turn and with confidence draw a straw. "Oh bugger," I say as I show the short straw to the gang. We select a goal, either a tree or a flagpole, that everyone touches and tags in. I cover both eyes and start counting to one hundred by fives. The players scatter to their secret hiding places. Upon reaching one hundred I yell:

"Apples, peaches, pumpkin pie.

Who's not ready holler I!"

The silence of the night is unpunctuated by voices yelling "I." My response to the silence is:

"Ready or not, here I come.

First caught shall be it."

Once the warning is pronounced, the game commences. Like a hunter I search the most likely hiding places. If I'm lucky, the person carelessly leaves a "tell," such as a moving bush, that is easy to identify. When a concealed player is found, I scamper to the goal, touch it, and yell, "One, two, three on Joe" or any kid I have found. The game rules demand that I don't whoop and holler meaningless babble because the one-two-three scenario must precisely be repeated lest an argument erupts about whether or not the hider gets in free. The downside is that if the hider beats me to the goal and yells "free," he or she can continue as a hider for the next game. If everyone gets in free, it dooms me to again be the seeker for the next game.

Bushes, trees, and hedges are favorite hiding places. Once hiders are located the ensuing footrace determines winners and losers. I am like a hunting dog flushing out game. Kids feverishly bolt from covert sanctuaries like formless herds of stampeding horses. I run at the speed of light to reach the goal first. I credit my amazing swiftness to my new black high-top PF Flyers sneakers. Nonetheless, experience teaches me additional tricks of the game. It never hurts if the hider accidentally trips over an outstretched leg or inadvertently takes a longer path to the goal as I give them a slight sideways push. Okay, I'll admit it isn't the Christian thing to do, but this isn't church. Once a new seeker is caught, the game is concluded by yelling, "Ollie, ollie, oxen free." The origin of the strange phrase is unclear, but it works. At the sound of my melodious bellowing, players emerge and tag in for the next game. The game continues until our parents start the nightly howling that beckons us home.

During the day spontaneous pickup sports in vacant neighborhood fields occupy my time. One kid in the group always has a ball and another kid always has a bat. My brother and I have neither, but we do have hand-me-down softball gloves that we share. One imprudent incident sticks in my mind. At dusk near the end of a softball game one day, someone proposes the bright idea of a wiener roast. We scamper home to rummage through cupboards and pilfer refrigerators. After procuring the hot dogs, buns, marshmallows, and condiments, the older boys dig a shallow pit and build the fire.

Eventually all fun comes to an end and Mother's familiar voice shouts, "Joseph, Jimmy, and Megan, time to come in." She always calls us home by our birth order. We start to disband, but Joe points out, "Guys, we can't leave with the fire burning. Anyone got any good ideas?"

"One of us can run home and get a pot of water," I suggest.

"Not so good," Joe replies, "we'll be here all night if we do that." Huddling together we use our collective creative brilliance to devise a field expedient solution. "I got a great idea," I say. Mighty Mouse, a movie cartoon hero, always enters the rescue scene singing, "Here I come to save the day; you know that Mighty Mouse is on the way." The girls leave and we unpretentiously take out our Mighty Mouses to extinguish the flames with nature's yellow fluid. Our streams hit the fire, and malodorous steam rises from the hot ashes. "Good God on Earth, what have we created? This is terrible. Whose bright idea was this?" Joe asks accusingly.

"I don't know," I meekly answer, "but he ought to be hung." The terrible stench attacks our nostrils. It stinks to high heaven. The sizzling fire hisses, gasps, and wheezes as it reluctantly gives up the fight to stay alive, but our powerful yellow streams prevail. The teensy-weensy wienie fire hose brigade victoriously extinguishes the fire. Smokey the Bear would be proud of us, but I venture to say that water is a better option.

All is right with the world, and the earth revolves slower in the early 1950s. The slow pace of life reflects the manner in which people interact. On hot summer days, between dusk and full darkness, the families gather on Aunt Betty's front porch. Main Street is a busy and bustling thoroughfare, with cars and pedestrians streaming in all directions. Aunt Betty's porch is strategically located to view the plethora of small-town activity. Car horns honk and people drive by, waving to us porch dwellers. Neighbors on their nightly walk exchange cordialities and often engage in casual conversation: "How's your mother? Is your boy going out for football? What do you think of those damn Republicans?" and a sundry of other conversations keep the sidewalk traveler cemented in place. Chatter abounds and often the neighbor comes up on the porch and joins the family in amicable fellowship.

I love sitting and listening to the adults tell stories, discuss events, and hash over the politics of the day. "Those damn Republicans" precedes a litany of grievances about what is wrong with the country. Brockway is a Democratic town and everything wrong is the fault of those damn Republicans. As the evening wanes the group thins, and by nine o'clock the porch reverts back to its vacant state. As years pass the art of visiting is supplanted by the isolating art of watching television. The glass picture tube captures people in their houses. Casual visiting gradually erodes and becomes as extinct as dinosaurs. Our small-town society changes, and interactions with friends are increasingly distant and void of warmth. The mesmerizing effect of the electronic boob tube takes an unsuspecting public totally by surprise. Must have been the fault of those damn Republicans—they're always up to no good.

CHAPTER 7

NOTHING VENTURED, NOTHING GAINED

Father constantly investigates ways to bring additional prosperity to his family, and in 1948 he enters the oil business. With three partners, he purchases eight oil wells in the vicinity of Titusville, Pennsylvania. Titusville is famous as the location of the first oil well drilled in the country. Once a month he drives to the wells to do maintenance. There are many trips when the entire family spends the day at the site. "Edith, tomorrow pack a lunch and we'll drive to Titusville," says Dad. "We will be there all day."

"I want you kids to go to bed early tonight," Mom announces, "because we are getting up at six tomorrow morning to go with your dad to the wells."

Twice Dad takes Joe and me when they are about to complete the drilling of a new well. On the way to Titusville, Dad calls attention to a huge hollow in the road. "See that big dip in the road? That's where a nitro truck blew up. Pretty big hole, isn't it?" I am hard to impress, but his comment makes a big impression.

After the metal pipe casings are placed in the hole and the boss is sure they have drilled to the proper depth, explosives are brought in. Oil doesn't trickle to the surface; it needs a wake-up call. A red Dodge Ram truck filled with gallon containers of nitroglycerin carefully approaches the well. Nitro is an extraordinarily powerful explosive and a temperamental, unstable, highly volatile liquid. A sudden jarring or dropping of a can may cause a disastrous explosion. Nevertheless, I am standing fifty feet from a truck full of the crazy stuff and have no real understanding of the clear, viscous fluid's power. Hopefully, hitting the hidden oil deposits will be the reward for the hard work and financial risk taken.

Only the nitro-man handles the explosives. I hold my breath and intently watch as he carefully removes one gallon at a time. He slowly carries them to the well and carefully pours them into the hole. Once the allocated amount is consumed by the hole, everyone stands aside. He takes three sticks of

dynamite, lights the fuses with his cigarette, and drops them down the hole. The boss yells, "All right, everyone get back."

Joe grabs my shoulder and says, "Let's get outta here. Dad wants us over by the tree, but we can better see if we are closer."

"Do ya think we are far enough away? I think we're too close. Dad did say to stand over by that tree."

"Of course we are. What are you, a scaredy-cat? Ya think I'm dumb or sumpin?" Joe knowingly says. Within a few minutes the ground rumbles and we hear a kazoo-like sound as the oil works its way to the surface. Suddenly, a tall gusher of black oil leaps toward the sky. As the gushing stream penetrates the clouds, we are certain it will turn and fall on our heads. "Look out, it's gonna get us," Joe shouts as the oil plume succumbs to gravity and starts to fall. "Let's get outta here." We instinctively turn and run, but it's too late. Dad's gonna kill us. He told us to move over by the tree and we didn't. Dad approaches and gives us his famous dirty look. We are covered from head to toe in greasy black oil. I consider my options, but they are limited. We really screwed up this time. Suddenly, without warning, Dad flashes an unanticipated smile and begins to laugh. "Are you boys alright?" he asks. "This is God's way of telling you two that you should listen to your father." Joe looks at me and we chuckle. We're oil drenched, but we're okay. "I'm sorry," Joe says repentantly, and I nod my head in agreement.

With smiles on their faces, the men rush toward the flowing oil and cap the pipe, giving Father and his partners another producing well. It is a scary but exciting adventure. As a tradition Dad collects a gallon of raw oil and places the glass jug on a shelf in the garage. Unfortunately, the price per barrel of oil is low and the business isn't profitable. His venture does give me the chance to see an oil well in action, something most people don't see in a lifetime.

Dad's spirit for adventure and entrepreneurship draws him into a new business enterprise, the coal business. Northwestern Pennsylvania is rich in natural resources. For the uninitiated there are two types of coal. Hard coal called anthracite, located in Northeastern Pennsylvania, requires deep mining. Hard coal is in demand by the steel industry where it is converted into the coke to fire huge steel ovens. Bituminous coal, or soft coal, is plentiful in our part of the state and is extracted by strip-mining. I watch in fascination as large earth-eating machines consume entire hills. In their wake the machine leaves deep gouges that expose shiny black veins of coal. As the steam shovel moves deeper into the hillside, it creates a progressively higher cliff, known as the high wall. Mining is stopped when the overburden of the rock above the coal is so voluminous that it is no longer economically feasible to remove it. At that point the machinery is moved to a new site. Pennsylvania is famous for hills that look as if a giant has taken a huge bite and spit out the remains to prove he can dine anywhere he wants.

At one particular site Dad purchases one hundred acres of land and strip-mines fifteen acres. The majority of the property remains untouched. Trucks haul their lumpy black cargo to the coal tipple near the Brockway railroad tracks and load it into railroad hopper cars for distribution throughout the United

States. Inevitably the work comes to an end, and like all strip mines it is abandoned. What remains adjacent to the slightly wounded hill is a beautiful valley with an abundance of trees and a flowing stream. Dad doesn't make much money in the coal business, but he inadvertently gains resources and property. That piece of untouched land is Wilburt Run and it becomes the home for his dream.

After his venture in the coal business, Dad forms an association with a chemist named Jude Paterson. The mid-1950s see an expansion of the arms race and the production of ballistic missiles. The missiles' outer casing is a light, but strong metal called titanium. Titanium is hard to manufacture and isn't cooperative when machining it into missile components. Removal of the white "flux" that coats the metal during production is one of the foremost problems in the manufacturing of titanium. Jude Paterson has the answer to the problem, and he and Dad form a company called Ferrous Glow. Dipping titanium in the magic liquid produced by Ferrous Glow easily removes the flux. The only challenge is selling the idea to the big companies that produce the metal.

A small Ferrous Glow plant is started in Ridgeway and later relocated to Brockway. The operation centers on a huge one-thousand-gallon vat in the middle of the plant floor. Even though Dad only completed eighth grade, he is a quick study of the chemical industry. "Now you boys get back," he orders. "As a matter of fact go into the office and wait. If anything happens I don't want you to get splashed with this stuff; it'll make your skin look like Swiss cheese." We learned our lesson at the oil wells, so we comply. Dad dons his rubber gloves, puts on an acid-resistant apron, and positions his safety glasses as he moves the 55-gallon drums of acid with a hoist. He removes the bunghole stoppers and gently transfers the liquid into the vat. Almost as if alive, the *glug, glug, glug* of the metal container gasps for air as the clear liquid pours from the drum. A plethora of other chemicals mixed into the vat produce a white vapor that clings to the top of the liquid stew. The chemical formula for Ferrous Glow is written on a piece of paper, and Dad follows the recipe religiously.

Joe and I often accompany him to the plant and watch him mix chemicals. We keep a safe distance, but Dad is in the middle of the action. One day after mixing and bottling a batch of Ferrous Glow, twenty gallons of the liquid remain in the vat. Dad leaves to go home for a while. "Joseph and Jimmy, you boys stay here and watch the place until I return. Now, boys, remember, don't touch anything," he instructs. "I mean it, guys."

"Okay, we'll keep an eye on everything till you get back," answers Joe. "You can trust us."

Neither Joe nor I are much good at sitting around doing nothing. A small junk stream populated mostly by bottom-feeding catfish flows past the plant. "Hey, Jim, let's bait a couple of hooks and go fishing for those ugly catfish."

"Okay, Joe, sounds like fun. There are a couple of poles in the office. I'll go fetch them."

"Yeah, you do that and I'll dig up some worms."

It's a good way to pass the time until Dad gets back. A person doesn't need talent to catch bottom-feeding fish. Catfish bite at anything. Within minutes we catch a catfish. What are we going to do with the ugly thing? We look at each other, shrug our shoulders, and then do a horrible thing. "Jim, do you think this fish can swim in Ferrous Glow?"

"I don't know, Joe—let's throw it in and see what happens." Splash, we drop the catfish into the liquid. While watching the grotesque scene, we both gasp and let out a series of "Ahhhhhh, geeeez," "Oh my God," and "Would ya look at that." The poor creature initially starts to swim. Quickly a red liquid oozes from its gills and soon all motion stops. Within five minutes the fish completely dissolves in the liquid. Whoever gets the last batch of the chemicals receives a concoction of "Catfish Ferrous Glow." Joe and I are aghast at the travesty we committed. I hope God isn't watching us act like boneheads. Still it does give us a healthy respect for staying away from whatever chemicals Dad uses. "I guess that answers that question—they can swim in Ferrous Glow," says Joe with a pained smile, "but not for long."

Dad and Jude make many trips to Pittsburgh, demonstrating their product for the big steel companies. They work hard, but to no avail. The companies won't have anything to do with them. They aren't part of the steel establishment.

Though none of the explorations into business other than the restaurant business are huge successes, they teach a valuable lesson in life. Nothing ventured, nothing gained, and Dad willingly tries. He isn't a careless man who jumps into situations without thought. In many respects he is a visionary willing to take a prudent chance. A pessimist sees only trouble when good fortune knocks at his door, but Dad sees opportunity. I inherit his sense of adventure because I always find myself creating new experiences that test my ability to adapt. Success does not require winning, but it does require trying. The only thing not trying produces is regret. What will life be if I never summon the courage to live it?

CHAPTER 8

C-C-C-C-CANCEL THE HOT DOG

Every boy has heroes. You may think my heroes are people resembling Captain America or Superman, but they aren't. I've got to tell you about my uncles. They are characters, and two in particular leave a lasting impression. Uncle Sam and Uncle John are the two most prominent in my life. When Uncle Sam arrives to give Father a work break, my brother, sister, and I taunt him. He is my favorite uncle and if you don't know him, you may think he is a bit grouchy and gruff, but he isn't.

Uncle Sam, the oldest of the three DeAngelo brothers, was born in Italy and immigrated as an infant with his parents. He is a pillar of the community and serves as an elected public official on the Brockway Borough Council. In my opinion he would make a good President of the United States, but being born in the "old country" prohibits him from holding the office. At five foot, ten inches tall, his most prominent characteristics are his thin golden wire-rim glasses, his ever-present stubby cigar, and his red suspenders. Uncle Sam is the most fiscally conservative of the three brothers. He never lavishly spends money, even after acquiring a great deal of wealth. His spending habits are rooted in a depression-era mentality. Joe tells me, "Uncle Sam is so rich that he stuffs money in his mattress." Never one to let a rumor linger, I put it to rest; because when the family visits his house, I sneak upstairs and look. "Joe, you don't know what you're talking about; there ain't no money under Uncle Sam's bed."

"God, you're stupid; you'd believe anything. Ya dummy, he really hides it in the cellar."

"Ding-dang it, I'll have to check," I say, never thinking he might be putting me on.

Aunt Betty, Uncle Sam's wife, wears housedresses with opaque nylon half socks that fit over her knees. She fixes her dark honey brown hair in a bun at the back of her head. The fastidious lady covers all the coal furnace hot air vents with cheesecloth to prevent dust and dirt—she hates dust and dirt. Her home is hospital clean, and she covers her new furniture with clear plastic so it won't get dirty or wear out. There

57

is nothing like sitting and sticking to Aunt Betty's plastic couch on a hot day. She wants the furniture to last a lifetime, and it does. Most of the time you'll find Aunt Betty cooking in the basement and not in her new upstairs kitchen. Maybe it's because that's where the money is hidden. You get the picture—conservative, but with good reason. Old habits are hard to break.

Uncle Sam's smelly King Edward cigar chokes the air, and the pungent smoke it produces is a disguised kid weapon. That stinky cigar smell is indelibly etched in my mind. Whenever Uncle Sam gets out of his car, we tease him with a song:

"Sam, Sam, the dirty ol' man.

Washed his face with a frying pan.

Combed his hair with the leg of a chair.

Sam, Sam, the dirty ol' man."

Sure enough, he chases me for a couple of steps and when caught I scream. On every occasion he rubs the wet tip of his cigar in my face—unpleasant but not painful. Gruff Uncle Sam is a great guy; all I want is a little attention, but there must be a better way.

It is fun to be with Uncle John. What a sense of humor Uncle John has when he tells his vintage stories. He has a quick mind and a ubiquitous wit. When wearing a suit, he puts his thumbs under the lapels and comments: "I told my wife to go down to Cox's and buy me a seersucker suit, and she went to Sears."

Another Uncle John story:

"I went into this greasy spoon restaurant and ordered a hot dog, and my friend ordered two hamburgers. The huge cook came out with the frozen hamburger patties in her hands and slapped them under her armpits. I asked her, 'W-W-W-What are you doing?' She replied, 'I'm thawing the hamburger.' C-C-C-C-Cancel the hot dog!"

You must pause and think for a minute, but he never says anything that is outright risqué. The interpretation of the humor is left to the mind of the listener.

Uncle John, the youngest of the DeAngelo brothers, is a unique guy. A little shorter than Uncle Sam but a bit taller than my father, he is definitely the flashiest and the best-looking of the trio. He has thick, wavy black hair and a noticeable idiosyncrasy is that he talks fast. Joe says he mumbles, but I think his tongue just gets ahead of his brain. Uncle John, his wife Aggie, and his kids live in the house next door. In the late 1940s he buys a Cushman Motor Scooter and I hear him putting down the street from a half mile away. "Come on, Jimmy, Uncle John is coming down the road. Let's sneak over and see if we can get him to give us a ride," Joe urges.

"Yeah, Joe, better move fast. Mom's standing on the porch. Let's go before she sees us."

Before we can move one step, Mom yells out, "You boys stay away from that contraption; it's dangerous."

"How in the hell does she know what we're thinking," Joe complains.

Mom views motor scooters as unsafe, so she never lets me or Joe catch a ride with Uncle John.

Crosley Motors builds an ultra-small car shortly after WWII, and Uncle John buys a Crosley convertible. The Crosley is a mini-mini car powered by a small four-cylinder motor. On long hot summer days, he puts the top down, piles us in the car, and takes us for a "Crosley ride." Sometimes he drives to Cook's Forest State Park and sometimes he just drives around. When the stock car races come to the Airport Speedway, Uncle John introduces me to the thrill of watching the races. I want to be a stock car driver, but other things soon distract me.

The most astute and intelligent uncle is my pipe-smoking Uncle Eddie. He works as an executive in the glass company's corporate headquarters. I know him to be a highly respected businessman and a man of character. Other executives say Uncle Eddie would have been president of the company if he had a college degree. A kind and gentle person, he tries to teach me the art of fly-fishing. Getting up before sunrise and tramping through the woods to his fishing spot doesn't fit my idea of fun. I never catch a fish and if I had caught one, I wouldn't know what to do with it. After my experience with Ferrous Glow, I have no inclination to mess with fish. I do have a pocketknife and I am relieved that I don't have to touch the critter to cut it open. For me fishing is best accomplished at the grocery store, where they come in square frozen boxes. Uncle Eddie never speaks a harsh word, even about my attempt at fly-fishing.

Every time affable Uncle Jack appears, he produces a box of Bazooka Bubble Gum and gives me something to chew on for the rest of the day. Bazooka Bubble Gum is far superior to Dubble Bubble gum for making giant bubbles that often burst and invade my hair. Mom isn't happy about my bubble-blowing escapades. "James, you got bubble gum in your hair again."

"Well, I sort of had a little accident. I was blowing this humungous bubble, bigger than my head, and then the accident happened. Joe came by and burst my bubble—he was the accident." Sometimes Mom is forced to take scissors and cut swatches of gum-infested hair when it can't be removed with a comb. It is easy to tell when bubble gum is the culprit; all a person has to do is look at my uneven haircut.

Uncle Jack is also the Democratic Committee Chairperson in our community and informs me about politics early in life. "When you grow up you're going to be a Democrat," instructs Uncle Jack. "Democrats are the people who will save us from those damn Republicans." True to his word, when I reach voting age, he escorts me to the voting office, where I register as a Democrat, but I still don't know what a Democrat is. Nevertheless, my becoming a Democrat makes him happy. Now I can blame everything on those damn Republicans, whatever they are.

Uncle Jim works at a dam construction site as a truck driver and takes me along for a day. Spending a day riding in a huge bumpy truck removes truck driver from my career choices. As a licensed beautician, he and Aunt Ruth open a beauty parlor in Brockway. Women's hair is better work than driving a truck. Brother Joe's Brillo head is a product of Uncle Jim's creative endeavor. He is a great guy, but for some reason he never participates in the family's activities. Joe and I speculate that religion has something to do with his strained relationships. Joe tells me, "Uncle Jim married a klu-clucker, and they hate Catholics."

"So, what the heck is a klu-clucker?"

"How the hell am I supposed to know," Joe says in an irritable voice. "This is America; you can hate anyone ya want to hate, no crime in that. For Christ's sake, you are dimwitted."

"Oh, I get it now. Klu-cluckers are people that love America so they can hate Catholics." The division between religious groups is a big thing in the 1940s. When Uncle Jim marries Aunt Ruth, he leaves the Church and converts to her religion. Leaving the Church is one of those burn-in-hell transgressions. I sense Aunt Ruth's covert anti-Catholic feelings and know that ours is a strong Roman Catholic family. The theory sounds plausible, and therein may lie the seeds of discontent. The rift that causes him to move out of the family circle is buried along with Uncle Jim.

My family, my uncles, and my aunts expose me to many life experiences. Even in a rich human environment, my knowledge of the outside world is limited. When anyone asks, "Jimmy, why don't you become an engineer?" I agree, because who doesn't want to drive a big steam engine? The front door to my house always remains unlocked. People out of the norm stick out like a sore thumb, so Brockway isn't a criminal's paradise. Unusual things such as elevators, escalators, and skyscrapers are outside the realm of my encounters. Among the experiences I am missing are crime, violence, and drugs—isn't that great?

The trappings of a modern urban society are neither important nor relevant. I can learn about "things" as long as I can define myself. My uncles help mold me as a person. I recognize that someone walking in another person's moccasins is usually a thief, so I set out to be my own person. My job in life is to make me my own hero—a tough job indeed. I would never trade "things" for the beautiful relationships developed with caring people who nourish me in body and spirit. Some gifts are priceless.

CHAPTER 9

HOOCHIE-COOCHIE

Between 1949 and 1950, two significant events occur. One is an innocent boyhood experience that fuels my playful imagination. The other pushes aside the innocent boyhood fantasies, and provides a preview of what is to come. The first event is when Curley Miller's Horse Show comes to town and Joe takes me to see the extravaganza. "Come on, bozo, a bunch of us guys are going down to the park. We heard in school that there is going to be a performance of some sort," says Joe.

"Gee, that's great—is it gonna be fun?"

"Ah shut up—you're either going or you're gonna stay home and shoot off your big mouth. Now make up your mind." How can I resist such an inviting invitation?

My gaze is focused on the back of a large truck with its tailgate lowered. The tailgate platform is where Curley performs his theatrics. A string of bare bulbs illuminates the makeshift stage upon which I see Curley Miller looking like someone out of the movies. He is wearing a long jacket, a cowboy hat, and he talks a mile a minute. Another guy with two braided pigtails, dressed as an Indian, begins beating a drum and chanting some kind of nonsense—"hi-ya, hi-ya, hi-ya." Finally, there is a nondescript stagehand providing Curley and the Indian with props as Curley cavorts back and forth across the makeshift stage. He sings, plays music, and dances for the enjoyment of the crowd. I certainly enjoy the show, but my sister's tap dancing requires more talent than Curley's wild and undisciplined romping.

The show is spectacular. I have never seen anything like it. After ten minutes when the crowd grows big enough, Curley suddenly stops his antics and produces, from a hidden pocket in his bright yellow and brown plaid jacket, a bottle of red elixir. "Laaadies and gentlemen," Curley loudly proclaims, "have you ever felt down, depressed, or just out of sorts?" People in the crowd nod their heads yes as Curley pauses and the Indian beats the drum faster and louder. "Let me tell you a secret I learned in my

61

travels to the far-off corners of the world. In my journey to South America, I lived with the now extinct Xanabina tribe. They taught me the formula for this potion made from exotic herbs and plants found only in the tropical Amazon jungle. Yes, I am one of the few people on Earth with whom God has shared this knowledge." Curley again pauses and the Indian continues his drum-beating routine. "Laaaadies and gentlemen, this ruby liquid will not only keep you healthy, but it cures most of the ailments known to mankind," Curley shouts as he holds the bottle high over his head. "My fountain of youth elixir is guaranteed to cure arthritis, lumbago, kidney stones, stomach problems, the vapors, and sleeplessness."

I ask Joe, "What are the vapors?"

Joe laughs. "They're farts, you dummy. What's wrong with you?"

"Oh…" I didn't think farts could kill you. "Curley's magic elixir sure is great. Got any money? Maybe we can get some for Dad."

Sarcastically Joe says, "Explaining things to you isn't worth the effort. For Christ's sake, are you crazy?"

"My good friends," Curley continues, "I am willing to share my life-enhancing fluid with you for the paltry sum of one US greenback dollar. Yes, just one dollar, ladies and gentlemen." The stagehand dressed as a farmer rushes to the platform and bellows: "I'll take three bottles; it saved my life—God bless you, Curley."

"Halleluiah, halleluiah, halleluiah, praise the Lord—you heard it, folks, halleluiah," chants Curley. That's enough to start the stampede. The citizens buy many bottles of the stuff, and if I had money I would buy some.

Dad supplements his diet with a liquid called Serutan. As advertised on television's *Ted Mack's Original Amateur Hour*, Serutan is "natures" spelled backward. This is my first exposure to a flimflam man, and I languish in the excitement. For weeks after Curley's one-night stand, I play in the backyard and pretend to be part of his horse show. Boy, am I glad I tagged along.

Prior to 1949, except for the occasional flimflam man and weekly movie, my entertainment is listening to the radio. On Saturday morning I hurry downstairs and tune in to the Cream of Wheat theater, where fantasy stories such as "Jack in the Beanstalk" and "Rumpelstiltskin" titillate my imagination. The art of audio imaging reaches its zenith in storytelling radio programs. The word pictures painted are vividly dramatic. After that I search through the AM radio channels to find *The Lone Ranger*. So engaging is the narrative that I picture myself riding side by side with him and his trusted Indian companion, Tonto, as they conquer evil. At the end of each episode, the Lone Ranger mounts his trusty steed, Silver, and gallops off into the sunset. The "William Tell Overture" announces the program's conclusion, and I join the Lone Ranger in yelling a final and resounding chorus of Hi-Ho Silver Away.

By the time I am in elementary school, Joe and I have a FADA radio on the dresser between our beds. A long string extends from the toggle switch on the wall to a post at the head of Joe's bed. He is able to turn off the light without getting out of bed. We are inventive, somewhat in the vein of Tom Swift in the kids' books. At bedtime Joe moves the dial, searching for *The FBI in Peace and War* or *Gang Busters*. When the opportunity presents itself, he tunes in the scariest of the scary programs. Joe says, "Let's turn on *Inner Sanctum*." He knows that Mom doesn't approve of us listening to this kind of stuff. From downstairs Mom yells, "Don't turn on any spooky programs, you boys understand?"

"Yeah," Joe answers. Miffed, he pauses and says, "How does she always know what we're up to?" We understand, but being boys her warning makes listening even more imperative. Except for the movie *The Thing*, my radio imagination frightens me more than any motion picture. Scare radio has a way of playing on my innermost fears. Everything is left to the imagination, and my mental picture exacerbates and exceeds the spoken dialogue. The program begins with a creaking door sound, boding evil, followed by the deep, ominous voice saying, "Now open that squeaky door." Falling asleep after *Inner Sanctum* is impossible, because I hear panic in the beating of my heart. Lying in the dark, listening to the sounds of our old wooden frame house creaking, squeaking, and rasping throughout the night makes me shiver with fear. "Joe, are you awake? There's someone in the house. Do you hear him?"

"Aw geez, go to sleep. There's no one in the house. Quit your babbling before I take my pillow and smother you."

"Yes there is. Can't you hear it coming up the steps? I can still hear it—I know it's here. When you wake up dead in the morning, remember I told you so." I am sure a nameless creature is coming up the steps and the stairs warning sounds that announce his presence. Some nights the stories are so frightening that Joe lets me sleep with him. On the lighter side we listen to *My Friend Irma*, *Life with Luigi*, *Our Miss Brooks*, *The Bob Hope Show*, and *The Jack Benny Program*. Jack Benny is special because like me, he has no musical talent. I smile, laugh, oooooh, aaaaaw, and recognize all humans have quirks, even if their peculiarities are being a tightwad or playing the violin poorly.

My radio-listening habits change drastically when cable TV arrives at the end of 1949. Previously, the only TV in Brockway is a five-inch circular black-and-white screen at the Brockway airport. The tiny television is hooked to a giant rooftop antenna, and on a clear day a person can make out fuzzy images of people playing baseball. Seeing things is revolutionary, but television also turns my imagination to mush. Things imagined when listening to the radio are much scarier than what I see on TV.

Entertainment isn't restricted to radio, TV, and movies. Once a year Dad, Mom, Uncle Sam, and Aunt Betty gather the families and take us to the Clearfield County Fair. The expectations and the excitement of the carnival atmosphere are overwhelming. Upon arrival my senses are bombarded with a milieu of sounds, sights, and smells, blending together to produce a high-energy atmosphere. The muggy July weather acts like an invisible lid, capturing and concentrating the sounds of carnival music and the smell of French fries bubbling in the deep fryers. Entering the fairgrounds brings me face-to-face with a person dressed as an Indian medicine man, barking out the benefits of his herbal medicine, something akin to Curley Miller's Horse Show. We fight our way through dozens of pitchmen hawking their products and move toward the grandstand. "Hey, get your cotton candy here," "Come on over and try your luck at the ring toss," "The best candy apples produced by Mother Nature—only twenty-five cents," are a few of the many high-energy hustlers vying for my attention.

Undistracted by the inexorable cacophony of blatant capitalistic zeal, we purposely focus on our primary goal. The family bought tickets to the live stage show, and that's where we are headed. Before the show, Dad and Mom make sure everyone visits the bathroom for a pit stop, because once the show starts, I must remain seated until intermission. Dad uses a secret signal to announce our restroom stop. "Well, it's time to go see a man about buying a horse."

"Better get your money out, 'cause it looks like we're going to buy Trigger again," I joke.

Joe nudges me and says, "Why in the hell can't he just say it's time to take a piss?" Joe makes a good point.

In the bathroom an old lanky black porter keeps things clean and provides a medley of chants, songs, and verses, for a slight gratuity. I get a kick out of his verses: "Shake it but don't break it. Zip it up and make sure you take it."

"Hey, Joe, ya think if I shake it hard enough, it will break?"

"With that thing, not a chance. Just wipe yourself, little girl, and let's go."

"Aw, wiping myself is gross. You're kidding, that isn't fair."

"Well, life isn't fair when you're stupid. Now zip up and let's get out of here." As said in the Maxwell House coffee advertisements, even our bathroom break is "good to the last drop."

From my seat in the grandstand, I watch a myriad of acts—clowns, magicians, singing groups, and slapstick comedy. The seamless parade of entertainment continues for two hours, but as far as I am concerned, the show can go on all night.

After the show it is customary to walk around the midway. The midway entices us with exciting rides, assorted concessions, and tempting adult burlesque shows. It seems strange that every year Uncle Sam and Dad separate from the group and disappear. To keep us amused, Mom and Aunt Betty let us go on the Ferris wheel and the Tilt-a-Whirl. The thrill of being pummeled and pinned against the wall of the Tilt-a-Whirl as it spins faster and faster is exhilarating. Out of curiosity I ask Joe, "Where did Dad and Uncle Sam go?"

He flashes a Cheshire cat grin and says, "They went to the hoochie-coochie show."

"Oh, I know what that means." Thus starts the second event—my expanding awareness of grown-up girls.

After we finish the rides, Mom and Aunt Betty escort us to the area where the burlesque shows are playing and wait for Dad and Uncle Sam. When the show is over, the guys, with smiles on their faces, pile out of the tent. Dad and Uncle Sam are easily spotted. They look like toddlers passing gas—a little guilty at what they have done, but still proud of themselves. Even more exciting is watching the lady performers bait the audience for the next show. I am thunderstruck as the hoochie-coochie girls appear on the outside stage to demonstrate a teasing look at their physical talent. They certainly capture my interest. I try moving my belly like those girls, but I can't.

The barker's titillating talk is better than the grandstand show. It is imperative that I see the performance. "Step right up, folks, get your tickets now. Seating is limited," he says. "Ten beautiful dancers with body movements you've never seen before. Blaze," he quips, "give 'em a little demonstration of what they'll see inside. Now remember, honey, not too much; we don't want any heart attacks out there." The dancer starts to demonstrate her unique talent. "Look at her go, folks—she squirms, she jiggles, she wiggles—this lady has more moves than a reptile. You can see it all for the paltry price of fifty cents. Hurry, hurry, hurry, step right up; we're filling up fast."

Instantaneously, precisely, and maddeningly, I focus my eyes on the stage. The top performer is Blaze Starr, a beautiful redhead readily recognizable because of her shapely body. Amazingly, she moves her hips in one direction while her chest goes in the opposite direction, almost as if they are unconnected. There is no question about the significance of the shapes and curves barely hidden beneath her meager diaphanous garments. My probing eyes move up and down as I explore every inch of her undulating body. My chest heaves and excitement ripples through my gut. "Holy cow, would you look at those," I marvel.

"Shut up and pretend you're not watching," Joe warns. "If Mom sees ya she'll get pissed and it'll be all over for us."

I try, but I can't help myself. My eyes are glued to her huge, well-shaped hooters. Surely one of them will fall out as she does her jiggle-wiggly dance. I am a saint with a sinner inside struggling to escape and if I stare too much Mom will stuff that sinner back inside. Discreetly I put my hands in my pockets and make needed adjustments. This lady has two attributes that need intense inspection. I am gawking—how can I not be?—but, ever vigilant, Mother is watching my roving eyes. She squints her eyes and her lips disappear into that familiar tight, thin line across her face as she orders, "Come on, you kids, we are leaving."

Joe looks at me disdainfully and says, "I told you not to stare, you moron."

Mom firmly grips my hand, gives me a tug, and quickly escorts me away from the hoochie-coochie girls, but I do get a good look at their aptitude for attracting a crowd. Mom suggested that in music I am a good listener; now I want to develop my eyes and be a good watcher. Sounds innocent enough, doesn't it?

In my mind looking is fun. I rationalize that looking isn't a sin, plus at least I'm not doing it in church. Sister Scholasticia's far-out words capture my mind, "Thinking it is the same as doing it," and I am thinking it without doing it. The only problem is I have no idea what "it" means. My imagination grows bigger than a breadbox, and the welcome mat is rolled out for the carnal thoughts that fill it.

At the County Fair everyone gets what he or she wants and everybody goes home happy. As an unanticipated bonus, I fantasize about the beautiful girls. My thoughts are sinful, but they put a smile on my sleepy face. I don't know how all the nifty equipment displayed works, but I know their equipment is different from my equipment. The only thing I can figure out is the difference must be the fault of those damn Republicans. They are always meddling and they have a way of screwing up everything.

CHAPTER 10

THE VACATION

Where do you think my family visits when we go on vacation: Florida, Washington D.C.? No, no, what a dumb question—we visit relatives. Our cousins in Niagara Falls invite us to visit, so that is our destination. Mom and Dad pile us into the car and off we go. The car is an eight-cylinder blue 1948 Dodge four-door sedan with the innovative semiautomatic transmission called fluid drive. Superhighways don't exist, so we start our six-hour trip by way of narrow, serpentine secondary roads.

Mom says, "Kids, keep an eye open for the Burma-Shave signs." They are an immediate hit. We spot the first in the series of signs and begin to yell in unison as each comes into sight: MY JOB IS—KEEPING FACES CLEAN—AND NOBODY KNOWS—DE STUBBLE I'VE SEEN—BURMA-SHAVE. I impatiently keep watch for the next Burma-Shave signs. By golly, after another half hour of driving, I spot the second set of signs. HE TRIED—TO CROSS—AS FAST TRAIN NEARED—DEATH DIDN'T DRAFT HIM—HE VOLUNTEERED—BURMA-SHAVE. It doesn't take much to entertain me because everything on my first vacation is new. Many gas station bathrooms are visited as Megan or I shout the well-known warning, "I have to go. I have to go!" When a gas station can't be located, the local roadside vegetation is liberally watered. Out of utter frustration, at every stop Dad huffs, shakes his head from side to side. "Again? Didn't we just stop a few miles back? What's wrong with you kids," he snips as he pulls to the side of the road. "Can't you hold it?"

"No, I gotta pee, you know, I gotta see a man about buying a horse," I say. When you gotta go, you gotta go. There is no way of predicting when the urge will overcome me. Truthfully, I can hold it, but let's keep it a secret; our stops keep the ride from getting boring.

On our big vacation the direct route to Niagara Falls is not followed. We first drive to Lake Ontario in New York State. Dad has directions to a place called Camp Keenan, where Joe is deposited for a week. "Well, here we are, Joseph. I think you will enjoy your stay. Oh, please be careful," Mom reassuringly says.

"Joe, I want you to listen to the camp counselors, and no monkey business," Dad lectures. "You understand?"

"Yeah, I'll be okay," Joe answers as he walks away with his cabin's counselors. Mom waves good-bye and Dad pulls away from the camp. I think I detect a small tear in her eyes. The camp is for boys, and my folks think camping will be a good experience for Joe. Truth be told, I believe they may be trying to get rid of him. They probably want to dump him off for a week so they can have a peaceful visit with the relatives. Unlike me, and my compliant behavior, Joe is a real pain in the posterior. He has an irritating way of getting under Dad's skin and he is very good at it. In preadolescent language Joe is a pain in the ass, but I would never say that.

As a second child I continue learning from Joe's mistakes. Passive-aggressive behavior rather than direct confrontation works best for me. It doesn't take a genius to figure out that if I'm going to do battle with the folks, do it between the ears; otherwise, I don't stand a prayer of winning. Nothing works better at getting in their minds than my weapon of choice—pouting and sulking. Yes sir, pouting and sulking are my atomic bomb, and I can drop it at will. The most I am able to milk the sulking-and-pouting routine is two days before I notice that my parents enjoy the peace and quiet. Mom and Dad weren't born yesterday. Atomic bomb or no atomic bomb, a kid can never actually win.

The four of us continue our drive to Niagara Falls. Sal Rizzoli, our cousin, is a smart man and one of the first to build motels in Niagara Falls. He has three sites where his cottage motels are located. Motels are relatively recent phenomena on the tourist scene, and consequently they are great moneymakers. Our bungalow has two beds, one for my parents and one for my sister and me. Walking out the front door of our room, I see a bluff overlooking Lake Ontario. It's a breathtaking sight and the golden-red sunsets are beautiful.

The visit starts with the familiar hugs and kisses and progresses to the usual boring, but familiar, adult dialogue. The Rizzolis welcome our family with open arms. Sal talks to Dad about building motels in Florida, which stimulates Dad's sense of business acumen. "Joe, I see a bright future in starting a motel business in Florida," Sal says. "I believe that we could do it for a hundred thousand dollars, but it will probably cost another fifty thousand to get it running right. It could be a big moneymaker." Dad's eyes light up, and he looks at Mom for an approving nod that never comes. It frightens me to think my future depends on a single nod from one parent to the other. Either a blessing or a curse, it doesn't take much to get Dad interested in a new business adventure.

After our stay with the relatives, we travel to Niagara Falls. The falls are fascinating. My young mind processes the aquatic panorama and determines the obvious: there's a lot of water in the Niagara River. We view the falls at night under colored lights and the sight is worthy of note, but the Tilt-a-Whirl is time better spent. Canada is the first foreign country I visit, and to my chagrin the Canadians sound like the Americans.

In the late forties there are uncountable numbers of shops filled with stuff that appeals to kids. I want an Indian bow and arrow as a souvenir and set about to get it. "Mom, look at this nifty bow and arrow—can I have it?"

"No," Dad answers for her.

"But, Mom, this is really nifty," I say in a begging voice.

"I said no," Dad again answers. "Didn't you hear me the first time?"

"I hear," I answer, "but, Mom, it sure is nifty. Won't ya consider it?" Mom smiles, because Dad has an irrational prejudice against my coveted bow and arrow set. My attempt at conversation with Mom is a failure. My wants and desires are subservient to Dad's pocketbook. To me it is a weapon of war, and I am a warrior. I get the idea, look all you want, but you are not getting anything. Dad never has a problem saying no, but if I work on Mom, I have a shot at getting something. The official term is nagging.

The week passes quickly. We visit the tourist stops, look at flowers, walk the streets, and hypnotically stare at the perpetual cascade of water. At every stop Dad chronicles our vacation with his new Kodak 8mm movie camera. Finally it is time to go to Camp Keenan and pick up Joe. Haw, haw, I'll bet Joe is miserable and can't wait to see us.

To my surprise, Joe is ecstatic about his camp experience. In my mind he is supposed to hate being away from us. Instead, he went swimming, shot a rifle, and hung around with a bunch of guys. Somehow, I assumed he would feel left out of being part of our visit to the relatives and Canada. Although Joe can irritate Dad to no end, he has a way of schmoozing him. I call it the firstborn, older brother finesse. I never do master finesse. Joe and his instructor show Dad a single-shot rifle. "Dad, look at this twenty-two rifle. They let me shoot it at the rifle range and I hit the bull's-eye five times," Joe brags. "Pretty good—huh?"

"It's a nice rifle, so what?"

"Yes, Mr. DeAngelo, your son is sure a sharpshooter. You ought to encourage him to practice. He could be a really good marksman," says the instructor.

Dad's eyes open wide and he has trouble hiding his smile as the instructor massages his ego. After all, Joe is his son and Joe's accomplishment reflects on Dad's family. "Well, how much would a rifle like this cost?" Dad inquires.

"This is a really good rifle and it retails for thirty-five dollars, but since it is used I could let it go for twenty dollars."

"I'll take it," says Dad. Imagine, one week away from home and Joe's suddenly a marksman. Without blinking an eye, Dad forks out twenty bucks and buys the rifle. The rapidity of the transaction amazes me. I almost get a whiplash injury trying to follow the lightning-fast exchange of money for the gun.

Joe gets a rifle, but I can't get an Indian bow and arrow. I never figure out the big difference between getting a rifle and getting a bow and arrow. Joe pounds two nails over the doorway in our bedroom and mounts the rifle. That's where it stays unless he uses it in the woods.

Being second born certainly helps build character and an appreciation for delayed gratification—because I have plenty of practice getting it right. You see, in life, everything has a way of leveling out. No one ever said life is a level playing field or that it is fair. The only requirement is that as long as you are alive, you have to live it. I make up my mind to make the best of it even in the worst of times.

CHAPTER 11

A HOLIDAY SIGHT TO BEHOLD

The happiest time is the holiday season, from Thanksgiving through New Year's. The house bustles with constant activity in preparation for the holidays. The center of our world shifts to the kitchen table with family, friends, and good food. In preparation for Christmas, Mom starts baking immediately after Thanksgiving. She is a great cook and knows exactly what I like. Mother and my aunts take pride in baking holiday cookies. In a subtle game of one-upmanship, the sisters bring plates full of cookies to the house, and she returns their plates filled with her goodies. Honey, nuts, or powdered sugar are the coatings that make her baking delectable. "Mom, please don't put any of that yucky stuff in your pizzelles this year," I beg.

"You mean anise?"

"Yeah, that's the stuff—it tastes like licorice and makes me want to throw up. Maybe, we can give Dad the anise ones Aunt Betty made—they're terrible, but they will keep him from getting constipated."

"Jimmy, now that's a good idea. We'll save your aunt's cookies for Dad."

As a compromise two batches of pizzelles are made, one with vanilla flavoring and another with anise flavoring. I avoid the anise pizzelles because the licorice smell conjures Dad's Fernet Branca cure.

White powdered sugar is my nemesis. The residue leaves a detectable trail on my faces and clothing when I sneak into the cookie tin. Mom's knowing eyes look at me. "James, have you been in the cookie tin?"

"You know I wouldn't sneak into your cookie supply. Must have been the White Sugar Fairy." I burst out laughing.

"Well, you got some white sugar on your shirt. How did that happen?" She doesn't have to be much of a detective to know what is going on. She knows who pilfered the cookies, but never lets on. When the container gets low, the canister is refilled with more delightful baking. "My, my," she says as if surprised, "it looks like the mice ate all the goodies. I guess I'll have to set some mouse traps and bake some more."

"Sure does, Mom. It wasn't me and we got to control them critters. They are nasty animals," I proclaim, even though I know it is a little white lie. You can fool some of the people all the time, and all of the people some of the time, but you can't fool Mom. I don't mind her catching me with my hands in the cookie jar.

The night before Christmas is amazing. As many relatives as possible squeeze into our small kitchen and sit around the dinner table talking, laughing, and eating. Christmas Eve dinner is traditionally a meatless Italian dinner, with an overabundance of pasta, fish, salads, nuts, fruits, and special Italian treats. As usual, Aunt Betty feels it necessary to give special Christmas advice: "Eat everything on your plate." According to her if I don't consume everything, it has an adverse effect on the world. "Those poor starving kids in China would give anything to have what you have," she continues. "You kids don't know how fortunate you are."

I nudge Joe. "Thank goodness there isn't a rice dish or Aunt Betty would accuse us of taking food out of the Chinese kids' mouths."

"Just be quit and eat," Joe replies, "unless you want her to start talking about Africa."

How I am linked to the poor kids in China, I don't know, but there is enough food to feed an entire Chinese village. Every Christmas, the local beer distributor gives Dad a two-pound box of Whitman's Sampler chocolates. At the end of the meal, he magically produces it for our consumption. All the chocolates look beautifully delicious, but as I bite into some, I discover I don't like them. Often I secretly push a hole in the bottom and if I don't like what I see, the chocolate is deceptively placed back into the box. Nobody knows who did it.

Astute Dad never passes on an opportunity to teach about life, even if it is as mundane as chocolates. "You know, kids, chocolate-covered candy is a lot like people." He holds the damaged milk chocolate up to the light and looks at the broken underside. "They are pretty on the outside, but you can't tell much about them till you look inside." We laugh as he eyes each of us. "Let that be a lesson, even though someone has already learned it." He knows we punch holes in the bottom and look inside. The man knows people and chocolates.

Wine is present at the dinner table. If I want some I am allowed to drink it. Wine and alcohol are part of the family culture, and it is never abused. "Do you want a taste of wine," Dad offers, even though he knows full well I don't.

"Nah, I think that stuff tastes terrible."

"I'll have a glass full," shouts Joe.

"No you won't," Dad answers, "you'll only have a half a glass."

Why be curious about alcohol when it is available any time I want, as long as it is in the family setting. As far as I'm concerned, wine is bitter. Personally, soda pop is my preference, especially my favorite,

Nehi grape soda. My parents are wise and know that making anything a mystery to a kid is like putting a magnet near iron—the attraction is there.

The big joke one year is when Uncle Sam and Grandpa Gamelo make wine using kegs that once contained a Coca-Cola type of liquid. The taste of the wine is closely associated with the wooden barrels used in fermentation, and that year the adults joke about drinking Coca-Cola wine. "Mom, do you mind if I have a Coke? You know, the good stuff Uncle Sam and Grandpa made?" Joe asks.

"Joseph, get those thoughts out of your mind right now. When you are twenty-one we'll discuss it."

My parents attend midnight Mass so as not to disrupt the Christmas Day festivities. Our culture centers on eating, visiting people, and celebrating with family. The Christmas Day ritual includes visiting everyone's house, and thus the eating and visiting seem to go on for days. We know that Christmas morning is for opening gifts, and Christmas evening is for visiting, a friendly formula for sharing the holiday season.

The holidays are also delightful because on Christmas Eve we are treated to a sight to behold. "Oh my god, Joe, here they come. This is hard to believe. Give them a mask and a horse and we got Zorro. Ya think there is any possibility that we can claim we don't know these guys," I cry out.

"Well, the good news is we only have to live through this once a year," says Joe.

Dad and Uncle Sam are members of a church honor guard called the Knights of Columbus, and for midnight Mass they dress in full regalia. The organization is a Catholic fraternal service group devoted to patriotism and a love for one's country. That is a noble goal. Their outlandish and ostentatious uniforms depict them as Soldiers of Christ. All I can say is that if they are soldiers, then Christ is in big trouble. They wear black tuxedo suits, white dress shirts, white bow ties, and a white sash, punctuated with a red and a blue stripe running diagonally across their chests. The sash is where they hang their three-foot swords. I must comment that their swords are nicer than the paltry $4.95 swords Joe and I bought from the *Popular Mechanics* magazine. As added pomp, a black cape lined with red satin material is worn over the uniform. Even Batman doesn't have a cape this fancy. As a crowning glory these merchants of peace wear a naval-type chapeaux that rivals anything Napoleon wore. A magnificent display of white ostrich feathers adorns the black hats, and the organization's red, white, and blue crest is emblazoned on both sides.

"Well, how do we look?" Dad proudly asks, smiling and winking. "Edith, is everything on right?"

"You look great" she answers in a reassuring voice.

In an audacious display of pageantry, Dad and Uncle Sam unsheathe their swords to demonstrate their ceremonial stance. "Oh my God, Joe, get down," I say as I duck for cover.

"Damn right. I don't want to be decapitated," Joe laughingly says.

I know their garb is for religious ceremony, but do they have to go to such extremes? Their uniform is similar to the outfit worn by Jackie Gleason in several episodes of *The Honeymooners*. "Joe, I don't mean any disrespect, but Dad and Uncle Sam remind me of Ralph Kramden and his buddy Ed Norton."

"They sure do. You would think they are dressing to attend a meeting at the Raccoon Lodge," Joe answers.

These soldiers are only a danger to themselves, and the chance of tripping and impaling themselves on those long swords is a possibility that Ralph and Ed never have to face. So like playful little boys, they depart for midnight Mass and do their special thing, but oh what a sight to behold.

One Christmas, Dad buys Joe and me a Lionel electric train that we are supposed to share. The beautiful black New York Central 773 Hudson steam locomotive, with its coal tender and assorted orange, black, and blue boxcars, begs us to play with it. In our basement we place a 4x8-foot sheet of plywood on two sawhorses as a platform for our railroad. We have a water tower and an automatic crossing gate that lowers to stop traffic as the train sweeps down the track. Occasionally, Joe lets me at the controls, but for all intents and purposes, he is the boss. Sharing with an older brother means he eats the bread and I scoop up the crumbs. As usual, Joe tests limits, even when it comes to electric trains. "What are you doing," I inquire.

"I'm fastening two large screws on either side of the railroad track, and between these screws I'll stretch rubber bands. I'm creating an elastic barrier. Watch this," he says. "Just make sure the train doesn't fall on the floor." Joe speeds the train down the tracks, ramming it into the springy barrier. The rubber bands stretch, rebound, and fire the train in the opposite direction from whence it came.

"Wow, that's brilliant, Joe, let's do it again." I don't think Dad ever gets wise to our antics. The hours spent in our old dank cellar are fun hours. Amazingly, we don't ruin the train.

My parents aren't rich as far as money goes, but the family is rich in love and caring. When I turn six Joe breaks the bad news to Megan and me. "There is no Santa Claus," he boldly announces. "It's the truth and you gotta live with it." The shock of his revelation stuns us. We decide to play dumb for the next two years on the outside chance he is wrong. One Christmas when I am nine years old I leaf through the J.C. Penney's catalog looking for my dream bike. I finally find it, the bike of my dreams, the best-looking bike in the world. Clearly it is fantastically beautiful, and I want it more than anything. The bike is a red Schwinn Black Phantom with chrome fenders, a front shock absorber, a horn, and a front and rear light; it is the cat's meow. Though beautiful, the bike costs ninety-eight dollars. Nonetheless, I continue to hint to Mom and Dad about my desire for a Schwinn. I make sure the catalog is accidentally on purpose left open to the page where I have circled my dream bike. Certainly, on Christmas morning it will be waiting for me under the tree; no other possibility exists.

With eager anticipation that only a kid can experience, I wake early and rush down the stairs on Christmas morning to look at my new Black Phantom, only to be greeted by a maroon JC Higgins bike from the Penney's catalog. I hide my disappointment because I know from the catalog that the JC Higgins bike cost twenty-seven dollars. I believe my parents did the best they could.

I never forget about my dream bike, and when the Schwinn company begins remanufacturing the Black Phantom, I purchase one. A lesson in life is: "It is never too late for dreams to come true." You only have to make it so.

CHAPTER 12

THATSA BULLAMA SHIT

By the end of the 1940s, the pace of change in our community accelerates. Everything has a beginning and everything has an end, and in the 1949–1953 era, I see the end of our old iron friend, the steam locomotive.

A flurry of activity precedes the day the first diesel locomotive passes through town. On a bright fall day, people line up by the railroad tracks as the large, but relatively quiet, black and yellow monster lumbers into town. Dad captures the cheering crowd on his Kodak motion picture camera. "Here she comes. This is a great thing for our community," he announces as the locomotive blasts its electric horn. The horn doesn't sound like a steam engine. It's loud, nothing like the raspy, tooting sound of a guy trying to clear his throat with steam.

"At least we don't have to worry about the smoke anymore. Finally, I can hang the laundry out to air dry and not worry about it becoming soiled with gritty smoke," Mom observes.

The first time I see a diesel locomotive, I dislike it. Something about it doesn't hit me right. Every steam engine passing our house talks to me and has its own personality. The diesels are boring and blah. They have no pizzazz. That day is the beginning of the end of the friendly huffing, puffing, chugging steam locomotives. Within two years they are as extinct as the horse and buggy.

The good news is the diesel locomotives do help solve Mother's laundry dilemma for a while. I say "for a while," because the family purchases a modern work saver. It is a shiny white Westinghouse front-loading electric dryer with a glass view port in the door. In many ways the dryer looks like a big old television set. This marvelous machine amazes me. The first time Mother uses the machine, we line up the chairs in the kitchen. Initially, we watch the tumbling clothes drying—how exciting. The excitement soon wanes and transitions into boredom as expectations catch up with reality. Watching clothes dry is like watching ice cubes melt. The dryer ushers in the age of electrical appliances.

Business is good, so Dad also purchases the family's first television, a 21-inch black-and-white Stromberg-Carlson. A Stromberg-Carlson is the Cadillac of televisions. It costs over five hundred dollars, a hefty sum of money. Television is possible in 1949 because cable is installed in Brockway. The town folk post a twenty-thousand-dollar bond, and Dad is one of the community fathers pledging a thousand dollars. We receive three channels, and regardless of the program, I watch it. TV is a novelty that completely captures my attention. The first event I view is the 1949–1950 New Year's Eve celebration at Times Square. Mom and Dad celebrate at the Knights of Columbus dance, and the babysitter allows me to welcome the new year of 1950. All the hype and festivity is great. I have never seen so many people. Nevertheless, I feel exactly the same one minute after midnight as I did before midnight. New Year's Eve does not meet or exceed expectations—it just happens.

My favorite TV show is *Howdy Doody*. Buffalo Bob, Clarabell the Clown, and Princess Summer, Spring, Winter, Fall are new vicarious friends. The daily old-fashion silent movie clips are fascinating. As I a teenybopper I rush home from school to watch *American Bandstand*. There is a beautiful black-haired girl on *American Bandstand* that I am in love with. Every night I dream of her, but our TV relationship never gets serious. *The Mickey Mouse Club* and the programming on early TV are fun to watch, and watch them I do. On Thursday night our vibrant little town is a ghost town between the hours of 8:00 and 9:00 P.M. Not a person is found on the streets; everyone is home watching the *Texaco Star Theater* with Milton Berle. His live comedy TV antics bring communities across the United States to a standstill. Like I said—no more front porch visits. Now, we visit with Uncle Miltie.

Grandpa Gamelo has an entirely different perspective on television. He doesn't believe anything on the glass tube. He is a real hard-nose doubter. Mother brings him to the house twice a week, and he visits with us in his long-sleeve flannel shirt. After dinner we gravitate to the television and watch the NBC Nightly News, with Chet Huntley and David Brinkley, before searching for our favorite programs. Anything that hints of cowboys, mysteries, or action/adventure is preferred. Grandpa sits upright in a hard, straight-back wooden chair, and I sprawl on the floor with my favorite pillow. I especially like the cowboy programs of *Gunsmoke*, *Rawhide*, and *Bonanza*. As I watch the fictional plots and the characters perform feats of daring, Grandpa frequently mutters in broken English, "Thatsa bullama shit." He is our homespun entertainment critic of three words.

Joe taunts him, "Hey, Grandpa, what did you think of that program?"

Of course the reply is always "Thatsa bullama shit."

"You mean you don't believe that happened? Well, I certainly think it's true," quips Joe. We giggle and don't pay much attention to Grandpa as he analyzes the relationship of the fictional events to reality. From my point of view everything is possible, but to him everything is bullama shit.

The marketing industry quickly recognizes television's potential and inundates our home with commercials. Indelibly etched in the neurons of my fragile mind are jingles that persist for a lifetime. For instance, the leading brand of toothpaste is Ipana, as sung by an animated Bucky Beaver. Throughout the day the refrain repeats in my mind.

"Brush-ah, brush-ah, brush-ah, here's the new Ipana.

Brush-ah, brush-ah, brush-ah, it's healthy for your teeeeeth."

Probably the most distasteful jingle makes me aware of a terrible affliction called halitosis, better known as bad breath. Until this ditty appears on TV, I am not aware of stinky breath. After seeing the jingle, I am insecure about breathing. A never-before-mentioned product suddenly transitions into a household necessity. Although a catchy exhortation, it is not a classic. The ditty is sung as follows:

"He said that she said that he had halitosis.

He said that she said, it's true of some girls too.

He said that she said that he had halitosis.

Here's what she said to dooooo.

Try Listerine, buy Listerine.

Make breath clean and sheen with Listerine.

Try Listerine, buy Listerine.

Make breath clean and sheen with Listerine."

At the end of the Saturday movie matinee, the cowboy inevitably kisses the girl good-bye before riding into the sunset. We mock the romance by singing; "He said that she said…" One of them assuredly has bad breath. Why these advertisements are memorable is a mystery. I try to fall asleep, but the bad breath jingle plays repeatedly in my mind. The song refuses to sleep. I am brainwashed. Although never a subject of violence or mayhem, I do worry about bad breath.

I watch *The Three Stooges*, but I know the Stooges are slapstick. Moe, Larry, and Curly aren't for real. They are the best belly laughs in town. Humor is based on the ridiculous, and the Three Stooges are totally ridiculous. As a juvenile, I flourish watching their unpredictable, ludicrous behavior. My parents understand that not everything in life is to be taken seriously—they, too, enjoy a good belly laugh. Dad is crazy about Abbott and Costello and he cries with laughter watching their performance of the "Who's on First" baseball routine. Underneath his stern facade is a little boy like me, enjoying a laughable situation.

I grow up in the best of times with the best of people and the best of families. The boundaries and rules are clear and followed until I am an adult in both mind and body. I don't like all the rules and sometimes rebel, but they do make me feel comfortable. As I grow and mature, my parents gradually give me more leeway, but always within the framework of a strong value system. The boundaries and rules never disappear; they only become wider. My home environment and my family support network are a sociologist's dream, and that's no bullama shit.

II.

THE SCHOOL YEARS

CHAPTER 13

GETTING READY FOR LIFE – ELEMENTARY SCHOOL

Late in summer Mom announces, "Joseph, Jimmy, and Megan, get dressed. We're going to Dubois. It's time to get ready for school."

"Golly, Mom, that's not for two weeks. Couldn't I just stay home and play with the guys?"

"James, no, now clean up and get ready. We're leaving in five minutes," she firmly replies.

Oh-oh, there's that James word again. She's not kidding. Her directive is a signal that summer is about to end. Getting prepared for school is an expensive proposition, costing as much as ten dollars for each of us. We drive to Dubois to buy new shoes at Brown's Boot Shop. After purchasing shoes, we make a trip to J.C. Penney's, where we each select two new shirts. As a second male child, there is plenty of opportunity to grow into Joe's castoffs, so more than two new shirts are considered a waste. If my black high-top sneakers are in good shape, I use them for gym class until they die a natural death. Otherwise, new sneakers are purchased at the ungodly price of two dollars. Thankfully, Mom never makes me wear Joe's old sneakers. To top off our back-to-school necessities, we purchase a fully equipped pencil box. A new pencil box is a status symbol, and I can't wait to show it to my classmates.

Preparing for school means saying hello to the Western Pennsylvania's fall season, and we know what follows fall. As I move through the grades, I become friends with my classmates, but even more important I am buddies with three special guys.

The Brockway Area School District consists of two buildings, the 9th Avenue Elementary School and the 7th Avenue Secondary School. In the 1940s we are exceptionally smart, because there is no such thing as kindergarten. Everyone starts school at the first-grade level. The excitement and anxiety of getting ready for first grade is overwhelming. In the fall of 1947, Mom drops me off for my first day, and my life is forever changed. Society replaces the security of home with a new and alien environment. I am fifty inches tall, weigh fifty-seven pounds, and I am ready to take on the world. Mrs. Rallton, my first-grade teacher, is a nurturing person. Her blue dress with pink flowers and a lace collar enhance her matronly appearance. Every day we start class activities with a cheerful song:

"Good morning to you.

Good morning to you.

Good morning, Mrs. Rallton.

Good morning to you."

To our chant she replies, "And good morning to you, boys and girls," after which she immediately outlines the tasks to be completed that day. My report card rates me on a one-to-five scale, with the number one meaning "outstanding" and the number five representing "unsatisfactory." Now my worth is expressed as a number from one to five. Thank goodness Mom doesn't view me in this manner; I'm sure there are days she would rate me as a five.

During my first year in school, I quickly improve in all categories. Even my social traits and work habits improve from threes (satisfactory) to ones. I think it is partly because I like my teacher.

The structure, rules, and classroom regulations are uncomfortable, but I adapt since rules and regulations at home are plentiful. My new friend Nick sits beside me and he adapts by becoming rebellious. I prefer to be a free floater and do whatever piques my interest, and now I am regimented and must conform—not a good situation. One of the first things I learn is to raise my hand with one finger to pee, and two fingers to do something else. It sounds reasonable. I catch on fast and go to the bathroom to do a number one or a number two, sort of like talking in secret Captain Commando code. If three fingers are raised, it is truly an emergency.

I already know the ABCs, and being around books is part of my home experience. The teacher only has to put everything together to get me ready to read. The ever-present "Dick and Jane" reading textbooks are exciting, and sight-reading skills are rapidly learned. Dick and blond-haired Jane do things together and they have fun, so they must be fairly nice kids. "LOOK, JANE, LOOK," yells Dick, and Jane often says, "SEE SPOT RUN." Yes, Dick and Jane are exciting, but they do have a limited vocabulary. I like learning about letters and numbers and soon master what is required of a first-grader. Nick struggles, but by midyear he is up to speed. I am easygoing and easy to get along with. Learning school stuff is a cinch.

There is one special time in first grade when our class has dress-up day. Nick and I dress as cowboys. Upon entering the classroom, we crouch under the desks, take out our cap pistols, and pretend to shoot each other. Ronnie and others in the class soon join in the fantasy battle. Mrs. Rallton is not in the room, but the principal's office is nearby. The principal, Joe Saffer, hears all the commotion and the racket of kids yelling, "Bang-bang you're dead, bang-bang you're dead," and bursts into the room. He points at me and shouts, "You kids stop that and get back in your seats right now." Yikes, he's mad and he's going to slaughter us. To me, Mr. Saffer is a fifty-foot-tall giant. He was a Marine in the Pacific Theater during WWII and speaks with the authority of a drill sergeant. He doesn't disarm me, but he does make Nick and I holster our six-shooters. That marks the first time that I get reprimanded by the authorities.

What is wrong with hiding under the desk? Hunkering under the desk for protection is something we are trained to do. Throughout my school years the dark clouds of war hang over the nation like a vulture stalking its prey. Even though I don't understand what is going on, I do know that in the 1940s there is big trouble in the world. Someone calls it a "cold war." How do these major events affect an elementary school kid in the middle of nowhere? The truth is nobody will waste a bomb on us. Nonetheless, at least twice a year the school conducts the infamous civil defense drills.

The drill makes me feel safe, because there is nothing like a school desk to protect me from an atomic bomb. By the time we enter junior high school, the "duck and cover" drills are commonplace. Nick's standard joke is, "The only reason to crouch under our desks and put our heads between our knees is so that we can kiss our butts good-bye." Nonetheless, it is better than doing nothing. The classroom drill consists of crouching, closing my eyes, and remaining in this position for three minutes as the fire company's siren screams its fearful message. Some families construct bomb shelters in their backyards. I want one; what a great play fort it will make. Just think, if that girl Dorothy in *The Wizard of Oz* had a bomb shelter, she would have never gotten into all that trouble.

From first grade on, friends are increasingly important in my life. Every morning, rain, snow, or shine, Nick walks past the house and like clockwork, I join him for the trek to the elementary building. Now, Nick isn't the brightest bulb on the Christmas tree, but he is a good guy. He doesn't directly tell me, but from our chatting I pick up that he doesn't have a happy home life.

"How ya doing today, Nick?" I inquire.

"Not so good. The old man pissed me off, and I got a whooping last night." After that he clams up and we continue our usual banter. They don't treat him well, and in turn he keeps his family in turmoil. I can't imagine such a household. He carries a chip on his shoulder and brings the chip into the classroom. From the beginning, the teachers don't cater to Nick and often put him on the back burner. Unlike his positive relationship with me, social skills among adults are not his strong point. Nick and I are more than friends; we are best buddies in our everyday walks to and from school. When he is with me, he behaves himself, but not with adults.

Ronnie Faust is another friend in the early years. As Nick and I journey down the main street sidewalk to the elementary school, we walk past Ronnie's house, where he regularly falls in beside us. Like me, skinny Ronnie has black wavy hair and crooked teeth. He isn't tall, but he does have one remarkable feature. He has humongous feet and is prone to stumbling over the joints in the sidewalk. Nick and I have great fun watching him play "step on a crack and break your mother's back." He sure does a lot of harm to his mother's back. Ronnie is a squeaky-voiced kid, a nice kid, a good person, and Nick and I like him. We look forward to his daily high-pitched greeting. "Morning, guys—what's up?"

"Why do you ask the same stupid question every day?" Nick asks.

"I don't know—I just do," Ronnie says, shrugging his shoulders.

Walking to school with a bunch of guys gives us a chance to talk about everything. We often joke about our common problem, and misinformation abounds. "That damn morning tent pole keeps me from rolling over in bed," Nick comments.

On a serious note I say, "Be careful, a quick morning rollover can cause it to break, and then what will you tell your parents? Yes, sir, I repeat, it'll snap like a dry twig. I'm not sure how they repair a broken boner, but it can't be fun."

"Boy, that would be hard to explain," Ronnie muses. "I think I came close to breaking mine one morning."

"Ohhh, that'll really hurt," moans Nick. "A guy needs to take these kinds of things into consideration."

I speculate, "Ya know, guys, I don't think there's a bone down there so why do they call it a boner? Why not call it a marshmallow instead?"

"It would be pretty hard to roll over and break your marshmallow—now wouldn't it," Nick says.

Our great intellectual conversations assist in understanding the world of preadolescent confusion. We are free from prying ears, and that's where friendships develop. I get my first buddies.

The elementary building is a small one-story brick structure with a gym and two classrooms for each grade level. Regardless of the weather, I stand outside until the principal opens the doors and rings his handheld bell, ushering in the beginning of the school day. Into the building rush the horde of kids, each making his or her way to their assigned classrooms. Once inside the room, my routine is to hang up my coat, sit at my desk, and wait for the beginning of class. Before class the teacher reads a verse from the Bible and we recite the Lord's Prayer, followed by the Pledge of Allegiance. The practice never varies in the twelve years I am in school.

My academic life takes a downturn. In second grade my love of learning is a different story—the teacher bursts my bubble. She systematically tears out my self-confidence and eats it. She has a voracious appetite for independent boys, and eats them up and spits them out. On the first report card, I receive an overabundance of fours. The number four is defined as "merely passing, needs improvement." Miss Ramero must think fours are my favorite number since she uses them a lot. Her six-week assessment of my performance is:

Works out for himself pronunciations and meaning of new words: 4

Reads aloud so that others enjoy it: 4

Understands what is read: 4

Does workbook carefully and accurately: 4

Sits, stands, and walks correctly: 4

Does not bite nails or put fingers in mouth: 4

Obeys his teachers: 4

Is ready and begins work promptly: 4

Tries to complete work: 4

Follows instructions well: 4

Makes good use of time: 4

Gone are all the ones I worked so hard to receive in first grade. I am devastated. Halfway through second grade I think of myself as a failure. What a revolting turn of events after riding high in first grade. "Nick, Miss Ramero is an ugly, mean, and miserable person," I assert. "She is out to destroy me—I mean it, Nick."

"Ah, quit giving her so many nice compliments. She's a witch," Nick remarks.

"Yes, something like the Wicked Witch of the North," says Ronnie, "or is that of the East?"

At home I am compliant, but with this woman I am profoundly mutinous. The nice Jimmy takes a vacation and leaves me with the noncompliant Jimmy. For some reason we just never connect. I try getting back at her by secretly resisting her dictatorial approach to my education.

My specific nemesis is mathematics, and multiplication is a problem. For some reason I can't master my times tables. I quickly lose confidence. As an independent free thinker, Miss Ramero doesn't appreciate creative math solutions. She wants me to memorize the math facts by rote. Particular problems are the eights and nines time tables. I am fearful that Dad will find out I'm doing poorly in her class. Imagine thinking of myself as a failure in second grade.

"Gosh, Nick, how am I going to explain flunking second grade to my parents?"

"Will it make them feel better if they know I'm flunking too?" says Nick.

"Do youse guys care if I tell my parents ya both are failing?" Ronnie inquires. "'Cause I'm failing second grade too."

The apprehension of being a second-grade failure grates on my fragile ego. There is nothing like the specter of failure to ruin a positive self-concept. This will bring disgrace upon the family name. Me, the only DeAngelo to flunk second grade. Joe knows my dilemma and teases me, "Well, Mr. Brilliant, you're about as sharp as an ice cube," and that makes matters worse. Nothing like an encouraging brother to help me out of a jam.

It is possible that I have contracted brain stupor. Perhaps a less-than-cooperative attitude hinders my learning. My irrational attempt at punishing Miss Ramero backfires and I find myself behind in my studies. Even at an early age I am hardheaded and resist the attempt of others attempting to impose their will on me. The art of catering to authority figures is hard to master.

Mom says that I should do better and signs my report card. She looks me in the eyes and teaches me a lesson I'll always remember. "Jimmy boy, I want to tell you something that may help. You are having some kind of a problem at school with Miss Ramero—am I correct? Do you think you may be part of the problem? I want you to face your personal dragon, or you will never be able to slay the nasty beast. Confront your problem. Look it straight in the eyes, punch it in the nose, and watch the beast that's kicking at you scurry away. Remember, son, for every problem there is a solution; you only have to make it so—it's your responsibility to make it so."

I get her message and know it is my responsibility to take charge of my attitude and change the situation. I work hard on punching dragons in the nose. By golly, it works, and by the end of the year, my grades are all twos (very good). I finally realize that sometimes there is no choice but to bend. I struggle through second grade and memorize my times tables. Yes, I even master "sits, stands, and walks correctly" and "does not bite nails or put fingers in mouth." With as much dignity as can be mustered, I swallow my pride and am nice to Miss Ramero. It works, because I don't think I get any smarter. Nonetheless, I never master "makes good use of time," and it haunts me for the next ten years. I am constantly in disagreement about what is good use of my time; after all, it is my time.

Self-confidence is regained in third grade with the nicest teacher I have ever met. Mrs. Edith Maurino is a wonderful person and teaches me everything Miss Ramero failed to teach. Her gentle and encouraging nature is what I need. I'm beginning to realize that I don't do well with authority figures. To me a little kindness is like a small bar of soap—though small, it makes bushels of suds that go a long way toward cleansing my disdain for authority. She looks me directly in the eyes and says with confidence, "Jimmy, you can do the work and I know that you can do it very well—do you agree with me? Then let's get on with it. We've got a lot to learn this year." What a boost to my self-esteem. Mrs. Maurino makes my hit list, and I want to learn. She knows how to encourage a viable seed to blossom into a beautiful flower. She reminds me of Mom, and they both have the same first name. I flourish in third grade and like school again.

On parents' day Mom comes to school for her annual visit. Parents sit in the back of the classroom and watch as the teacher continues her lesson. The teachers know Mom from the restaurant, and I am proud to have her in my classroom. Mother is a naturally beautiful brunette, but when she dresses up, she is really spiffy. High on her prepping routine is checking her nylons and her slip. "Are my seams straight? Is my slip showing?" she inquires.

"Straight as a white picket fence and your slip isn't showing. You're all cleared for takeoff," I answer. Of course, I provide truthful feedback. Leaving the house with crooked seams or a slip showing is an emotional tragedy. God forbid that her seams are crooked like the lady's in church. I am as proud of her as I am my new pencil box. Sizing up the mothers who visit our class, I conclude that Mom is the best-looking. She radiates love from the inside out. I never thought much about it, but when you grow up with goodness, you naturally believe that's the way the world is.

Mrs. Conners is my fourth-grade teacher, and her claim to fame is producing the holiday operetta. "Each one of you children will be assigned a part in the operetta," she announces. "This year's operetta is called *Fairies and Garland*. If you have any questions, see me after class." During recess I ask Mrs. Conners if I can talk with her. "Of course," she replies.

On the following day Mrs. Conners announces, "Children, I have your assigned parts for the operetta." As she goes through the list, she finally says, "Nicholas and James, you will do a duet and play the parts of the Good Fairies from the East." As we read the script, we find our task is to search for the magic shoes. In reality the magic shoes are sneakers covered with tinfoil, but the audience will never know that. This is my first stage appearance, and who knows where it may lead.

"Nick," I say, "these parts will make us famous."

"Are you deranged?" he replies. "Do you realize we are going to dress up like fairies in front of the whole school? Fairies are queer, three-dollar bills, bogus, and anything else you want to call them. Jim, somehow I know you put Mrs. Conners up to this, and I'll get even with you. You're screwed up enough to do a stupid thing like this."

"Oh, come on, Nick, it'll be fun. I wouldn't do anything like that."

"Yes, you would," he says in a displeased voice. Apparently, Nick and I have different ideas about fairies, but he isn't far from the truth. I did ask Mrs. Conners to assign Nick and me to a part we could share.

Operetta day finally arrives. We are dressed in full costume and Nick is not pleased about our attire. I believe he has social anxiety. The excitement surges through my body as I am about to make my first appearance on stage. After days of practice, Mrs. Conners gives us last-minute backstage instructions. "Remember, boys," she coaches, "sing loud, very loud." I think loudness is the virtue that got us the parts. "Alright, boys, it's almost time for your performance. When I wave my hand, it will be your cue to go on stage. Now break a leg." I search my mind for reasons she wants Nick and me to break a leg, but find no logical answer. We wisely ignore her overture for bodily harm. She cues us. I take a deep breath and we skip our way across the brightly lit stage, singing:

"We are the Good Fairies of the East,

We are in search of our magic shoes,

We know the magic within,

And we will do good."

Here we are, two guys wearing white tights, skipping across the stage like injured frogs. The humiliation of white tights shatters my manly persona and the floppy fairy ears don't help. We approach a bench on the stage and abruptly stop. Nick boldly points and in a muddled monotone voice says, "Look, we have found the magic shoes." In front of the bench are two pairs of glistening tinfoil-covered metallic silver sneakers. After days of practice I yell my only line—the line that will make me famous—a line that will launch my acting career. "Let's try them on and see if they fit." I speak the line with such gusto, embellishment, and emotion that I know the audience is amazed with my unfettered acting talent. Nick and I sit down and begin to put on our magic shoes. Nick has no trouble fitting his feet into the shoes, but I am having difficulty and struggle. Somehow my feet won't slip into the sneakers. Hells bells, what's going on here? Glancing over at Nick I wonder why he is sitting beside me with a coy snicker on his face. I say to myself, *There's nothing funny here.* As I place my hand on the shoe, I notice that someone has tied the top of the shoelaces in a knot. Oh my god, what am I to do? I mentally scream, *Nick, you dirty rat!* How I do it in my panicked state I don't know, but I do. With superhuman effort I unknot the shoelaces and thrust my feet into the silver sneakers. Must be a reflex action, because everything is a blur. With beads of sweat flowing down my brow, I cock my head and give an audible sigh of relief. This is a serious part of the operetta, but there is giggling emanating from the audience. Oh boy, Mrs. Conners won't like this. We stand, face the audience, and say, "We have found the magic shoes and now we must continue our journey." Together Nick and I prepare for our exit. As we skip off the stage, we again sing our duet.

"We are the Good Fairies of the East,

And we have found our magic shoes,

Hurray, hurray, hurray,

We are off to do good."

Backstage I intensively stare as Nick bursts into a raucous belly laugh. With furrowed brow and lips tight as guitar strings, I let loose with an accusation. "You tied my shoelaces in a knot, didn't you?"

Laughingly he responds, "No, I didn't—why would I do a thing like that?"

I end the conversation with "You're an asshole." As far as my acting career is concerned, I am a mere relic of my former self, but I can't stay angry for long. I guess I got my "just rewards" for volunteering him to be a fairy. We have trouble living down our performance in girlie-boy white tights, but we survive. The operetta is the beginning and the end of my stage career. I know that I'll never see Broadway. I am relieved, and never again allow myself to wear white tights.

Mrs. Conners is a good lady, but she is a taskmaster. My performance in the operetta doesn't endear me to her. Absolutely no talking is tolerated in her classroom. Good manners get me in trouble as I whisper, "Excuse me," to a classmate blocking me from getting my coat for recess. Mrs. Conners' voice accusingly echoes, "James, I told you there would be no talking." I instinctively know that when anyone calls me James, trouble follows.

"But, Mrs. Conners, I only…"

"James, no talking means no talking," she affirms before I finish my protest. Okay, I get busted and get detention. I'll admit, maybe I did purposely push the envelope to test her resolve. Her rules are absolute and inflexible. Neither a court of appeals nor an explanation is allowed. I do the time, but I'm not angry. No matter what, I broke a rule and that's that. The lesson learned is that a rule is a rule and don't break it if you don't want to pay a consequence. There are no lawyers to mitigate my case, citing the injustice of the punishment, but who can afford lawyers.

The big deal in fifth grade is riding my bike to school. My customized black and pink JC Higgins bike is a reliable mode of pedal-power transportation. Riding certainly cuts down the time to travel home for lunch. Yes, Nick and I go home for lunch every day. At home there is a sandwich waiting, a glass of milk, and a piece of warm pie from the restaurant. I gobble my food and quickly return to school. Aunt Betty is amazed when water fountains, complete with cold water, are put in the school. She can't get over it and repeatedly says, "Imagine, chilled water fountains in the school—what will they think of next?" Nonetheless, Aunt Betty does adapt, but rather slowly.

During class I have an unpleasant experience. I sit at a desk behind a kid who stinks. This kid is still having accidents in class, and he wets himself or does even worse. "Nick, did you notice what happened on my side of the room today? Stinky boy crapped himself."

"Ya mean he took a dump in class?"

"Yes, he surely did—it was disgusting. What am I going to do?"

"Maybe you need a shovel and broom like the guy who walks behind the circus elephants." I knew I could count on Nick for some words of wisdom. Our desks are screwed to the floor, so the opportunity to gradually move away from stinky boy is impossible. Mom teaches, "Be kind to others less fortunate," but the situation requires action.

Phew, the choking smell makes me nauseous. I finally ask the teacher, "Mrs. Carlson, will you please move my seat? I don't want to be mean, but Johnny Steel stinks."

"Oh, I think I understand," she says. "I'll see what I can do." Thank goodness, she honors my request. I feel sorry for the kid, but the unpleasant experience sticks with me. Besides, what if the odor is catching? What if I start to smell like stinky boy just because I am near to him?

Our curriculum in school centers on developing interest in things other than comic books. I read *Popular Mechanics* magazine and find science fascinating. To me scientists are people looking to the future. On the other hand, historians are people excelling at predicting the past. I am particularly fascinated with space and the planets. Mrs. Carlson picks up on my interest and encourages me. "Jimmy, here is a book you would be interested in. Why don't you read it?"

"Gee thanks, Mrs. Carlson," I politely say. "What's it about?"

"Well, the title of the book is *Planets*, and it will intrigue you."

I read the book and devour its contents. It talks about space and the planets, with chapters discussing the possibility of rockets and traveling to the moon. Fascinating, maybe I can grow up to be like my comic book hero Flash Gordon and slay Ming the Terrible.

A requirement for graduating from elementary school is proficiency in pen and ink writing. Mr. Green, a chubby, but likable guy employed by the state, comes to school to give writing lessons. Our old desks are arranged in five columns. Each desktop has a two-inch inkwell hole that waits day after day to fulfill its mission. On writing days, the teacher issues glass ink containers that fit into the vacant inkwell in the same manner as a hand fits into a glove. Ahhh—finally the inkwell hole fulfills its destiny. From a scraggly black box, I pick a wooden stylus. The stylus has a bottom groove into which the pointed metal pen is inserted. On command from Mr. Green, the ink jar is opened and my pen is dipped into the opaque black liquid. Devilish Nick encourages me, "Jim, you dip the pigtails of the girl in front of you in your inkwell, and I'll do the same to the girl in front of me—okay?"

"Nah, Nick, you have a better chance than me 'cause her pigtails are longer. I'll make you a deal. Let's get Ronnie to do it first and then we'll do it at the same time."

Nick leans over, points, and whispers, "Ronnie, dip her pigtails in the inkwell."

Ronnie hesitates, nods, and says, "Okay."

A shrill scream fills the room and the angry teacher says, "Ronnie Faust, go to the principal's office immediately."

"Boy, that Ronnie is sure stupid," says Nick.

I am tempted to dip the blond pigtails of the girl sitting in front of me into the ink container, but successfully resist. Unlike dumb Ronnie I know the consequences will be catastrophic. I continually practice making the smooth cursive curves, circles, and lines essential for meeting the requirements of the Palmer Writing System. I am happy to report that I receive my writing certificate that year—another successful life experience.

The most trivial and unimportant thing is learning to spell the word geography. Phonics isn't taught so I lack the tools to sound out and spell complex words. But I never misspell it again because I can mentally recite the phrase Mrs. Carlson teaches me: "George Eats Old Gray Rats And Paints Houses Yellow"—a meaningful technique, isn't it? I like Mrs. Carlson; to me that's important. Later, Dad tells me she is the wife of his workout buddy.

School is great and with the exception of second grade, little effort is required. Sailing along without expending much energy suits me fine. I never think of myself as smart. I only know that I don't have to do much to get by.

In early 1952, the state consolidates school districts and moves the adjoining district into the larger Brockway schools. Thanks to the state, my circle of friends expands. My first encounter with Wolf is as a fifth-grade student. His real name is Wolfgang McGuire. Wolf's mother admired and named him after Wolfgang Amadeus Mozart—you figure it out. He is fresh off the farm, and somehow the name Wolfgang doesn't fit. Our first meeting is awkward. As this lanky boy approaches me, he holds out his hand and says, "Shake." When I extend my hand, he plunges his open hand into my midsection, yelling, "Spear!" My response is, "Boy, that is witty, like I've never heard that line before." The fake handshake is as ridiculous as slapping a kid on the back and in the stomach while using the old WWII saying, "Glad to see you back (slap) from the front (slap)."

"My name is Wolf," he says. "What's yours?"

One good turn deserves another, so I shrewdly retaliate. "My name is Peter McCain; ask me again and I'll tell you the same." How's that for an ingenious comeback?

"You look familiar. Aren't you the kid that dressed in white tights for the fourth-grade operetta?"

"No, you are confusing me with someone else." My god, will people never forget about that fourth-grade operetta? After we finally introduce ourselves, Wolf starts to laugh and I know that our awkward meeting is no more than a clumsy way of breaking the ice.

Wolf is a bus kid and I am a town kid. I envy him. He gets to pack his lunch every day and rides a bus to school, whereas I have to walk home to eat lunch. Going home for lunch is worthy of note because most of the teachers eat lunch at my father's restaurant. Frankly, I have to toe the line, given Dad's direct line to the teachers.

When I return to school, the bus kids are in the playground playing "pump-pump-pull-away." The rules are vague, but go something like this. Initially, one person is "it" in the middle of the field. All other players line up at the end of the field, and the person yells "pump-pump-pull-away" and calls a name. The person whose name is called runs across the field. The job of the person in the middle is to tag the kid and have him or her join him. Progressively the number of people in the middle increases as the number of runners decreases. The objective of the game is to be the last person, the winner, the swiftest and most elusive person to run the field. The game is usually not completed because the bell for afternoon sessions rings.

Except for getting some new kids in school, fifth grade is uneventful. It doesn't matter who you are, everyone is placed in the same classroom. That is why I sat behind stinky boy. I feel good when Nick tells me that a girl in our class likes me. "Dorothy Smith told me she has a crush on you. If I'm lying may my mother wear army boots. Cross my heart and hope to die, I wouldn't lie to you."

"Then your mother wears army boots. Nick, if you think I believe you, then there is a bridge in Brooklyn I'll sell you cheap. Ya know—liar, liar, pants on fire? Well, your pants are on fire. Now forget about it." Other than inflating my ego, such rubbish doesn't interest me. I have absolutely no interest in girls. Why God made man give up a rib to create them, I'll never know.

I develop a circle of friends who remain with me until I graduate from high school. Nick Manceni is affectionately known among the guys as "Nick the prick," but I never call him that. In school I am secretively seditious, but Nick is outright defiant. Nick is different and those differences increasingly manifest themselves later in life. Nick takes himself down a different pathway, but when in school he is my best buddy. Although tough on the outside, I know him as a loveable marshmallow. He remains a good friend in the same manner as Fonzi is to Richie in *Happy Days*. Other friends are Stump, Liver, Spike, Kike, and Tank—nicknames are the thing. Unfortunately, I'm known only as Jim. Another friend, Mot, uses his first name spelled backward as a moniker. I try doing my name backward, but it is a girl's name, Mij.

Like a revolving door, friends come and go, but the three of us stay buddies for a long time, and buddies are one notch above friends.

Except for a bad experience in sixth grade, I don't get into fistfights, but I do create age-appropriate mischief. At this time male bonding with buddies is important. I never acquire a nickname, even though a name like Rocky, Crusher, or Flash is appropriate. They are hard to come by.

In sixth grade we are the big shots because this is our last year in the elementary building. I still have not mastered "makes good use of his time" on the report card. I think of myself as average, but my sixth-grade teacher thinks I am dogging it. She spills the beans by writing a note to Mom on my report card:

"According to tests administrated in the fall, Jimmy shouldn't get anything lower on his card than a 2. More careful work would improve his card."

The jig is up; those damn tests scores betray me. Why work for a two when a three is easy to achieve without sacrificing playtime with my pals? Good grief, did you ever get a good look at those "pansies" who get twos and ones on their report card?

Life is one long adventure, and spectacular grades aren't important. Secretly, Mom knows that when ready I will blossom, but in the interim I drive her crazy. Dad remains silent on the topic of grades, but I sense he is frustrated at my average performance. My flower does blossom, and I assist nature by giving my intellectual seed ample time to germinate—good rationalization, isn't it?

I am five-feet, one-inch tall, weigh 108 pounds, and grow another three inches during the school year. My body is a solid mass of undeveloped muscle, and fat is nowhere to be found. I grow so fast that I often go to school wearing flood pants with cuffs one or two inches higher than the top of my shoes, until Mom drives to J.C. Penney's and purchases new trousers.

In sharp contrast to my growth spurt, two sixth-grade students overshadow us all—they are Bo-Jo and Jessy. More than six feet tall, they physically tower over my classmates and the teacher. They are the only sixteen-year-olds in our class and the only students in the sixth grade who drive cars to school. In the 1950s, social promotions do not exist, and Bo-Jo and Jessy are proof of that. A person either earns a promotion or they don't pass.

The administration warns the class that if we get in Bo-Jo or Jessy's cars, there will be dire consequences. That is a message they don't have to issue. A person would be a lunatic to get in either of the junk cars driven by Bo-Jo or Jessy, and none of us is that demented.

Bo-Jo and Jessy have a memorable effect because they are the first persons to use dirty language. Cuss words are common, but dirty talk is something else. If it hadn't been for sneaking peeks at Mother's nursing books, I wouldn't know the difference between boys and girls. Even though Wolf lives on a farm, he isn't any different from me when it comes to girls.

In order to keep her classroom under control, the teacher places Jessy in a front row seat and Bo-Jo in a back row seat. I am watching one day as the two boys silently banter and gesture. Their antics increase as Miss Huntly turns her back to the class and writes notes on the chalkboard. Jessy slyly turns in his seat and, with a gap-tooth smile that only can be displayed by a person never visiting Doc McGrin, mouths to Bo-Jo in the rear of the room, "Fuck you." As a follow-up, he clandestinely puts the middle finger of his left hand in the air. Remarkably, no one knows what they are talking about. That is my first introduction to the F-word. I never know when an opportunity to increase my vocabulary will occur. Nonetheless, it is best not to ask Mom what it means. I recall how upset she got when I asked the meaning of "bastard," and "fuck you" sounds a lot worse than that inauspicious word. The word is tucked away in my mental folder for use on appropriate occasions. I figure, someday I will blurt out "fuck you" in a conversation and the shock value will be tremendous. Of course, I first have to find out what the F-word means.

Bo-Jo lives two blocks from me on Railroad Street. His house is a modest, old-fashioned, two-story, brown asbestos-shingled building that screams *I'm livable but nothing special.* When his car isn't working, he takes the forbidden shortcut home through the woods, which is totally against school rules, and if caught he will be reported to the principal.

One morning before class Nick taps me on the shoulder and says: "Boy, have I got a great idea. The hell with school rules; let's take the shortcut home tonight."

"Nick, ya think we'll run into Bo-Jo? I don't see his car, and he goes home by way of the shortcut."

Nick loudly proclaims, "Nah, that big stupid ape will be long gone by the time we get there."

At that precise moment, which only could have been orchestrated by God, Bo-Jo walks by. He glares the meanest glare I've ever seen. He points to me, yes, to me, saying, "I'm gonna get you for that."

"Oh my God, I didn't say anything and now he's after me; he's gonna kill me."

"Aw, forget about it. He's all talk. Ya worry too much," Nick advises, dismissing my concerns. "He's a mental defective. Bo-Jo can't remember anything for over a day or else he wouldn't be in sixth grade at the age of sixteen."

"Hope you're right, Nick. What's our plan? How we gonna keep from getting killed?"

Well, we fool the giant dingle head and don't take the shortcut home that day. The next day Nick and I feel secure in sneaking through the woods to go home. Halfway into the woods something larger than a bush but a tad smaller than a tree blocks the sunlight and casts a shadow over the path. Suddenly it moves. "Oh-oh," I mutter to Nick, "trouble ahead."

"Hey you two shitheads, I want to talk to you," the deep, angry voice bellows. Oh my God, it's Bo-Jo. His huge body blocks the trail, and it is too late for us to retreat—we are trapped. I can see in his fire-red eyes that he wants a piece of us and won't be happy until he satisfies his desire for revenge. "I remember you two birds. You're the two queers that dressed up in white tights in fourth grade, ain't ya," he gruffly says.

"No, you must be mistaken," Nick abruptly interjects. Some things are really hard to live down.

"Aw, shut up, I know what I saw—youse think I'm stupid, don't you. What did you call me?" He slaps me across the side of the head. "And you, you little fart," he addresses Nick, "you were laughing." Wham,

his hand strikes Nick across the side of the head. The one thing I can say about Bo-Jo is that he is an equal opportunity hitter. "I'm going to teach you guys a lesson ya ain't gonna ever forget," he threatens.

"Now, Bo-Jo…offffffff" are the two defensive words I am allowed to utter. With his clenched fist, he delivers a compelling belly blow that knocks the wind out of me and drops me to my knees. The same medicine is given to Nick. We are both breathless and on the ground crying in pain. "Nick, I know the next hit will be the killer deathblow," I say as I wait for its delivery, but the deathblow never arrives. What a surprise.

Bo-Jo walks away. "That'll teach you assholes what a big stupid ape can do," he says as he glances back.

We quickly get up and recover what little dignity we have left. We learn a painful lesson. Never bad-mouth a guy sixteen years of age and a hundred pounds heavier. We pay the price and never report the incident to the principal, but we avoid the shortcut and Bo-Jo whenever possible. If his idea is to terrorize us, he does a great job.

A week later it is my turn to help the teacher clean the classroom after school, and I leave the building later than normal. Mounting my trusty JC Higgins bike, I discover that the chain has slipped off the drive sprocket. I dismount and try to reengage the chain, but to no avail. I start walking the bike home when a car door slams. Looking up I see Bo-Jo walking slowly and purposefully toward me. My mind races as I contemplate what is about to happen. Yipes, he's smiling. Oh God, what's he going to do to me now? Should I run or scream for help? Nah, only a sissy would do that. What should I do? Within seconds hundreds of thoughts stampede through my mind. I feel the adrenaline pumping. I freeze, stand my ground, and look him in the eyes as he approaches. Too scared for flight means the only alternative is to fight. Something inside me snaps. Enough is enough; time to take a stand. Courage, not fear, is summoned. I mentally prepare myself: *This time he isn't going to have a piece of me. I'm going to viciously attack him.*

Bo-Jo stops inches in front of me, looks me in the eyes, and says, "What's the trouble?"

I size up the situation. Something is wrong. What gives here? "My chain came off the sprocket," I defiantly reply. "If I had a screwdriver, I could probably get it back on." I'm not about to let my guard down.

"Wait a minute, I'll go to the car and get one." Bo-Jo returns with the screwdriver and says, "Here, let me help." Christ almighty, I'm talking to Bo-Jo and I am still alive. We work together and in less than a minute fix the bike. Death is not at my doorstep, and another thrashing does not occur. Everything is hunky-dory. Boy, is this weird. Unexpectedly, Bo-Jo announces, "Ya know, you and your buddy took your licking in the woods like men. Ya never reported it to the principal, did ya? That's important," he says. "Ya won my respect. You didn't squeal on me."

"No big thing, we had it coming. We acted like a couple of jerks."

"Thanks anyway. They wanna get rid of me and they woulda thrown me out of school if you guys woulda squealed on me," he says. "Well, youse guys is okay with me. Oh, by the way, you guys did a good job in the fourth-grade operetta. I got a good laugh out of it, but for god's sake, lose the white tights," he says as he walks back to his car.

I get to know Bo-Jo and realize he isn't a bad guy, just a little slow when it comes to book learning. It's funny that the guy I fear is now the guy who befriends me. Underneath all that size is a gentle, lonely, and kind person who has been dealt a bad hand from nature. He was in the back of the line when smarts were handed out. For the rest of the year, he watches over us like a big brother. I feel bad for him. I don't think he ever had friends like he sees in Nick, Wolf, and me.

Bo-Jo drops out of school at the end of sixth grade, and as he drives by in his jalopy, he honks the horn and waves. Life takes many strange turns, and this is just one of them.

An important part of sixth grade is that we are now considered mature enough to accept policing responsibility. Living in town increases the possibility of being selected for the school Safety Patrol. Nick and I are townies and we are chosen for the praiseworthy task. I wear a white belt apparatus that goes diagonally over my shoulder, across my chest, and around my waist. Adding to all the pomp, a shiny metal badge similar to a police officer's is provided. Nick and I are now law enforcement agents. The Safety Patrol's job is to assist the smaller kids in crossing the street. We are assigned a busy corner near Railroad Street and Main Street. One day while Nick is on patrol, he decides to exercise his authority as a Safety Patrolman. "I'm getting sick and tired of waiting for this traffic to stop," he proclaims.

"Not much you can do about it, is there? Nick, you're not going to do something stupid, are you?"

"Oh yes, I am. I'll show 'em who's boss." Nick positions himself in the middle of Main Street and, with his arms spread like a "T," stops traffic so little people can cross. Angry drivers line up in the traffic jam he creates. It doesn't take long for a disgruntled driver to report Nick to the principal, and thus ends his fledgling career in public service. Though his intentions are honorable, his execution is poor. Wolf and I think he pulled off a cool and gutsy caper, but no one else agrees.

About this time, Aunt Freda gives me my first and only sex talk, though I'm not entirely sure. The social norms are so far to the right that the Catholic Legion of Decency prohibits movies depicting a husband and wife sleeping together in the same bed. In a society that represses the discussion of anything sexual, Aunt Freda's talk is revolutionary. She has a slight lisp, and often swallows to ensure her tongue says what her mind is processing. While sitting in lounge chairs in her backyard, she swallows and makes an abrupt announcement. "Jimmy, don't ever let those girls taste your candy stick."

"Oh, I won't, Aunt Freda." She uses a metaphor to make her points, but I don't have the foggiest idea of what she is talking about. Nonetheless, I don't want to appear dumb, so I never let on. The beautiful thing about Aunt Freda is that I never know what golden gems of wisdom are about to be foisted upon me. On the other hand, I don't think she knows either. She is totally candid, totally unpredictable, and mistakenly assumes that what she is saying is understood. Needless to say, I heed her warning, and for many years hence, I never give a candy stick to a girl. Up until that time it's about as close to talking about sex in my family as I ever get. Around the dinner table grown-up relatives jokingly smile and say, "Someday we'll have to tell you about the birds and the bees," wink, wink. However, no one ever does tell me the birds and bees story. I figure it must be either something dirty or a way of getting out of having an embarrassing chat.

There is a big difference between being stupid and being ignorant. Stupidity is a permanent condition, whereas ignorance is situational. Education cures ignorance, but truly stupid people are doomed to live with their affliction the rest of their lives. Our naiveté is so pervasive that when Wolf, Nick, and I find squished white balloons on the ground, we are unaware of what they are. Wolf observes and asks, "What the heck are these? A kid would be downright stupid to throw away perfectly good balloons."

"Yeah," Nick interjects, "somebody filled them with something 'cause they're gushy inside. What a waste of good balloons."

An older boy sees us gawking and poking at the spent objects. He shakes his head and says, "They're called rubbers and they're used for screwing. Are ya stupid or something?"

Aha, finally an answer about that sex stuff. In my subsequent high-powered intellectual peer discussion, we come to a conclusion. We are amazed as we ponder the difficulty of how the older girls get these long, narrow rubber tubes over their tits. "Yikes, it's gotta hurt," I comment. "Can't see how this can be much fun." Imagine, balloons for tits, who woulda ever thought. This sex stuff sure is strange.

Yes, at last a moment of youthful enlightenment, I figure out what titties are for. Golly, it is great to know because knowing takes some of the mystery out of this sex stuff. It all begins to makes sense. Ignorance is bliss, but knowing is better. We don't know it is proper to call a woman's chest appendages breasts, so we call them tits or titties. In sixth grade, the chests of girls are similar to the chests of boys. Conspicuous topics have yet to fully develop. I'm amazed by our ignorance, but at least now I have some answers.

The mothers are peeking into the gym and saying low-down, egg-sucking, disparaging remarks. "Oh, look how cute they are." I feel like estate jewelry on display at an auction house. It is downright embarrassing. The adult world tries to socialize us by means of a sixth-grade prom. Girls certainly don't interest me, but I know my folks want me to attend. They like to see me dress up and wear my Sunday church suit. Wolf, Nick, and I sit at a table in the highly decorated elementary school gym. Twisted two-inch blue and white crepe paper is draped from the ceiling, and colored balloons adorn the walls. The tables are covered with a white plastic, and the record player blares in the background. The music consists of dull tunes played to entertain adults. Sitting like fish on display in a fishbowl makes me uncomfortable.

When in a swamp, it makes me feel better knowing everyone else is up to their necks in alligators too. Weeks before the prom, my cousin Mary Jane teaches me the basic four-count box step. I hold the girl awkwardly and stiffly shuffle through the repetitive motions of the box step, regardless of what music is playing. I count over and over—one, two, three, four—in an attempt to get my feet coordinated to move in a repetitive pattern. Looking around I see my buddies are also counting. Mother made me get flowers and someone else pins them on, because the flowers are placed close to the girl's private parts. I wonder if the true purpose of the prom is to please my parents or me. I think parents win.

The girl I bring is Judy, and she dates ninth-grade boys. Nick's date, Janet, is also a mover with older boys. Wolf brings Diane to the prom. The one thing we have in common is that we are uncomfortable with the opposite sex. Judy and Janet quickly get bored with us immature boys and want to go to Joe Adalino's and dance. Joe's teenage hangout, located across the street from the junior-senior high school, is the town's hotspot. Dad warns me to stay away from that place because a lot of white balloons are found abandoned in Joe's alley. Little do we know that the girls previously made arrangements to meet older and more experienced boys. So Nick and I do what smart sixth-graders do: we leave the prom and bring the girls to the hangout. Once there, we make the swift decision to ditch the girls and go back to the prom. As I reflect, maybe we aren't so clever and slick, because in reality, the girls actually ditch us. We rejoin Wolf and the dance is more fun without the girls.

As a graduation reward our teachers take us on a field trip to Pittsburgh. Never having visited a big city, I am excited by the trip. Golly, gee whiz, me in a big city—wow. I get up earlier than usual in order to meet the bus at school. As expected, Nick walks by the house and I join him. Mom prepares a bag lunch with more food than any human can possibly eat. In addition she provides an enormous amount of spending money, two dollars. Walking past Ronnie's house we expect him to pop out and walk with us, but he doesn't. "Oh my gosh," I exclaim. Nick and I instinctively know something is wrong. We dash onto the porch and start pounding on the door. Ronnie's mom answers in her housecoat and has a panicked look in her eyes—she forgot to set the alarm clock. "Wait one moment and I'll get Ronnie," she says. Mrs. Faust scurries and quickly gets Ronnie ready for the trip. She pushes him out the door and off we go. If not for Nick and me, he would have missed the greatest trip of our lives.

The bumpy school bus ride to Pittsburgh is joyful, with singing and loud noise emanating from a bus full of early morning juveniles. We boldly sing, "Ninety-nine bottles of beer on the wall, ninety-nine bottles of beer. Ya take one down and pass it around, ninety-eight bottles of beer on the wall…" all the way down to no bottles of beer on the wall. It must make the bus driver crazy.

I see my first skyscraper when I get off the bus at the Carnegie Museum. The building is the University of Pittsburgh's Cathedral of Learning. I am told the Cathedral of Learning is an ugly building, but to me it looks huge, tall, and powerful. In the Carnegie Museum, life-size fossils of mammoths and other prehistoric animals fascinate me. I have never visited a museum and I am awestruck. Small-town USA has many advantages, like learning how to avoid cow pies, but does lack the educational opportunities that are part of city life. It is a delightful day filled with *wows*. If I say wow once, I say it a thousand times.

There are miles of plants and flowers mixed among an army of vegetation at the conservatory. Maybe not miles, but it is big. I learn that the streets are lined with fan-shaped leaf trees called ginkgo. The guide tells us that ginkgoes were once thought to be extinct but, rediscovered in China, they now grow vigorously in Pittsburgh. As a bonus we get a little sex talk. "The male and female ginkgo trees when planted together produced a stinking fruit. Never plant a male and female tree next to each other because when they do the dirty deed, it is indeed dirty. Their golf ball-size offspring fall and slowly decay."

I say to Nick, "God, it smells like fresh cow-poo. Let's get out of here before I throw up." Now I know why the tree is tagged with the nickname "Ginkgo-Stinko."

I'll be honest. The big city overwhelms me. I feel insignificant and alone. In Brockway I know everybody. Where would a guy go blackberry picking or take a hike in the woods? I couldn't possibly have an uncle on every corner; even my family isn't that prolific.

Soon I am back in my old routine with familiar people saying, "Hello, Jimmy," as I walk to and from school. Sometimes it's great to think small. At the end of sixth grade Ronnie Faust's family moves out of town and I never see him again. Other than that one downer, sixth grade is another good year.

CHAPTER 14

DAD BUILDS HIS DREAM

Near the end of my sixth-grade year, Dad decides to build a camp. It is his long-standing dream. His venture into the coal business leaves him with a hundred acres of forested land two miles outside of town, in a place called Wilburt Run. The first task in molding his dream into reality is clearing the land of trees and shrubs. "Jimmy and Joseph, here are two axes and they're sharp. Be careful with these—do you understand?" Dad asks. "We're going to start cutting these small trees by the stream and work up to the higher ground. As you cut them drag them up here and put them in a pile. They'll make a good bonfire for us to roast our hot dogs. Get busy, boys, but be careful." For two months, in early spring, the family, relatives, and friends meet at the campsite with chainsaws and axes in hand. Cut, slash, and burn is our motto. Three- and four-inch ironwood trees are particularly challenging to my eight-pound ax. As the blade meets the toughness of the wood, the tree often rejects the ax. Sometimes it feels like my arms will be ripped out of their sockets when the ax bounces and recoils from the intrusive blow. Nonetheless, perseverance triumphs, and I eventually prevail over the tenacious tree.

After clearing the land, Dad uses his business world connections to purchase a batch of long, straight pine logs. The logs are hauled on a large logging truck to a sawmill where they are cut flat on two sides. When finished we transport them to the campsite.

Life is filled with tempting choices and options. Dad tells me he is going to pick up the logs at the sawmill, and a choice must be made between attending a school roller-skating party or tagging along with the adults. "I got a problem, Mom. I want to go with Dad, but my buddies want me to go to the skating party."

"Jimmy, trying to please everybody usually results in pleasing nobody," Mom counsels. "It means do what's right for you." I want to be with my friends, but an insatiable quest for adventure pushes me to choose the trip to pick up the logs. There will certainly be another roller-skating party, but building a log cabin is a once-in-a-lifetime experience. The enormity of the task is overwhelming and hard to comprehend. Clearing the land and getting the logs to the site propels us into a summer of hard work and toil.

Traveling to the campsite in our 1948 Ford pickup truck, I find that being sandwiched between Dad and his buddy Frank Lytle is an adventure. Frank is a good friend of the family, and predictably stops by the tavern every day to drink his two beers and scurry home to his wife. Frank's drinking routine never changes in twenty years. My olfactory nerves reverberate and sting from the malodorous experience of sitting between Father, eating Limburger cheese, and Frank, chewing snuff. As Dad is driving and forking the smelly cheese into his mouth, Frank calmly spits his brown snuff juice into a paper cup. The synergetic smell of the Limburger cheese and freshly chewed snuff is like an unflushed toilet bowl. Adding to the mayhem, Dad can't hear in his right ear and Frank can't hear in his left ear. This unfortunate circumstance places me in the middle of some exceptionally loud conversations. During their dialogue they yell to assure each understands what the other is saying. Their vociferous attempts to be heard causes them to spew debris from their mouths, and stuff always lands where I am sitting. My fear is the truck will hit a bump and Frank's half-full snuff juice cup will spill on me. I am sure Mom will burn my clothes if they are infested with snuff juice. Never will a snuff-stained garment be allowed in her washing machine. These situations are classic moments I wish I could forget.

On our daily drive to camp, I take note of events in the neighborhood. Wilburt Run Road is remarkable for its cast of characters. The area is Northwestern Pennsylvania's version of Li'l Abner's town of Dogpatch. The people run their intellectual engines on two speeds: slow and slower. The term *inbreeding* comes to mind. Wealth cunningly eludes the residents, but they never motivate themselves to pursue it. I once heard a definition of failure as "a person setting low expectations and then consistently failing to meet them."

The Barr brothers exceed this definition. They own a small farm and cannot be construed as prosperous or mental giants, but they save enough money to buy a workhorse. The brothers strike a deal. Each agrees to take his turn at feeding the horse. The brothers, being of disagreeable temperaments, do not work as a team, even though it is mutually beneficial. During an ensuing argument over feeding the critter, each accuses the other of being a slacker and shirking his duty. The obstinate brothers refuse to accept responsibility, and neither feeds nor cares for the horse. In such a standoff the inevitable happens, and the horse dies. One day we drive past their place as they are pulling the horse out of the barn, its four legs stiffly protruding from its bloated body. "Dad, look, the horse died," I angrily say.

"Yep, it sure does look that way. Well, son, there's an old saying. As best as I can figure," Dad explains, "you should use a little common horse sense and teamwork to feed your dreams, or you'll never be able to put them out to pasture." I laugh and Frank gives an extra nod and "snuff spit" to show approval. You get the idea of the people in the area. They aren't bad people; they are just different people, and I am happy my family isn't like them.

We spend the next months skinning bark from the logs and cross-stacking them neatly in a pile. Stacking allows air to circulate between the logs and dry them. The pungent smell of pine bark saturates the air as the debris pile underneath our workstation grows larger and larger with each passing day.

"Jimmy, fetch me a beer," says Frank.

"What kind?" I mutter.

"No, I don't think it will rain," the hard-of-hearing Frank answers.

"No, no, Frank, I didn't…"

"Nope, no rain. Now be a good boy and get me that beer," he repeats before I can explain.

Frank works at a one-beer-per-log pace, and by my bottle count estimation, he skins a dozen or more. Frank's large bulbous nose is a beer barometer. The more he drinks, the redder it gets, and he has a nose that is hard to miss. Put antlers on this guy and you've got yourself a human Rudolph the Red Nose Reindeer.

One day while working with Frank, I observe something with disgust and admiration. Frank blows his nose without using a hanky. Wow, this is something they don't teach in school. His technique is fascinating. One finger presses on the side of one nostril, and in one continuous motion he swiftly moves his head forward and downward while forcefully blowing out from the unobstructed nostril. In one swift movement the gummy contents are expelled. The process is repeated on the opposite nostril with the same result. Boy, is he good at it, but could I do it? "Hey, Joe, come on over here; there's something I want to show you. Watch this." I prepare to imitate Frank's actions. "Here goes." I place one finger on the side of my nose to block a nostril and forcefully blow out of the other. "Oh, you doofus, you got snot all over your shirt. You are a cool dipwad," Joe declares as I try to clean the mess. I try twenty times, but never get the hang of Frank's technique—it isn't a pretty sight. Besides, even if the technique is mastered, Mom will never approve of her son clearing his nasal passage in such a crude manner. The venerable handkerchief is still my weapon of choice in combating a runny nose.

Dad doesn't have an architectural plan or a diagram; the plans for the camp are in his head. When imagining a typical camp, I see a picture of a shack in the woods, but Dad's vision is different. The foundations are poured and the dimensions of what we call the lodge are thirty feet by forty feet, a considerable size. The entire family spends summer and fall constructing the walls by stacking one log on top the other and fastening them with ten-inch spikes. Between each log, tar and fiber material called oakum forms a weather-tight barrier. Oakum is the stuff sailors put between the planks to make wooden ships waterproof. The repetitive nature of stacking, sealing, and pounding logs into place is tiring, but rewarding. Clunk, clunk, clunk is the metallic sound reverberating through the structure as the sledgehammer kisses each spike on its journey through the logs. As the walls are constructed, window openings are cut, holes are drilled for electrical wires, and the building slowly takes form.

The excitement mounts as we spend hours finishing the shell by pounding and fastening the red shingles to the wooden roof. I am on the roof fastening shingles when Dad yells down, "Frank, how about bringing up another bundle of shingles."

"Yeah, good idea, I think I will have another beer."

"No, Frank, I need another bundle of shingles."

"Sure, Joe, I'll bring one for you too."

"No, Frank, we need more shingles," bellows brother Joe.

"No way," shouts Frank, "you kids are too young to drink."

Joe and I look at each other in amazement. Slapstick comedy isn't better than listening to a conversation between Dad and Frank.

Finally, with the building fully enclosed and protected from the elements, a huge stone fireplace is constructed. Coal is plentiful and a combination of coal and logs make a roaring fire that heats the entire building. The inside work consists of constructing three bedrooms, a bathroom with running water, and a kitchen with a bar that opens into the huge main room. It takes the better part of the year to finish the building. When completed the lodge is a showcase for Dad's accomplishments. However, he gets carried away with his fondness for the camp. "Edith, what do you say we move up to the camp and live there," he says during Sunday dinner. Mom takes a deep breath, firms up her lips, and says, "I don't think so." She refuses the offer and sanity again prevails. Thank God for Mom.

Dad also designs and plans the landscaping. From his coal mining experience, he has a tractor, a bull-dozer, and a backhoe available to scoop out two large ponds in the front of the building. A tragedy is averted by pure luck and fortunate circumstances alone.

"Hey, Dad, I'm going down and finish pulling out that stump," Joe declares.

"Now you be careful, Joseph."

"Yeah, yeah, I will," Joe placates Dad. As usual Joe is a bulldog and challenges the capacity of the trac-tor to do its job. He aggressively attempts to pull out a stump—something tractors aren't designed to do. Dad yells, "Joseph, you take it easy on that tractor," but to no avail. Joe vigorously steps on the gas and tugs on the rope. The stump doesn't move so the tractor obeys the law of physics and rotates upward and back-ward on its large rear tires. Like a bucking horse, Joe is thrown off the tractor and onto the ground, and the huge tractor, with front wheels pointing to the sky, is about to fall on him. His life is spared because the tractor is equipped with an anti-roll bar that stops the rearward collapse of the metal mass. Mom screams, "Oh my God!" Mom, Dad, and I stand helpless as we witness the entire incident. Never again are we allowed to drive or ride on a farm tractor. It is a razor-thin close call, but at last we have our own pri-vate swimming hole.

For an eighth-grade graduate, Father is the smartest man I have ever met. "I hope you boys never confuse education with intelligence," he informs us in a matter-of-fact tone. "They are two different

things. Always remember this, intelligence is a gift of God, whereas education is a gift from man. Education will help you land your first job, but intelligence will enable you to earn a decent living. That's the big difference."

Our piece of paradise is ten minutes from home. I suggest we call the place Twin Pines because of two prominent pine trees on the property, but Dad insists the camp be called Sugarbush Lodge. I never do find out how he picked the name.

What good is a camp if the fruit of Dad's loins can't use it? As fall gives way to the winter hunting season, Joe and I make preparations to become big-game hunters. Well, maybe medium- to small-game hunters is a more accurate descriptor. Joe is sixteen and I am twelve, which in Pennsylvania is old enough to go hunting. Early winter introduces me to the challenge of a turkey-hunting safari and by mid-winter we begin deer-hunting season. We make a trip to Moody's Variety Store to purchase hunting licenses and ammunition.

"Excuse me, Mr. Moody, we'd like to buy two hunting licenses," I ask.

"Okay, boys, fill out this paperwork while I fetch the licenses."

The expense is considerable—three dollars for each license. The vast expanse of land upon which we stalk our prey is the hundred acres of wilderness at Sugarbush Lodge.

An outrageously loud directive booms, "Okay, guys, rise and shine; it's time to get up." Five o'clock in the morning comes too soon, but that is the hunter's wake-up time at the lodge. The nippy winter air infiltrates the cabin, and the first order of business is building a blazing fire; the second order of business is eating a mountain man breakfast. Joe orders, "Go out and get some logs for the fire." I comply, but think, *Why me? Couldn't one of your hunting buddies do it?* It is still dark and frosty cold outside, but I abide by my brother's order—size does count when dominance is an issue.

As the sun starts to peek over the hills, I glance out the window and see the wind blowing and trees bending in an effort to get out of the way of the gusts. Keeping comfortable is as important as keeping warm. Never will I wear unbearably itchy red woolen long johns. They remind me of my scratchy wool suit. Thinking about wool on my skin gives me the willies. Red wool long johns are popular apparel with many hunters, but I save enough money to buy soft, cotton thermal underwear, and a pair of red rubber, lace-up, thermal-insulated hunting boots. To complete my outfit I wear a hand-me-down hunter's red Woolrich jacket and hat. Real hunters dress in the Woolrich brand.

Out into the cold wintry mist I venture in search of my elusive prey. The cold is pervasive, and when my boots compress the sparkling pristine snow under my feet, it screeches, screams, and crunches as I tread upon it. The wretched sibilant winter wind pushes against my outer garments in an effort to reach my cloistered body. I venture into the wilderness with Joe on one side and his buddies on the other side. We militantly walk in line through the snow, carefully avoiding encroaching snowdrifts and staying a healthy distance from the numerous ice-encrusted streams. Since I do not own a gun, I am relegated to using Joe's

22-caliber rifle. Joe and his buddies have 16-gauge shotguns and that's okay because shotguns kick like a mule. The chances of hitting a wild turkey with a .22 are slim to none. I probably could do just as well with the cheap bow and arrow set I found in Niagara Falls.

The winter air scintillates my nostrils, and each hunter leaves a vapor trail as he exhales. Up hills, through fields, and into dense forest, we stalk the stealthy wild turkey, but none is found. Apparently dumb turkeys are smarter than brave hunters. Throughout the morning Joe commandingly cautions, "Keep your gun pointed up and down range," a fallout skill learned at Camp Keenan. Finally, when the timid sun reaches its zenith, someone shouts, "Hey guys, let's go back and get some chow."

"A great idea," I echo and since nobody protests we follow our snowy footprints back to the camp-site.

At camp, I go to the log pile to load up on firewood without being asked. Why cause conflict. We warm ourselves at the fireplace and each person selects a can of his favorite culinary delight. My preference is Dinty Moore Beef Stew, which in reality has no resemblance to the picture on the can. Once comfortable and warm nobody has the desire to again venture into the harsh winter environment, so out come the cards, and a poker game commences. This we do until twilight, when we get into the trucks and start the ten-minute journey home. Thus ends my first day as a great Northwestern Pennsylvania hunter and stalker of the elusive wild turkey.

Later in the year I try my luck at deer hunting, but with the same results. Year after year we hunt without ever shooting anything. A pattern of morning hunting and afternoon partying is established. Just as well since none of us knows what to do if we do bag anything. "Joe, I want you to know, I ain't gutting no animal," I proclaim.

"Listen, Davy Crockett, with the way you hunt, you have nothing to worry about." Never in my life would I gut an animal, and since we are in the restaurant business, meat is plentiful. Hunting is an adolescent social activity that gives me the opportunity to act like a predatory human carnivore. Nonetheless, there is nothing like a brisk walk in the woods followed by a card game to lift a person's spirit. What do I like best about hunting? The picturesque and transcendent beauty of the seasons in Northwestern Pennsylvania paints a changing panorama of nature at its best—that's what I like best about hunting.

My hunting career ends at the age of seventeen. I am standing by a large oak tree with my rifle at the ready, waiting for deer. Every year farmers lose a cow or two when the infamous city slickers go on a drunken hunting spree, shooting anything that appears brown. More ingenious dairy farmers paint "COW" in twelve-inch script on the side of their livestock. While standing by a tree I hear the distinctive but commonplace crack of a rifle shot. Four more booming shots quickly follow, and the wounded branches directly above my head tumble to the ground. Oh my God, I frantically realize, some crazy loon is shooting at me. I scream, "Stop your shooting, stop your shooting!" Silence permeates the woods as I hug the ground. Slowly I get up, brush myself off, nervously look around, and sing a child's song very, very, very loud.

"Row, row, row your boat gently down the stream.

Merrily, merrily, merrily, life is but a dream."

Even foolhardy hunters know deer can't sing. That's the last time I venture into the woods during hunting season. Seeing my life coming to an abrupt end is a sobering experience. Yep, hunting can be deleterious to my health and well-being, and I intend to keep my being healthy.

CHAPTER 15

SQUIRRELLY JUNIOR HIGH SCHOOL BOYS

In September 1953, I move to the junior-senior high school. The school, an old three-story brick building, has oiled honey-brown maplewood floors and windows that pivot outward to open. An engineering masterpiece sixty years ago relegated the building to the values of that era, cold in winter and hot in summer. The old secondary building is known as the "big house" because it bears a resemblance to a prison without barbwire, although I'm sure it will be installed.

About this time Mother proudly buys me a jock strap. A guy never forgets his first jock strap. This momentous occasion recognizes my impending manhood—what little there is of it. Rumor has it that the senior high school basketball coach, John McDuff, has his eye on Wolf and me as future players for his varsity team, and that especially feeds my adolescent ego. We are aware of the varsity coach scouting us, and wearing a jock strap is important.

"Wolf, I got a jock strap. Did you get one yet? Imagine what Coach McDuff would think if he finds out we don't wear a jock strap?"

"Mom bought me one last week. The damn dog chewed on it and messed it up, but it's still wearable," Wolf responds.

Without a jock strap the coach will think we are a bunch of girly, sissy wimps. I don't want him thinking I'm one of those guys who wears underwear underneath his gym shorts. "One way or the other, we gotta let the coach know we are men and wear jock straps," I comment. "I'll think of something—maybe let it fall out of the gym bag in front of him. Just give me some time." Important, irrelevant thoughts like this dominate our conversations.

Even though our junior high school team has a losing season, I have a good year, scoring a total of twenty-two points. I won't go down in the record books, but for a seventh-grader it isn't bad.

Our seventh-grade physical education teacher, Harry Christie, is a likable guy. "Listen up, guys," Mr. Christie says to our class as we sit on the gym bleachers. "You're not little boys anymore, and I don't expect little boy behavior out of any of you. Everyone understand that? So let's get something straight. First, I don't want any horseplay in gym class. If you guys want to play grab-ass, do it after school. Second, everyone, and I repeat, everyone will shower after class." Mr. Christie pauses. "Am I clear so far? Okay, third and most important. No one pisses in my showers. I take it personally, and I will be like dark death to those who test me. Do you boys understand what no pissing in the shower means?" Everyone silently nods his head yes. "Well, then let's go have some fun."

In the 1950s, everyone takes a shower after gym class, no exceptions. To Harry the greatest sin is peeing in the shower. If caught, staying after school and scrubbing the shower with a toothbrush is the consequence. Even though the showers are dank, old, cruddy, and disgustingly dilapidated, we have to respect them. To avoid the embarrassment of being labeled a "shower scrubber," we control our weenies and make sure the hoses are drained in the designated place. Coach Christie is right, even today I don't want to shower in a toilet bowl.

Harry's fellow PE teacher, Mr. Wetzell, is a strange bird. We call him "Stryker" after the tough Marine Sergeant John Stryker played by John Wayne in the movie *The Sands of Iowa Jima*. One of Sergeant Stryker's notable quotes is "Life is tough, but it's tougher if you're stupid," and it fits Wetzell perfectly. He makes life tough for stupid kids. "All right, you guys, today we are going to learn the game of softball. Are you ready?" says Mr. Wetzell. "I don't want no screwing around or I'll tear you limb from limb. This isn't a playground—ya understand?" We all shake our heads yes. By this time we are getting used to being terrified. Wetzell has a nasty habit of verbally intimidating kids. If he doesn't like you, he places his hands on either side of your head and picks you up by your ears. He never bothers Wolf, Nick, or me, but he makes it a point to pick on the less athletic kids, especially if they act girlish and don't wear a jock strap. Yes, we do fear him and whenever possible avoid him.

Seventh-grade math class is taught by a relic from the caveman days named Marvin Piller. For obvious reasons we call him "Baldy Piller." An extremely strict and nasty teacher, he never hesitates to slap kids around if he thinks you aren't paying attention. My best guess is that the old codger is about 150 years old. He wears the same tobacco-stained suit every day, which creates some personal hygiene problems. Baldy chews snuff when teaching and that annoys me. Only a brave soul has the guts to look him in the eyes, because the sight exposes snuff juice oozing from the sides of his mouth. Occasionally, I observe him spitting in a cup or taking a big wad of chewing tobacco from his mouth and throwing it in the waste can. I nervously watch him move his hand around the edges of his mouth in an attempt to control the flow of the brown liquid—but to no avail. The effluence leaking from his lips is temporarily displaced to the back of his hand as he wipes the corrupt spittle from his mouth. After he does these revolting, sickening things, he walks from desk to desk, stroking our hair with his moist, brown, repulsive, snuff-infested hands. "Oh-oh, Nick, here he comes. What are we going to do?"

"Maybe I'll duck my head this time and he won't be able to touch my hair," says Nick. "Better yet, ya think if I fall on the floor and throw a screaming fit, he won't pat me on the head?"

"Not a snowball's chance in hell. Snuffy hands is heading our way, and he'll probably stroke your head a little more if he thinks you are retarded." I shudder every time he pats me on the head. I have pride in my shiny black hair, and don't want it violated by snuff juice.

Discipline is in the forefront of education in the 1950s. Only boys take shop class and the girls take home economics. In shop class, if a kid fools around the teacher bends him over a table. "Hold your balls," Mr. Johns instructs. Whap, whap, whap is the sound of three rapier-like blows delivered to the butt of a disorderly student. "Now stand up," Mr. Johns orders. "You act stupid again and I'll paddle you again—understand? Don't forget to say 'thank you' for taking the time to build your character."

"Thank you, sir," says the student. With a paddle ventilated with holes for less air resistance, Mr. Johns paddles ass right then and there, but it's good to know he doesn't want to damage my balls. You see, in school everything is black and white; there is no such thing as due process or mitigating circumstances. You screw up, you pay the price, and if my parents find out, I pay the price twice. In all fairness, fooling around in shop class makes a person a danger to himself and to others. Kids with half a brain don't horse around, but in every class there are a couple half-wits, and I calculate that together they equal one complete wit.

Our principal is Jonathan Hysing. We call him Captain Muncy after a warden in a prison movie. He is also feared, and Wolf and I are only sent to his office twice. We are considered good guys, so he lets us off with a stern warning. Captain Muncy rules the "big house" with an iron fist. This fear thing works well for the teachers and the administration. The fear of consequences is a deterrent, but what the heck, the excitement of straying is sometimes overwhelming. Without risk, life is awfully dull. Wolf and I never receive a taste of the wood, but Nick does.

Think about being cooped up every day with a group of squirrelly adolescent boys whose voices range several octaves, from a not-yet-manly deep bass to an annoying, high-pitched screech. Mrs. Methy, my homeroom teacher, is a sweetheart. More like a mother than a teacher, she is a saint, and in return we treat her well. Behind her back we daringly call her by her first name, Virginia, or even more affectionately by the name of Ginny.

At this time, about nine years after WWII, I am infatuated with the military, so we invent the beloved "Order of the Claw." The significant aspect about the order is that upon greeting a claw brother, my hand is raised to my shoulder and formed into a chicken claw. In response the other claw brother renders a similar salute, accompanied by the secret call sign, caw, caw, caw. Our call sign sounds like either a sick eagle or a dying crow. Sometimes, I swear flocks of birds invade the room as we greet each other with "caw, caw, caw."

Every morning during homeroom each claw brother is saluted with the secret greeting. "Good morning, Claw Brother Wolf—caw, caw, caw. Claw Brother Wolf, there's Claw Brother Nick; let's greet him—caw, caw, caw. Greetings, Brother Nick." We greet every claw brother, and the discordant sounds echo throughout the classroom. Secretly during the pledge I defiantly, daringly, and covertly render our secret sign rather than holding my right hand over my heart. This is on the edge of being un-American. If Senator Joe McCarthy knew, he surely would expose me as a decadent American youth. I would be one of his alleged triumphs over the communistic red menace. We even invent a song sung to the tune of "Rudolph the Red Nose Reindeer." We call the song "Adolf, the Blackhanded Jew Killer," and it pokes fun at Hitler. Ignorance is bliss, and I have no idea about the magnitude of death and destruction brought about by Adolf; in fact I don't even know what a Jew is.

Virginia, to her credit, tolerates us. Our antics are great fun, but totally meaningless—just something young boys do to establish common bonds and belong to a group.

As I grow and struggle for identity, I do what all kids do. I experiment with my image. Wolf, Nick, and I decide to make outlandish hats and wear them to school. This will be cool. Coolness is an indefinable quality, but I recognize it when I see it. Age-appropriate, wild, and almost revolutionary—huh? This must be some form of rebellion, against what I don't know. Maybe crazy hats are just fun, and being cool is the thing to do.

"Jim, what's your hat gonna look like?" Nick inquires.

"Well, I'm going to take this red corduroy hat and pin the brim on three sides to make a triangle. Then I'll borrow a black feather from one of Mom's old hats and stick it in the hatband, but wait till you hear the crowning glory. Ya see this gold cowboy belt buckle? I'm gonna sew it on the back of my hat to add a little pizzazz."

"Oh, I see, it will be something like a pirate hat. Are you gonna leave the hatband the way it is?" Nick inquires.

"Naw, I think I'll paint it a bright yellow."

"Boy oh boy," says Nick, "that will be a stunning and spiffy sight. I gotta go and get busy working on mine."

Wolf's work of art is a black baseball hat covered with buttons, pins, and crazy logos that are equally nifty.

One day we synchronize our efforts. Friday is a good day to celebrate the end of the week by wearing our hats to school. A pirate's hat, a wild baseball cap, and Nick's nondescript creation, mimicking either the movie version of the Bowery Boys or a gangster's headpiece, appear on the school's campus. Other than the flamboyant hats, our dress is normal. The principal sees us and makes a point to briskly walk toward our group. We believe he is coming to compliment our ingenious wardrobe. But no, he looks at us with intense, almost hateful eyes. "You guys are just a bunch of punks."

Surprised, I say, "You mean us?"

"You heard me, DeAngelo. So quit being a wise guy." He does burst our bubble and we do feel bad. Maybe he is having a bad hat day? Imagine what he would say if he ever saw Dad in his flashy Knights of

Columbus outfit! Nevertheless, it is good to know that for whatever reason, he flipped out. We got to him without trying. Boy, I never thought I had that kind of power. Our clowning should be labeled as finding a healthy outlet for our youthful exuberance.

Once again, the strength of my family is tested. This time it is my brother. In eleventh grade Joe becomes mysteriously ill. Mom calls the doctor, who stops at the house to examine him. After the examination the doctor opens his black satchel. "Edith, here are some pills that will help take care of whatever is ailing Joseph," says Dr. Longo. "Make sure he takes them twice a day. One in the morning and one in the early evening."

"Dr. Longo, what do you think is causing this?" Mom inquires.

"I'm not sure," the doctor answers.

Whatever the medication is supposed to do, it doesn't. Joe's condition does not improve. During the night his temperature jumps dangerously high to a fiery 105 degrees and he is delirious. Mom is alarmed and calls Dr. Longo early the following morning. The doctor again makes a house call, and we wait downstairs as he examines Joe. The steps begin to creak as Dad slowly walks down the stairs. I am distressed; he has tears in his eyes. I have never seen him shed a tear, so I know the situation is serious. Usually solid as a rock, he never shows this kind of emotion. Mom follows him down the stairs and says in a calm voice, "Jimmy and Megan, we are taking Joseph to the DuBois Hospital. Aunt Betty will stay with you until I return."

"Mom, are you sure I can't go with you," I plead.

"I'm sure. Now do your school work and I'll see you later tonight." Clearly, she is reassuring and has control over the situation.

The doctor has no idea what is causing the high fever and knows Joe needs help. The next day the hospital calls a specialist from Pittsburgh to diagnose Joe's illness. However, his condition continues to deteriorate. By the end of the fourth day, the conflagration in his body rages and we begin to think the unthinkable. We are going to lose my brother. So serious is his situation that Father Goodler confers upon Joe the Last Rites of the Church. He anoints Joe and makes him ready for heaven. Tears fog my vision as I try to be brave. The Last Rites are only administered to those who are about to die. Joe is more than a brother; he is my buddy. I tell God, "I will put all our boyhood bickering aside, it doesn't matter. I'll be the best-behaved boy in town. Honest, I'll even quit having dirty thoughts in church, just let Joe get well."

Rumor of our family's plight becomes known to some of the old-time Italian ladies at church. I am told they have a special flower brought from the old country and they perform a prayer vigil. As best as I can understand the story goes that if the flower opens, the sick person will be okay. Though I never witness the event, the family is told the flower opens. These are the only words of encouragement provided to us, so we are inclined to believe the story.

Through the turmoil Mom makes sure Megan and I continue to attend school. Joe's classmates ask how he is doing, but there is nothing I can tell them. The one lesson I learn is never underestimate the power of prayer. It may be possible that the ladies' prayers are what enable Father to make an accurate observation.

At the hospital Dad watches Joe come out of his delirium every day for a short period, and at that time the nurses administer his medication. After about fifteen minutes, fever again ravages his body and he slips back to his incoherent state. Dad notes the pattern and takes the risk of making a life-and-death decision. "I want the medication stopped," he orders in a forceful tone.

"Mr. DeAngelo," pleads Dr. Longo, "this is not a wise thing to do." The learned doctors, with all their degrees, are shocked and unhappy with the order. "But Mr. DeAngelo…" Dr. Longo attempts to retort, but is interrupted by Dad.

"You heard me, no more medication," Dad says with finality. With his eighth-grade education, he initiates another bold action. "Enough of this nonsense. Edith, you stay here with Joseph and I'll be back in a little while." He buys vitamins and begins administering them to Joe. Remarkably, by the next day the fever diminishes and his condition improves. Joe never again becomes delirious and is on the road to recovery.

I believe the only thing that saves my brother is Dad's intervention. We never find the root cause of Joe's illness or what triggered the high fever. We only know that God is with us, and it isn't my brother's time to check out. One way to deal with fear is to joke about it. When Joe is back to normal, he starts bugging me again. "Hey, pinhead, did you take my red striped shirt? Keep your hands off my stuff or I'll slaughter you."

"Joe, I think that fever fried your brain and that's why you act so stupid. If I want any crap from you, I'll squeeze your head." Nick taught me that last retort, and I have waited a long time to use it. There's nothing that can take the place of brotherly love.

Junior high school years are the in-between years. Not old enough to drive, but too old to be considered a kid. This leaves limited choices. I have measured freedom to come and go within certain parameters. Generally, on Saturday nights I stay out until 11:00. Nick and I combat boredom in various ways. Getting together and shooting the breeze is a favorite pastime. Being manly we often interject phrases such as "holy cow," "that's a bunch of crap," "hell's bells," "ya gotta be kidding me," "get outta here," or "damn if I know" to spice up the conversations. In the absence of adults, the F-word is liberally peppered throughout our banter. Yes sir, when alone we certainly use colorful language; after all, I've got to have something to tell the priest in the confessional.

After the Saturday evening movies, Wolf and I go to the City Restaurant. We invent a new pastime never before practiced by humans, called "hanging around." Nick gets a weekend job pumping gas at Navan's Gas Station, so after the restaurant and movie, I walk to the gas station and hang around. Like clockwork every Saturday the owner gasses up his shiny new Buick Roadmaster and goes out with his girl-friend. He leaves the entire station, including the candy counter, in the hands of Nick. Navan's Gas Station is the place to watch cousin Tom Varni drive his black Ford V8 hot rod, with dual exhaust, on the road out of Brockway. Tom has his hot rod hooked up so that he can pump raw gas into the duel exhaust system and upon his command the gas ignites. The visual effect is moving and dynamic. It is similar to two jet engines producing a flaming exhaust. The sight dazzles my eyes and leaves me wanting more. I wouldn't miss it for the world. Some nights a local guy comes in with his Jaguar XE sports car and brags about its great performance. "Nice car," Nick says. "Ya ever wind it out?"

"Sometimes I press the pedal to the metal and burn some rubber," he replies. "I can beat the ass off any car in the tri-county area. The English make a sweet car," he says, "goes like hell."

We stand in awe of this beautiful machine. The car does go fast. Unfortunately, it goes too fast. Within the year he kills himself after losing control and running into a boulder on the DuBois road; those boulders just didn't want to budge. Visiting the gas station and talking with the cast of characters is a necessity for my social life. I try to get there by 9:30, and if it is a dead night, Nick and I watch our favorite TV programs: *Have Gun – Will Travel* and *Gunsmoke*.

Do you ever wonder what the gas station attendant does when he cleans the windshield? On dull nights we talk mostly about girls and I watch Nick clean car windshields while he pumps gas. The practice in the 1950s is the gas station attendant pumps the gas and washes the windshield. Nick constantly tantalizes me with stories of the sights he sees as he peers through the front windshield. "Whew, what I see when cleaning those bug splatters from the windshield would blow your mind. Ya gotta see it to believe it," he says. "It's amazing."

"Hells bells, see what? What do you mean? Explain?" I query.

"The wonders of the world," Nick says with a wink. "Come on, you're not stupid. Ya know what I mean." Nick continues his efforts to remove bug splatters. "Boy," he taunts, "you should have seen what I just saw." Nick smiles, shakes his head, and proclaims, "What legs on that chick—wow. Her legs went all the way from her toes to her ass."

According to Nick, young adult women are not modest about how high their skirts are hiked up or how their blouses are buttoned when they are behind the steering wheel. I ruminate about the situation for some time and come to a conclusion. Why should he be the only one to get a free show?

In response to my inquisitiveness, I start assisting Nick by washing windshields as he pumps gas. Perhaps I, too, can become a voyeur and sneak a peek. Why should only Nick get to see the forbidden sights? I lust for a peek, and coyly inspect every female who stops for gas. In spite of snooping through windshields and removing zillions of bug splatters, I never see any sights to behold. There are no show-and-tell stories that I can discern, and nothing blows my mind. What's going on here?

The thought enters my head that maybe, just maybe, I have been suckered. Is it possible that Nick read about Tom Sawyer getting his buddies to paint the white picket fence as he sits and watches? Did he play mind games with me? Have I been conned, snookered, and duped, or am I just plain stupid? Nah, they never taught that in shop class, and Nick would never think of that on his own. The idea is absurd, preposterous, out of character for him, but not improbable.

Our parents want us young RC adolescent boys to attend the church-sponsored dances. Attending the dance fulfills an obligation and keeps my parents happy, which in turn keeps the nuns happy. To the nuns dances are like the TV game show *The $64,000 Question*. Catching us doing anything semi-sinful is the jackpot and demonstrates their commitment as a bulwark against evil. Whenever slow dancing my chest doesn't touch the girl's chest, lest one of the nuns has a stroke, seizure, or God forbid throws a conniption. I like semi-sinful stuff, but know I can't get away with anything. Since I only slow dance the box step, church dances are boring. At one dance under the watchful eyes of the nuns, we meet a group of nice girls from Ridgeway.

"Hi, my name is Jimmy DeAngelo and these are my friends Nick and Wolf."

"I'm Rita, and these are my two friends Ann and Carol."

"Ya want to dance?" I ask as slow box-step music begins. After the music stops I ask, "May I call you on the phone?" The girls willingly give us their phone numbers, and this changes the Saturday night routine. My regular movie, ice cream, and visit to the gas station continue, but now a new dimension is added, calling the Ridgeway girls. Weekly, Nick and I talk to them on the pay phone, and I'm sure our conversations are not stimulating, but the phone calls are an attempt at maintaining boy-girl relationships. We now have electronic girlfriends, and our first phone dates.

Life continues changing. Between the eighth and ninth grade, a series of cataclysmic events sneak up on me. One traumatic event is getting little red marks on my forehead and my back that turn into white spots. First a few spots appear, and they multiply like rabbits until they are constantly harassing me. Squeezing them only provokes anger and they retaliate by becoming redder and easier to see. Ever-vigilant, the first person noticing this phenomenon is Mom. She talks to me with a smile on her face. "Jimmy, you're getting pimples." Oh my God, oh no—what should I do? I pause to digest the bad news. Pimples are nothing to smile about; they are serious business. I've seen older kids with pockmarked faces, and don't want that. What can I do to combat this boyhood scourge? The nurse part of Mom rescues and instructs me. "Make sure you wash thoroughly with soap and make sure you rinse well, do you understand? Wash your face three times a day, morning, noon, and night—and use plenty of soap and water. Above all, don't pick at yourself or you will only make the situation worse, especially if your hands are dirty. You've seen those boys with big pimple scars on their faces," she says. "How do you think they got there? By picking at themselves with dirty hands—that's how."

"Yeah, I get it—sure don't want my face looking like the surface of the moon."

The third and perhaps most important thing she does is buy a tube of an acne medicine called Clearasil. That does help. At a minimum the brownish cream hides the pre-eruption zits. The greedy red zits are replaced by polka-dot brown patches of Clearasil dispersed on my forehead and cheeks. Regardless of what Nick and Wolf say, pimples are not a punishment for having dirty thoughts; otherwise, I would have gotten them much sooner.

Mom is a fount of knowledge. In addition to coping with my skin condition, she teaches me other life-enhancing skills. "Dress properly and practice good grooming. Keep yourself neat and clean. As a minimum, change your underwear, wash your face, tie your shoes, brush your teeth, and comb your hair. Keep this in mind; if you ever have to go to the hospital, I don't want you to embarrass the family by wearing dirty underwear." To that she adds, "Oh, also use a deodorant, and remember, don't pick at yourself." She always ends with "and don't pick at yourself." If I hear it once, I hear it a thousand times, but she is right. There must be a reason why God made the word MOM spelled upside-down read as WOW. After all, I don't want to embarrass the family by going to the hospital in dirty underwear.

The other distressing development is growing hair where I never had much hair before. The most obvious place this occurs is on my face, with hair that is darker, thicker, and much more noticeable. God, I'm getting a beard. This causes a great deal of anxiety. I'm unsure where the hair will grow next; it keeps popping up and spreading like weeds. Perhaps I am evolving into an ape. I inspect myself and guard against thoughts of swinging from vines. I learn not to shave with a razor. The pimply surface turns my face into a red river of blood. "Jimmy, what have you done to yourself," Mom says with a shocked look on her face.

"Just shaving with Dad's Gillette razor."

"Here, use Dad's septic stick. It will help stop the bleeding."

From that day forward, Dad's stubby, three-headed brown Remington electric razor becomes my weapon of choice in the struggle against the rampage of facial hair. The only place I want hair is on my head. My voice changes, and now I am able to sing bass in the choir. I have a great body, but a body cursed, defiled, and violated by zits and hair. Well, I survive, and fortunately, I don't turn into an ape. As with all things in life, my family helps me work through this period of change without ever letting me know they are helping. Nonetheless, when I think Mom won't catch me, I do pick at myself. How can a kid resist?

CHAPTER 16

SENIOR HIGH SCHOOL, BECOMING BIG BOYS

Wolf and I enter high school as male virgins. To my disappointment, it appears that we are also predestined to graduate from high school as male virgins. When talking to us you would never know, because we maintain a macho image. "Hey, Jim, ya get your wick wet yet?" Nick inquires.

"Now, Nick, you know a gentleman never talks about his exploits, but if I did your ears would fall off."

"Yeah," laughs Wolf, "I'm going to have to go to the doctor 'cause working these chicks is probably damaging my health. Why do you think people call us studs?"

"The only reason your health is damaged is because you whack off more than a zoo monkey," Nick says with a smile on his face. "You two will only be studs if you become a two-by-four." He laughs and adds, "I've heard bullshit before, but now I know where it comes from. Youse guys are real asses."

I get sex education where all boys and girls get it, on the streets, talking to my equally ignorant peers. As a ninth-grade high school student, I have choices to make. Am I to become an Academic Student, a Commercial Student, or a Vocational Student? Wolf and I are assigned to the academic pathway. We are never asked to choose. Our friend Nick is a Vocational Student. By senior high school Nick defines himself by his dress and noncompliant behavior. Marlon Brando's behavior in the movie *The Wild One* influences him to a greater extent than I thought possible. He wears a black leather jacket, buys an old Indian motorcycle, and smokes a pack of Chesterfields a day. To reach his life goals, Nick takes vocational shop courses. He is talented and clever in some endeavors. I overhear the shop teacher telling the guidance counselor, "That Nick is sure good with his hands. Too bad he's such a pain in the neck." For instance, Nick makes beautiful eighteen-inch wooden clubs for us. His clubs are the best in the school, and he takes extra time to drill holes through the center and fill them with lead. He builds a quality club. "Gee Nick, this is a nice club," I observe. "I'm so glad you took the time to do this for us. Well, Wolf, it's time to go back to class, but after class we'll go and club someone senseless. What do you think?" I taunt.

"Yeah, it's just what I've always wanted. I'll treasure this the rest of my life," Wolf says with a huge smile on his face.

"You guys are douchebags," says the aggravated Nick. His workmanship gives the clubs a special property, making them a prized weapon for Attila the Hun. It feels good knowing he is developing into a skilled craftsman.

Nick spends part of the school day hiding in the shop's wood storage room. There he secretly smokes and never gets caught. The storage room is known as Nick's Office. One moment of carelessness on his behalf could accidentally burn down the school. The possibility of starting a fire doesn't bother him. This may sound outlandish, but Nick puts his rudimentary engineering skill to work building a sex machine. One day while visiting his storage room office, he makes a heartless comment. "When I'm done you guys can have your first sex experience, 'cause that's the only way you're going to get it." At that point, I secretly think Nick had a vision and could possibly be right. He describes his intricate plans, and we give him hints on how to improve his machine. Something like the blind leading the blind.

"Nick, do you think you could get a patent on your invention?" I inquire. "You'll put a smile on a lot of guys' faces. If it works you will be famous with the teenage crowd."

"Don't forget, Jim and I are the first to try your contraception," says Wolf.

"Ya know, guys," Nick comments, "I think you two dipshits will be better off doing what you're good at. Just keep pulling your pork—'cause that's as close as you're gonna get."

"Jim, did you hear that? He wants us to indulge in self-gratification," Wolf remarks.

"Can't do that," I explain. "It would be a sin and I don't want to disappoint the nuns. Some buddy you are, Nick. You know God will punish me and make me wear glasses if I self-indulge. Quit trying to lead us into a life of sin." Our banter is good-natured and Wolf and I laugh, but wonder if ingenious Nick ever completes his dream.

Academic students have the choice of studying French or Latin, and I choose Latin. Why? Because Latin is easier than French. Water always seeks the path of least resistance, and my academic behavior mimics running water. Two years of Latin are required, so it is fairly important I do okay during the first year. Wolf and I don't want to tick off the school's one Latin teacher because such behavior dooms us to two consecutive years of hell. Miss MacCarty has taught Latin for fourteen years; however, the first day in class, she is uptight and stiff.

"Wolf," I whisper, "she looks like an uncomfortable grimacing person experiencing the symptoms of constipation."

"You're right." Wolf laughs. "She needs a good crap. Her on the pot is a awful thought."

"Wolf, you're so gross; that's hard for me to imagine," I moan. "Two years of Latin with a neurotic rubber band that can snap at any time."

Initially, Miss MacCarty is stern, aloof, and cautious. Her anxiety concerns me, but as the year progresses, she morphs into a different person. I find her to be great fun and in turn she makes Latin fun. Picture Wolf and me in front of the class with sheets draped over our shoulders, speaking and acting Latin dialogue from textbooks. It is hard to keep a straight face, but Latin class is an enjoyable part of the school day. Miss MacCarty gives us passing grades because she likes us, not because we master the language. After all, I have no intention of visiting Latin America.

Across the hall from Miss MacCarty's room is Mr. Neff's social studies classroom. Everyone knows he is a National Guard officer. As boys often do we tag him with the nickname of Combat Kelly from a popular comic book character. Allegedly, if Captain Neff doesn't like a person, he holds them by the legs and hangs them out the second-floor window. I believe the allegations. Nevertheless, why test the validity of the rumor? Being dropped from a second-story window isn't good because I don't bounce well.

We study American History during the Civil War period. After class Nick makes a profound observation. "Hey, Jim, I got a question. Well, you know we've been studying about all them there Civil War battles. How come they were all fought in the National Parks?"

"Good question, Nick, I'll ask Mr. Neff tomorrow." Of course, the question never makes it to the ears of Mr. Neff. Not only do we get along great with him, but we also learn social studies in a meaningful context.

Gym class consists of seasonal activities. In the fall the teacher throws out a football, and we play football. During winter the teacher throws out a basketball, and we play basketball. In the spring the teacher throws out balls and bats, and we play softball. Thank God we don't live in Spain, because during bull-fighting season the teacher more than likely would throw out a bull, and you know the rest. We don't need a teacher to do this stuff, but the teachers have the balls, bats, and equipment. The best recreational activity is vocal music. Many great experiences result from an early introduction to chorus.

A frightening and disturbing rumor circulates. Wolf and I have a reputation as good guys. As Perry White, the editor of the *Daily Planet* newspaper, says in Superman comic books, "Great Caesar's ghost!" We've got to put an end to this nonsense. It would be different with tough nicknames such as Slick, Blade, Bullet, Rocky, or Killer, but names like Jim and Wolf don't sound menacing. We visualize ourselves as rough-and-tumble guys ready for a rumble, like Matt Dillon on *Gunsmoke*. My nice-guy image is a boyhood dilemma. A good reputation has the same effect as Kryptonite has on Superman. I will never be known as Killer DeAngelo or Rocky DeAngelo or Jimmy the Tiger. Wolf and I endure the burden of good reputations since it serves us well. Better well thought of than well hated.

Junior high school basketball is the sport of choice in ninth grade, and as a bonus Wolf and I make the first string. We have a fair record, four wins and four losses, and continue to show promise. During this period I believe I want to be a professional basketball player like the five-foot ten-inch Bob Cousy of the Boston Celtics. I cannot imagine life without basketball. Again rumors circulate that Coach McDuff has his eye on us. I'm unsure if it is to boost our egos, or if it is the truth. This type of baseless banter does build self-confidence for my still fragile ego. It's funny how any hint of a positive remark said about me boosts my self-esteem. I feel bad for Nick. Even though he is a good guy, people are stingy with positive comments. Wolf and I tease him about his well-hidden but generous nature. "Nick," you're the kind of guy that would gladly give us the shirt off somebody else's back. You could be the poster boy for the mob."

"Now, Jim, that is cruel. He would make a better poster boy for the Hell's Angels."

"Christ almighty, will you dorks get off my back?" says Nick.

People's perception of him is partly his own fault. If the teachers knew him as I do, they would shower him with praise. What other kid in the school makes clubs for his buddies? Nick will do anything for a person he likes.

In junior high school the idea of dating girls never enters my realm of possibility, though my interest in females increases. What a turn of events from three years earlier. Girls are a mystery, but my comprehension of the physical differences is catching up with reality. The school library is the place to indirectly expand my knowledge. "Wolf, want to go to the library during study hall? I got something to show you."

"Yeah, Jim, do you think the study hall teacher will let us both go at the same time?"

"Sure. We'll tell her that we have to complete a book report. Okay, we can be a bit disingenuous." Wow, I just used a new word from English class in a sentence.

The most sought-after magazine in the library is *National Geographic*. I have a special interest in issues focusing on developing tribal countries. The pages depicting bare-breasted women are well worn by anxious fingertips, and the tattered remains of the magazines telegraph their frequency of use. In stark contrast to the relatively boring narrative, the pictures are spectacular. I find myself in a reluctant transition from being totally with my friends, to a curiosity about girls. The tug-o-war between buddies and girls vacillates for the next four years.

At home the beauty of the female form is further affirmed by means of a purposeful accident. One day Mom and Dad are out of the house, so Joe and I decide to go through Dad's desk. We constantly snoop around. This time we find the bonanza of bonanzas. Concealed in the corner of the bottom desk drawer is a cylinder with something rolled up inside. The poorly hidden tube naturally piques our curiosity. "Hey, Jim, look at this. I wonder what's in here."

I look out the door to make sure our parents are not on the way home and reply, "Let's open it and see."

Joe slowly unrolls the paper and exclaims, "Holy cow, would ya look at this?"

With eyes wide open I see a sight to behold—Marilyn Monroe nude. The picture leaves me breathless. It is the Holy Grail of nude photographs. "Ooooooh, my God," I excitedly stammer. Before my eyes is a colored calendar photo of Marilyn lying naked on a red satin background. She is beautiful, gorgeous, stunning, and provocatively spread out with most of her nubile hardware exposed for viewing. If I could read lips she would say, *Jimmy boy, I want you.* Blaze Starr couldn't run a close second to the iconic Marilyn. After catching my breath and my heart starts beating rhythmically again, I tell Joe, "Oh my God, what if Dad finds out we've been looking through his stuff? He'll kill us."

"Yeah, we better put it away," Joe agrees.

It never enters my mind to ask why Dad has the picture in the first place. With deliberate action we carefully roll up the picture and place it into its container. "Joe, when you place it in the desk drawer, make sure it is in the exact position as when we found it. I could stand a steady diet of her," I declare as I take my last glance of Marilyn. Dad will never know we feasted our eyes on her. There is nothing sinful in something so beautiful, so I forgive myself for the transgression. This is not a topic for the confessional. A couple of months later we again brave the perils of entering Dad's space. To our surprise she is gone. Somebody kidnapped Marylyn. Did Dad know we found the picture, and did he remove it? Some questions are better left unanswered and this is one of them.

As a result of Mother Nature's intervention, the girls in my class are developmentally and socially light-years ahead of us. When a girl bends over, I explore the gaps in her shirt. Looking is the natural thing to do. Girls wear girlie jock straps called "bras." If lucky, I see cleavage. "Believe me, Nick, breast cleavage is more exciting than the toe cleavage I see when they wear black flat shoes. I'll let you know if I see anyone we should focus our attention on," I promise.

"You do that, Jim, and I'll walk by and drop my books," Wolf says. "There are some great melons growing in those hidden valleys."

"Why would you do that?" I ask.

"Ya dummy," Wolf says with an expression of disbelief, "we can all watch as she leans over to pick them up."

I concur with an approving nod. Every opportunity to sneak a quick look is exploited; it is like a game of chance. I reason that peeking is a sin-free pastime. It is nonintrusive window-shopping; look all you want, but don't touch. Like everything else the bra is renamed a hooter holder or, in a more graphic, utilitarian term, the double dunce cap. One girl in our class develops the biggest set of boobs ever seen on the face of the earth, and every guy wants to grab them. "Wolf, did you get a good look at the set of gabooms on her?"

"My God, her chest looks great in a sweater," says Wolf. "I'll bet when she walks through a door, her tits arrive twenty minutes before she does."

"She must have the biggest melons north of the Mason-Dixon line," Nick comments.

We unkindly call her Big Boobs. The only problem is that Mother Nature treats her chest well, but never gets around to fixing her face. Nonetheless, the bra design and the tight sweaters of the era give the impression that Big Boobs has two large, solid, triangular cones sticking out from the wall of her chest.

By ninth grade Wolf, Nick, and I have one major goal: to feel up girls. We occasionally accidentally bump into Big Boobs' chest, but a man can't count that as getting a feel. Getting a feel isn't as easy as you think. Wolf reports, "Hey, Jim, wait till I give you the latest scoop. I just got a feel from Big Boobs."

"Okay, give me the down-and-dirty details," I reply.

"I was standing in front of her and went to turn and I nudged her boob with my elbow."

"Nah, Wolf, that's bogus, that's not a feel. You can't get credit for that one."

"Why not?" Wolf challenges.

"'Cause it's just not a feel," I retort. "Come on, Wolf, you know that a nudge is a nudge, not a feel. If nudges count we'd all be feel-up kings." Even though there are a lot of accidents, nudging a breast is cheating and doesn't count. Reporting a genuine feel requires three standards are met.

1. The feeler must use the palm of his hand.
2. The feeler must grab hold of the boob.
3. The feeler's elbows, shoulders, and the back of the hand don't count.

A feel takes lots of planning, and has to be on the up and up. It is good to have standard criteria. Even though my goal is to feel up every girl in our class, it never happens. In fact, I don't come close to achieving the goal. Okay, I don't even get started, but still it is good to have a goal. By ninth grade, most of the girls in class date older guys, and we are left with the few that even the older guys won't hit on. The best flowers get picked first, and we get what is left over. Yet among those left behind, are some hidden gems that blossom over the next few years.

My buddies and I are fairly immobile. I am a foot jockey and to get somewhere I walk or ride my bike. A big time on Saturday night still consists of going to the movies and visiting the City Restaurant to have a pizza, talk, screw around, and play the pinball machines. By high school inflation occurs. The price of movies increases to twenty-five cents, but the pinball machine continues to cost a nickel a game. Fortunately, it is possible to pool our money and buy a pizza and drinks for less than two dollars. A dollar bill in my pocket makes me rich and I can experience the good life.

My buddies and I perfect the art of beating the pinball machine and winning free games. "Nick, you work the left flipper and I'll work the right," I instruct. "Are you ready?" I pull back the spring-loaded plunger and it strikes the waiting steel ball. The energized ball races toward the obstacles and traps on the machine. As a team we are more likely to win free games. Thump, bam, thump, bam, we pound the edge of the machine with the palm of our hands in a feeble attempt to influence the path of the metal ball. "Careful, Nick, don't shake the machine. I'm telling you, you're shaking the machine too hard," I plead.

"No machine is gonna beat me. You worry too much," says Nick as he continues vigorously pounding the machine. Without warning the machine gets its revenge. We elicit the dreaded TILT light that terminates our game.

Invariably, fooling around at the City Restaurant gets us in trouble. Nick and Wolf think it is a big joke to fill the sugar shaker with salt. As their accomplice, I have a voyeuristic experience of watching people drink coffee sweetened with salt. Our transgressions end when Marvin, the owner of the restaurant, catches us. He lectures in a harsh tone, "Listen, you nimrods, if you ever do this kind of stupid thing again, I'll ban you from coming in the restaurant. You understand?" We nod our heads slowly and deliberately in agreement. Yeah, we get caught red-handed, and we never do that dastardly deed again.

Candor, not tact, is one of Dad's strengths, and he sure proves it to me. At the beginning of tenth grade I receive the first of two lifelong sex talks. No, the conversation isn't anything you would expect. Dad has old-fashioned ways when it comes to raising kids. He figures that anything I do reflects on the family. I have my eye on a red-haired girl named Carol Jones, and she is rumored to be a hot commodity—chronologically a year younger, but experience-wise at least five years ahead of me. To my youthful mind this is excellent math. As a ninth-grade girl she rides the roller-skating bus from Brockway to Reynoldsville, and the older boys talk about her as easy. Being eager, curious, and normal, I am interested in easy and available girls. I begin to talk with her at school. She is good-looking; in fact she is beautiful. The hackneyed cliché "beauty is only skin deep" is wrong since good looks get my motor running. Beauty does count and given a choice, beauty comes out the winner. Why date ugly when beauty is available? At a football game I make the bold move of holding her hand. I am especially careful to keep my activities hush-hush from my parents. Surely they will never find out about my clandestine desires. I feel ready to make my big play. The exciting fantasy with the red-haired girl plays over and over in sinful dreams. Yep, this is a great way to sin.

Shortly after the hand-holding incident, Dad and I get into the truck to go to camp. Without any introduction or hesitation, he looks at me and says, "I hear you've been nosing around that Jones girl." Shocked silence is my only response. Oh my God, how could he possibly know? I sit motionless and continue staring straight ahead, purposely avoiding eye contact. He continues, "Stay away from that girl, do you hear me?" I nod my head yes. That ends the conversation, and that ends my association with the red-haired girl. All the time and effort invested in a clandestine relationship and I didn't even get a feel. Dad never again brings up the subject, but the paranoia planted in my mind tells me that he is keeping an eye on me. How am I going to break into the big league with him watching? Things are simple in the 1950s. Young guys aren't supposed to have interest in girls who are easy—damn it.

Dangling participles, contractions, prepositions, adverbs, and all the stuff perceived as insipid trash are low on my priority list. Mrs. Feeney is my tenth-grade English teacher. She is a slight woman in her late forties, but who can tell about matronly ladies—they all look old. Because of her petite stature, knobby knees, and fuddy-duddy appearance, we call her Canary Legs. Mrs. Feeney doesn't allow horseplay in her class; she takes the teaching of English seriously, but because of the carelessness of youth, I don't. I do learn some unimportant facts in her class. "What is the longest word in the Oxford English Dictionary?" she asks.

"Who cares, we'll never use it," I whisper to Wolf.

Mrs. Feeney glances in my direction and continues. "The word is floccinaucinihilipilification," and she writes it on the blackboard. We laugh since pronouncing, let alone spelling, the word is a challenge. "The word," she notes in a cutting tone, "means the act of estimating something as worthless." She looks directly at Wolf and me. I briefly pause to ponder if she is delivering a covert message about my classroom behavior.

One day I am offensive and inattentive in a subtle but undermining manner. Haw-haw, I'm really getting to her and grating on her nerves. My buddies encourage me. In fact, I am a pain in the neck, only the pain is about two and a half feet lower. She reciprocates by striking where I am most vulnerable. After casting a few warning glances, she stops teaching, looks me straight in the eyes, and says in a threatening voice. "Well, James DeAngelo, what would your father think if he knew you acted like this in school?"

"Oh my God," I ponder, "my father?" Instantaneously I melt and turn to putty as she surgically opens my chest and tears out my heart. Immediately after the panic attack subsides, I get my act together. In two nanoseconds I change into a gentleman. Dad will kill me if he knows I am disrespectful. The fortunate part is that if it had not been for old knobby-knee Canary Legs, none of us would read Shakespeare or other classical literature. Nonetheless, thank God for Classic comic books, for without them Mrs. Feeney would never receive a book report.

Mrs. Feeney is a wonderful teacher, but my overactive imagination generates an epiphany of blasphemous thoughts. I learn a few concepts from English literature class and apply them to religion. I confide in Nick, "Philosophically, without evil and goodness as antagonists, the world can never have good and bad as outcomes." I learn in literature class that comparing and contrasting can't occur unless there is a standard to compare and contrast against. "Think about it, Nick. Without sin there is no need for forgiveness, and without the need for forgiveness, why would we need religion? Am I right? Take it one step further," I hypothesize. "Without sin what would fiction writers write about? So you can say that sin guarantees full employment for the clergy and fiction writers, thus eliminating the need for a clergy/writer welfare state."

"God, you're dangerous. What the hell are you talking about?" Nick asks with a confused look on his face. "Christ almighty, get off this weird crap."

"Well, Nick, I don't want you to underestimate the power and need for sin in shaping modern society." How's that for obtuse reasoning? If those damn Republicans don't beat him to it, the Devil probably will sell me a teenage discount ticket to hell.

Our Problems in Democracy teacher, John McDuff, is also our varsity basketball coach. At six feet, five inches in height, he appears easygoing on the outside, but it's turmoil on the inside. His stature makes him hard to miss since he is the tallest person in Brockway. Every day he enters the classroom, sits at his desk, takes a bottle of chalky white Maalox, and gulps a sip. He then opens the *New York Times* newspaper and tells us what is going on in the world. Thankfully there isn't a newspaper strike or class would be canceled. Occasionally the *Times* generates some serious classroom discussions about current events. We are the best-informed kids on national events in Brockway. Mr. McDuff also teaches Drivers Education. The only thing I learn is his theory on straightening a curve by cutting it short at the beginning and swinging to the outside to complete the turn. When I receive my driver's license I find straightening curves works fairly well, as long as there is no opposing traffic. Telling kids they are forbidden to do something ensures that they will try.

Our upper-level math teacher, Miss Barwell, is the school's only guidance counselor. We call her Aunt Carolyn since she is the aunt of one of the boys in our class. One kid receives a passing grade in math only after he promises not to take more math courses. Wolf and I struggle through nasty math courses such as algebra, plane geometry, and trigonometry. An indicator of learning is the application of the knowledge gained. At the end of all those math classes, I can't provide examples of practical applications of the content foisted upon me. I do okay, but I never brag about my grades. Just enough to get by; no more, no less. I classify myself as an academic minimalist.

Music is increasingly important. My favorite song is "Sixteen Tons" sung by Tennessee Ernie Ford. By the tenth grade I can go into Joe Andolino's teenage restaurant and listen to the jukebox. We tough guys act out the words and sing the song without hitting each other. I sing, "One fist of iron," Nick follows, "the other of steel," Wolf holds his right fist up and sings, "If the right one don't get you," we all join and sing, "then the left one will." This manly phrase is the symbolically tough refrain in our adolescent lexicon.

Since driving is not yet possible, we find other ways to entertain ourselves. Our log cabin outside of Brockway offers exciting opportunities for boyish experiments. The guys agree to go on an overnight excursion to the camp. Nick brings some munchies, and I know where Dad hides the hard stuff. We make it to the camp and immediately begin playing penny poker. In poker the dealer changes with each new hand of cards dealt.

"Okay, Nick, it's your turn to deal," I say as I hand him the cards. "All right, gimme the cards," he instructs. Unknowingly, Nick procured a deck of French nudie playing cards from one of his gas station buddies and switches decks. As the cards are dealt, I try to maintain my cool and collected composure. None of the other players reacts to the porn cards except Wolf. His eyes get big like saucers and he blurts out, "I certainly won't have a hard time identifying the ace of spades."

Cursing, smoking cigarettes, using foul language, acting like fools, bellicose bantering, and talking about chicks is the order of the night. Our talk speculates about girls who do the dirty deed and girls who don't. I verbally theorize, "Guys, if we don't get some action, we'll come down with the dreaded lovers' nuts or the feared blue-balls disorder."

Wolf inquires, "What the hell are those? They sound as bad as the black plague."

Nick laughs. "I think it's too late. Ya sorry shits both look like ya got them and have already built up an immunity."

What these two ailments are, and from whence the medical myth originates, is unknown. Speculation is that new blue denim overalls worn on hot, humid summer days sometimes stain jockey shorts blue along with a guy's vital parts, but I'm not sure this is blue-ball disease. Nonetheless, if they exist there is a distinct possibility we will succumb to the afflictions. Each of us secretly recognizes that even if we find one of these legendary loose girls, we won't know what to do with them.

It just so happens that guys our age also get a near lethal dose of brain warp manifesting itself as groin fever. Mother Nature simultaneously kicks in the pimple factory and strange hormone juices. The internal conflict to break the shackles of childhood and move into the realm of near adulthood rages inside. My body is a busy chemical factory working overtime to produce a plethora of sudden change. Brain warp is more of a mental disorder than a physical disorder. I'm sure that many times I have brain warp. It is pervasive among my age group.

The pot in poker is pennies and nobody gets rich, but we have a great time. The fun lasts until late in the evening. In the mid-1950s the dangers associated with drinking alcohol are not stressed, and even if they were, we would ignore the warning. Nick and I find a fifth of hard whiskey called Seagram's Seven. Whiskey smells terrible, tastes bitter, and burns my throat, but when I'm with my peer group, I never let on.

Nick puts out a challenge. "Jim, I double-dog dare you to a drinking contest," and promptly splits the whiskey into two water glasses. Nobody refuses a double-dog dare.

"I accept the challenge; all right, you're on."

The rules are that you have to chug your drink in one gulp. Nick loudly proclaims, "Through the lips and over the gums, look out, stomach, here she comes—chug-a-lug," at which time we both gulp the entire glass of golden liquid. "Holy crap and double hell's bells," I gasp as the acrid liquid punches its way down my gullet. The secondary reaction is goose bumps over my entire body. Mother Nature is warning me that I have done something stupid. The next morning, as I pick myself off the floor, I wish I were dead. The toilet bowl and I become best friends. The dry heaves, along with pseudo-retching, signal a clear message that I have exceeded anything classified as responsible drinking. I am a ten on the stupid scale. Nonetheless, there is an upside to any bad experience. From that day forward, I avoid the smell or taste of hard whiskey. Nature teaches me a valuable backhanded lesson.

In 1957, at the end of our sophomore year, our class moves from the old Seventh Avenue School building to the newly built high school on the west end of town. Wolf still rides the bus, and Nick and I remain town kids. The bad news is every day I have to walk farther to school, and the good news is I don't have to walk as often. Why? Because we now have a cafeteria, and for the first time in eleven years, my buddies and I eat lunch together. Aunt Betty comments, "And now we're feeding them—imagine that. What will they think of next?" Nick, Wolf, and I think cafeteria food is great, especially the mysterious ground meat sandwiches. The cafeteria ladies know healthy appetites, and scoop a little more food on our trays.

Their theory is, when the boys are eating they aren't getting into mischief, and it works fine because we are always eating.

What would a bunch of guys do if they found a sanitary napkin? Wolf finds an unused woman's sanitary napkin, and he and I agree it will look great taped to the outside of Nick's locker. A sanitary napkin is an unmentionable, sacred, and mysterious thing that none of us is supposed to have knowledge of. It doesn't matter that half the humans in the civilized world use them. We decide that a little catsup from the cafeteria applied to the napkin will add realism. "Great idea," Wolf says. "All this schooling must be doing some good." Wolf waits until the coast is clear and tapes the napkin to the outside of Nick's locker. It's a tough and dangerous job, but he is up to the task. Wolf brags after he clandestinely slithers away from Nick's locker, "Mission accomplished." Daringly we wait nearby to see what will certainly be Nick's embarrassed reaction.

Nick walks to his locker and is nonchalant about the situation. The sight of the slightly red-stained lily-white object taped to his locker greets him. "Geeeez," he says as he shakes his head, takes it off the door, and puts it inside his locker. He looks askance at us, bent over laughing like silly fools, again shakes his head from side to side, mumbles, "Assholes," and goes on his way. He is unflappable. What a guy.

In the years I know him, the only time I am truly angry with Nick is during my junior year. Walking from gym class I stop at the ceramic water fountain for a drink. Nick, horsing around as usual, pushes my head down as I am preparing to sip from the arching stream. His action forces my mouth to hit the metal part of the fountain and severely chip my front tooth. I want to physically strike out at him. I cannot contain my anger. "Goddamnit, Nick, look what you've done—you broke my tooth. You stupid sonofabitch, I could kill ya."

Nick apologizes, "Geez, I'm sorry."

"Ah shut up," I tersely say, and walk away.

I find myself in a strange paradox. For the first time I want to visit Doc McGrin's office. Maybe he can somehow perform magic and make me whole again. Doc McGrin examines the damaged tooth. He stoically says, "Hmmmmmm," followed by an enlightened "Ahhhhhhhh. I think we can do something about this." Quicker than John Wayne draws his six-shooter, he pulls out his trusty drill. He grinds the tooth until it feels smooth to my tongue. It doesn't matter that one tooth is shorter than the others; there are no options since none of the dentists in the county do caps. When finished he again examines his work. He proudly announces, "Hmmm, you're okay," and sends me on my way. Every time I place my tongue in the front of my mouth and feel my damaged tooth, I think about that day.

Horseplay is either a genetic aberration of adolescences or maybe it is just fun; either way it creates problems. The new school needs volunteers to assist in getting the building and grounds fully operational. During study hall Nick, Wolf, and I are assigned the task to tie down the newly planted trees. Being good school citizens we position the stakes and then realize that we don't have a hammer.

"Wolf, do ya have a hammer so I can pound in this stake?"

"Where in the hell would I get a hammer?" says Wolf. "Here, use this."

"Hey, bright eyes, you want me to use your history book?" I ask.

"Brilliant, Jim, you are absolutely brilliant. Why do you think I handed it to ya?"

Using heavy history textbooks to pound stakes in the ground is a good idea. Little do we realize everyone in the building is watching. I look up and see our gaping window-wall audience. They are aghast at the sight of a beloved history textbook being used as a pounding implement. Does it really matter? I guess it does, because again we are called on the carpet, but this time serious trouble is not a consequence. As a matter of fact, our school newspaper, *The Buzzard*, picks up the action and writes a story about the incident. We are now famous tough guy abusers of history books.

In 1958, Grandpa Gamelo's health seriously deteriorates. He suffers a stroke, and Mom, Aunt Betty, Aunt Jenny, and Aunt Helen stay by his side. They know he is failing fast. Mom asks, "Jimmy, do you want to come into his bedroom and say good-bye."

"Is he going to die?"

"Yes, son, he is."

When I enter the room, Grandpa is breathing in a shallow and infrequent pattern. After fifteen minutes his chest no longer heaves, and he stops breathing. Mom, with tears in her eyes, quietly says to me, "He's gone."

He was eighty-five years old, and although he didn't believe in the church, the priest administers the Last Rites. It makes us feel better knowing God will now welcome him. At the time of his death, Aunt Jenny opens the window. "Why did she do that?" I ask.

"By opening the window his soul can get out of the room and find its way to heaven—it's an old country tradition," she replies.

"Gee, what a nice old-country ritual," I say. "I'll bet he's in heaven telling God about the bullama shit he's seen on Earth."

The funeral is held in his house with Grandpa laid out in the living room. Friends, relatives, and neighbors visit and say good-bye. Old-time Italian ladies dressed in black visit and do their obligatory wailing beside the casket. The wailers give me the willies. I know Grandpa would disapprove of all the fuss. He would say, "Thatsa lotta bullama shit." The ladies from the Rosary Society recite prayers, and the priest gives him a final sendoff before he is interred at the Saint Tobias Cemetery. Ya know, this religion stuff isn't as stupid as I thought. Part of my life and part of my past disappear with the passing of Grandpa Gamelo.

CHAPTER 17

THE BOYS BECOME MOBILE, YIPPEE!

The tempo of life quickens as I move to the eleventh grade. The most significant events are getting a driver's license and discovering I like girls. They drive me crazy. The transition from male bonding to a more sociable creature with the opposite sex accelerates. "Meet ya up at the City Restaurant tonight. If you chip in fifty cents, Wolf and I got enough for a pizza," says. Nick.

"Nah, not tonight."

"Whadda ya mean?" Nick inquires. "Are you going out with some hot tomato tonight? Must mean she's another one of those religious nuts. You're never gonna get any dating those semi-nuns."

Understand, being with my buddies is a healthy outlet for my youthful zeal. It is nice to have sufficient time to grow and remain a kid, but those days are gone. School continues as usual, except I take courses requiring that dastardly word, "effort." This is against my minimalist philosophy. Wolf and I take chemistry from old Pop Shoofer. Chemistry is an exercise in survival. Pop's only teaching credential is a diploma from a Teacher Normal School. Admittedly, we aren't good students, but Pop never masters the art of teaching. Arguably, he never approaches the fine art of teaching. His lack of technique is only surpassed by his inability to motivate developing minds.

As a budding chemist, Wolf summons me to a lab table for a surprise. "Hey, Jim, come on over here. Wait till you see this; it'll blow your socks off."

I walk to where Wolf is working and we huddle around the table. "Wolf, what the hell are you doing?"

Wolf reaches in his pocket. "See this penny? Now watch this," he instructs. He drops the penny into a beaker filled with liquid. The brownish liquid sizzles like a newly opened bottle of vigorously shaken Coke.

"Wolf, you crazy ass, what are you doing? Pop is going to see us. Let's get out of here." We make a hasty retreat to another work area.

"Which one of you blockheads did this?" Pop's booming voice echoes throughout the classroom. "You people are so dumb that you are dangerous." Wolf's surprise consists of placing the penny in nitric acid and watching the penny dissolve into choking brown fumes. Granted, the Tom Terrific penny trick catches my attention, but once the reaction starts, we don't know how to stop it.

I do master the technique of coating old dimes with mercury. "Jim, I don't think we should be doing this," warns Wolf. "While you were sleeping during class, Pop told us mercury is a poisonous heavy metal that shouldn't be handled by humans."

"I didn't know that," I respond, "but mercury certainly does make old dimes bright and shiny."

Did I learn anything? Probably, but I can't remember. Memories of chemistry class are Pop's veins popping out of his head as he yells at Wolf and me. "You blockheads" always precedes a litany of uniquely degrading remarks. I'm sure he flunked out of charm school.

Only two guys, the Mole and Will, understand the stuff Pop is attempting to teach. They aren't much smarter than the rest of us, but they doggedly study. They are non-jock-type academic students. Everyone has different priorities in life, and textbooks are their priority. Fortunately, they are humanist and share the results of their lab experiments and homework assignments. In study hall before chemistry class, fellow students fight to sit by them and check the answers to the homework they never do.

I decide in eleventh grade to try out for football. Now, the catch-22 is that the prerequisite for playing football is Typing I. Why? Because the football coach is also the typing teacher. Learning to type is the most useful thing Wolf and I do, but the challenges are great. Wolf, Nick, and I sit side by side in typing class, with Nick in the middle. Typing is an elective course, and any breathing student can sign up for it. I spend hours learning the key positions and practicing repetitive typing drills. The rhythm of ASDF; JKL echo in my mind as my fingers blindly search for the correct key. Our typewriters, old black mechanical Underwood machines, have a finicky temperament. Wolf and I do our best to pass the speed test final exam so we can get out of Typing I class. Imagine the anxiety, tension, and fear of making a typo. Then imagine our surprise when our hands automatically reach to hit the manual carriage return lever, only to see the carriages fly off the typewriters and plummet to the floor. Wolf and I look at each other in startled amazement. Mechanically inclined, Nick has discovered that if he loosens a screw on the carriage return, the carriage will fly off the typewriter. It must be get-even time for the sanitary napkin caper. Frankly, I think Nick wet his pants laughing, but the teacher didn't seem nearly as amused.

Thank God Mr. Z understands boys and maybe, just maybe, his need for football players helps ameliorate the situation. I know one thing; Wolf, Nick, and I are treated extra special at practice that day. After our warm-up exercises, the coach pulls us aside. "Manceni, McGuire, DeAngelo, over here. I've got something special in mind for you three clowns. You see that hill?" Coach Z points his finger. "It needs you three to conquer it, up and back—do you understand? I'll tell you when I think you guys have completed conquering it. Now get going." He orders us up and down the side of an enormously steep hill, which we doggedly do, not once, but four times. By the third time we are crawling up the hill, not running.

"Wolf, do you really think he is doing this to get us into better physical condition?" I ask between deep, panting breaths. Coach Z. refers to this as advanced character building, and I have got enough character to last a lifetime. Next to running additional laps around the field, chugging our bodies up that damn hill makes us appreciate the folly of our behavior. The price paid isn't harmful, but it is memorable. I do make it out of typing class, but only by the skin of my teeth.

A person must take the attitude "every day is a good day, but some days are just better than others." I do play second string on the football team. Coach wants me to be a halfback on offense and play in the backfield on defense. The team isn't bad that year, so we second-stringers do a lot of bench time. Being on the bench at football games is agonizing, not because I'm not on the first string, but because of the bitterly cold Northwest Pennsylvania late fall weather. Getting splinters in my behind is one thing, but freezing my sweet cheeks off is another thing. With no expectation of getting into a game, I get smart and dress for comfort and warmth. We sit on the bench for the first six games, and the coach certainly won't put us in during the last game of the season. The coach values us as good bench-warming material. Under my equipment are five sweatshirts. I am so bulky that my arms can't rest at my side; they sort of puff out.

Wouldn't you know, the team gets far ahead and Coach decides to give us a break. He puts in the second string. "DeAngelo, get in there for Smith," he orders.

"Okay, Coach," I respond in a confident voice.

The entire second string is on defense, and our task is to maintain the lead. The opponent's first play is a pass to my general area, and with my bulky uniform, I can hardly move. Like something akin to running chest-deep in water, I move in slow motion. Our opponents quickly score on us and "touchdown" is announced over the PA system. Back on the bench I go, but at least I am warm. So ends my illustrious football career. That day is a good day, but not one of my better days.

Receiving my driver's license creates an opportunity to remove myself from the scrutiny of Brockway people. I am a born-again teenager. The girls in my class are so-so, something akin to lukewarm water, neither hot nor cold. I have known them all my life. So, Wolf and I look for the proverbial greener pasture. As junior varsity basketball players, we don't always suit up for the varsity games, giving us ample time to scout for girls. At a game in Brookville, we meet a couple of girls sitting in the bleachers. Wolf's great conversation opener gets their attention. He is smooth. "Hey, are you girls from Brookville?"

They smile and say, "Yes we are. Who are you guys?"

"I'm Jim and this is Wolf."

They both giggle and repeat, "Wolf." Those introductory remarks are enough to start a trivial conversation that ends with us asking them for a date. Surprisingly they say yes, and give us their phone numbers. "See you tomorrow at six," I comment as we leave to get on the bus. The girls' names are Rhonda and Mary. Rhonda, the more robust built of the two girls, is outgoing, but Mary is shy and reserved. Both girls are good-lookers. Wolf decides to hook up with Rhonda and I get Mary.

The following day Wolf picks me up in his family's Oldsmobile 88 and off to Brookville we go. We pick the girls up at their houses and take them to the movie. My courting protocol starts at the movie as I hold Mary's hand and put my arm around her. She does not protest. I give her a gentle caress. Still, she does not protest. She snuggles closer and is perfectly happy with the situation. After the movie, as planned, I sit in the backseat with Mary, and Wolf is in the front with Rhonda. Wolf and I are batting zero, so what do I have to lose by risking bold moves? We pull over on a little-used road and start necking. Mary still does not protest. I can't tell you what Wolf is doing because I am completely occupied. Mary starts breathing heavily, and I think her panting is possibly a covert sign that she is hot to trot. She continues not to protest, and her accommodating behavior gives me the courage to try another daring move. May as well reach for the golden ring, I reason. I put my hand under her blouse and slowly, carefully, calculatingly, inch by inch, methodically work my way up to her breast. She still does not protest. She groans, "Awwwwwwwww," and I take it as a good sign. Putting my hand under her bra increases her heavy breathing. She does not protest; instead the groaning machine kisses me even more passionately. Oh boy, nothing shy about Mary. Finally, I make it to first base with a girl.

Suddenly, without warning a disturbing thing happens. Like an emergency brake on a car, my conscience kicks in. Flurries of conflicting thoughts gallop through my mind. Oh my God, what am I getting myself into? What will my family think of me? What will the Church think of me, and even more important, what will God think of me? She feels soft and so good that I know there must be some sort of terrible retribution to follow. Nothing this good goes unpunished. Lead us not into temptation is past tense—I'm already there. Not only does the self-reproach and guilt of committing a forbidden act manifest itself in my mind, but also inexperience limits my capacity to take advantage of the situation. After conquering the challenge of her bra, I have no idea what else to do, so I leave it at that. My inability to exploit the situation makes me the one who ultimately does protest, but it is a relatively weak protest. I get a hit, but a homerun is not in the cards.

Contrary to contemporary thinking, fear is helpful. Fear is the brake slowing down my engine of passion, and my engine is operating at high speed. My biggest worry is getting a girl pregnant or getting a disease. Nobody wants to explain either of these situations to their parents. Dad's words, "Don't ever bring disgrace on the family name," echo in my head. The consequence of careless behavior surely will bring disgrace to the family.

Despite my raging internal conflict, legitimate concerns, and irrational fears, the audacious deed leaves me in a state of euphoria. I feel manly, and I am floating on a cloud of pride. It is the first time the three criteria for a legitimate feel are met. Her firm, soft, smooth flesh felt super great. This was no accidental bumping with an elbow. This was the real thing. It actively involved the palm of my hand and the caress of a breast. Imagine, I had a breast in my hand and life is great. I'm an eleventh grader and just got a certifiable feel. On the way back to Brockway, Wolf and I debrief each other about our groping exercise. We discuss the details of our first successful double-date adventure. "Ya know, Wolf, sooner or later, even a blind chicken pecking gets a worm. We finally hit pay dirt," I comment.

"Yep," Wolf replies, "it sure is great. I like getting my worm pecked, only this chick wasn't blind. Ain't no arguing about it—this was a real feel."

We made it to the big-time, and we are on our way to becoming studs. Our time of heaven on Earth has arrived.

The next day at school, neither Wolf nor I can banish the smile from our faces. We feel ambivalence toward the girls in our class because we have sipped from the fountain of passion. A sin, yes, but what a boost for the morale of two teenage boys. Our escapades end when Rhonda falls and breaks her pelvis. As only insensitive teenage boys can do, Wolf and I tell our buddies, "Well, we can't see Rhonda anymore; she fell and broke her ass." The comments do get a good laugh from our equally insensitive buddies.

In sports the enemy of good is better. The most significant effect of the new high school building is on the varsity basketball team. Wolf and I are on the junior varsity team, but we are also part of the varsity team. That year, it looks as if the varsity team has a good chance to win the sectional championship. At the old Seventh Avenue building, the small, enclosed, cracker box gym didn't have much playing room. In comparison, the gym at the new school is a large, expansive place, and we are unaccustomed to such an unrestricted area. The old, small Seventh Avenue gym was a distinct advantage for our team. We lose that advantage in the new gym, and we lose the championship game to Reynoldsville. It is a bitter night and one in which many senior players cry. Luck bounces the ball off the rim, and the rebound goes to the other team. Brockway is a good team, but that night the other team is better.

Eleventh grade is noteworthy because Wolf and I start to become music stars. As a result of our participation in chorus, we are selected for county chorus. That means we are invited to go out of town for two nights. Brockway is a sheltered environment, and going out of town is a big deal. As seniors, Wolf and I are selected for district chorus in East Brady, Pennsylvania. The music director for district chorus is Aunt Betty's son Blasé, and that means I have to mind my manners. I have loads of fun, and county chorus proves to be a great opportunity for meeting chicks.

Our singing abilities improve and Miss Thomas approaches me with a special request. "Jim, I am forming a boys' quartet. Would you consider being a member?"

"Gee, thanks, I guess I would. Who else is going to be part of the group?"

"I'm considering you, Wolf, Chester Charlie, and the underclassman Norman Green. You'll be the bass, Wolf will sing baritone, Chester the alto, and Norman will be the tenor."

Chester is a classmate and somewhat effeminate. Like his name he can't decide which way to go. Pudgy Norman's voice changes later in life because he has a testicle that hasn't descended and the doctors are working on it, but for the time being his one hanging ball makes him a tremendous tenor. Look in the "Sunrise" yearbook and you will see our picture.

Miss Thomas likes us and puts up with a lot of crap, but we do make her look good. The quartet entertains at social events in church basements and meetings throughout the community, singing our beautiful harmony. Funny, but the words we crooners sing continually resonate through my head: "Coney Island Babe," "The Tack," "Madam Jeanette," and others are etched in my brain. We are so good that our quartet wins first prize at the school's annual talent show. First prize entitles us to the first choice of the donated items. Wolf selects a black lamp with gold trimmings, and I take its mate. They aren't beautiful lamps, but they are reminders of our vocal accomplishment. Mom is proud of me, but Dad remains stoic. Even Marco, my frustrated accordion teacher, would be proud of me. With the help of my buddies, I have become more than "a good listener."

CHAPTER 18

WILL IT NEVER END? SENIORS FINALLY

Twelfth grade is a year of decision and transition. I don't continue my football career, but Wolf and Nick do. Truthfully, I didn't like football and don't view it as a loss. Some things I try and like, and other things I try and don't like. The important thing is that a person tries. After getting a taste of the forbidden fruit, I find that sports are no longer my only priority. How I look is important. I perceive myself as a cool dresser and pattern my wardrobe after the teenage pop culture models. Elvis is a big influence on my mannerisms and my appearance. Being cool means wearing a pink polo shirt with the collar pulled up in the back, sleeves rolled up past my elbows, cotton khaki trousers, and Vaseline Hair Tonic liberally applied. I wisely abandon the Jeris Hair Dressing. Shiny hair is a good thing in the 1950s. I even wear white buck shoes and white trousers when Pat Boone becomes a teenage idol. Nick adds that extra bit of panache by carrying a pack of cigarettes either in his shirt pocket or rolled up in his sleeve.

As a punishment for struggling through chemistry, I have the honor of taking twelfth-grade physics from Pop. "You blockheads back for another year of making my life miserable?" is Pop's initial greeting.

"You know, Wolf," I whisper, "at least he remembers us."

"Yep, he's damn lucky we're giving him another chance to make scientists out of us. In life you don't get many second chances," Wolf jokingly responds.

Physics class mimics the experiences of chemistry class. In a small school two consecutive years with Pop is equivalent to getting the double-whammy. Who said God doesn't have a sense of humor? Sometimes He enjoys a good laugh and wants to teach us that life isn't fair all the time or even part of the time. I never take a book home. Studying isn't important and my comfort level continues to be unperturbed with grades of C or an occasional B. Studying and applying myself will come later in life.

Hormones control my intellectual ability, and they aren't about to take a backseat to rational thinking. The only necessity is a grade good enough to keep my parents off my back.

As a senior, I am co-art director of the 1959 yearbook. My partner is Debbie. Debbie is the cat's meow, and I am secretly fond of her. The black-haired, blue-eyed girl makes me swoon. She is hot. The only problem is she has a crush on Wolf, and nobody else will do. It is interesting that Wolf doesn't give her the time of day. I can't figure out his lack of attention; he must be crazy. "Wolf, what the hell's wrong with you? Debbie is crazy about you. Why don't you give her some attention?"

"You'll find out," Wolf says in a warning voice.

"What do you mean," I ask, and Wolf only responds with a smile. It tortures me to work with Debbie on the yearbook, knowing she wants Wolf but not me. All the "Jimmy charm" in the world can't change that.

I design the yearbook cover that year. The red-and-white cover depicting the rising sun signifies a new day, and it is an artistic triumph. Miss Cranford, the art teacher and the yearbook advisor, likes my work. I am flattered. She believes I have talent and encourages me to become an art teacher. Yikes, me as an art teacher. I reason that given a choice of vocations, the likelihood of being an art teacher far exceeds that of becoming a priest.

By the time Wolf and I enter our senior year, we date not only girls in our class, but also girls from other towns. Girls, girls, girls everywhere, but not a one who suits me. I am drowning in a sea of possibilities.

My dream of becoming a basketball star quickly evaporates. Wolf and I are on the varsity team, and Nick is the team's student manager. After winning our first game, the road to victory takes a detour. It isn't that we aren't good; it's just that everyone else is better. Our senior class consists of sixty-eight students, and the pool for talented players isn't competitive when compared to large schools. When playing against Clearfield, their team is so good and their gym is so large that we are lost in its cavernous interior.

"Wolf, do you see the size of the guy I'm supposed to guard? He must be seven feet tall."

"You can handle King Kong—just rough him up a little" is Wolf's sarcastic remark. "He's going to eat you up and spit you out."

"Never gonna happen," I boast. "I'll stand on a chair, look him in the eyes, and growl. That'll intimidate him. Yeah, I'll punch him in the knee a couple of times. That'll get him pissed off." What a menacing environment. At five feet ten, I am a midget compared to my counterpart. He is eight inches wider and a foot taller than I am. After the first quarter Clearfield gives us a break and puts in the second string. "I think they're getting tired," Wolf comments. "We are getting to them. We've got them on the run." The second string continues the trouncing. The most embarrassing moment is still to come. They put in their third string, and the third-string players carry on the thrashing. How humiliating. From that point I know I will never make it to the professional arena.

Coach McDuff isn't happy and expresses his unhappiness in a scornful manner. He takes his charm school lessons from Pop Shoofer. I'm sure Coach McDuff's consumption of Maalox doubles during the season. The coach values a winning season, but our record is a lackluster two wins and fourteen losses. Somebody has to lose and more often than not, we are that somebody.

An accident is caused by an unfortunate set of circumstances leading to a physical event caused by ignoring the laws of nature, ignoring the laws of probability, and disregarding the use of common sense. In other words, doing something stupid. With the advent of the new building, Physical Education class becomes more than games. Harry Christie remains our gym teacher and he tries to teach us gymnastic skills. I get better and better at gymnastics and Harry encourages me to push the limit. Like a good coach, he prods me to explore my abilities with an encouraging "Way to go, keep up the good work, Jungle Jim." "Jungle Jim" is the closest I come to a nickname, but it doesn't stick. One day on the rings I perform an exercise called a dislocation. The rings hang suspended from the ceiling by nylon straps, and a boost from a spotter is required to reach them. A dislocation is an exercise in which a person does a complete 360-degree suspended summersault while maintaining a grip on the two rings. The operative words are "maintaining a grip." Two dislocations are completed without incident. Nick urges, "One more for the road, Jim. C'mon, you can do it." As I attempt a third dislocation, I lose my grip and plummet to the floor. The fall is broken with my right hand and it stings a little. I shake it off and continue my activity.

"Nick, every time I listen to you, I get in the shits." The problem is too much ambition and too little skill or strength, which is the prerequisite formula for the ill-fated plunge. My enthusiasm exceeds my capability.

After class my hand starts throbbing, and throughout the day the throbbing increases. Finally, during English class I inform my relatively new teacher, "Excuse me, Miss Thompsel, something is wrong with my hand. May I please go down and see the nurse? My hand is hurting."

She stops grading papers and glances up. "No," she says without making eye contact. "Go back to your seat and finish your assignment." She probably thinks I am trying to pull something over on her. So what's a guy supposed to do? I go back to my desk and continue working. After school the pain increases, and it is necessary to tell Mom. Usually the discomfort of bumps and bruises goes away by itself, but my wrist is progressively getting worse. Unlike Miss Thompsel, Mom knows that I never complain and takes me seriously. She calls the local doctor, who directs us to the DuBois Hospital to have my wrist X-rayed. The emergency room doctor says, "By golly, son, the X-ray shows you broke a bone in your right wrist. I wouldn't have thought it when examining you. Don't worry, we'll fix you up."

I mumble, "Oh shit," softly so Mom won't hear. The doctor applies a stark white plaster cast from my hand to my elbow. The next day at school Miss Thompsel is mortified. She didn't mean me harm and I never hold it against her; in her shoes I would do the same. The plaster cast is a great conversation piece, and friends rush like stampeding buffalo to memorialize their names on it.

On Saturday night, we pursue the unrelenting quest for merriment and entertainment. Often we gather on the sidewalk outside the City Restaurant to decide who is going to drive to Reynoldsville, where a place called the Pink Panther sponsors teenage dances. For a slight cover charge, I see many famous people such as Frankie Avalon, and other lesser-known stars. The plaster cast is worn as a badge of honor. Wolf and I leave the dance and are standing outside the Pink Panther when we spot a familiar guy smoking a cigarette. "Wolf, is that Conway Twitty standing over there?"

"Yeah, Jim, it sure does look like him. Unless he has a twin—but you never know."

A teenager is a teenager, and as hokey as it sounds, I approach him. "Ah, excuse me, aren't you Mr. Twitty? Huh—Mr. Twitty, would you sign my cast? How about right here under Nick's name."

"Sure, son, it'll be a pleasure," he says as he scrawls his name on the cast. I thank him and walk away. The cast is more than a badge of honor; it is a novelty that I wear with pride. My valued cast is stored in my bedroom for many years until Mother decides to throw the smelly thing away.

Wolf and I meet a couple of Reynoldsville girls at the dance and start dating them. By this time, we don't always double date. Wolf dates Lisa, an incredibly tall, slim female with a bubbly personality. She drives me nuts with her constant giggling. Ask her what day it is, and she giggles. Say hello, and she giggles. No matter what is said or asked, she giggles. Her behavior is beyond a nervous tic. Imagine a six-foot, two-inch giggler.

"Wolf, does that string bean always giggle?"

"Well, Jim, the truth of the matter is yes, with one exception. When I get her hot, she goes from a giggler to a moaner. Yep, a real live moaner. I call her the Moaner Lisa," Wolf remarks with a big grin.

I date an attractive full-bodied person about five feet eight inches tall, but we don't get along. I secretly call her "Norma Nasty" to reflect her one overriding personality trait. We have fun with the Reynoldsville girls, but still date girls in other towns. What they don't know won't hurt them, and besides, neither of us make any sort of commitment.

A new meaning is given to the term "double dating." In the usual lexicon, double dating is two couples going out together. Wolf and I redefine double dating as a guy going out on two dates in one night. The logistics of such an arrangement are simple. Pick up the first girl at six o'clock in the evening and attend the seven o'clock movie. After the movie, take her home and give her a kiss good night and immediately proceed to the second girl's house to pick her up by nine thirty. It is best to take the second girl for a snack, followed by some light petting and necking and deliver her home before midnight. The scheme keeps the first date's parents happy since she is home early, and the second date gets a free snack. The system is beautiful, but risky. Lucky for me the girls never discover my disingenuous Machiavellian scheme. After a period of time the scheme is abandoned. It isn't how nice guys treat girls. Having a conscience does change my behavior. Double damn those nuns. Besides, neither I nor Wolf can afford the expense of two dates in one night.

I have my first case of puppy love with a girl in our class. My heart swoons for her the same as a honeybee swoons for flowers. I must say, I'm getting good at this swooning stuff. We date and do some passionate necking in the front seat of my car. I'm sure she is hot for me. Heavy breathing and fully clothed body contact is the norm, but that's as far as it gets. Our hips naturally grind together, but our bodies never meet in intimate contact. Wow, I am nutty in love with this foxy girl. Her father, a redneck from the old school, finds out she is dating me and bans her from going out with a Catholic, and even worse with an Italian. One of her girlfriends tells me of her dilemma, and it makes me angry and sad. Every time Ricky Nelson sings "Poor Little Fool," it is as if someone rubs salt into my emotional wound. This is 1959. What right does her father have to judge me? How can a man hate someone he doesn't know? It hurts, but I sadly cope with the situation. For the first time, I experience prejudice. I feel sorry for the girl, and what she endures. As time passes I realize how fortunate I am that her father is such a bigot and our puppy love never blossoms. I recognize that unenlightened humans must maintain the protection of their prejudices to fully justify their ignorance.

During the summer we drive to Bailey's on The Bee Line in DuBois for a hot dog and a drink. The Bee Line is known as the million-dollar highway and in the 1950s anything costing that much is considered special. Bailey's is the "hot spot" where the Falls Creek and DuBois chicks hang out. Like a cool stud I get out of the car, order my food, and while waiting circulate and talk to people in other cars. Inevitability, carloads of girls appear. After a period of time I become acquainted with people and establish the necessary connections. I meet a cute girl and she seems different, so I ask her for a date. Maybe this is that special girl I have been looking for. A friend tells me on the sly that she is a girl of questionable morality, only he doesn't say it in polite words. A guy can't always believe gossip, and often that's all it is. My instincts are correct; she is nice and she is different, only I don't yet know how different.

I embark on the strangest date of my young life. The date is so weird and bizarre that I expect Rod Serling to suddenly appear and say, "Welcome to the Twilight Zone." I drive to her house and knock at her front door. "Come in," a voice beckons from afar. Upon entering, I see an older man wearing silver-rimmed spectacles and sitting at a black grand piano. He is dressed in a black satin smoking jacket with a white silk ascot around his neck and he is smoking a cigarette inserted in a four-inch holder. I instantly recognize that his complementary color scheme is coordinated with everything else in the room. What is the significance of all this strange behavior? I have no idea.

As if on cue from a Hollywood set, he sways from side to side and begins to play a crescendo on the piano. Something akin to a cheap B-rated melodramatic movie. Everything happens in dreamlike slow motion. With mouth agape, I am immobilized as the incredulous recital unfolds. A thought races through my mind: *This comic opera must be some sort of nasty gag. Nick and Wolf are behind this.* I peer to the left and to the right, looking for a director and camera, but the *Candid Camera* crew is not found. Almost as if from a staged scene from *The Donna Reed Show*, I watch in utter amazement as my smiling date slowly walks down the stairs in her high heels and promenades into the living room. Every hair of her bouffant-styled head is immaculately in place. Heavy blue eye shadow frames her big brown eyes and gives her the appearance of wearing a metallic mask similar to the one worn by the Lone Ranger. Her mother, sitting on the couch, stands as her beauty queen daughter walks into the living room. I was waiting for applause to erupt from the parents. She formally introduces me. "Mother and Father, I would like you to meet James DeAngelo."

I gain my composure and say, "Glad to meet you," and press their flesh with a firm handshake.

"Will you and James be late tonight, darling?" her father inquires.

"I think not, Father."

I am observing reality, but it may be just a bad dream. The only character missing from this soap opera is the nightmare Devil that chases me in Hell. I pinch myself as a reality check.

"One more thing before you leave, darling," says her mother. Like a monkey in the zoo, her mother primps and fusses her one last time before we leave. I am completely befuddled. I take her out a couple of times and I am proud to say that is all I do. She is a nice girl, but a strange girl. I have a reputation to protect as a levelheaded guy, and even more important I don't want to be associated in any way with that eccentric family. My last stale words to her are, "I'll give you a call, see you later," but I don't mean it and quickly transition out of her life. When assessing the situation I remember Dad told me, "An apple doesn't fall far from the tree," and I certainly don't want that apple falling on me.

Wolf and Nick date other girls we meet at Bailey's, but none are memorable or long lasting. The big morale booster is the knowledge that I can get a date. Bailey's is a training ground to develop social skills that get me absolutely nowhere.

As young guys we think ourselves immortal. One night driving from Bailey's to Brockway, we have an unexpected surprise. That night Nick borrows his father's 1954 Chevy, and he babies the car by driving at a reasonable speed—this in itself is unusual. As we approach a sharp, blind, hairpin curve, we spot a railroad train blocking the railroad crossing. We have never seen a train at that crossing before, but that night a train claims the crossing for its own. Nick slams on the brakes, causing the tires to squeal like newborn pigs. "Hold on," he yells as he pulls sharply to the right. Up on the bank we fly, and the car comes to a sudden stop. "You guys okay?" Nick turns and asks.

"Everyone's okay, but I crapped my pants," Wolf informs us.

After a few deep breaths, Nick puts the car in reverse and backs onto the road. We get out, look the car over, and find a few shrubs on the bumper, but no damage, so we continue our journey home. Nick says his usual cliché, "Uh, no big thing—a miss is as good as a mile."

In the back of my mind, I ponder the possibilities. Why did lead-foot Nick drive sanely that night? What would have happened if we had been going at the usual barn-burning high rate of speed? The possibilities for a disaster are frightening. Hmmm, somebody up there likes us.

Now the girls in Punxsutawney, Pennsylvania, are a different story. Punxsutawney is a mouthful of letters, so local folk and groundhogs call the town Punxsy. Before getting to Punxsy there is a little town called Anita, and we sometimes journey there for dances. Wolf and I are relatively harmless individuals, but Nick continues to stray from the centerline. He develops a persona as a "hood." Nick has his own car and gladly volunteers to take a bunch of guys to social events. Hidden underneath the backseat of Nick's 1953 Nash are a .22 rifle and an assortment of Nick's lead-filled clubs. I ask, "Why do you have that stuff in your car?"

Wolf inquires, "Christ, are you preparing for war or something?"

Nick says, "These are here just in case."

"Just in case what?" Wolf and I ask in unison. We are a little anxious since we don't entirely know what "just in case" means. Now, Nick has no problem carrying knives and clubs on his person. This he does, and during a dance at Anita his belt breaks and the knives and clubs tumble onto the dance floor. The loud clunking noise made by Nick's war tools brings the dance to a screeching halt. "Huh, huh, it's okay. Nick, pick up your things," Wolf says loudly.

"Yeah, everything is cool. Excuse us, but we gotta get going," I stammer. Everyone stands looking as we awkwardly pick up Nick's implements and make a speedy exit. Why wait for an invitation to leave or, even worse, be arrested? Nick's actions are an embarrassing social liability that destroys the cool image we are attempting to portray. To symbolically have the last word, on the way out of town, Nick abruptly pulls his Nash to the side of the road and commands, "Hold on, guys, wait a minute."

"What the hell are you doing?" I ask. Without saying a word, he proceeds to get his rifle from the backseat and promptly shoots at some guy's porch light. "Holy mackerel, are you crazy?" I yell at Nick.

"Yes," he replies as he gets back in the car and speeds away. I must admit that even though I laugh, Nick's impulsive behavior scares me. He appears not to be crazy, but there is an element of doubt in my mind.

Now, Wolf and I aren't angels by any means. When riding with Nick from DuBois to Brockway, we take turns leaning out the window to shoot at the Glade Isle ESSO gasoline station's metal sign. At the moment, I am thrilled to use Nick's .22 in a competition to see if Wolf or I can score the most hits. When with the guys, I sometimes do crazy things. I rationalize that a sign is a lot different than some poor guy's porch light. A short article in the local newspaper describes unknown vandals shooting at the sign. There is no way to justify our behavior as age-appropriate mischief it is just plain screwball stupid. When thinking about it I'm not proud and worry that if Dad finds out, there will be hell to pay. Thank God he never does.

Sometimes a guy bites off more than he can possibly chew. The corresponding dinner table analogy is "Your eyes are bigger than your stomach." Well, everyone has the same opportunity to make a fool of himself, and I take full advantage of it. Wolf and I date a couple of girls we meet in Punxsutawney. My date is Fran and we take the girls to the Punxsy drive-in. The common name for a drive-in movie theater is the passion pit. I think, boy oh boy, what a beautiful and shapely body on Fran. She has more curves than the road to Punxsy. Fran's bee-sting puffy lips, dark, probing brown eyes, deep, husky voice, and sexy body remind me of Sophia Loren. Every sexy inch of her makes my blood want to boil. If I were a wolf, I would surely howl at the moon for her. Her provocative come-and-get-me smile tells me she is "experienced" and wants to get serious—how serious, I have no idea.

Wolf and his date sit in the front seat and I sit with Fran in the backseat. Fran keeps getting closer and closer as she invitingly makes moves on me. I lose my cool and nervously start to babble like an idiot without having anything to say. My mouth goes on automatic pilot. I am rattled and lose any semblance of composure. The smooth, sophisticated moves perfected with other chicks are nowhere to be found. Fran and her aggressive body moves unnerve me.

"Huh, huh," I chatter, "I think it is a beautiful night for a movie."

"Yes," she responds.

"Oh look, there's a radio tower in the corn field."

"Yes" she responds.

"The blinking red light on top sure is bright."

"Yes," she responds.

"I'll bet it costs them a fortune to keep it lit."

"Yes."

Oh-oh, I suddenly realize, *she keeps saying yes to everything.* Meaningless babble continues to dribble from my mouth until Fran takes control of the situation. Fran's motor is revving and wants to get started. We begin to passionately neck, and that does shut me up. Before I can make another stupid remark, she sits on my lap and paws at my chest. She isn't just hot to trot, she is preheated fast food. For the first time a girl pries open my lips and puts her fully erect tongue in my mouth. I am so taken aback by her probing intrusion that I freeze as my mind gropes for what to do next. Fran doesn't understand that I am a French-kiss virgin and her tongue has just deflowered me.

I catch my breath and realize she is preparing for another round of sucking out my tonsils. By this time more than my eyes are bigger than my stomach. I mull over the situation. Oh my God, she's the predator and I'm the prey. I'm doomed. How do I handle this man-eater? My God, this girl has a healthy appetite for guys. Instinctively, I know she will eat me up and spit me out. I hardly know her and she is anxious to get it on with me. Incredibly, I contemplate, *How is she with other guys?* In truth, she is much too much for me to handle. What a contradiction between my desire and the reality. I hit the jackpot, and don't know how to spend the money. Mom told me that someday I will meet a girl and I will become breathless and see stars. As the marauder again pounces on me, I say to myself, *This ain't her, this ain't her, this ain't her.* I envision myself as a well-mannered charmer, but I'm also smart enough to know that I am not that charming. No use kidding myself. I entertain the possibility that the girls think we are movers, but they soon find it a misperception. Even though Wolf and I talk the talk and walk the walk, we are still inexperienced teenage virgins.

In this type of situation, old taboos concerning disease and knocking up a girl haunt me. Maybe "haunt me" is too strong. A better way of phrasing the sentence is "protect me" and control my carnal desires. Dad says, "Look at every girl you date as if they are the girl you are going to marry." Now I know what he means. As much as going wherever Fran wants to take me will be a rapturous experience, I instinctively know she isn't the girl for me. Sometimes a guy gets what he wants only to find it's not really what he wants. The adventurous date is an exciting and memorable flop. Fran wants the lead dog of the pack and not a person like me. At best I am puppy chow. So ends my association with the man-eating Fran. Triple damn those nuns.

Toward the end of the year, our class takes a senior class trip to the "Big Apple." For years, war stories of the crazy things other classes have done circulate throughout the school. Wolf, Nick, and I hope to break the dry spell and score big time. You have to give us credit, we aren't lucky, but we are persistent. Everyone pairs up with a girl. Before checking into the hotel, we make arrangements to meet in their rooms later that night. To keep things under control, the girls' rooms are on a different floor than the boys' rooms, and it doesn't take a genius to figure out why. Coach McDuff and Miss Barwell are the chaperones. After screwing around in the room and throwing glass ashtrays out the window onto an adjoining roof, we decide it is time to join the girls. It is one o'clock in the morning and we are confident the coast is clear. I eagerly anticipate a night of wild, unrelenting passion.

McDuff and Barwell aren't as dumb as expected. They don't go to sleep, and they do raid the girls' rooms. All our scheming, planning, and plotting go down the drain as McDuff and Barwell gain entrance to the room. "Well, well," Coach McDuff says. "Who do we have hiding under the sheets?" McDuff yanks the sheets off the bed. Although I am fully clothed, he finds me hiding under the covers of a girl's bed.

"How did I get here?" I confusingly express myself. "Must have been sleep walking." I meekly shrug my shoulders and smile. What else can I do?

"Well, lover boy, it's time to wake up. Now, who could possibly be hiding in the closet? I'll bet it's one of the Three Stooges," comments Barwell, "and since we already nabbed Larry, it's got to be either Curly or Moe."

"Yep," says Coach McDuff, "Curly and Moe or Wolf and Nick, take your pick; they are the same."

That night Nick is literally forced to come out of the closet. Barwell opens the closet door. "Nick, come out," she orders.

"Can't a guy have any privacy," says a belligerent Nick as he grabs the doorknob and closes the door on himself.

"Nick," yells Barwell, "come out of that closet right now."

"Okay, okay," says Nick as he complies with her demands.

"I suppose we better check the bathroom since Moe is still missing," says McDuff. "It seems like someone is taking a shower; should we look?"

Wolf's words are memorable for their brevity and wit. McDuff pulls back the shower curtain, and Wolf nonchalantly stands there smiling as if he has just entered the room. He grins, gingerly waves his hand, and greets the chaperones with a casual "Hi there—what's new?"

Well, we get busted and sent to our room with a stern warning that if we misbehave one more time, they will send us home. And thus ends the precisely planned, but poorly executed, scheme to spend a night with the girls.

As seniors the possibility of an all-night senior prom depends on raising money from the community. Nick, Wolf, and I are on one such collection team. Our team goes door to door and business to business asking for donations. To accomplish soliciting in such a large area requires the use of a car. Uncle Sam is on the Brockway Town Council, and the council sponsors the prom, so I borrow his blue 1949 Ford sedan to collect money. Even by late 1950s standards, the car is considered a disaster, but a car is a car.

We are doing rather well in our efforts and decide to canvas houses further out of town. Traveling down an old, twisty dirt road at a reasonable rate of speed, I suddenly come upon a hairpin turn and the car starts to skid on the loose gravel. The car lurches to a sudden stop, but the sideward momentum of the vehicle keeps it going. As if in slow motion the car slowly tips over and comes to rest on its side. "Is everyone okay," I ask.

"Yeah, I'm okay," answers Wolf, "but I'd be a lot better if Nick got his ass out of my face."

I frantically reach and turn off the ignition, because in most movies the turned-over car explodes. I quickly look around. In stark contrast to my behavior, Nick and Wolf are laughing like hyenas. Some situations aren't funny—are these guys insane? We wiggle out through a window, push the car back onto its four wheels, and to my surprise it starts. The passenger side front door is caved in a little, and I think if I take the car to a service station, they can easily pop the damaged door back in place. It is a great idea; then no one will ever know.

I drive to the local Chevy garage, get out of the car, walk to the service area, and tap the mechanic on the shoulder. "Excuse me, mister, can I talk to you? Can you take the dent out of this door?"

"Listen, kid, there is no way I can immediately repair it. I'm busy right now. Make an appointment and bring the car back some other day," he snaps. This is a big disappointment.

"Can't you just push the door out so it looks okay?" I plead in a groveling voice.

"What part of 'no' don't you understand, kid?"

"It is all over. Surely Uncle Sam will kill me," I tell Wolf and Nick. I mull over the idea of fleeing to Canada, but soon abandon the plan as an impractical solution to a complex problem. "Well, there's only one thing left to do," I sigh. "Go home and tell Uncle Sam."

I dread the moment. When caught with my hand in the cookie jar, I can only smile, remove my hand graciously, and say sorry. The sad part is I am caught with my hand in that damnable cookie jar too often. The trepidation overwhelms me. On the edge of despair and with my heart pounding, I approach Uncle Sam. Holding my breath I look him in the eyes. "I got some good news and some bad news to tell you. The good news is we collected forty dollars—huh, and the bad news is I wrecked your car."

To my surprise he isn't angry. "Did anyone get hurt?" Uncle Sam inquires. He glances out the window. "Okay, I'll take care of it." What a relief. I told him the bad news and I am still alive.

At school the next day, we are heroes, and a topic of discussion among the students. Our tip-over turns into an embellished story about rolling the car over. In some of the stories my unwelcome screw-up is cast as a group of young boys surviving a serious accident. People continually ask, "Are you all right? Did you get hurt?" and a series of other irrelevant mundane questions. Me, I just want to forget about it and move on.

I view the senior all-night prom as an anti-climactic gala. Unfortunately, the girl I want to take is not permitted to go with me—you know, the Catholic and Italian thing. For convenience, I ask Debbie, the yearbook co-art director who has a crush on Wolf. It is annoying knowing the chances of scoring with her are zero. I don't even get a nudge. At best, the prom is a date of mutual convenience. The non-passionate good night kiss is more like a good night peck, and that's all I get. The next day at school, I meet Wolf in the hall. "Wolf, Debbie sure didn't score big in my hit parade. Now I know why you're not interested in her. Somebody needs to stoke that girl's fire, but it isn't going to be me."

"Yep, you would have been better off going out on a date with a nun." Wolf chuckles. "Live and learn."

Dates of convenience have their limitations. The expectations do not live up to the reality of the event.

About mid-year, Wolf and I start to apply to colleges. I haven't the foggiest idea of what I want to do. Wolf and I feel fortunate, because the dreaded SATs are not a requirement for college. We both take the Indiana State Teachers College exam, and Nick takes the exam for Lockhaven State Teachers College. Nick doesn't do well and takes another exam for a job at the glass factory. Indiana State Teachers College accepts Wolf and me. Attending college is an unwritten family expectation and I meet that expectation. The prospect of college excites me. My parents are pleased and Mom congratulates me. "Good going, Jimmy." Dad treats me as if it is his expectation and never voices approval or disapproval. He's a tough nut to crack.

CHAPTER 19

THE HORSE LADY

A bell can never be unrung, and I can never undo stupid mistakes already made. I'll be the first to admit an unforgettable mistake made near the end of my senior year. I rationalize it in this manner. I have a bag of marbles, and every day I take one out. When I lose all my marbles, I agree to go on a blind date with Nick. What a looney-toon decision. Aunt Freda's advice should be heeded. In one of our many conversations, in which I mostly listen, she says, "Always be honest and sincere even though your intention is to lie."

"You mean that I should never lie unless I'm telling the truth?" I pause and add, "So if I'm going to be a phony, be sincere about it?"

For the slightest moment Aunt Freda processes my comments, swallows, and says, "Yes, yes, now you understand; always be truthful when you lie."

Most of the time I don't comprehend Aunt Freda's advice, but now I finally understand. Nick has found a nice-looking but fairly wild girl from Falls Creek, and she won't go out with him unless her girlfriend accompanies her. Even though an adventurous girl, she wants the security of a girlfriend. What the heck, what do I have to lose? Maybe I'll get lucky, and maybe this babe will be something special. Reluctantly I agree to go along to keep the girlfriend busy.

We pick up the girls in Nick's Nash and drive to DuBois for a snack. I sit in the backseat and Nick is in front. On an attractiveness scale of one to ten, Nick's girl is a six. My date is indeed special. She is a solid minus one.

"Are you a senior at Dubois High School," I ask.

"No, I don't need no school," she abruptly answers.

"That's interesting," I say and then silently stare out the window. There is nothing remarkable or alluring about my blind date, except she isn't blind. My first impression is that she doesn't take pride in her appearance. Cheap shower flip-flops expose her black, crusty gypsy heels. Poor dental hygiene further degrades her large, rotund, and unattractive body. I muse, *Geez, lady, I may not be Clark Gable, but the least you can do is comb your scraggly hair.* As an added bonus she smells like the inside of a barn. My oh my, this is not a good day. I sense she really doesn't want to be on this date. In all fairness, I think we both want to be somewhere else. The unpleasant news is that calling her mediocre in intellect is a compliment. The good news is that she is breathing without assistance. Whatever the situation there is always something positive to comment about.

After our snack, Nick starts driving and puts his arm around his date. They snuggle closely as if they are Siamese twins. It looks like only one person is sitting in the driver's seat. Their cuddly closeness concerns me. Nick is not the best of drivers and numerous times he is downright careless, especially when distracted, and he is distracted. Nick and I have had many close calls, and he dismisses them with the same nonchalant phrase: "Don't worry, a miss is as good as a mile." When fear lodges in my stomach, excuses aren't relevant or reassuring. Anyway, I relax and reluctantly put my arm around my date, but only out of politeness. "What are you doing?" she asks.

"Oh nothing," I defensively reply and withdraw my arm. "Just trying to be friendly."

"Well, don't get any bright ideas, buster."

I pray to God that fleas or other infectious critters are not infesting her body. Mother's lecture about brushing my teeth, changing my underwear, and other hygiene tips are appropriate for this girl. Certainly her family would be embarrassed if she had to go to the hospital. I have no carnal craving to conquer her fleshy virtue.

Nick drives to the Catholic cemetery, and travels as far back in the cemetery as possible. The hot June night has a waning moon that casts dark blue-gray shadows from the tombstones. Ah, fresh air. We get out of the muggy car. A quick survey reassures me that creatures from the movies featuring the living dead are not residing in the vicinity. On the other hand, some of the chicks from *The Night of the Living Dead* look better in their afterlife than my live date. Nick fetches a blanket from the trunk of his car and heads out among the tombstones. "See you later," he flippantly announces as he and his date disappear into the darkness.

"Huh, what? Uh, Nick wait," I plead. That damn Nick stiffs me. He planned ahead, but he didn't share his plan with me. What a predicament. Here I am, stuck with a girl I have no particular interest in. I ask myself, *What would a gentleman do in this situation?*, so I start a conversation. For ten minutes I try to initiate a conversation and am about to give up when I hit upon something of interest to her. "Oh, so you like horses." Her interest is horses, and I immediately tag her with the name "Horse Lady." A fitting name when combined with her compelling barnyard odor. She talks and talks about horses, and I feign disingenuous interest in her conversation. She is completely, totally, and mercilessly one-dimensional. I interrupt, "You really do like horses, don't you," in a vain attempt to sidetrack her conversation.

"Yes, horses are my life." She pauses and quickly continues her narrative. Once started, she will not stop.

"Oh my God," I quietly moan, "I'm going to inadvertently learn more about horses than I ever care to know." Her irrational predisposition for horses needs curtailed, but how? Morgan horses, Clydesdale horses, Arabian horses, and any other of the thousand breeds are included in the monologue. *For Christ's sake,* I mentally scream, *will ya shut up?* My civility, insincerity, and attempt to politely ingratiate myself with the Horse Lady are my downfall. The rambling monologue is undeniably my fault. I should never try to be a nice guy and fake sincere interest. Aunt Freda, why didn't I listen to you? Maybe I am wrong. Maybe Mother did raise a fool.

The people under the tombstones must be wildly laughing and rolling over in their graves at my preposterous situation. I look to the heavens and prayerfully ask: "Why, God, do you punish me like this? What heinous sin did I commit to deserve such terrible retribution? No mere mortal deserves punishment on such an apocalyptic scale." When life is at its darkest, when all seems lost, when I think it can't get any worse—it usually does. I perch myself on top of Joseph Saraphini's tombstone, bombarded by mind-numbing horse dialogue. My thoughts drift to the guy buried in the grave. "Hey, buddy, do you want to trade places for an hour?" Suddenly, giggling noises escape from the darkness, and to my delight smiling Nick and his date emerge from the shadows. "Well, that was good," Nick says and winks. "How are you two doing? I knew you'd be happy." He snickers.

"Great, Nick, I'll always remember you for your thoughtfulness." My encounter with the Horse Lady and her discourse on equine proclivity have shut down my testosterone production. Someday it will regenerate and the desire for the opposite sex will gradually return.

Well, partner, I have to tell you I can't wait to saddle up and charge out of that cemetery. Yeah, the sanctity of the graveyard was violated and God adequately punished me, so let's call it even-steven. As the Nash gallops out of the cemetery I only recall the Lone Ranger's famous words to express joy, "Hi-Ho, Silver, away." I never tell anyone about the embarrassing date, but Nick does, and for that I'll never forgive him. To my delight, the Horse Lady is never seen again. Nevertheless, every time I pass a barn, memories of her emerge. The encounter with Horse Lady is one of those things I want to giddy-up and forget.

Never again do I go on another blind date. On the upside, I sometimes reflect back to my feeble attempt at establishing a relationship with the Horse Lady and mutely have a raucous belly laugh. This is one misadventure that I can't blame on those damn Republicans. I completely understand Aunt Freda's advice and never again lie unless I tell the truth. The one consolation is that I now have a better appreciation of horses.

CHAPTER 20

THE SUMMER OF TRANSITION

To get along in life I continually adapt, but I'm uncomfortable with change. The older I get the more complex the changes become. Wolf and I apply for temporary summer employment at the Brockway Glass Factory. In the interim, I wait and hope to get called to work. During our waiting period Nick and Wolf hatch a brainstorm. "We are going to go on an excursion to Conneaut Lake," Nick announces.

"And when will this event take place?" I ask.

"This week," Wolf informs me.

I raise the question, "How are we going to get there, fellows?"

"Don't you fret one iota; we got it all planned out," says Wolf.

Oh boy, Wolf and Nick planning something. This I gotta see.

Conneaut Lake is an amusement park located forty miles south of Erie, Pennsylvania. We are people of little means and the logistical question is "how." On his farm Wolf has an old black 1951 Chevy pickup truck. The day before the excursion, he drives to Nick's house and they construct a makeshift cap. Maybe Nick did learn something in his four years of shop classes. A wood frame, clad with a cardboard top and sides, are used in its construction. It's functional, not beautiful. One additional problem, what if it rains? Cardboard won't hold up in a downpour.

Our trip begins early the next morning, by way of State Route 28 to Brookville. Wolf drives, and Nick and I lounge in the truck bed of our pleasure palace. On the outskirts of Brookville, we spot a farm tractor covered with a canvas tarp. The tractor shouts, "Stop, I have a canvas tarp—do you want it?" Hallelujah, either God or the Devil provides a solution to a rainy day predicament. To avoid an ethical dilemma, we credit God. Wolf pulls to the side of the road and backs the truck up to the tractor. Before I can say, "Oh boy, a canvas tarp," we are out of the truck cutting it loose. Quick as a wink, it is removed and put it in the bed of the truck. This time we pull a clean caper. We drive through Brookville and are on our way to Clarion when a guy behind us furiously blinks his lights and motions us to pull over. Implausible and irrational as it sounds, we are good citizens and comply. A huge, gruff man in bib overalls gets out of his pickup truck and lumbers toward us. He sternly drawls: "Youse boys seem to have taken sumpin that belongs to me." We say nothing. "Give it back before I blow youse asses to kingdom come," he says, clutching his shotgun. The look in his eyes makes me think he's serious. "Ya see, boys, I don't put up with your kind of crap. There won't be much left of youse for the cops if I don't get my tarp back right now." The angry farmer, with shotgun in hand, stares at us and continues to give us hell.

"Whadda ya think we should do?" asks Nick.

"What do you mean, what should we do?" I exclaim. "Are you crazy or something? Give him the damn tarp." We quickly throw out the tarp and he takes it. The clear sky signals it is not going to rain, so we continue our journey.

Somewhere past Clarion we spot two young kids hitchhiking. Nick yells through the back window, "Let's pick up those guys."

"Ah Nick, what are you up to now?" I shout. "Please, Nick, no more screwing around. Almost getting shot is enough excitement for one day."

Wolf is driving, and he pulls over and the boys eagerly jump in the back with us. Nick is wearing his black leather motorcycle jacket and tight Levi blue jeans. He looks like a poor man's version of Marlon Brando in *The Wild One*. We greet the boys, and Nick immediately starts acting like a lunatic madman character from a James Cagney gangster movie. Naturally, I play along with him. I can't help myself. "Hey guys, I'm really glad to meet ya," I remark. The boys smile and politely nod.

"Where ya headin'? Ah, don't worry, it doesn't matter; just ride with us," says Nick. "We're gonna have a lot of fun. I need some cash. Let's go pull a heist at the next store we come to."

Oh no, where is Nick going with this? I don't want to be a store bandit. Nevertheless, I continue playing the gangster roll. "For Christ's sake, don't you ever get tired of holding up those damn stores? What are you, some kind of pervert? Why dontcha try one of them there gas stations," I bellow. "I'm tired of knocking off those goddamn nickel-dime stores."

"God, you're getting awful picky—ya on the rag or sumpin," says Nick. The look of fear in the boys' eyes escalates at a rate directly proportional to the increasingly feral rhetoric. Nick continues his verbal shenanigans and gangster-like threats against humanity. "I gotta better idea. Maybe we can beat someone up. Ya know, like stomp them a few times once we get 'em down. That's always a lotta fun," Nick suggests as he runs the blade of his hunting knife through his fingers. "Damnit, Nick, settle down or we'll take you back to the prison so ya can be with all your weirdo friends. Those idiots paroled you too soon. You need treatment. You're a damn psycho. Those nut doctors don't know squat about crazy people." I turn to the two boys, smile, and reassuringly say, "Honest, guys, he's got a few screws loose, but he's harmless. I'm pretty sure that he took his medications today, didn't you, Nick?"

"They'll never take me back there alive," Nick dramatically proclaims. "I'll never let them put me in that cage again." Nick's pompous oratory is better than any gangster movie character. He changes his tone and calmly says to the boys, "Youse guys look like pretty good guys. Do ya wanna join in? We could have a lotta fun. Whadda ya say?" The boys' lips quiver and they nervously shake their head no. "Ya mean ya don't want to join our gang? What's wrong with youse boys?" Nick asks in a threatening tone. The boys sit motionless. I'm sure they think fanatical Nick is going to harm them. As the truck approaches a stop sign Wolf slows down to a crawl. In the blink an eye, the two frantic boys bolt from the truck and run across a cornfield. Deer can't run that fast. One boy stumbles and falls, but the other keeps running, never bothering to look back. If I knew those kids, I would tell them I'm sorry, but maybe they do learn a lesson about taking rides from strangers. We are harmless, but they have no way of knowing if Nick is for real, and of course neither do I.

The amusement park on the lake has many familiar rides, but an exciting and frightening ride we have never experienced before is the wooden roller coaster. Tossing, plummeting, and throwing us in every possible direction, it definitely tests my ability to tolerate extreme forces. I love the stomach-wrenching experience and ride the roller coaster until I run short of cash. We consume a plethora of hot dogs, drinks, and other amusement park food in a greedy manner. The Tilt-a-Whirl is my nemesis. After eating the greasy food, nausea inevitably results from the spinning. Later that evening we drive home with a pocket full of war stories.

The prospect of college creates a unique challenge. Initially, neither Wolf nor I has much money. Finally, the phone call from the Brockway Glass Company arrives. I am called to work at the plant. On the first day the foreman gathers the new employees together. We are called "gooney birds." A gooney bird is a flightless bird. Like a gooney bird, they know I am only a summer employee and will never become a full-time factory worker. The gruff foreman takes an accepting deep breath as he looks disdainfully at his new temporary employees. He isn't overjoyed and doesn't particularly like this part of his job. "Listen up, you guys," he orders. "Don't piss up my back and try to convince me it's raining. You ain't the first batch of gooney birds I've worked with, and you ain't gonna be the last." He pauses, looks at each of us, and sternly instructs, "Just do your work and we'll get along fine. Do ya understand? I'll call your name and you'll be assigned to group one or group two. James DeAngelo—group one, Wolf McGuire—group two," and so on until every gooney bird stands in one of two groups.

Temporary employees are assigned either to the yard crew or as all-around jacks on the conveyer belts. I am assigned to the yard crew. A factory is an intimidating place where inexperienced kids obtain a real-world education. The full-time plant employees treat us well, as long as we do our jobs. As expected we are at the bottom of the factory food chain. If I want to work, I must join the Glass Bottle Blowers Association union. No matter what I earn, the union gets their share, but I don't care.

Intelligence need not be displayed to do the work. The only prerequisite is to follow directions and complete the assigned job. Initiative and ambition are not a requirement, but compliant behavior is. Factory work makes me aware of my ignorance about the real world. I rapidly learn the well-established pecking order, and adhere to factory protocol. The foreman of the yard crew assigns me a different job every day, whereas an all-around jack stands at the end of a conveyor belt stacking endless cases of bottles and jars fed by a machine with an insatiable appetite for reproducing identical glass products. Wolf does all-around jacking, but I am lucky and work mostly on the yard crew. The foreman likes me and treats me well. Dad's teaching me to keep my mouth shut until I size up a situation works well at the plant. I sweep floors, clean bathrooms, tar roofs, and do any other task assigned. One day I am down in some dark, dank hole mucking up unbearable black gooey stuff, and the next day I'm on top of a glass kiln sweeping off dust and debris. I never know what job will be assigned.

Every day produces a surprise, but if the boss doesn't like a person, it is an unpleasant surprise. The job isn't bad, but to spend my entire life in a factory seems unthinkable. To punctuate the importance of education, an event occurs that cements the lunacy of plant life. The foreman says, "DeAngelo, I want you to start today by sweeping off the tops of these three ovens. Don't raise a lot of dust, and make sure you don't sweep the dirt on the guys working below. Here is a pail and a shovel. Put all the stuff you sweep up into the pail; do you understand?"

"Consider it done, boss." Sometimes I feel like Stepin Fetchit in the 1930s movies, but calling him boss is a sign of respect that massages his ego. When sweeping the top of the huge, hot kiln, I smell something burning. The smell has a pungent but unfamiliar odor. "Hey, you guys smell something burning down there," I yell to my fellow workers.

"Nothing burning down here except the kiln," a voice answers.

Suddenly, I glance down and the bottom of my thick cork-soled work boots are smoking. That does it; I know then and there whatever it takes, I have to get a college education. At the end of the summer, I clear a total of eighty-two dollars. Since tuition is fifty dollars a semester and room and board is relatively cheap, it means that Wolf and I can afford college life with little financial support from our parents. I take pride in that, because being a man means earning my way in life.

Toward the end of summer, Nick tells me an incredible story that makes our hitchhiking prank modest by comparison. The story is hard to believe, and at first I discount it. Nevertheless, on hot August days the guys do strange things to amuse themselves. Only upon reading a sketchy accounting of the incident in the newspaper, I give the story credibility.

Located in town the Hi Tide bowling alley provides adults and kids with healthy entertainment. If a guy isn't too bright and needs spending money, the job of setting bowling pins is uncontested. One particularly nice but inordinately dull pinsetter is Jim Heeber. Everyone knows him as a harmless teenager. Jim's mashed and flattened thumbs easily identify him as a pinsetter. More times than he wishes to remember, someone careens a bowling ball down the lane as he is setting pins. Catching his fingers between the ball and the pin causes excruciating pain. Except for Jim, pin-setting is not high on anyone's career path.

Jim is a dull but likeable guy, with all the emotions that drive a young guy. He never hurts anyone and is a fairly good citizen. Nick and a bunch of older boys win his confidence and concoct a fraudulent scheme. Nick asks, "Hey, Jim, why don't ya come with me tonight? We're going to have some fun with Heber."

"And what is your definition of fun?" I inquire. "What do you have in mind? He's harmless and he's a pretty nice guy."

"You know, just fun," Nick answers in an elusive manner. "Aw, just come along. We're just going to mess with him a little, maybe scare him."

"Nah, can't make it tonight." I wink and say, "Maybe some other time. I got other plans. You know what I mean." As long as Nick thinks I have a hot date, he won't insist. I don't have anything planned, but I don't want to mess with Jim.

They convince Jim that they can fix him up with a hot female, and for the first time in his life, he will get a little. The guys make arrangements to pick him up after work and drive to the girl's house.

The story Nick tells is a classic small-town tale. Off into the far horizon beyond the town limits and into the wilderness they drive. Unknown to Jim, the house is one of the many abandoned shacks in the middle of the woods. He sits in the bed of the old pickup truck with the guys, talking and joking as they navigate the twisty back roads. As planned, one of the pranksters is waiting in the shack with a double-barrel shotgun. Outside of Brockway a person can easily wander aimlessly for twenty or more miles. As the pickup truck approaches the house, the driver turns off the engine and extinguishes the lights. Nick says, "Okay, this is it. Jimmy, all you have to do is go up to the house and she'll let you in. From then on it's up to you. By the way, here's a pack of rubbers so you can dip your wick without getting her knocked up. Go get her, tiger."

With smiling confidence, innocent Jim starts walking toward the house. As he approaches a dim light flickers inside and a man bursts through the door shouting, "Youse guys think you're going to come out here again and screw my daughter."

"No, you must be mistaken," panicked Jim yells.

"It ain't going to happen again," he continues bellowing, "'cause I'm gonna kill the whole goddamn bunch of ya." At that precise, preplanned moment, he fires two bursts of the shotgun in the air. "I'll get all of you—you rotten sons of bitches," he shouts. As planned everyone feigns running from the house, but Jim does not fake it. He gets out in front of the stampeding pack and takes the lead. Off he runs faster than any of nature's four-footed creatures. As far as Nick knows, he keeps running and never bothers to look back, because when the laughter subsides, he is nowhere in the area. After searching for a couple of hours, the guys decide to go back to town. They have the good sense to report Jim lost to the local authorities.

The next morning the town folk form a search party. Happy to say, they do find Jim. He made about eight miles in the dark. He is a little scratched and hungry, but none the worse for wear. Jim asks, "Did the rest of the guys get out of there without getting killed?"

The police chief answers, "Yeah, Jim, they're in good shape but they ain't gonna be for long."

The boys get a tongue-lashing before the town's justice of the peace, but it is not as punitive as it might have been. Jim's adventure becomes local folklore. He continues as a pinsetter for many years until the Hi Tide bowling alley is destroyed by fire in the 1960s. Thus, the summer of transition comes to an end.

III.

THE COLLEGE YEARS

CHAPTER 2 1

COLLEGE, HERE WE COME

College is an adventure into an unknown world. Wolf and I request to be roommates at Indiana State Teachers College. We receive official notification that our room is located in Whitmyre Hall and meals are served three times a day at the dining facility. Whitmyre Hall is a three-story men's dormitory with common bath facilities. The building is a cookie-cutter replica of the buildings on hundreds of other college campuses. Finally, the ever-present spying on the adult world is behind us. Each building has an adult dormitory mother occupying one apartment suite. Throughout the dorm a scattering of resident hall student advisors live in cubbyhole rooms. This is the student governance system for dorm life.

The odds of not getting the only apartment across the hall from the dorm mother are overwhelmingly in our favor. Nevertheless, ours is the only dorm room, in an isolated hallway, across from the infamous Ma Butler. It has to be those damn Republicans who did this. "Wolf, there is bad, badder, and baddest luck, and we rolled the snake eyes of baddest luck."

"Good morning, boys, I am Mrs. Butler and I want to welcome you to Whitmyre Hall. I take it you boys have read the rules and regulations for campus living? I expect you to follow them to the letter."

With tongue-in-cheek I say, "Oh yes, we have meticulously read them all." Initially there is a thin veneer of a smile. This is the last time she displays a hint of hospitality. Instantly I sense bad karma. By my calculations, she is about 3,000 years old. With wire-rimmed glasses halfway down the bridge of her nose, she stares at us with accusing intensity. Her black penetrating eyes perforate my being as if I am guilty of committing vile and despicable acts. Well, so much for positive first impressions. Honest, I try to appease her, but it doesn't matter. In her mind, we are the rowdy recidivists upon whom all blame for disturbing her complacent world is focused. Yeah, we smoke pipes and make noise, but compared to other guys in the dorm, we aren't bad. Out of sight, out of mind is a good saying, but we are in her sight and on her mind. The college requires freshmen to live in the dorm one year, so we cannot escape the silver-haired beast.

Wolf registers as a science major, and I register as an art major. Why not develop the creative part of my personality? Two weeks into the first semester, I decide to change majors from art to science. "Wolf, those guys in my art class are effeminate fruitcakes. I don't know if I can take it; they live in their own weird world." I am creative, but not that creative. The one positive thing about my short stay as an art major is that the chicks are outrageously gorgeous.

In 1957, the Russians launch the first satellite, and science, not art, is the hot area of study. Making a decent living as a science major will be more lucrative than as an art major. The tragedy of switching majors is that I don't see another good-looking girl in class for the next four years. By the time I get to the class selection process, the easy courses are full. As a second choice, College Chemistry is placed on my freshman course list—my favorite subject. The teacher administers a pre-test focusing on the simple facts about the periodic table of elements. Thanks to my lack of interest in chemistry, I can't identify the elements. The professor probably thinks I am putting him on. Even by osmosis, some knowledge should have been absorbed.

Somehow I manage. Getting serious about chemistry is like loving an ugly girl—it takes a lot of effort, but it can be done. Feeling sorry and expending energy is nonproductive behavior. Taking charge of the situation requires that terrible "E" word, effort. It's not that I am stupid; it's just that I never apply myself until college. Education cannot create intelligence, nature already took care of that, but my life experiences help compensate for innate academic shortcomings. Initially, I struggle, but now there is a reason to learn.

Knowledge about people is an invaluable commodity. Avoiding dorm life pitfalls is as important as academics. If not dealt with properly, living in a dorm is deleterious to a person's health and well-being. Experience and consequences make me wise to the ways of the world. In my dorm there are naïve loners who are academic winners and social misfits. A lack of life skills makes them easy prey for dorm hustlers. The dorms are filled with such predators.

One nice but naïve kid, named Vince, wants to belong to a group at any price. Wolf and I see him stray and give him a fast lesson in life. "Vince, you know those guys down the hall from you?" Wolf says.

"Yes, they are really nice guys."

"No, no, Vince, you really don't understand what you're getting yourself into," I warn. "Vince, it is in your best interest to put some distance between you and them."

"What do you mean?" Vince asks in an astonished voice. "I don't understand."

"Mark my words, Vince, they'll do you harm," I repeat and conclude my unwelcome advice. I liken him to a protected person lacking immunity to the appallingly bad things that come along in life. It doesn't take long for the hustlers to gain Vince's confidence and talk him into participating in a "circle jerk." Wolf and I aren't rubes, and much too wise to have anything to do with these guys, but not Vince. One night Vince is in a dorm room with five other guys. Each throws five dollars into a pot at the center of their circle. The guys in the circle pull down their trousers and underwear and with their tools hanging out say, "The first guy to cum wins the pot." As soon as the lights are off, the yank-off competition commences. The hustlers slap the sides of their legs, giving that flesh-on-flesh sound, but Vince doesn't know that. "I won, I won!" yells Vince as the lights are flicked on. The humiliating laughter must have stayed with that poor kid the rest of his life, because his reputation on campus as the object of a circle jerk does. "Wolf, you heard about Vince, didn't you?" I remark.

"Yeah," answers Wolf, "maybe now he understands." Neither Wolf nor I would do this to another human being. We both laugh, but think humiliating Vince a cruel joke. He is a nice kid and doesn't deserve such degrading treatment.

At our initial orientation in the auditorium, the dean directs, "Look to the student on the right and the student on the left." *What gives here,* I think as I dutifully look. He then emphatically announces, "Two out of three of you will not be here to graduate."

"Wolf," I whisper, "their goal in life is to flunk us out, and we haven't even got started yet."

He may as well hit me over the head with a baseball bat. Oh boy, do his comments make a lasting impression. A hard-nosed professor sums our situation up in one succinct statement. "If you think you are indispensable, put your finger in a cup of water and observe the hole that remains when you pull it out." An extremely powerful and graphic word picture delivered to anxious students. The courses we fear, dread, and despise are Communications I and Communications II. Comm I and Comm II, as they are called, are tough five-credit-hour courses taken in sequence, and each proves a test of a student's true grit. Together, the two courses make or break a freshman. To fail Comm I as a freshman means failing one-third of my total credit hours, and that is a near fatal blow to maintaining a decent grade point average.

I struggle through Communications I and II and receive a well-deserved mark of C. I still don't know the difference between a gerund and a dangling participle. In jest, I tell Wolf, "Watch out for those dangling participles hanging from a tree when driving. They can do a lot of damage to the car."

"Almost as bad as sideswiping a stupid oxymoron," Wolf jests.

I guess some of what old Canary Legs taught did sink in. A grade of C is a respectable grade. "Wolf, got my grade report today in the mail. Did you get yours? How'd you make out?" I ask.

"As best as I can figure, it is a 2.0," says Wolf.

"That's what I got too. We're both some kind of genius," I exuberantly proclaim. Halleluiah, there'll be no academic probation for us. The college has a waiting line of students ready and willing to take my place. If I don't achieve a 2.0 grade point average, I will be placed in the dungeon of academic probation. If I still do not produce a 2.0 average during the following semester, I will be executed and tossed out of school.

Who says you can't teach young dogs new tricks? I'm ill prepared for college, but quickly adapt. All those sleeping brain cells are suddenly jarred awake. "Ya know, Wolf, it's not how you fall down that counts, but how you pick yourself up."

"You're right 'cause we've been doing a lot of picking ourselves up this year."

Wolf and I go from never bringing books home in high school, to studying nightly for hours. Neither of us has study skills, but in time we learn to study efficiently. I am determined not to be a student who flunks out.

In many ways, bunking with a person is like being married. You never truly know a person until you live with them, and there is a lot of truth to it. I inadvertently discover one of Wolf's little idiosyncrasies the first week in school. He listens to classical jazz and he loves to fall asleep to jazz music. "Wolf, I got to tell you something. I'm sorry, but I can't stand jazz." I need either quiet or a hissing steam locomotive outside my window to fall asleep. To me, jazz has no beginning and no end. It just keeps going on and on and on, something akin to listening to my heartbeat. We have a little talk and Wolf graciously agrees not to play the radio at bedtime.

"Jim, there is something I have to tell you. I don't like sleeping with the window open."

"Fair is fair," I reply. So in turn I capitulate on that bone of contention. We are easygoing and accommodate each other as much as possible.

For relaxation, every night between 7:00 and 8:00 we visit the Student Union located in Whitmyer Hall. The only reason to take a breather is that the girls are permitted to leave their dorms between those hours. I never meet nifty chicks at the Student Union. This is probably because the interesting girls are in their dorms studying and not because I lack charisma, but there is the possibility that I'm wrong. No action means retreating back to the room to continue studying. "Is Ma's door open?" Wolf asks.

"Let me peek out and check. No, it's closed, the beast is hibernating," I report.

"Good, let's light up." We light our pipes packed with a sweet, aromatic blend of cherry tobacco and Mixture 79. Most nights a smoky haze permeates the room and the soothing sweet smell of the tobacco invades every part of my being. Neither of us is a serious smoker, but it is fun to sit like big shots puffing on a pipe. No wonder Ma Butler accuses us of smoking; we smell like a plantation tobacco factory.

All freshmen take either Physical Education or ROTC courses. I had enough PE classes in high school and make a no-brainer decision to enroll in ROTC. In 1959, I have to contend with the draft after college. "Wolf, we're gonna spend four years going to college and then be drafted into the Army. All this education and we will be earning less than seventy bucks a month as a draftee."

"Doesn't seem fair to me," Wolf comments. "There is an alternative."

Wolf and I decide it is better to go into the Army as officers than as enlisted persons. Besides, officers make more money and we are tired of being broke. Twice a week, on Tuesdays and Thursdays, we dress in our green uniforms and, along with other cadets, parade around campus. Drill and ceremony are fun, and the uniform does provide the perception of belonging to a special group. Along with marching, academic military courses are required three days a week. Due to the introduction of tactical atomic battlefield weapons, the onus of Army doctrine centers on the "Pentomic Division." Fortunately, the concept never becomes operational in a battlefield scenario. All the time studying about how to avoid becoming crispy critters is wasted—thank God.

A back-home saying is, "Once you dip your feet in Toby Creek, you'll never leave Brockway." The old saying conveniently omits that Toby Creek is a polluted, acidic stream. The reason you can't leave is that once you dip your feet, they could possibly fall off.

Maintaining ties with our old lifestyle never diminishes. Throughout the four years at Indiana, Wolf and I spend weekends at home. Only one problem—how do we get home? Even though Dad can afford to provide me with a car, he never permits me to have one while attending college. The guy is a genius when it comes to understanding what is good for kids. If I have a car, a plethora of ingratiating car buddies will hang around to distract me. Car buddies are an odd life form. God forbid the car breaks down, because you not only lose the vehicle, but also the pseudo-buddies. Wolf and I don't have to contend with such primitive behavior since the leeching relationship is predicated on the use of an automobile.

As a solution to our transportation dilemma, we take up the art of hitchhiking. Hitchhiking is both an art and a science. The first time we stand by the highway wearing our high school varsity B jackets and blue jeans. As cars pass we stand and stand and stand, with thumbs pointed in the proper direction. Rides do not come easy. After several weekends I realize our dismal hitchhiking technique isn't successful. Eventually someone feels sorry for us and picks us up, more often than not some crazy kid wanting to show what his car will do.

"Wolf, we're not getting rides. What are we doing wrong? There's gotta be a better way." I give it some thought and a bulb lights in my head. "Wolf, I finally figured it out. It's simple—people don't want to pick up high school kids. We need to market ourselves so that people want to pick us up. If the TV guys can do it to sell their products, why can't we?" The plan calls for a change in tactics and a change in perception management.

Perception and reality are not mutually exclusive or inclusive; they are what the person manipulates them to be. I speculate that by looking like typical Joe College persons, we will increase the probability of hitching a ride. We prepare to test our hypothesis. The first thing is to ditch our varsity B jackets. We wear khaki-colored trench coats, brown semi-dress trousers, put on our reading glasses, and start smoking pipes at our hitchhiking station. As frosting on the cake, we carry a small suitcase with a big sign, BROCKWAY, taped on the side to announce our destination.

"Ya gotta be kidding me. Where in the hell do you come up with all this crap?" Wolf asks.

Amazingly, the plan works, and it works extremely well. We hit the hitchhiking jackpot. The scheme even endears us to little old ladies as they stop and offer a ride. Looking like everybody's son or nephew attending college is the answer to our quest. From this time on, hitching a ride is never a problem.

There are basic rules for hitching. The master rule is: always ask drivers where they are going and never accept a ride that will deposit us in the middle of nowhere. Generally, we try to get a ride from our corner in Indiana to at least Punxsutawney, and preferably DuBois. At Punxsy and DuBois we scout the best corners to continue to our final destination. The last rule learned is never accept a ride with young screwball, lunatic kids. The beauty of hitchhiking is saving a bundle of money, whereas the frightening part is the danger of getting picked up by weird people.

I must tell you about the one and only time we feel lucky in our travels. Nick offers Wolf and me a ride back to college, and we eagerly accept. Though Nick is still a good friend, he has ample opportunity to expand his skills as a cool cat who can beat the system. His 1953 red Nash is still running and he acquires a second "Indian" motorcycle. Nick picks us up at my house and we start our trip to Indiana. Halfway along our journey he asks, "Anyone hungry? Let's stop and get something to eat."

"There's a nice mom-and-pop diner about a mile up the road," Wolf informs us.

"Good, we'll stop there," says Nick, "and, guys, don't worry about the bill. Order whatever you want." We are thankful that Nick will pick up the tab. We eat our sandwiches and are ready to leave. Nick says, "Come with me," which we dutifully do.

Nick gets up and I ask, "Don't we have to stop and pay before we leave?"

"Just keep walking and don't you worry about a thing, Jimbo," Nick instructs, intently focusing on the exit. He walks at a fast pace and as he approaches the cash register, he accelerates his velocity and scoots out the door with Wolf and me closely following. In less than a minute, we are in the car, traveling down the road. Wolf and I laugh nervously as we look behind for either the cops or the owner. I am relieved that no one chases us, but I realize I can't risk my future on such foolish nickel-dime schemes. "Wolf, imagine, placing our entire future in jeopardy for a few lousy bucks—such craziness. I don't know about you, but that's the last time I'll let anything so stupid happen again." Wolf nods his head in an affirming manner. From that day forward we never accept a ride from Nick; hitchhiking is safer.

Upon attaining a respectable college grade point average, I ease up on the studies and devote more time to my social life. Wolf and I know that we have to get out of the dorms. Ma Butler and her clones hang around like black clouds and they drive me crazy. The opportunity arrives during my sophomore year when the fraternity rush period begins. Wolf tries out for football, but never puts forth the effort to play at the college level. His association with football makes him a candidate for the fraternity rushing jocks. The Sigma Deltas are known as the campus animals, and with their jock mentality, they act like animals. Wolf likes them, but he isn't comfortable with them.

Several other fraternities rush us. Getting rushed means attending many parties, some on campus and some off campus. Indiana is a conservative community where everything, including the movie theater, closes on Sunday. On Sunday, it's a great town to sit around and watch clouds form. The town is the last bastion of the old Pennsylvania Blue Laws. Drinking alcoholic beverages is considered a serious offense, and can result in suspension. I am not interested in the Kappa Delta fraternity, but we do attend their beer party at an off-campus site. There is an abundance of alcohol, and many dorm students attend. Wouldn't you know bad luck follows us to college, and a most unthinkable disaster falls upon us.

A bunch of us get caught and have to report to Dean Shnell, the dean of students. Dean Shnell lets us off with a stern warning, but threatens to throw the book at us if we ever get in trouble again. I think the dean is one of those damn righteous Republicans. I know this makes Ma Butler grin, and I hope that as she smiles her dentures drop out. Nice guy, am I not?

CHAPTER 2 2

FRATERNITY TIME FOR THE BOYS

Wolf and I are interested in the Alpha Tau Kappa fraternity. They are the good-time party guys, and we fit in. The Alpha Tau brothers invite us to a first-class rush dinner at the Indiana Lodge, where we receive a beautiful brandy snifter etched with the fraternity's Greek symbols. That impresses us country boys. For a partying fraternity the snifters are symbolic of their image and highly appropriate. During bid time we receive several invitations to be brothers in various fraternities.

"Jim, look at all these invitations; we gotta make a decision. Are we gonna join the same fraternity?" Wolf asks.

"Of course, Wolf, we've come this far together, might as well go for broke."

"All of the fraternities are okay," Wolf remarks, "but one stands out."

"Alpha Tau," I suggest.

Wolf and I decide to pledge Alpha Tau. On bid night, we dress in a jacket with a tie and walk to the Alpha Tau fraternity house.

The brothers stand on the porch, wearing their blue blazers with the white Alpha Tau emblem, and wait for pledges to arrive. As we walk toward the house, they let out a loud cheer, followed by enthusiastic applause. We are welcomed, escorted into the frat house, and attend our pledging ceremony. I receive a blue-and-white pledge ribbon and declare my intentions to become a brother, but I am not a brother until my probationary period is completed. Tradition dictates I must prove myself worthy by means of a prolonged initiation established by generations of undiagnosed mentally ill brothers. After soaking the pledge ribbon in a saturated solution of sugar water and drying it until the ribbon is as stiff as unyielding cardboard, I pin it on my shirt and am now ready to endure my rite of passage.

The sordid details of the initiation process start the next day. Initiation requires my participation in disgusting and degrading activities. One brother, the pledge master, is in charge of the pledge class. At four feet, eleven inches tall, he is known as Big Dick. How he came across such a nickname is never revealed, and I don't push for an explanation. "So, you dickheads want to become brothers. Well, I don't want you in my beloved fraternity. To get into this brotherhood you damn well better prove yourself worthy, and none of you look worthy," Big Dick proclaims.

Wolf whispers, "He doesn't like us."

"Nah, Wolf, the guy's just got a personality disorder. It's called the asshole syndrome." We expand his name to "The Big Dick"—it is more appropriate. I always watch for those short guys, because a little Napoleon lives inside each of them.

As a pledge, I am assigned a mentor brother. I report to Korky Kazamareski daily, something akin to being an indentured servant. Korky, an art major, isn't a bad guy and he doesn't harass me. Nonetheless, the pledging process is composed of animalistic rituals, which neither increase my academic astuteness nor expand my social awareness.

The first ridiculous trial of worthiness includes the Peter Pencil exercise, and it is an amusing challenge. The object of the Peter Pencil is to obtain ten sorority girls' signatures. There is a catch. It is called a Peter Pencil because it is tied to a string and the string runs under my shirt, to under my belt, to under my skivvies, and finishes its journey tied to my manly appendage fondly known as the Peter. If a guy thinks every girl on campus doesn't know where the pencil is attached, he is kidding himself. "Ah, excuse me," I say to a good-looking campus girl, "would you do me the honor of signing my pledge book? I have to get ten girls to sign my pledge book by tonight."

"You must be one of them Alpha Tau pledges," she remarks with a foxy smile. "Be glad to oblige you." She giggles. "You got a pencil or should I use my pen?" she taunts as she winks.

"Oh no, all the signatures must be in pencil." I hand her my pencil and try my best to hide the attached string.

"You mind if I keep the pencil?" she teases.

"Uh, no, I must have the pencil back. I've sorta become attached to it."

"Well, if anything ever *comes up*, let me know and I'll sign it again."

I can easily tell the girls who have been around by the extra tug they give the pencil. Wolf and I do obtain the required signatures and we don't forge them; after all, we are men of honor. Besides meeting a lot of chicks, there is nothing socially redeeming in the assigned task.

In the basement of the fraternity house, the brothers conduct what are euphemistically called pledge parties. They aren't fun parties; they are harassment sessions. In my class there is no paddling of the butt. Nonetheless, the brothers sometimes get carried away and commit acts that make paddling preferable. The advantage of paddling is that it is quick and I can go back to the dorm and study. No matter what the scenario, some rule is violated, and if a rule doesn't exist, one is quickly improvised. Often the brothers knock at our room at midnight and roust us out of bed. Like drill sergeants they order us to run down the middle of the now vacant streets yelling, "Alpha Tau Forever" until we reach the frat house. When we arrive, huffing and puffing, the brothers herd us to the basement and announce we are going to have a pledge party.

The warped minds of college boys conjure up sadistic activities to amuse them. The hot and cold treatment is a standard for breaking the ice and getting things started. "Face the wall," The Big Dick orders. "Now lay down on your back with your legs propped upright against the wall. Pledges, are you ready?"

"Yes, Pledge Master," we holler.

Whitey the Albino and Bull, two obliging brothers, slither up from behind with two pitchers of water—one filled with hot water and the other with ice water. The yellow-eyed, nefarious Whitey moves to my right leg trouser opening, and massive Bull goes to my left leg trouser opening.

"Upon my signal commence with the hot-and-cold treatment," he shouts. The Big Dick commands, "Go," and they simultaneously pour the water down the legs of my pants. As the water works its way to my crotch, my nerves deliver mixed messages to my brain. I pray that the brothers won't get carried away and make the water unreasonably hot or cold. After all, I don't want the family jewels damaged.

During initiation the brothers do stupid things. The primitive part of the brain supersedes rational behavior. Humanity and all the years of evolving into a civil society are flushed down the toilet. I am consumed by a primal culture. An out-of-control brother has the bright idea that pledges will appear more representative if they are painted blue and white, the fraternity's colors. Down to our skivvies we strip, and out come buckets of blue and white paint. The brothers coat our bodies with crude blue-and-white designs, none of which win an award for artistic creativity. As playtime ends we are instructed to hose off and go back to our dorms. Only then do we learn that the brothers made a miscalculation—the paint does not wash off with soap and water. Some stupid brother used oil-based enamel paint for our body art. Whitey the Albino is the chief suspect since he is the most animal-like brother possessing the least mental ability. Carter's has more "Little Liver Pills" than Whitey the Albino has brain cells. Unlike tempera paint, enamel paint clogs our pores and isn't willing to relinquish its grip on our skin.

"This pisses me off," says Wolf.

"Ya know, Wolf, when pledging is over, we should take up a collection and give Whitey the Albino a sun lamp. Maybe he will disappear in a spontaneous combustion reaction when the light rays hit his super-white skin."

"Ya got a point, Jim. That dickhead could be some sort of vampire with a low IQ. His old man should have let him drip into the coal bucket."

"I think he did and that's where Whitey came from," I respond.

We are pissed and spend the evening removing paint with turpentine. Thank God no one suggested using gasoline. Whitey the Albino isn't too bright, and he is a heavy smoker. As unthinkable as it may seem, I can visualize him carelessly flicking a cigarette butt in the direction of a gasoline container.

"I'll keep a keen eye out for that butt-head Whitey," Wolf promises.

It only goes to show that putting a bunch of guys together without rules or limitations is a recipe for disaster. In college, I read *Lord of the Flies* and easily make the connection with the group's aberrant mob behavior.

In keeping with tradition the hose exercise is also crude. The brothers cut six feet from a garden hose and fill it with a liquid concoction. Depending on what is available in the house, the contents vary widely from pledge class to pledge class. The one consistent ingredient is Tabasco sauce. Holding the hose upright in the shape of a U, two pledges are stationed at opposite ends. Each pledge blows into his end until its contents are forced into the other pledge's mouth. The loser has the privilege of drinking the remaining gunk—a gastronomical disaster.

Yes, many nonproductive things are learned during my pledge period. To top off the initiation, the infamous hell night must be endured. Hell night, the last obstacle to becoming a brother, is the pinnacle of non-achievement. The house is converted into a multi-station challenge and each pledge moves through the stations as an individual. The fun starts in the TV room. Goofy brother Buck says, "Take off your socks and stand on the table. Uh, dis is an exercise in trusting. Put on this blindfold." Before being blindfolded, Bull rattles a bucket half filled with glass shards. As I am blindfolded the sound of glass falling out of the bucket onto the floor titillates my imagination. In reality, the sounds are glass shards poured from one container to another, but I'm not supposed to know that. Buck orders, "When I count to three, you will jump off the table." This could be a protracted period because I'm not sure Buck can count to three. I jump, and upon hitting the floor experience sharp objects on the bottom of my feet. Corn flakes feel similar to glass when you think it may be glass.

After the trusting exercise is Station Two, the goldfish station. The Big Dick says, "This is an exercise in obedience." Dad often stated, "If somebody tells you to go jump off a bridge, will you do it?" and the answer is no, unless it is during hell night. "Here is a live goldfish and your job is to swallow the critter," the smiling Big Dick orders. The Big Dick hands me a goldfish. I smile back at him and say thanks. I glance at my squirmy golden-orange victim and think, *You're a goner, buddy.* The first goldfish easily slithers down my throat. The ease of the operation displeases The Big Dick. He doesn't understand that the enemy of good is better. "Here, take another one," he orders and he hands me a second one. Again, I say, "Thank you," and dutifully swallow it, no big thing. I can swallow those critters all night long if necessary. The Big Dick is frustrated and pissed, but he has a limited supply of goldfish and passes me to the next station. My culinary accomplishment is a victory for our pledge class.

After the goldfish station is the raw liver station, and I easily chew and swallow the raw delicacy. This bothers me because I always eat meat cooked well done—I don't want to get a tapeworm. There are rumors that a fraternity at another college did the raw liver routine, and a pledge choked to death. Thank God I chew my food thoroughly before swallowing. Queasiness is not tolerated.

The toilet bowl station requires that, blindfolded, I reach into the smelly toilet, pick up a long, squishy, cylindrical object, squeeze it until it becomes gooey, and eat it. The banana isn't that bad and tastes better than raw liver. After a few stations the distasteful tasks are redundant, and the pattern of events established. Nonetheless, the brothers must have fun, so I play along with their pranks.

The intent of the last station is to throw the pledge out a window. The frat house has internal double-hung windows connecting the old addition to the new addition. Still blindfolded, I feel the breeze coming through the window and hear voices from afar cheering, "Jump, jump!" I know hell night is a ridiculous hoax, but dutifully jump and land on a soft mattress. In reality the embellished folklore is more terrifying than the experience. Hell night enters my repertoire of war stories that are increasingly glorified over the years. The Big Dick, Whitey the Albino, Bull, Buck, and a myriad of other kooky characters welcome and accept us as brothers in the Alpha Tau Kappa fraternity.

Fraternity life releases me from the forced incarceration of dorm life and the intolerable dorm food. I relocate to the frat house and begin a new adventure. Wolf and I find a fresh source of fine cuisine at the Student Union. My palate is titillated with a semi-gourmet meal of a plump hot dog and a Coke for the bargain price of fifteen cents. If money is available I splurge and buy a delicious hot meat loaf sandwich with mashed potatoes for forty-five cents; the Coke is extra. For less than two dollars a day, I gorge myself on the best culinary delights the Student Union has to offer. If I budget closely, I have fifty cents left over by week's end and buy a quart of beer at Lefty Richmond's Tavern.

During my sophomore year the rules for girls are relaxed, and there is always something going on at the Student Union. After all, this is the progressive 1960s. Imagine the challenge of living in an unregulated environment with a group of party animals. More often than not, there are four persons to a room and over thirty brothers in the house. My first room, a poorly insulated back addition, is best described as cold in winter and hot in summer. I room with three other guys. Wolf is assigned a second-floor room. He comments, "I notice your bunkmate drinks a copious amount of alcohol."

"Yes, Wolf, that's true. I'm convinced that at his tender young age, he is an alcoholic. I can't be certain, because I've never see him sober."

"Well, Jim, if you can overlook that one minor character flaw, Saul is a great guy and a great drunk."

Saul has the top bunk and I sleep on the bottom bunk. Like clockwork, he stumbles in every night soused to the gills, climbs in his bunk, lights a cigarette, and falls asleep. Well, I'm not sure if he falls asleep or passes out. After Saul burns up two mattresses, I dread going to sleep. I fear fire, and either he or I has to leave. I discuss my dilemma with Wolf.

"Wolf, the panic of waking up in a smoke-filled room is always on my mind. Saul's character flaw of drinking and smoking can be fatal to my health. I don't want to become a burnt ember or a jar of ashes on someone's fireplace mantel. It's enough to give a guy a nervous breakdown. It sure isn't a good environment for longevity," I jokingly state. The problem is solved when another brother, Bob, replaces Saul. He is a challenge of a different sort. Whereas Saul is passive and easygoing, Bob is an extreme right wing paramilitary guy who thinks the best thing in life is freedom from the government and hunting in the woods. My new roommate has an abrasive personality, akin to sandpaper grating against a person's behind—a polite way of saying he is a pain in the buttocks. His small, scraggly body and thick, round-rim glasses make him hard to miss. I classify him as a small, skinny Napoleon. To make a short story long, the cast of characters in the fraternity is unique, endless, and changing.

A few brothers occasionally go beyond the point of good taste and proper decorum. Linda is a homely coed who is periodically invited to the house to service the brothers. She is available to anyone, and best of all she doesn't charge. "You guys want to try her?" asks Whitey the Albino.

"No, Whitey, I have no desire to participate in getting my wick wet in someone else's baby batter. I'll keep my peter in my pants. There isn't enough booze in the world to make her appealing," I said and Wolf agreed.

"Oh, you guys are crazy—she's a premium broad," Whitey boastfully retorts. Regardless of the opportunity, we wisely choose not to participate. Taking advantage of a poor soul lacking self-respect is not my idea of entertainment. Nonetheless, the possibility exists that she just likes to do the dirty deed.

The biggest night in the house is Wednesday night. That's when Bugs Bunny and Road Runner cartoons are shown on television. In a relatively small room, the brothers crowd around the TV to clap and cheer for Bugs Bunny, Wiley Coyote, Road Runner, and the Tasmanian Devil. It is age-appropriate entertainment for Brother Buck. Yes, we have fun watching the "wascally wittle wabbit" and the stupid coyote do their thing.

There are academic advantages to belonging to the fraternity. For instance, the fraternity's test master maintains an up-to-date file on the latest test given by the professors. A lazy professor who does not change exams every semester is appreciated. I search the files, but none of the exams are science related, because science instructors change their tests often. For all our horsing around, the fraternity maintains one of the best grade point averages on campus.

Alpha Tau is a partying fraternity and on occasion we join in the frivolity. Our motto is "Party hard and party often." Once a year the fraternity throws a special party. Our biggest and best is the Playboy party, sponsored by *Playboy* magazine. *Playboy* provides napkins, coasters, paper cups, and decorations—great advertising at little cost to the company. Outside the house a twenty-five-foot Playboy Bunny is erected, announcing to potential pledges that the Playboy party is about to commence. Wow, me a playboy—Hugh Hefner, eat your heart out.

Sometimes Wolf and I stay over on weekends and visit Lefty Richmond's Tavern in downtown Indiana. The brothers congregate in the back room of Lefty's place. His establishment is an important part of student life, since Lefty, either knowingly or unknowingly, serves alcoholic beverages to minors as long as they don't cause trouble. A minor in Pennsylvania is defined as anyone under the age of twenty-one.

A quart of beer cost fifty cents and a quart of Carling Black Label is enough to get sloshed. Being a cheap drunk is a distinct advantage. Neither of us has a car; hence, we are harmless to our fellow motorists. Wolf and I walk back to the frat house in an erratic path and flop into bed. No harm done, except the inevitable headache and bad taste the following day. I always ask myself, "Why in the world did I do something I don't enjoy?" and never come up with a good answer. There is something inherently alluring and challenging about picking the forbidden fruit. What other reason could there be for drinking a beverage that I neither like nor desire? If Adam and Eve couldn't resist temptation, what makes the authorities think that an older teenager will do any better?

CHAPTER 23

LOOKING FOR LOVE IN ALL THE WRONG PLACES

Dating hometown girls keeps distractions at college to a minimum. Homegrown girls also give us an active social life during the summer doldrums, when we have ample time to spend on social issues. In my sophomore year, Wolf provides me with a hot lead on a girl named Sue in Brookville. She is rumored to be adventurous, and that titillates my imagination. He informs me that she is a hot item. "Wolf, where did you hear that? Someone feeds you crap and you willingly eat it."

"Hey, where there's smoke, there's a hot chick," Wolf responds. "I was talking to a guy who knew another guy who said he heard she is hot."

The scenario sounds similar to hundreds of fictional stories I hear about other nice girls. Who knows what truth lies within the rumors spread by the gossip line, but calling her is worth a try. When a guy heads down an unknown trail, he never knows where the path will lead. I muster the courage and call. As fate will have it, a female voice answers and tells me that Sue isn't home. I have no remorse; in a sea of green why be limited to looking at one blade of grass? There will always be another opportunity.

Several months later at the Pink Panther Dance Hall in Reynoldsville, I meet a tall, slim, and exceptionally attractive golden-haired beauty. She carries herself like a goddess, and has the poise and demeanor of a princess. I decide to turn on my charm and try to book her for a date. I take a deep breath and mosey over to where she is standing. "Say, would you like to dance?" She smiles and says okay. The song is "Twilight Time" by the Platters and it is perfect for getting close. Near the end of the song, I ask, "Will you consider going out on a date with me next Friday? I'll call you next Thursday and we can work out the details. My name is Jim and I'm from Brockway. Would you please give me your phone number?"

"I may," she teasingly says. Her buttercup blond hair complements her smooth, milky white skin. The prudent use of makeup and ruby red lipstick accentuate her petite, straight nose and high cheekbones. She doesn't wear a revealing or sexy dress, but she is sexy. Sexy is a quality hard to define, but I know it when I see it. I use all my Jimmy charm, and she finally gives me her phone number. She is a good looker, and I want to get to know her. I'm impressed when she tells me she is one of eight children.

When I call, a young girl answers. Thinking it is her sister, I begin my charming introductory banter. The girl won't have anything to do with my amiable dialogue and starts interrogating me. "Where do you live? How old are you? What does your father do?" On and on she continues. After five minutes I end the irritating conversation by calling her a neb-nose. Neb-nose is appropriate, since she asks so many prying questions. Suddenly, the irritated girl hands the telephone to my potential date. Finally, I get to talk to the classy blonde and ask her for a date. She tells me to call me back in fifteen minutes, and she will let me know. I feel supremely confident—I give her one hundred and twenty percent of my charm. I call back and say, "Can you go out with me next Friday night?"

"No, I can't go out with you. You called my mother a neb-nose," she responds. "Thanks, and goodbye." The feisty girl I bantered with on the phone wasn't one of her sisters. It was her mother and now I am off limits to her daughter. Oh-oh, I screwed up. How was I to know her mother did telephone interviews?

Never trust a telephone voice. In the dating game, sometimes I win, and sometimes I lose. This time I lost, but I feel bad about it. Wolf and I continue looking for other blades of grass in the vast expanse of green. I'm a sophomore in college and still a virgin—what a mortifying situation. There must be some high-quality action for me, but where? I reckon a guy has to keep looking; she's out there. If I keep throwing darts, eventually I will hit the bull's-eye.

As fraternity guys Wolf and I wear blue suede leather jackets with three-inch Greek letters emblazoned in white leather on the left side of the jacket. We also purchase navy blue blazers with the fraternity's crest sewn on the pocket. In my mind I am a true chick magnet. During my sophomore year we continue to be weekend warriors. Saturday nights are mostly spent moving and a-grooving on the prowl at the Pink Panther. There are many girls I meet and date, but for a guy portraying himself as the cock-of-the-walk, life is an embarrassing façade. God, it's like I am a closet heterosexual desperately trying to come out of the closet. How long can I present myself as the epitome of masculinity knowing I am a strikeout king when trying to score the big home run?

Will the tabloid magazine *Confidential* pick up my story and make me the laughingstock of the world? Will my drought ever end? There are many questions that need addressed. Nick makes a philosophical statement about my situation. "Ya know, guys, sometimes when you gotta itch, ya gotta scratch it."

"What do you mean?" I prod. "Be specific."

Brain warp proliferates like a malignant growth as good judgment is thrown to the wind. Wolf counsels, "Guys, we've got to get some and it doesn't matter what ya get."

"That's what scratching an itch means, ya dummy," Nick exclaims. He thoughtfully adds, "Remember, guys, if you turn 'em upside down, they all look alike."

"What a revolting idea," I interrupt. "Don't forget, fellows, eventually you have to turn them right-side up and look them in the eyes."

Nick scolds, "Jim, you sound like a goddamn priest. What's wrong with ya? Ya chicken or something? They ain't gotta be beautiful; all they gotta do is screw." Nick, the sorry soul, completely misses my point.

I try to make him understand. "I just don't want to raid a pigpen when I'm looking for a sleek race horse."

Wolf interjects, "Too much college for that boy; his brain is full of shit."

"I'll second that," says Nick. "If he wants to screw a race horse—let him."

The situation is desperate and we reluctantly decide to hit on some real dogs. It is totally out of character for Wolf and me, but Nick doesn't set the bar so high. We meet a small herd of wild girls at the Pink Panther. They can only be described as double-bag girls. At least two double grocery bags over their heads are required before going out with them in public. Their hidden beauty is exceedingly well hidden, and should remain so.

The girl dubbed "Snake," a rather rotund, fleshy morsel, takes a liking to Wolf. We tease him that she is a doggie's delight. Snake hangs around him like the lingering bad smell of someone passing gas in a public restroom. She's hard to shake. Nonetheless, all dogs have the ability to bark, if you get my drift. "Wolf, any way you look at it, these chicks are three hundred sixty degrees unattractive."

"Remember, guys, there's no such thing as ugly in the dark," Nick responds. "You losers gotta take whatever ya can get. Listen, Jim, all you gotta do is close your eyes and pretend they are beautiful."

"I take exception to that," I retort. "Even a blind person won't have anything to do with these dogs."

I tag Wolf's mate with the moniker Snake because if you are foolish enough to do the dirty deed with her, you will surely do it with a snake. The girls Nick and I talk with aren't much better, but Snake is a perfect ten on the bow-wow scale. It isn't their unattractive looks that turn me off—that I can deal with. The entire herd is composed of low-class characters, openly soliciting our manhood. The girls are beyond moral bankruptcy; they haven't even started a savings account.

"Damn hell, Nick, I now understand why some species eat their young," I explain.

"Who cares, don't mess it up. I think I am in love," Wolf says in jest.

"You'll be in love when you get rotten crotch and your tool falls off," I caution. Even though I have a biological destiny to fulfill, they frighten me. I don't want to devalue the family jewels, so I make an on-the-spot decision. "My guy and I are going to take a raincheck." I want to be able to look at myself in the mirror without throwing up.

"God, Jim, they're ready and willing—what more do you want?" Wolf pleads. I'm lucky, I have the power of attorney for my guy and can speak on his behalf. I am not about to dive into the cesspool where so many others bathe. Imagine, getting someone like Snake knocked up, having to marry her, and then living with her the rest of my life. Dad once told me, "Quit worrying about going to hell; marry the wrong girl and you'll have your hell here on Earth." Another bit of prudent advice results in viewing Snake and her pals as the earthly manifestation of that nightmare scenario becoming reality.

One of Uncle John's stories is appropriate for getting us out of our predicament. I pull the boys aside and tell the thought-provoking story.

"There is a cat sitting with its tail on the railroad tracks, when a train passes by and cuts off a piece of the cat's tail. As the cat turns its head to see what happened, the train runs over its head." I continue, "The moral of the story is don't lose your head over a little piece of tail."

The guys laugh, but the point is well taken. It must be that when you have natural urges, the brain is somehow short-circuited. It is a temporary form of insanity. Beauty is in the eye of the beholder, and the girls are about as beautiful as a fire hydrant is to a dog—use them and walk away.

After reevaluating the situation and bleeding off excess hormones, we agree the show isn't worth the price of admission. Sometimes a guy's primitive emotions take over, but this time rational thinking prevails. The situation is similar to putting lipstick on a pig—the pig sure does look good, but it is still a pig. Besides, horrible post-traumatic nightmares will haunt me if I mingle among the bow-wow people. I don't relish therapy for the rest of my life.

By chance, at the beginning of my junior year, I again meet the attractive buttercup blonde at the Pink Panther. It has been fourteen months since our last encounter. I'm pulled to her like metal is to a magnet. She is even more attractive and appealing than when I first met her. She blows my socks off. I am googly-eyed. Is meeting her again fate, or an accident? There is something special about this girl. She mesmerizes me and turns me into jelly. My big head tells my little head that she is a classy lady and we should behave ourselves. Dancing with her is a pleasure, and unlike the Horse Lady, she smells good. I still do not venture past slow dancing. Learning comes hard to some guys.

She feels good, looks good, and is a nice person. My heart goes thumpity-thump. What the heck— no risk, no gain—I again ask her for a date. She accepts my offer. On the way home that night, I rehash my feelings. There is a tenderness and kindness about her that is striking. I instinctively know she is out of the ordinary; she has the body and grace of a model, a great personality, a wonderful value system, and most of all, I sense she likes me. I can't get my mind off her and I can't blame it on those damn Republicans.

Thankfully, her mother doesn't remember my phone call or my verbal "neb-nose" transgression. We begin to date and I have fun with her. I kiss her lightly on the lips at the end of our first date and walk her to the front door. How could Mom possibly know? She is right, I am breathless and I do see stars. It isn't a passionate kiss like Fran gave me. Unlike man-eating Fran, who tried to eviscerate me with her tongue from inside out, her kisses are gentle, sweet, and innocent kisses that let me know I am also someone special. We talk without saying a word. I am beyond swooning. This is love. My hormones rage like a forest fire, and I want to ravish her body, but my Catholic morals kick in and stop my aggressions. Quadruple damn those nuns.

I do a lot of coaching with the little guy to make him mind his manners. Thankfully he takes the coaching in the spirit it is given. When dating her, I treat her as if she is delicate porcelain, because to me she is precious. Little by little I realize that I have hit the proverbial mother lode—the person I have been looking for. This is love and it feels belly-tickling good. After four months, I take her to the Brookville Country Club Ball and as we dance give her the band off a cigar. Looking into her eyes, I say, "Will you be my girl and go steady with me?" Delicately, she places the fragile cigar band on her finger, delightfully smiles, and softly says yes. I am absolutely euphoric.

We date steady throughout my last two years in college. God, even Beaver's TV parents, Ward and June Cleaver, would be proud of my gentlemanly behavior. She is magnificent, and I think about her day and night. That fair-haired person is everything I could ever want. In life some things are worth waiting for, and she is worth the wait.

Life is full of interruptions, and the military is one of those bumps on life's road. At the end of my junior year, Wolf and I travel East on PA Route 322 to Fort Indiantown Gap. There we receive our basic training. Initiation into the Army includes a full physical exam at an old reactivated hospital facility. Similar to cattle moving to slaughter, we are herded through the makeshift medical facilities, moving from station to station in assembly-line fashion. "Drop your drawers," orders the doctor. "Now bend over and spread your cheeks." Spread your cheeks doesn't mean the doctor wants to look in my mouth.

During the psychological interview the doctor asks strange questions. "Do you like your mother?" he inquires, giving me a blank stare. A rather insulting question, but I'd have to be crazy to answer with anything but the truth. "Yes." I can tell he never met Mom. "Okay, soldier, move on to the next station," he directs. Golly, I guess I'm not nuts.

In a tender, loving manner that can only be imagined by living the experience, shots are administered by troops training to become medical corps personnel. There is nothing comparable to having a trainee practice drawing blood and giving shots. "Roll up your sleeve," orders the rookie technician. "Make a fist. Now this won't hurt. Oops, guess I missed," he says as he pulls out the needle. "Let's try again" is the phrase he uses four times before hitting a vein.

After the physical exam, I am transported to a barn-like building to receive my GI clothing. Whatever is issued is worn, even if the uniform is only a near fit. When it comes to customer service, the Army is not competitive with J.C. Penney. Thus ends the first day at "Uncle Sam's" summer camp for wayward boys.

Egalitarianism is the operative word in the Army. In basic training we are all treated like crap. Indiantown Gap is an old semi-deactivated Army post near Harrisburg, Pennsylvania, with hundreds of lookalike wooden World War II barracks. The barracks have absolutely no privacy. The latrine (bathroom for non-military people) consists of eight commodes lined up side by side without privacy barriers between them. If a guy is shy, he will soon be constipated. I adjust to sitting on the throne and talking to others as we complete our biological functions.

One valuable lesson learned and transferable to civilian life is making a bed Army style. Every morning at five o'clock, I awaken to the melodious sound of our platoon sergeant pounding a stick against the metal trashcans. "Rise and shine, up and at 'em, you losers," he affectionately yells. "Ya ugly bastards got enough beauty sleep. We got another exciting day planned for you adorable college boys." Somehow, I feel he is having the time of his life mocking us. "Get your sweet asses moving, formation at 0600."

The last thing before falling into formation is making my bed. The bed meets military standards when a dime can be bounced off the top blanket and fall to the floor. Even Mom can't do this, but then again, why would she want to? Living conditions are unpleasant and leave much to be desired. The Army acts like a surrogate parent; they feed us, clothe us, and doctor us—what more could a person want?

The drill sergeant likes to run, and we run everywhere. We run to the mess hall, do our pull-ups, eat whatever is offered, and run back to the barracks. Up hills, across airfields, and anywhere he can possibly imagine, he makes us run, and run we do. When not running, I'm marching: first in platoon formation, then in company formation, and finally as a battalion. All the time we are marching, the drill sergeant keeps us in step by singing what we call "Jody calls." Jody calls are a technique for maintaining a marching cadence. The right foot is supposed to hit the ground when the numbers one and three are called or when the words "you're right" are sung. The Army is mostly males and little attention is given to what is sung. My favorite Jody call goes like this:

> I got a girl in Kansas City
>
> She's got a mole on her left elbow
>
> Am I right or wrong—you're right
>
> Am I right or wrong—you're right
>
> Sound off—one, two
>
> Sound off—three, four
>
> Bring 'em on down—one, two, three, four
>
> One—two—three—four.

Followed by the next two lines, Jody calls finish with the same refrain:

> I don't know but I've been told
>
> Eskimo girls are mighty cold.

GI parties are substituted for pledge parties, but now we clean billets that are impossible to keep clean. Cleanliness is more than godliness; it is the only avenue by which we can attain a weekend pass. Every activity is done according to a tightly controlled training schedule. Even break times are controlled.

After four weeks the possibility of a free weekend is within our grasp. We collectively hold our breath. Saturday morning finally arrives and after three tries our platoon passes the barrack's white glove inspection. No dust on the platoon leader's white glove is a liberating and welcome sight.

After four hectic weeks a weekend pass is earned and we decide to drive to the big city of Harrisburg to do some partying. We rent an upscale hotel room in the Hotel Harrisburg and plan to go out on the town to explore the nightlife. Nonetheless, it is six o'clock in the evening and a hour's nap is in order. I lie down, dead tired. It is comforting to climb into crisp, fresh sheets that aren't on a sagging Army bunk. When I wake somebody asks, "What time is it?" The answer, "It's ten o'clock," doesn't make sense. The sun is still shining. I am disoriented. It is the next day, Sunday morning, and our little nap turns into a fourteen-hour sleep-a-thon. I had not planned on this type of pajama party. Reluctantly, we get dressed and make our way to the base to continue our training. Thus ends my first weekend pass. Some war story, huh?

I do Army stuff like fire machine guns, fire rifles, fire pistols, throw grenades, learn how to read a map and use a compass. Mainly I do what millions of others have done before me. To best describe the state of my physical fitness is that at the end of the six weeks, I go from size 36 trousers to size 32. My butt disappears and I am lean and mean; well, maybe not so much mean as nasty. The military wisely do not worry about the uniforms' fit at the beginning, because they know no matter what is issued, after six weeks of rigorous training, it won't fit. The civilian trousers worn on arrival gape so much that I must tie them with a string to keep them from falling down. I am proud to have survived and accomplish another of life's challenges.

The fortunate part of my decision to participate in ROTC is unanticipated and comes in handy in my junior and senior years. As upper class ROTC cadets, Wolf and I receive a monthly allowance of $27.50. That is a bundle of money. Not only does the money help in the last two years of college, but also we are guaranteed a job for at least two years upon graduation.

I want to fly airplanes and while a ROTC cadet apply and am accepted into the Army Flight School. Snoopy, Charlie Brown's dog, will be jealous. Imagine me a pilot, a dream come true. I easily pass the rigorous physical examination. The only remaining requirement is to attend Saturday morning ROTC classes, and complete flight training at Fort Rucker, Alabama. As circumstances would have it, I cut some mandatory classes and get dropped from the flight program. That old elementary school comment, "makes good use of his time," gets me again. In retrospect, God is good to me. Cutting class is a fortunate event, because in 1964 many of my friends finish rotary wing school and spend their extra third year of service in a place called Vietnam.

Indiana is a land grant college, and all officers are commissioned as quartermaster officers. There is nothing glamorous about the Quartermaster Corps, but the corps' mission is an essential element in the combat force's ability to complete their mission. Anything the Army needs in the way of supplies, equipment, food, clothing, and petroleum passes through our hands. In civilian life we would be called giant storekeepers. Our standing joke is "The Quartermaster Corp—every man a trained killer." To properly function all parts of the organization must work as a team. Soldiers need food, and tanks need fuel.

By my senior college year, I save over seven hundred dollars and journey to a jewelry store in DuBois with one thought on my mind. I buy my sweetheart a diamond engagement ring. Mom accompanies me to help pick out the ring and I choose a beautiful three-quarter-caret diamond solitaire. There is no doubt that the buttercup blonde is the person I have been seeking as a life partner. She keeps getting better and better. The question is, how best to propose to her?

We are traveling on PA Route 28 on the way from Brookville to Brockway when I ask, "Would you please open the glove compartment and get that package for me?" She reaches in to get the wrapped package and hands it to me. I smile and hand the petite packet back to her. "Will you please unwrap this for me? Just open it. There is something I want to show you." Apprehensively, she unwraps the box. When she views the diamond ring, she cries and accepts my commitment to her. It is cute to see her so taken aback that she loses her composure. "I love you. Will you marry me?"

"Oh yes. I love you too," she responds. We are officially engaged and want everybody to know. She is the girl I take to the Playboy parties, she is the girl I am in love with, and she is the girl I marry. Just a side note, I never do tell her or her sister that I am the guy who once called for a date. So let's sort of keep this our own little secret—okay?

During the last semester of my senior year, I complete student teaching. To keep cost down, Wolf and I student teach in Punxsutawney. The advantage is I can live at home and drive to Punxsy each day. One semester of study at Indiana is lost when I contract infectious mononucleosis, known as the "kissing disease." This puts me a semester behind Wolf. He does his student teaching in the spring of 1963, and I student teach in the fall of 1963. As fortune will have it, we both have the same mentor teacher. His name is Melvin Michaels, and he is the best of the best at teaching tenth-grade biology. Every day I write lesson plans and every night I drive to Brookville, where my honey types them. Lesson plans are a great excuse to visit on a nightly basis—who can object to such a business relationship? I learn the art of teaching from Mr. Michaels and receive an A for my efforts.

One day in November the principal interrupts my class and announces over the public address system, "I am sorry to announce, our President, John F. Kennedy, has been assassinated." We are shocked and the kids start crying. I don't know what to do, but Melvin does. He sees my distress and takes over the class. He asks for silence, and we all join in prayer. Once the prayer is over, Melvin does the right thing and gets us back on task. Boy, what a curveball fate throws me that day. We finish one of the most memorable days in history and go home for the next three days to mourn the nation's loss. That Sunday, as I am scrubbing the floors at Dad's restaurant, I have the TV on and witness the shooting of the President's assassin, Lee Harvey Oswald. What a memorable month.

Even though I am in college, I help Dad with the family business whenever possible. When I turn twenty-one, I help the family by tending bar on the weekends and during the summer. Bartending is an enriching life experience. Throughout the period unwritten rules that are neither found in textbooks nor taught in college classrooms are learned. For instance, I observe the CEO of a major world-class corporation bring young upstarts to the establishment, where he buys the drinks. The CEO is an accomplished executive, and an accomplished consumer of alcoholic beverages. As the evening progresses, the junior wannabe executive becomes relaxed, more informal, and sloppy with his comments. There is no way the young executive can keep a drink-for-drink pace with the sardonic old CEO. At a predetermined moment, when the upstart carelessly crosses an invisible line, the CEO cuts loose and lambasts the individual loud enough for everyone to hear. The startled novice is purposely humiliated and dissected piece by piece. At first I think I am seeing a unique situation until I observe him systematically do it to others. The lesson learned is that there is no such thing as informal with your boss. The thousand-pound hammer can assert his dominance and pound you into the ground whenever he chooses. Life is much more instructional than college courses.

Every person should tend bar for one semester during their college career. A psychology book hasn't been written that provides such insight into human behavior. The lessons serve me well, and many times assist in identifying potential landmines before stepping on them. Alcohol is to be enjoyed and not abused, because once a person's social filters are down, stupid things easily pour from their mouth.

The wide variety of people I interact with is enlightening. Daily old codgers throughout the neighborhood stop for a visit and their vintage wake-me-up libation. Beer and muscatel wine are the popular beverages of choice. It takes some of the old-timers many drinks over an extended period of time to wake up. I joke that "some people are slower at waking up in the morning than others, and getting them on the move is part of my job."

Every day at ten o'clock in the morning and two o'clock in the afternoon, Andy stops by for his daily consumption of draft beer. Andy is a retired blue-collar factory worker. He often brags about his ability to change the leer belt that transports fired glass products. His dirty manual labor job was an important part of keeping the plant productive and efficient, but his faded glory means little outside the confines of the plant environment. Andy is a cantankerous and argumentative individual who knows everything about anything. His opinionated knowledge is tolerated most days, but some days he gets on my nerves. I am tending bar one day as he is expounding on world events. I get so worked up arguing with him and trying to nurture a civil conversation that I find myself on the edge of anger. If I say something is white, Andy automatically retorts that it is black. I get sucked into squabbling with him. He only disagrees more intensely as I point out the fallacy of his argument. I'm losing it fast and know I have to get out of there. I interrupt Andy and say, "Excuse me, Dad's in the kitchen cleaning the grill and I have to check to see if he needs any help." I go back to the kitchen where Dad is working and blurt out, "I've never met a person as stupid as Andy Pulacki."

He looks up and says, "Oh, well, I have. We both know he is ignorant and stupid, and only a person more ignorant and stupid would argue with him." His words freeze me in my tracks as the full impact of what he said sinks in. Dad continues, "Son, if you learn one thing in life, learn never to get into an argument with a stupid person. You'll never win and you'll become very frustrated. Stupid people never change their minds." Thus, another worthwhile lesson in life is learned. Never argue with a stupid person. I add this to my bag of valuable life tools. How can a guy who never went to college be so damn smart?

My favorite customers are the factory workers who stop in daily for a shot and a beer and to talk to their buddies. They are unique characters and are classified as the local color. My least favorite people are the wannabe crowd from the corporate office. Generally, they are persons who wannabe but don't know how to be. Many live and drink beyond their means in an attempt to impress their peers. Given the choice between the "suits" and the local characters, the local folks win every time. The restaurant and tavern business is the place to observe human behavior at its best and at its worst. All in all, a relatively cheap form of education worth a million bucks in real-world experience.

IV.

MY NEW FAMILY—
MOVING ONWARD

CHAPTER 24

GRADUATION AND GETTING ON WITH LIFE

Wolf graduates a semester before me. He receives a bachelor of science degree with a major in biology and a minor in general science. One semester later I receive the same degrees. I work hard for my diploma and I am proud of my accomplishment. Underneath the cap and gown, I wear a Class A military green uniform. Immediately after the academic ceremony, I am commissioned a second lieutenant in the United States Army. A second lieutenant is comparable to a private in the enlisted ranks. A junior "butter-bar" is as low as you can go as an officer.

Every officer commissioned is provided a two-hundred-dollar clothing allowance. I purchase two Class A uniforms, browns for summer and greens for winter, and an Army dress blue uniform. Wolf anxiously waits at home for his military orders. Once received, he goes to Fort Lee, Virginia, to complete the eight-week Quartermaster Officer Basic Course. I follow half a year later in April 1964, but by that time Wolf is at another duty assignment.

As a typical young and dumb second lieutenant still wet behind the ears, I think I have a say in where I will be assigned. In 1964, the nation has a draft system and my obligation is for two years' active duty and four years active reserve duty. My requested assignments are the United States and for an overseas assignment, the Far East. If possible, I want to be within one day's driving distance of home.

Of course the Army tries to please its new officers, and certainly they will assign me to my first choice. However, upon receiving the first set of official Army orders, the only part I can decipher is my name, a date, and a destination. My assignment is a place called Baumholder, West Germany. In disbelief, I immediately sit down and reread the orders. Surely this is an error on the Army's behalf. "Nah, it must be a mistake—would you look at this," I point out to Mom. "I can't believe what I am reading; I don't want to go to Germany."

"Let me look," she says and carefully examines the letter. "It does say Germany."

"Doesn't the Army know Germany isn't one of my choices?" I retort. Like death and dying my mental energy focuses on denial. I call the personnel officer at the Pentagon.

"Hello, this is Major Kuvak at the Army Personnel Center speaking."

"Major, my name is James DeAngelo and I have just received my active duty orders."

"Yes, is there a problem?" the major inquires.

"I have been assigned to West Germany, and I didn't put that as one of my choices. Is there some sort of mistake in the orders?"

"Lieutenant, the orders are correct—you are assigned to the 56th Quartermaster Company in Baumholder, West Germany." It takes the major a few short seconds to curtly make me realize no mistake has been made. There is no court of appeals. Reluctantly, I accept an overseas assignment to Europe.

After recovering from the shock, I talk to my sweetheart. "Honey, I got my orders for active duty and have been assigned to Germany."

"What?" she says as the sparkle drains from her eyes. "What about us?"

We plan to wait a year after graduating from college before getting married. As a logical science major, I do logical things. I have carefully planned a timeline to ameliorate financial stress. Saving money is a good idea, but my duty assignment means decisions need to be made, and made quickly. Out the window flies logic and planning. "Let's get married now," I say.

The sparkle comes back to her eyes, and she says, "Okay—God, I love you."

Besides, I don't want some other guy beating my time while I'm overseas. We decide to make our commitment official and get married within the three weeks I have remaining in the States. We visit my parents to inform them about our plans and nervously break the news.

"Mom and Dad, we've got something to tell you," I announce as I watch Mom's face grow somber. "There is nothing wrong," I add, sensing her anxiety.

"What is it," Mom says as she breathlessly waits for the anticipated other shoe to drop.

"Well, we don't have to get married, but we are going to get married before departing for Germany."

"Congratulations to both of you," says Mom. Her lips transition from a firm line to a warm smile. Dad stoically stands beside her and states, "You don't have much time, so get started sooner rather than later." They are happy for us, but many obstacles must be overcome, and red tape must be cast aside.

In the Catholic Church a couple is required to take pre-marriage classes, and the bands of marriage must be announced two times at Sunday Mass. Why, I don't know, but a church rule is a church rule. Maybe it is as simple as giving the couple time to back out.

It is a race against time. An old-time priest at my sweetheart's church in Brookville, Father Kioli, bends over backward to help. The last bands of marriage are announced the weekend before my deployment, and that means the only time we can have the ceremony is on the following weekdays. No one gets married on Monday, unless a shotgun is involved. I'll bet our wedding stirs talk among the relatives. Aunt Betty is probably saying, "Getting married on a Monday—imagine that."

Our wedding is on Monday, July 6, 1964, at the Brookville church. For economic reasons I wear my military dress blue uniform, and my sweetheart borrows her sister's wedding dress. I get up like any other day except it is the day I am going to get married. Joe, my best man, drives me to the church. A large crowd of relatives and friends gather for the Monday wedding. At the altar my sweetheart radiates beauty from the inside out, and I am absolutely sure of the woman I love. She is the most beautiful person I have ever seen. After the religious ceremony, a reception is held at Sugarbush Lodge. The clan only gets together for weddings and funerals, and the celebration is a welcome event. My aunts bake cookies, and Dad furnishes the food and liquid refreshments. It is a first-class wedding costing two hundred dollars, a lot to spend in one day.

Before we leave for our brief Washington D.C. honeymoon, Dad provides the second fatherly sex talk of my life. As I am about to depart, he furrows his brow, looks at me, and says as only he can say to his 22-year-old son, "Now you behave yourself—do you hear me?" I smile at his awkward attempt at telling me to treat my new wife with respect and dignity. It isn't necessary, because he has been delivering that message all my life.

My new bride and I leave the reception and drive to Penn State, where we spend our first night together at the Holiday Inn.

Our honeymoon night is the only night I wear pajamas. In my haste to get under the sheet, I do forget to take out a few strategically placed pins from the newly unpacked garment. After a short honeymoon, I take my bride to Germany. Oh, by the way, I forgot to tell you the name of the golden-haired blonde I met at the Pink Panther. How rude of me—where are my manners? Her name is Betty Jane and like me, she is also a virgin. I'm not alone in the world. Aunt Betty's remark would have been a surprised "Imagine that, a virgin!" I am fascinated because Betty is increasingly beautiful every day of our marriage. She is the center of my new family.

I don't particularly like Army life. It reminds me of living in the dorms. Even as an officer everyone tells me what to do. Resentment of authority is not a good thing to have in the Army. My primary assignment is as a petroleum platoon officer, and I operate an oil depot in West Germany. Here I am, a 22-year-old junior butter-bar operating a multimillion-dollar facility. Hard to believe. The company commander is an obsessive-compulsive person and nervously spends his days stacking cigarette butts in his rectangular ashtray as if they are mini logs. Every day after work, including Saturday, the officers are required to meet with him for an hour. "Come in," says Captain Pear Head. We call him Captain Pear Head because of the peculiar shape of his head. "Well, boys what's new?"

Each officer briefly tells the happenings of the day, which isn't much different from the previous day. "Not much new," I report. "Everything is going as expected."

Captain Pear Head continues with a series of inane questions and incomprehensible babble. As he continues to chain-smoke and stack the butts in the ashtray, I sit thinking that this is insane. "Well, boys, we got to remember that those damn Russians can come across the border, and we must be prepared." We all know the Russians do not give a damn about what we are doing.

The captain has an obtuse sense of leadership. Whenever there is a bivouac, he is mysteriously ill. Such a strange character is featured in the book *Catch-22*. Nevertheless, the one thing learned is that I don't have to like the person, but I do have to respect the rank. The military protocol and lessons learned while bartending serve me well. I have no intentions of making the military a career and play along to get along, even though the Army of the 1960s does foolish things to keep soldiers dissatisfied.

Betty and I do not seek government housing, since that would obligate me to an extra year of active duty. I am anxious to get on with life. The world is a bit unstable, and soldiers are stationed in Korea, and a few troops are sent as advisors to a place called Vietnam. I have no desire to visit other foreign lands. We live on the local economy with a German family, the Kugles. Baumholder is a typical GI town with a population of less than 2,000 people. Lining its bleak downtown streets are fifty-seven bars primarily supported by military personnel. I spend nights and weekends at the Military Police station getting troops released from the brig. As a second lieutenant, I often counsel soldiers older than my father about paying bills, budgeting money, and staying on the straight and narrow path. It's like being a priest without the collar.

Ironically, there are many nights when we sit in our apartment and listen to the drama programs on Armed Forces Radio in the same manner as when I was a kid in the 1940s. Now that I have a regular paycheck, we purchase a new 1965 Mercedes-Benz 200, and Betty and I travel extensively. Traveling in Europe is exciting because unlike regimented tourists, we don't plan a specific destination. We just drive. Germany, France, Austria, Switzerland, Italy, Monaco, and the Netherlands are part of our travels. The Swiss Alps and the French Rivera are particularly noteworthy. We even visit Rome and have an audience with the Pope. It makes me proud to be a Catholic.

I complete the two-year active duty tour and, much to my surprise, continue to serve as an active reservist. For a guy who doesn't like authority or regular Army life, I feel obligated to help the nation in any manner I can.

Throughout my military career, continually upgrading my skills is essential. Unlike the civilian world, people's lives depend on my maintaining a high level of competence.

Reminiscent of my grandparents and my parents, I also have a deep-seated love for my country. Living overseas for two years reaffirms that the United States is God's gift to humanity. My family define themselves as Americans first, with a lineage that is traced back to Italy. When anyone asks if I am Italian, I answer, "No, I'm an American." Our heritage defines what we were; my family defines us by what we are. I return to the States in 1966 as a much wiser and more mature first lieutenant.

Dad decides to retire from the restaurant business about the time I am discharged from the Army. In his generosity he signs over the business to Joe and me. At that time, around 1967, the family is grossing over $150,000 a year, and in 1960 dollars that is nothing to sneeze at. Joe and I grew up in the business and know all aspects of the trade. We easily make the transition. A good living can be made as a business-man, and the take-home pay is twice as much as a schoolteacher.

After four months working in the business, I make a life-altering decision that forever changes the course of future events for my wife and my new family. "Joe, I'm leaving the business. I've got other things I want to do."

"What do you mean you're leaving the business? Why?"

"I don't exactly know, but I do know there are other things out there for me." I decide not to do what my father did during his working career. It is an agonizing decision, because it means leaving the security of my family and going on my own. I don't know what I'm looking for, and I must be crazy to venture into the wilderness—but I have the urge. "Joe, you are going to have to buy me out," I announce to my astonished brother. "Remember, Dad always preached that you never get something for nothing," I say. Anyone who thinks they are getting something for nothing usually gets nothing for something. "In keeping with Dad's philosophy, I'm going to need the grand sum of one dollar. I just hope you can afford it."

Somewhat surprised, Joe says, "That seems fair enough."

I sell my half of the business to Joe for a dollar and enroll as a graduate student at Indiana University of Pennsylvania. We live in a converted horse stable, and Betty works during the day while I watch our young son. My classes are scheduled at night, so there is always one of us to care for our baby boy. I have supreme confidence in my ability to make it on my own. In 1967, with the help of my wonderful wife, I graduate with a M.Ed. in biology.

My master's degree leads to a job teaching science at the Oil City Area School District in Oil City, Pennsylvania. Oil City is within easy travel distance of Brockway, and we are able to keep close ties with our families. After three years of classroom experience, I apply for a National Science Foundation Fellow-ship for a year of study at Syracuse University. I open the mail and say, "Honey, look, they accepted me as a NSF student at Syracuse."

"Oh sweetie, that's great—what are you going to do?" Betty asks. "You know I'll do anything you want and support any decision you make."

"Okay then, pack your bags, load up the car, and get ready to go. We leave in two months."

Off we go on another adventure. With my GI Bill benefits, my fellowship stipend, and the money I receive as an active reservist, I have more take-home pay as a student than as a full-time teacher. So con-voluted is the situation that my take-home pay is doubled. I prefer to think that Mother didn't raise a fool—some things I just learn on my own. I pride myself in being a fast learner and know a good thing when I see it. At mid-semester I approach the head of the department and inquire, "Dr. Barns, I would like to stay on at the university and work towards my doctoral degree. What do I have to do to make this happen?"

"Let's see how you do this year and then we'll make a decision," he responds.

"Okay, just watch, I'll do great." To me this is the mother of all challenges.

Joe teases, "Holy hell, Jim, you're becoming a professional student," and in many respects he is correct.

I draw upon my real-life experiences as a bartender and the armed forces to survive university politics. The powerful department chairman is a person short of stature, a little over five feet tall (he wears lifts in his shoes), and to top it off, he wears a cheap, puffed-up toupee. To say he is height conscious is a gross understatement. The rhythmic phrase uttered between graduate students is: He's not under-tall, he's just very small. Quickly say the sentence, give it a beat, and you've got a hit song. His little-man complex is a well-known no-no topic of conversation within the university community. I am mindful that my future is in his hands.

As in the past, one important rule is followed: There is no such thing as informal, especially when it applies to the academic chairperson. I now have a family and discipline myself to stay on task. While attending a social function where drinks flow freely, I observe the chairman's conversation with a student. Nature abhors a vacuum, and the person dominates the conversation as if he is filling an imaginary vacuum. After a few drinks tongues loosen, and the conversation somehow gets around to the person telling the chairman that he once sold caskets for a living. Not a pleasant topic, but engaging conversation. The department chairman politely asks, "Well, how much will a casket for me cost?" The slightly tipsy student stretches his arm in a measuring motion well above the vertically challenged chairman's head and slowly lowers his hand to the top of his five-foot frame and loudly blurts out, "Well, for you, half price." Funny, yes—appropriate, no. The crowd is horrified by his faux pas. The conversation stops and everyone freezes as the chairman turns and briskly walks away from the group. The stupid mistake reminds me of the old WWII poster, "Loose lips sink ships." My fellow student never recognizes discreet silence as the antibody protecting him from the germ of stupidity. Regret is not an outcome of silence, and nobody ever misquotes or misunderstands something never spoken. You can never un-ring a bell, and from that day forward, the imprudent student experiences difficulty completing his graduate studies.

In life sometimes you are the bug and sometimes you are the windshield. I am determined never to be the bug. I risk everything putting all my marbles in one graduate studies bag. Being successful in the academic environment requires more than academics; it requires well-honed life skills. I study hard and receive my first ever 4.0 grade point average for the year. Not bad for a blockhead kid from Brockway. Doing that well while taking tough courses such as statistics, astronomy, and microbiology proves to the department chairman that I am more than capable of doing upper-level graduate work. For the following two years, I study under a coveted National Defense Education Act Fellowship Grant.

During my second year of study at Syracuse University, an even harder decision has to be made when Dad becomes seriously ill. "Jimmy, why don't you come home and live?" he suggests. This is the first time he has ever asked me for anything. It breaks my heart to see the once hardy man frightened and in decline.

I sadly tell him, "No, I am sorry, Dad, I've got to do what's best for my family."

"I understand. You've done well, son. I'm proud of you." This is his way of finally saying, "Jimmy, I love you."

"Thanks for understanding. I love you, Dad."

My dream of living in Brockway with family and friends is not to be—something greater waits for me out there, what I have yet to discover.

Never before have I seen Dad afraid, but because of his grave illness, he is fearful for his future. I also know he is proud of his son, because when the tough decisions have to be made, I put my young family first—that's what he would have done. Nonetheless, every Friday while attending Syracuse University, we pack our bags and make the grueling seven-hour trip back to Brockway. If in some small way our presence gives him comfort for a short period of time, the trip is worth the effort. The only thing left that can possibly be given is my time. The agonizing hurt of watching Father slowly fade away continues in my heart.

Three hard years of study culminate in one four-hour oral dissertation examination. The oral exam is one of those make-it-or-break-it situations. My dissertation is "The Effects of Structured Overviews and Background Variables Upon Reception Learning in a College Audio-Tutorial Genetics Course," and I must defend my research. Dissertation mathematics compute like this: Three years equals four hours. For a moment fear and doubt prevail. Maybe I should just leave. Why put myself through this torture? What if I fail? I am on the verge of becoming mentally paralyzed. Just as quickly I give myself hell for having such self-reproach. I remind myself, "Jimmy boy, you're not in second grade anymore. Now get on with it, and punch that beast in the nose." I shore up my confidence. "You've come this far—go for broke, stop this nonsense of childish self-doubt. You know the research better than any of them." I put on a thin veneer of confidence and face the exam committee.

"Good morning, gentlemen," I say and begin the exam process. Defending a dissertation is like being a scab—you sit in a room and the professors pick at you. At the end of a grueling four-hour oral exam, the committee of learned professors ask me to leave the room. I am physically and mentally exhausted. They confer for fifteen minutes and summon me into the room. It is the longest fifteen minutes of my life. When I nervously enter, the committee is sitting stoically at the table. The chairperson gets out of his seat, sternly looks me in the eyes for what seems like an eternity, and says, "Congratulations, Doctor DeAngelo." I finally crack a smile as the committee applauds. I receive my PhD from Syracuse University in 1973. Imagine, me a doctor. That night I sit with Betty and over dinner get sloshed on champagne, even though I will hate myself in the morning. God is good to my family, and with assistance from me, He makes life even better.

I am able to make the tough decision to leave my father's business and blaze my own trail because my parents prepared me to be a man and do what is best for my family. In their lifetime Dad and Mom grew children who have confidence in themselves.

In his last days, Dad knows his son as a man of academic letters and an Army officer. The last gift he gives me is a beautiful Syracuse University graduation ring. He wants me to have the ring because he knows I can't afford one. In return my PhD is the last gift I am ever able to give my father before he passes away in the fall of 1973. He is proud of my accomplishments and no longer stingy with his compliments. To me the degrees are unimportant, but to Mom and Dad, they are more valued than gold. I am the first of my generation known as Doctor DeAngelo, and I am their son.

Thanks to my parents I know who I am and what I stand for. A degree is only a symbolic piece of paper; it is not what makes a man a worthy person. Paper is worthless, but humans are precious. The strength of a man cannot be measured in physical units, but is an attribute of his character, his mental resolve, and the good he accomplishes during his passage through life. In Dad's way of thinking, the success of his children is an ultimate measure of his success in life and his success as a father. He isn't wrong. I am proud to have the honor of having him as my father and to be the mirror upon which he judges himself a success.

At Dad's funeral Nick sends flowers, but he does not make a visit to the funeral parlor. During my tour of active duty, I completely lose track of Nick and never again talk to him. Nick does not return for any of our high school class reunions. Sadly, I hear that he passes away in the early 1990s. I never get to say good-bye. A lifetime of heavy smoking, and the big "C" takes its toll. His passing leaves an empty hole in me, and another part of my life disappears. Wolf meets a wonderful local girl and marries her, but since I am out of the country, I also lose touch with him. After his active duty tour, he moves his family to Michigan and works as an engineer for a large auto company. At the last class reunion, I talk with Wolf, but don't realize he is seriously ill. Almost two years later I run into a classmate, and she tells me that we have lost Wolf. I am again saddened. I never get to say good-bye to him either. My buddies are gone forever.

It is difficult to contemplate, but my hope is that we will all be someone's joyful memories someday, and if those memories aren't written, they will eventually disappear. Wolf and Nick were good persons and both are my buddies. On my road to adventure, I hope you are able to reflect back to your youth and have fun with us. Every person has a Wolf or Nick in their life, and their antics live in the memory of their children. Please, allow me to bring closure by saying good-bye to Wolf and Nick. It was a pleasure and a privilege knowing you. Only God knows why He chooses to pick flowers when they are in full bloom, and none of us is in a position to argue with Him.

Many people spend their entire life seeking answers to the meaning of life, and many die with the same questions as when they began. To me life is being among friends and living to the fullest day after day. What you are when you are here is more important than what you were after you've gone. Even though we all take different pathways in life, everyone ends at the same destination. Life is nothing but a transition to that destination, and if God is merciful, He allows that transition to progress slowly. When all the extraneous wrappings are stripped away, the truly important things are family, friends, and buddies. Don't feel bad for Wolf, because I know he is in heaven screwing around with Nick, and when I get there they will again be my buddies. So, a final "ciao," ol' buddies, I'll be seeing you someday, but until that time Dad and Mom are there to guide you. Oh, by the way, rumor has it that in heaven, no matter what you did as a youngster, nobody ever needs glasses. Thanks for sharing happiness with me.

REFERENCES:

Scarnati, James T. (2002) <u>Career Development International</u>. Leaders As Role Models: 12 Rules. MCB University Press Ltd. Vol. 7, No. 3. UK pp. 181–189.

Scarnati, James T. (2001) <u>Team Performance Management: An International Journal</u>. On Becoming a Team Player. MCB University Press Ltd. Vol. 7, No 1, UK pp. 5-10.

Scarnati, James T. (1999) <u>Career Development International</u>. Beyond Technical Competence: The Art of Leadership. MCB University Press Ltd. Vol. 4, No. 5. UK pp. 325–335.

Scarnati, James T. (1997) <u>Career Development International</u>. Beyond Technical Competence: Honesty and Integrity. MCB University Press Ltd. Vol. 2, No. 1, pp. 24-27.

CPSIA information can be obtained at www.ICGtesting.com
Printed in the USA
BVOW09s1842100416

443693BV00051B/269/P

9 781457 544774